THE BIRTH

With both elbows up Levine tried to clear the infant's breathing passages.

The baby coughed; everybody cheered.

"No, not yet . . ." said Levine in a low voice. "I don't know . . ." He was breathing rapidly. His hands were shaking.

Forgetting sterile procedure, Jill raised one of her gloved hands to her mouth and pressed hard, trying not to be ill.

"*Can't* be Thalidomide—nobody's used that in twenty years!" Levine was saying.

"Then what?" MacIntyre's voice was dull.

"God only knows." Levine's hands were working furiously, and his voice suddenly rose. "Oh, Christ. The kid's retracting. Look at his ribs. Oh, Jesus—"

Jill helped push the incubator into place. The infant's form was darkening rapidly; his almost inaudible gasps were now coming faster and more shallowly. The infant's features were indistinct—at two pounds it was like a tiny doll, a doll with four little stubs where there should have been arms and legs . . .

STRYKER'S CHILDREN

A NOVEL

JOYCE ANNE SCHNEIDER

JOVE BOOKS, NEW YORK

This Jove book contains the complete
text of the original hardcover edition.
It has been completely reset in a typeface
designed for easy reading, and was printed
from new film.

STRYKER'S CHILDREN

A Jove Book / published by arrangement with
Arbor House Publishing Company

PRINTING HISTORY
Arbor House edition / August 1984
Published in Canada by Fitzhenry & Whiteside, Ltd.
Jove edition / June 1989

ISBN: 0-515-10031-5

Jove Books are published by The Berkley Publishing Group,
200 Madison Avenue, New York, New York 10016.
The name ''JOVE'' and the ''J'' logo
are trademarks belonging to Jove Publications, Inc.

PRINTED IN THE UNITED STATES OF AMERICA

10 9 8 7 6 5 4 3 2 1

For Matt, Danielle and Bob

Acknowledgments

Special loving thanks go to Robert Schneider, M.D., for his patient technical help, and for countless hours of discussion in which many of the ideas of the book took form.

WAGNER:
A man is in the making.
MEPHISTOPHELES:
A Man? And what enamoured couple
Have you got locked up in your furnace?
WAGNER:
God forbid! We declare all that a farce.
That common mode of him-and-herness.

from Goethe's *Faust*

1

MARIA MORAN'S FIRST inkling of trouble was the coppery taste in her mouth. It had come suddenly, a rushing whoosh of something that made her gag, and when she reached up instinctively to wipe her mouth, her hand came away smeared with blood.

"What . . . ?" She heard her own high voice. Stopping in her tracks, she stood motionless, staring down in panic at the bright crimson smudge on her hand. Around her, on the sidewalk of Third Avenue in New York City, Monday morning pedestrians jostled her, but she was oblivious to them, oblivious even to the fact that a moment before she had been worried she'd be late for work.

A hurrying young man in shirtsleeves bumped into her. "Hey, fer cryin' out—oops, sorry." Maria looked up to see him staring down at her great, melon belly. "Jeez, lady, you shouldn't *stan'* there like that!"

Flustered, he rushed off and was swallowed by the crowd.

At Fiftieth Street the light was red. Maria stood a few feet away from the impatient crowd at the corner, out of habit, overcautious as usual. Probably every first-time mother feels like this, she thought. Stumbling over a sewer grating, falling over a curb, being pushed in the back of an elevator—these were all *serious things* in the Pregnant Lady Department. A faint, Madonna smile crept over her lips as she felt the baby kick. *Saw* the baby kick, she was certain—right through her white maternity dress with the lace eyelets that her mother-in-law had insisted on buying for her.

The light changed and she started to cross the avenue.

The first wave of dizziness caught her as she passed a jackhammer, working about ten feet from the curb. Swaying for a moment, she blamed her weakness on the ferocious July heat and the noise. A policeman flagging traffic around the work crew blew his whistle. Maria shook her head to clear it.

She made it to the yellow line before the second wave of dizziness came, and the avenue began turning slowly, sickeningly, on its axis. She held on desperately to her shoulder bag. People pushed past her. As the dizziness subsided she noticed that the crowd in the crosswalk had thinned. She worried that the light was about to change.

"My God," she said aloud. She took a step, then another, and was surprised that it was so difficult because her feet had just turned to granite blocks. A fat woman in a sleeveless dress cursed as she shouldered past her. Maria stumbled.

"Hey! You okay?" A man coming up from behind stopped and seized her by the arm.

She blinked at him, trying to smile. "The heat," she said. "I'll be all right."

He pointed ahead. "You better hurry," he said. "Light's gonna change."

He rushed off, and in the next moment Maria was sorry, because in a swoop of nauseating terror she knew that her problem wasn't the heat or bleeding gums or anything so absurdly simple. She was suddenly granite to the waist. The coppery taste came back, this time flooding her mouth too fast to swallow. She bent, gagging violently, put her hand over her mouth and felt a sticky wetness above her lip. Dazed, she looked at her hand again, then felt her nostrils streaming blood.

A nosebleed?

Horns blared, startling her upright again. The flashing red sign had turned to DON'T WALK. Through a blur she saw a line of glinting fenders begin to move toward her.

A whistle. A man's distant shout. The intersection was suddenly clogged with traffic again, and as she crumpled to the pavement she thought she saw cars swirling around her like a whirlpool. From somewhere came a squeal of brakes.

"Help me!" Her words came out in a feeble cry. She began to crawl on her hands and knees.

And then the pain in her middle came.

Not a little, crampy pain, the way contractions were *supposed* to begin, but a queer, viselike tightening, as hard as a rock.

Too soon! Not time yet! Through a fog she saw men running toward her, shouting; felt their hands on her, under her arms, lifting, but she could only focus on the pain. Getting tighter, unbearable. *Weren't contractions supposed to let up?* This was not what her mother and sister had described to her. Jesus, help me! She was vaguely aware of two men carrying her, a policeman and a man in a yellow hard hat, but her eyes came unfocused as the pain became more agonizing.

She felt herself lowered to hot pavement, saw feet crowding around and hands reaching down to her. Somebody was yelling for an ambulance. Weakly she tried to raise herself, and then the final pain hit and she screamed. An explosion of knives went off in her belly. She felt the soft, warm mass well up below her and pour rapidly down her thighs. She screamed again.

"They're coming, honey, they're coming." A middle-aged woman was on her knees, stroking Maria's shoulder, too rapidly, her eyes full of horror. Through the haze Maria lifted her head, tried to see the woman, and saw instead her own white dress, turning red.

"Help me," she whimpered, but her voice sounded slow, far away. Her last conscious thought was hearing the wail of an approaching siren. And then her head slid back down to the pavement, and blackness closed in around her.

2

TWENTY BLOCKS AWAY, Madison Hospital Medical Center rose shimmering above the waves of heat on First Avenue, inspiring fear and fascination in the people who passed. Not everyone stopped, but everyone looked at the imposing buildings with nervous, sideways flicks of the eye that acknowledged the world fame of the place; and the gratitude that, today at least, they were on the outside and not the inside.

At that moment Dr. Jill Raney would have preferred being on the outside. Standing in the hall outside the obstetrical suite, she tried not to look too destroyed as she watched her fellow interns troop out of the Special Procedures Room. Ten minutes ago she had nearly blown it. Four years of brutal studies in med school, working hard enough to graduate with top honors, and now this.

Morose, she leaned on a gurney and wondered: would it be professional suicide to have a shouting match with one's academic superior, right here on the ward floor?

"Damn," she said aloud.

"You say something, Jill?"

Chubby-cheeked Tricia Donovan, her friend since med school, was next to her in a green scrub suit and surgical cap, peering at Jill from behind tortoise-shell glasses. They were both July interns—beginners, raw recruits. And as much appreciated by the older doctors as an outbreak of hepatitis.

Jill Raney turned her remarkable green eyes to her friend. "No," she said. "It's nothing."

"Oh." Tricia's round face resumed its look of furious concentration, and she went back to scribbling on her clipboard. Jill watched her in amazement. Nobody ever destroyed Tricia's ability to concentrate, she thought.

It was nine o'clock; three babies had been delivered in the last hour alone, and today's schedule of gynecological surgery was unusually crowded. Nurses rushed up and down the corridors, pushing medication tables and baskets full of bloody linen. Patients, drowsy from the effects of medication, lay parked on gurneys in various staging areas, some just coming out of surgery, others going in.

Watching the corridor bustle, Jill brooded about how everyone *else* seemed so briskly confident. Suddenly she felt close to tears, and fought them down.

A clatter of gurney wheels nearby caused her to straighten and look in the direction of the Special Procedures Room. By the doorway, David Levine and Sam MacIntyre, third- and second-year residents respectively, were bending over a relieved-looking patient, smiling and joking with her. Both doctors wore scrub suits and surgical masks pulled down around their necks. Jill stared. She could not take her eyes off that trio, nor the pair of nurses who were also standing around the gurney, alternately smiling at the patient and gazing with something less than clinical detachment at the dark-haired Levine.

The only thing Jill knew about David Levine was that he was from Denver, and possessed that air of rugged stamina one usually saw in cigarette ads. At this point his good looks didn't concern her. It was the patient who attracted her attention. Mary Hollins, thirty-six, had just undergone an amniocentesis, the third that Jill had seen performed. Clinically, she thought, it wasn't such a difficult procedure: amniotic fluid was surgically withdrawn from the abdomen of a pregnant woman, then examined for abnormal cells or chemicals that would indicate whether or not the fetus was in any genetic trouble. For the doctor at least, the job was almost easy.

But what about the patients? Jill thought angrily. I'll bet

they just *love* lying there, fully conscious, having their bellies skewered by a twenty cc syringe.

Jill peered over again at Mrs. Hollins. Somehow she could not accept that this smiling patient, fervently clasping Levine's hand, was the same patient who had been hysterical only half an hour ago.

"God," said Tricia Donovan, looking at Jill again. The fluorescent lights above flashed off her glasses. "He's something else, isn't he?"

"Who?" Jill frowned.

"Levine. When you think of *some* of the residents we could have gotten stuck with—"

She broke off as Levine left the patient with MacIntyre and headed their way. Coming up behind him was another resident, George Mackey, a squarish and jovial sort who only two days ago had introduced the interns to fetal sonography.

"David!" Tricia called out. "I have one more question about using Procaine as a pain killer. Do you think if the patient—"

Levine stopped and looked at the troubled expression on Jill Raney's face. He half-turned in Donovan's direction.

"Listen, Trish," he said absently. "Why don't you ask Mackey here? He'll be glad to help."

Mackey and Levine exchanged glances. Mackey pulled a ballpoint pen from his breast pocket and glanced at Jill, who turned, stony-faced, and began walking away from the group. Levine followed after her. "Why sure," said Mackey heartily, turning back to Tricia. "*Always* glad to help."

"Why the scowl?" David Levine asked.

"Who's scowling?" Jill said, aware of the brittle tone in her voice.

"You are. Come on, what's the matter?"

Jill had made the mistake of marching up the corridor in the wrong direction, only to find herself blocked by the double swinging doors which led to the delivery area. There remained only one refuge: a walk-in linen closet. Levine had followed after her and now stood, leaning on the jamb, his tall, broad-shouldered frame blocking the exit.

For several seconds Jill kept her back to him, pawing furiously through a pile of sheets, pretending to look for something. She felt his eyes, silently watching her. Abruptly he said, "I'm sorry I yelled, Jill."

She hadn't expected that. She stopped, stared at a stack of white towels, then slowly turned. He saw with surprise that her eyes were red-rimmed, her cameo-perfect face blotchy. Quite a contrast to the way she had looked eleven days ago on the first day of internship. The new crop of interns had arrived on the floor looking like a bunch of awkward schoolchildren, except for Jill Raney. She looked confident and relaxed—not surprising since she was already an old hand around here. Coming from the med school, she had already spent her third and fourth years in clerkship on the hospital floors, caring clinically for patients and generally getting to know her way around. Her clerkship—like all of them—had been a rotating one, but David had seen enough of her, darting in and out, to decide that she was unusual. Brains *and* beauty—what a combination. Once, the week before internship began, he had shown the group around the OB floor. Their glances had met and she had smiled at him.

Now he leaned with his arms folded and watched her, disappointed. She wasn't smiling anymore.

He watched her slender hands clench. "Oh, you didn't yell," Jill said in a faintly supercilious tone. "All you did was make a complete jackass of me in a very ordinary voice. 'No comments allowed from the peanut gallery!' " she mimicked angrily. "Isn't that what you said? Everyone in the room laughed—including the patient!"

He dared a small smile. "They say it's the best medicine."

"Well, *I* call it lousy medicine!" She pounded a fist on the counter, sending packages of gauze flying. "Hollins wasn't *like* the other cases, dammit! She needed Pentothal, not five lousy milligrams of Valium! How can you do an amniocentesis on someone who's practically jumping off the table?"

Levine turned serious. Any other resident would have decapitated her for shooting her mouth off like that. She needed to be straightened out.

He unfolded his arms and straightened. "Well, we *did* it, didn't we? The less medication the better for the baby, and all Hollins needed was a few minutes to calm down. Procaine is an excellent pain killer—once it took effect, she was okay for the rest of the trip." He held up his finger. "Now you, kiddo—"

"Don't call me kiddo!"

"—spoke out of turn. You scared the patient! Anyway, interns are supposed to *observe* and keep their damn mouths *shut* and do what they're told!"

His face colored and he stepped closer to her. She took a step backward, her cheeks red, her eyes staring with fury. For a moment he was afraid she was going to punch him in the nose.

"Egotist," she hissed.

"Sorehead," he returned.

And then she burst into tears.

Levine blinked at her. "Aw, come on," he said. Awkwardly, he reached out to her as she yanked away, turned her back again and found herself quelling sobs before a pile of toilet paper.

David Levine suddenly felt foolish. Women. He could deal with male interns easily. Even drunks in a bar were easier than a crying woman. But here he was, confronted by a slender, delicate, and thoroughly mettlesome young woman, and he was at a loss. He decided to try a different tack. Inhaling, he brushed his dark brown hair off his brow and cleared his throat.

"Okay, Dr. Raney. Tantrum's over. I know all about your impressive scholastic background, and starting from square one again must be hard on your vanity." He waited for a response, and got none. Her back was still turned to him. She was sniffling quietly. He went on in a lower voice. "Listen. You're going to find out that putting an M.D. after your name doesn't make you a doctor. That takes longer. And if you can't manage a little give and take around here, you're not going to make it. You got that?''

God, how he hated making speeches. But something he said had pressed the right button. Several seconds passed, and her face unpinched a little. She turned her head slightly toward him. She looked at him with those achingly vulnerable green eyes, then looked away and stared miserably down at the floor.

He heard his name being paged. Well . . . they could wait thirty seconds.

"Jill—"

Now he felt guilty. He *had* humiliated her, and he was sorry. He bent his head, tried to look into her face. His voice became soft. "Hey, you're assigned to me," he said. "You and the others. Do you think we can work as a team? Get along?"

She hesitated, then, her face still downcast, shrugged and gave a weak nod.

Impulsively he reached out and slowly, gently, pulled off her surgical scrub cap. He realized he had wanted to do that since he had chased her into this place. Her long, honey hair fell to her shoulders and framed the high cheekbones, the beautiful face. He held his breath.

A harried-looking Sam MacIntyre poked his head around the door. "David, you're being paged. Want me to take it for you?"

Sam's perpetually cantankerous face peering in the doorway jolted David back to reality. "No, I'll answer," he said. "But do something else? Tell the interns to take the Hollins lab specimens up to Pathology."

Sam turned and glanced down the hallway. He brayed: "Looks like they've already *left* for Pathology. And took the lab rack with them, it 'pears." He snorted laughter and looked back in. "Hey, can you beat that? The pups are getting housebroken . . . Oh, sorry, Jill."

He gave her a wolfish grin. She glared at him.

Sam left and David turned to face Jill Raney. She was stuffing her long hair back into her surgical cap.

"Wait for me here. There's more I want to go over with you."

She nodded.

Levine left the door ajar and hurried down the hallway. Yanking the phone off the hook, he muttered his identity and listened intently. His face remained immobile, but he stiffened. Replacing the receiver, he walked rapidly back to the linen closet.

"No time to talk," he said. She sat on a chair, resting her head in her arms on a pile of towels.

"Up! The others have left the floor. Something just came in to Emergency, and they can't handle it. Woody says it's an obstetrical nightmare."

Jill stood up. "Elevator or stairs?"

"Stairs. Much faster. All set?"

"Yes." She gave him a timid smile. He turned and hurried out the door. She followed.

They rushed down the hall and past the nurses' station. At the far end they pulled open a door, and pounded down eight flights of stairs as if somebody's life depended on it.

$$3$$

ROUNDING THE LAST landing, they pulled open a steel door and turned down the wide hallway. Outpatients milled around and watched them curiously as they hurried past. The eight-flight plunge had left Jill breathless. She looked up at Levine. "You're not even winded."

"Try jogging," he said. They rounded the corner and emerged into bedlam. The hospital paging system was louder on the main floor to compensate for the constant stream of human traffic. "Dr. Levine. Calling Dr. Levine. Emergency Room, please."

They heard his name called, seemingly from everywhere above their heads, and elbowed their way through the chaos of the emergency room waiting area. The place was teeming: every chair around the periphery was filled; children cried, ailing or injured people and their relatives formed a check-in line that stretched all the way from the main entrance to the reception desk.

Jill thought: Wait till tonight, when it gets busy.

She could see the harried clerks and nurses at the reception desk. Multibuttoned telephones rang maddeningly, while tall stacks of patient charts threatened to topple. To one side, an anxious group leaned over a counter, arguing with an exasperated young doctor about an X ray. Bongo music blasted from a knot of Hispanics crowded around a transistor. Once again Jill wished she had studied Spanish in college. Their chatter sounded like gibberish to her, and, working among them, she was at a loss. As she hurried past she studied the faces in the group. None of them appeared injured or in need of emergency assistance.

Jill stopped and did a double take. A man in line stood about six feet away from her. Bright veins mapped his nose and cheeks; his tattered clothes smelled awful and he was having a coughing fit. Suddenly he bent over, clutched his ribs, and began to vomit blood. One of the Hispanics moved his sandwich out of the way. Two policemen at the main entrance stood by impassively. They were here for somebody else.

"David!" she cried. Levine turned, followed her gaze, and pointed to two orderlies who were fast approaching with a gurney. He reached for her arm, gesturing toward the entrance to the emergency room. "Come on," he shouted. "We've got a hot one in there too."

They rushed under the arch and down the busy corridor. Doctors and nurses whisked past in both directions, and Jill recognized another new intern carrying wet X rays. Levine weaved rapidly ahead. Trying to catch up, Jill collided with a rolling green laundry basket full of bloody sheets, turned to excuse herself to the orderly pushing it, and was rammed by a lab technician wheeling a table filled

with test tube racks. Jill felt dizzy. She heard David, far
ahead, calling to her; then he disappeared around the
corner.

She ran.

Passing a trio of policemen, Jill raced under a second
arch and through the busy, large gray room. She caught up
with David as he reached a far cubicle off to the right. The
only thing separating the cubicle from the pandemonium
outside was a flimsy nylon curtain. David flung it aside.

Inside four people crowded about the bed. Two nurses
were on the left, one adjusting a blood pressure cuff, the
other tearing open a package of tubing. Two doctors in
wrinkled scrub suits worked near the head of the bed, on
the right. The taller one, Jim Holloway, was nervously
eyeing a cardiac monitor. The other, Woody Greenberg,
was fussing with the position of the disk electrodes on the
patient's chest. Both were first year residents. Both looked
overwhelmed.

Woody glanced up at Levine and Jill as they entered.

"Oh my God, David, what do you make of this? We've
never ever *seen* it before!" Woody spoke so fast he stumbled over his words. To Jill, the already wiry young man
looked as if he had sweated off five pounds in the last ten
minutes.

David hurried around the bed; Jill held back. For some
reason she felt afraid. The shoulders of the nurse who had
moved in front of her made it difficult to see the patient.
Jill hesitated, then took a step forward; the white-uniformed
back moved away and Jill stared. On the bed lay a young
woman, about eight months pregnant, bleeding profusely
from her nose, mouth and ears. Her still face and closed
eyelids were grayish-blue. Her arms and torso were covered by spreading areas of black and blue, as if she had
been beaten and was still *getting* beaten. Blanketing her
skin was a sheen of sweat.

Jill heard Woody excitedly giving David the rundown
on the case. The young woman's name was Maria Moran;
she was twenty-five; she had collapsed on Third Avenue
and been brought in bleeding from every orifice. Her

blood pressure was already down to 70/40, her pulse was 140 and "thready"—too rapid and barely discernible, instead of "bounding" like a normal pulse.

"And look at the nails!" Holloway said, reaching down to lift a gray bruised hand by the wrist. A wedding ring glinted feebly.

"Cyanotic," Levine said tightly. To one of the nurses, "Nancy, I'll need sterile gloves and an OB pack." And to the two younger physicians: "Okay, what's been done so far?"

"Started an IV," said Woody Greenberg in his rapid-fire, piping voice. His hair of sandy corkscrews was darkened by perspiration. "Drawn blood for hemoglobin and hematocrit, ordered a type and crossmatch, sent off the SMA-12 blood chemistries and ordered a complete blood count . . ." He stopped, winded.

"We also ordered a bleeding and clotting workup," said Holloway in a low voice. His eyes were glued to the patient. "I'm not even sure *why* we ordered it, except that at the rate she's dropping . . ."

There was a snapping sound as nurse Nancy Hughes helped David on with his surgical gloves. Nancy looked up at him and shook her head. "She was pink when they brought her in, doctor. Honest, *pink*. I never saw—"

"Old story," Levine said, turning. He bent and his gloved hands explored the woman's abdomen. He frowned. "Uterus is as hard as a rock," he said. Holloway, watching, eased past David and stood at the other side of the bed. No one spoke. Sixty seconds passed while Levine's experienced fingers remained on the woman's abdomen, pressing gently. The titanic, knotted contraction did not even begin to let up. Levine's eyes became troubled; he understood.

Woody Greenberg was now by the door and peering anxiously outside the curtains. "Ginny Tata's supposed to be back from hematology any second," he said. "Jeez, what's taking them . . ."

"Forget it," said Levine.

They all looked at him.

"*Abruptio placentae*," he said softly. Jill's lips parted. She watched Holloway and Woody as they stared blankly at Levine. The disorder he had named was to most a word found only in textbooks. It was rare. It was the most bizarre of obstetrical mishaps, and it was bad.

With his left hand on the patient's abdomen, David Levine reached up with his right hand and pressed a red button. "Hematology!" he bellowed. "Ginny Tata, are you there?"

An electronic babble of voices answered him in the same pitch.

"Ginny!" he hollered. "Don't wait for the chemistries! Listen, run to the blood bank and get eight units of fibrinogen, stat! You hear me, Ginny? Also two units of whole blood and two units of packed red cells. Got that?"

There was a crackling, high-pitched response and David Levine switched off.

For three seconds he stood, staring into the hanging IV bottle, concentrating. Then he bent and began helping the other nurse, Cathy Mulvern, remove blood clots from the patient's nostrils.

Jill stood frozen at the foot of the bed. She realized there was nothing she could do, except watch, as Levine managed the case.

"Before anything," he was saying, "you have to get the blood pressure out of shock level. Then we can take her up to the O.R. and do a Caesarean." To the nurse he said, "Cathy, give her eighty milligrams of Aramine, will you?" And, glancing over at Holloway, "How's the fetal heartbeat?"

"One-sixty and rising," said Holloway, tense.

Levine said, "That's starting to sound like trouble, isn't it?"

"Yes," said Holloway. He rubbed his eyes and continued staring at the fetal monitor.

Jill had trouble finding her voice. "Do you *have* to do a Caesarean if you stabilize her?"

" 'If' is a big word," muttered Woody Greenberg.

"The worst," said Jim Holloway.

David Levine said nothing as he watched Cathy Mulvern administer the Aramine. Jill knew he was trying to elevate the blood pressure. She could hear his rapid breathing. "Nancy," he said, turning. "We're going to need two lines open. Start another IV in the left antecubital. When the stuff arrives from the blood bank I want you pushing in whole blood as fast as you can. And on the other side start the fibrinogen, right into the tubing, okay?"

"Got it," said Nancy Hughes. Cathy Mulvern opened a fresh box of cotton swabs. Jill glanced into the bin where Cathy was throwing the blood-soaked swabs. It was almost full. She looked away quickly.

"Dammit, where's Ginny?" David said to no one in particular. Jill helped Nancy hook up another bottle of 5 percent dextrose in saline, then heard Levine's voice again, sounding solemn.

"*Abruptio placentae*," he said, bending to check some tubing, "is sudden and dramatic. It involves the separation of the placenta from the uterus before the child is born. Usually, this is for reasons unknown, and the results are devastating. What happens is like a dam breaking. The amniotic fluid pours into the maternal circulation, the mother's veins, reducing the blood fibrinogen level, which in turn causes massive internal hemorrhaging."

He took a surgical sponge and mopped the glistening area from the woman's cheek to the ear. The patient's hair was matted; the pillow was soaked with blood.

"Due to blood loss," he continued, "the patient goes into lightning shock. Diagnosis is hypofibrinogenemia. It happens so fast, that's what makes it so hard to control. . . ." He stared down at the pretty, blue-gray face and inhaled. "The next ninety seconds will tell us if a Caesarean is academic."

As if by cue they heard a commotion and then, with a whisk of the nylon curtain, nurse Ginny Tata burst into the cubicle. "Need roller skates," she huffed, depositing four vials and four red-filled plastic bags on the supply table.

Levine looked over at Greenberg, who had just removed a blood pressure cuff from the patient's left arm. "BP?"

"Plunging," said Greenberg.

"Doctor . . . I . . ." Levine turned toward Nancy Hughes's tight voice and said, "Oh, Christ." Jill looked too and saw that the nurse had been trying and failing for the last three minutes to insert the new syringe into the vein on the patient's inner arm. It was no use. The patient was in deep shock; the veins had collapsed and gone too flat to penetrate.

Everyone started talking at once.

Levine's voice became suddenly loud. "Jill!" he called over his shoulder. "How fast can you do a cutdown?"

A cutdown?

"I've never done a cutdown," Jill said. Suddenly her heart was beating hard and she was terrified. "I mean, I've memorized the procedure from textbooks but I've never . . . on a real . . ."

"Here's your gloves, Dr. Raney." Cathy Mulvern stood before her holding up the surgical gloves.

Jill pushed her hands into them. She realized she was trembling.

Jerkily, she moved around the bed toward the patient's feet. Mulvern hurried a scalpel into her hand while Hughes pulled up the bloodied sheet to the patient's knees. David shouted for eight milligrams of Levophed in a stepped-up attempt to raise the blood pressure. Bending, he supervised the insertion of a nasal oxygen catheter through one of the patient's nostrils; turning his head frequently, he was watching, as were Holloway and Greenberg, both the fetal and maternal heartbeats on the two beeping monitor screens.

"Ninety over sixty, with a pulse of one-sixty," Jill heard Greenberg say.

"Shit," Holloway said.

"Fetal distress!" It was Levine's voice. "Fetal heartbeat's gone from 160 to 180 and dropped back down to 100!"

God, what now? Jill thought. Caesarean? *Here?* No, no way. More blood loss would kill the mother instantly. Only this cutdown might help. . . .

She concentrated. Lowering the scalpel, she held it

poised over the patient's ankle. Then she made a quick incision about an inch wide above the ankle. The skin gaped, like an eye opening wide, revealing a flat, blue vein. She blinked at the cut. The incision was neat, a perfect perpendicular to the vein. She began to breathe rapidly. Peripherally she heard voices at the head of the bed. Someone was yelling that the patient was fibrillating. She heard a command for Lidocaine—*good, they'll shock her out of it*—and tried to concentrate.

Vaguely she was aware of a white uniform injecting the Lidocaine into the IV line, of someone in a scrub suit placing the defibrillating paddles on Maria Moran's exposed chest. One paddle rested directly over the sternum, the other was placed halfway down the left side of the chest.

"Everybody off the bed!" Levine shouted. Without looking up Jill took a step backward. Levine activated the powerful electrical charge; Maria Moran's body arched violently; the arms flailed and then flopped inward, across the chest.

A moment passed. Jill heard the electronic blip reappear on the screen. At the "all clear" signal she stepped forward again with her scalpel. Quickly she threaded two silk sutures under the vein, tied the bottom suture and with her left hand exerted traction to pull the vein free. With her right hand holding the tip of the scalpel she nicked the vessel open, then took the polyethylene catheter Mulvern handed her and began to thread it into the vein and up the leg. *I'm doing it!* she thought. She felt a thrill of confidence surge through her. Only a few more inches of threading to go and she could hook up the other end of the catheter into the IV, and they'd have two good IV routes going and then they could push blood in faster than . . .

"Jill . . ." It was Levine's voice but she ignored him. She was almost finished, and her heart was pounding.

"Jill." Levine was now at her side. His voice was tired, flat. She inhaled, stopped what she was doing and looked up at him.

"It's all over," he said softly.

She stared at him.

"But she was only *fibrillating* . . ."

"She arrested four minutes ago," Levine said. Exhaling heavily, he started to pull off his gloves.

Jill felt her eyes mist over. Then she looked up to the head of the bed to where Jim Holloway was applying external heart massage.

For several moments Levine also watched Holloway's futile efforts, then turned back to Jill, his face drooping with fatigue.

"We gave her intracardiac epinephrine, mouth-to-mouth resuscitation, the whole works." He hesitated. "She was mortally ill when she came in, Jill . . . we did everything we could."

By the door Woody Greenberg sat on a wooden chair, his face in his hands.

Jill Raney, still wearing her bloodstained gloves, stared in disbelief at the dead woman stretched out on the bed. The woman's abdomen still looked as if it contained a beach ball. A dead beach ball. Six minutes before, Levine explained, the fetal heartbeat had abruptly stopped, probably because its own bloodstream had become as poisoned as the mother's.

Jill found herself fighting back tears. Her eyes traveled to the white maternity dress with lace eyelets, now bloodied, hanging on a peg in the corner. She tried to imagine the vibrant young woman who had put it on this morning: alive—no, *doubly* alive. Jill wondered if Maria Moran had been conscious before she and David arrived, tried to imagine her relief at finding the skilled doctors of Madison Hospital eager to help her.

And they hadn't.

It was time, as Cathy Mulvern was now saying as she moved numbly about the room, to "clean up for the next case." And just as numbly, Jill watched Nancy Hughes make out an I.D. card and hang it around the corpse's large toe. At the head of the bed, Levine was filling out a report. His jaws were clenched, and his pen hand was shaking.

Jill looked down and saw that the blood stains on her scrub suit, minutes before soaking and a warm, *alive* red, were now drying and turning brown. Just like that, she thought, and started to cry. She was aware of Greenberg rising from his chair and coming toward her; of Levine helping to remove her surgical gloves. One of the nurses looked up with a less sympathetic expression. *Interns,* her face seemed to say.

Holloway was already outside. Someone had looked in to announce that Maria Moran's husband, a fireman, had arrived. It would be Holloway's task to inform the man, offer solace, perhaps gather more background on the patient's case history.

Jill looked a last time at Maria Moran's closed eyes, the bloodless face, and then left the room. Levine followed after her. They walked silently down the busy, connecting corridor as far as the arch. Ahead she heard the blasting bongos, the howling babies, people arguing over their place in line.

She turned to David, pale and anxious.

"I don't want to go through there," she said.

He gave her a tired smile. "I'll run interference for you."

It was meant to lighten her spirits, but she saw that he, too, was as shaken as she felt. Somehow that made things a little easier. She nodded and let him lead the way. Together they went across the emergency room and headed for the elevators.

4

FLOWERS—RIOTOUS BOUQUETS, extravagant floral decorations —began arriving around 9:30 for the happy new mothers. When Jill and David reached the obstetrical floor, the bouquets had overflowed the desk of the nurses' station and were beginning to take up floor space. "Nurses' station looks like an altar," Jill muttered as they stepped off the elevator.

"Yes," Levine said. "Depressing, isn't it?"

They stood talking quietly in the elevator foyer, oblivious to the activity around them. "I don't think I'm up to doing patient rounds. I just couldn't put the face on," Jill said. David, hands on hips, nodded.

"I've got a better idea," he said. "We don't both need to visit well patients." He glanced at his watch. "You've got forty-five minutes before clinic duty, right?"

"Yes, 10:30 to 12:30, I'm due in *el clínico*."

He raised his eyebrows and smiled. "You're learning the lingo," he said. "Well, you could use a little space before going down to *that* pit. How about finding a quiet place to read charts? There's a lot of paperwork to be caught up on."

Jill stared at the floor. "Do you think forty-five minutes will be enough to get my head back together?"

"Do your best," he said.

Levine reached out to give her shoulder a friendly squeeze. She watched him walk over to the nurses' station and gather up charts. He seemed to remember something, and looked back at her.

"If I don't see you," he said, "don't forget Grand Rounds at one o'clock. In the old building."

She nodded, then gestured in the direction of the long corridor lined with patients' rooms.

"Act cheerful," she said.

He made a face. "Thanks a lot."

And then he turned and walked down the corridor, and disappeared into the room of a patient more fortunate than Maria Moran.

Motion, Jill decided, was the first step toward feeling better. Bypassing the nurses' station, she went into the women doctors' lounge, walked past the lockers and hard benches and into the shower room. There she tore off her stained scrub suit, threw it in a bin, showered, shampooed, and changed into a new scrub suit, all in less than ten minutes. Then, eyeing her waterproof watch, she spent another seventy seconds standing before a blasting wall hairdryer known as "the hot rod"; and before twelve minutes were up, she was back out in the hall, clasping her still damp hair into a tortoise-shell barrette and pulling on a stiff white jacket.

She forced herself to move. At the nurses' station Gladys Hemendinger sat behind the counter, ignoring a ringing telephone as she stapled together a pile of lab reports.

"Hello, Miss Hemendinger," Jill said, easing past her. "I'm going to be needing the floor charts."

"Why, hello Dr. Raney . . ." Jill was aware of Hemendinger swiveling on her secretary's chair and watching as she pulled out the chart rack and began wheeling it away.

The nurse was out of her seat and peering anxiously at Jill over the countertop. "*All* of them?"

Jill stopped, turned, "Half, actually. Anything the matter?"

"No. I mean, well, yes!" The nurse dropped her voice. "You *have* to have them back by eleven. Stryker himself is leading today's attending rounds. He's already destroyed a few people around here this week, and if he loses his temper again . . .''

Jill smiled, and promised to have the charts back. She hadn't been around this department long enough to fear Stryker as she knew others did; but on the other hand she did not want to annoy the chief of Obstetrics. She had already heard about his terrible temper. A nurse brushed by, then two strolling patients wearing pastel-colored robes. Visiting time was over and the squalling infants were all back in their isolettes in the nursery at the other end of the corridor.

Jill's thoughts wandered back to Dr. William Stryker.

It was, she reflected, impressive enough that he was chief of Obstetrics and Gynecology at Madison, one of the top teaching institutions in the world. But he was also a world-famous fertility expert acclaimed for his pioneering work in human reproduction, as well as chairman of the Genetic Counseling Committee at the university. Jill peered down at the rolling chart rack as she thought of the word "genetic." It was an important word in the hospital. Stryker, or Stryker's team, were always in the newspapers with their astonishing breakthroughs in genetic research. How ironic, Jill thought. Every discovery of Stryker's prompted either adulation or raging ethical debates—even among his own medical colleagues. Many said he had gone too far. Some said *science* had gone too far.

She approached the small room used for storing drugs and surgical supplies. Jill had seen this room before and liked it because it had a floor to ceiling window. She pushed the door open, saw the sunshine streaming in, and knew she had come to the right place. Kicking the door shut, she maneuvered the chart rack alongside the desk that stood perpendicular to the view of the river. She looked around. The room was narrow. The two facing walls were crowded with locked, glass-fronted medicine cabinets. Below them, on both sides, were long counter tops jammed with equipment. To her right was a stainless steel sink and a coffee pot.

Jill sat and attacked the pile of charts. This was what

she was best at: scanning quickly and absorbing reams of information. Beginning at the top of the pile she took down the first chart and opened it on the desk. She read, flipped pages, took notes, wrote orders. Then she went on to the second chart, the third. Pages in patient charts were color-coded, which made the going easier. Lab and X ray reports were pink. Doctors' order sheets were light green; progress sheets were yellow; TPR (temperature, pulse and respiration) sheets were light blue; and nurses' notes, like nurses' uniforms, were white. It made things less confusing that way.

Now *here* was the stuff of real life, Jill decided. Mrs. Andrews, who had delivered early yesterday, was constipated; Mrs. Mazzini had diarrhea; Mrs. Kowalski's episiotomy hurt—oops, missed that one, Jill thought. She turned back to green and wrote an order for thirty milligrams of codeine, Q4h, then flipped back. . . .

Where was I . . . oh yes, Mrs. Flaherty has sore nipples, Mrs. Horowitz wants to go home; Mrs. Dowe *doesn't* want to go home. "Ha!" Jill laughed out loud over that one. What else . . . Mrs. Hollins is running a fever. . . .

Jill stared. *Mrs. Hollins?*

She looked up.

Mary Hewitt-Hollins the attorney? The one who had had the amniocentesis this morning? Jill frowned, confused. All amniocentesis patients were sent home after an hour or so in the recovery room. It was really a minor procedure.

So what was she doing here as an inpatient?

Jill reached up and pressed a button on an intercom.

"Yes?" came the response. The voice was not Gladys Hemendinger's.

"Nurse, can you tell me if Dr. Levine is still on the floor?"

"No, he's not," said the voice. "I believe he was called into surgery. Dr. Holloway was supposed to finish his patient rounds, but he's not here yet either."

"And Dr. MacIntyre?"

There was a pause, the sound of urgent whispering, and then the voice came back on the line.

"Dr. MacIntyre and Dr. Mackey are in delivery, room ten."

"All right, thank you." Jill switched off, then pulled the Hollins chart out of the pile. After loading the rest of the charts back into the rack, she opened the door and wheeled it back to the nurses' station. The clock on the wall said 10:25. The floor seemed empty.

Two student nurses were behind the desk, trying to figure out all the buttons on the telephones.

Jill said, "Please tell Miss Hemendinger that the rack is back and the orders are updated."

"What?" said one of the students.

Jill went quickly down the hall, staring down at the Hollins chart, and trying to read as she walked. The patient had been admitted by George Mackey at 9:22—only half an hour after Jill and David Levine had left the floor. A terse note in Mackey's awful handwriting recommended admission for later evaluation of nonurgent symptoms. The letters F.U.O. were scribbled, then underlined, indicating a fever of unknown origin. But the fever was only 100.2. Definitely low grade. Mackey was just being extra cautious.

Jill stopped under a fluorescent light and flipped from the admission sheet back to the nurse's note. The note was clocked at 9:51. Within twenty-nine minutes after admission Mary Hollins' temperature had risen to 102.1.

Jill hurried down the corridor to room 824. MARY HOLLINS, the card on the door said. She knocked, then went in.

It was a semiprivate room. The bed nearer the door was empty; the blinds over the window were drawn, diminishing the light, and the figure in the second bed was a vague hump.

Jill whispered near the bed, "Mrs. Hollins." The patient's eyes were closed. She wore a hospital gown instead of the usual pretty nightgown, a giveaway that the patient had not expected to stay the night. Somewhere, probably in an office uptown, was a husband who had been notified, who would soon come rushing in with an overnight case.

"Mrs. Hollins—" she began, and the woman's eyelids fluttered and opened.

The patient stared at her for a moment, as if trying to place her. Then a wisp of a smile crossed her lips.

"Peanut gallery," Mary Hollins said weakly.

"Right," said Jill with a wry expression. "I was one of the interns observing you this morning." She glanced over her shoulder. "Do you mind if I raise the blinds? I'd like to have a look at you."

Mary Hollins rolled her head slowly toward the window. "Oh, please do," she said. "I was beginning to think a gloomy room was part of the cure."

Jill smiled. She drew the blinds. Midmorning light poured in; the sound of traffic became more audible.

"How's that?" Jill asked, turning back. Mrs. Hollins smiled wanly. Jill crossed back to the bed, pulled out a pen, and held it poised over the chart.

"Well," she said, resting an arm on the bedrail. "I notice here that you're running some fever, and I'd like to start tracking down its source. Is there anything specific that's bothering you?"

Mary Hollins half-closed her eyes and inhaled slowly. "Dizzy," she said. "Feel *so* dizzy and lightheaded. Can't think, can't . . ." Her voice grew thinner and then trailed off.

Jill scribbled. "Any sore throat or cough?"

"No." Mary Hollins shook her head.

"Any burning when you pass urine? Sometimes cystitis can cause—"

"No. No burning. Nothing like that."

Jill studied her for a moment; then, jotting on the chart, decided to order a urinalysis and complete blood count.

"Okay," Jill said, placing the chart at the foot of the bed. The history-taking part over, it was now time for the physical. "I'd like to look you over just a bit," she said, adjusting the white sheet.

With her penlight Jill examined the patient's throat. Next she put the stethoscope to her ears and listened for several moments to the lungs. The possibility of any kind of lung infection was remote, but it was still a possibility that had to be ruled out.

Removing the stethoscope, Jill lowered the sheet below the patient's hips, then raised her gown almost as far as the breasts. Carefully she began to examine the exposed abdomen. Removing a Band-Aid from below the navel, she checked the amniocentesis puncture wound for signs of infection. There was none. Then, fingertips pressing gently, Jill examined the rest of the abdomen. No sign of undue swelling. At five months' gestation the fundus of the uterus was just up to the navel, where it was supposed to be. There was nothing to suggest problems on the sides of the abdomen either, although the area above the navel was almost concave. The patient couldn't have eaten much this morning.

Without looking up Jill casually asked, "Have you noticed any change in your appetite?"

Several moments passed. Jill looked up. Mary Hollins' eyes were shut tight. Tears spilled from her eyes and ran down her cheeks.

"Oh, Mrs. Hollins, please don't be upset! You . . . you'll see . . ." Jill hurriedly finished her exam and drew the sheet back up to the patient's chin. "You probably do have cystitis or something." She made tucking-in motions about the bedclothes as she studied the patient's face.

Mary Hollins opened her still-brimming eyes. She had quieted somewhat, but her lower lip quivered.

"We had it all planned. Career first, then children. I started trying to conceive when I was thirty-two." She paused, inhaled as if it were painful. "What a joke. We spent so many years being careful and found out we were borderline infertile."

Jill looked at her. "But you're pregnant *now,* aren't you? You're going to have a baby!"

Mary Hollins turned her head on the pillow and stared out the window. "Yes," she said. Her voice rose. "Oh, we waited too long! Maybe that's why this fever is happening . . ." She began to weep again.

"Ridiculous!" said Jill, reaching for some Kleenex. She began to dab at Mary Hollins' face. "Why, more women than ever are postponing childbearing until their thirties or

more. Amniocentesis has extended the safe childbearing
years by a full decade—besides, you're young! And it's all
a moot point anyway, because there's *no way* your age
could have anything to do with an elevated temperature.''

The legal term, "moot point," seemed to light a spark
in Mary Hollins.

Jill pulled back and smiled at her. "I'll bet you're a real
whiz in the courtroom," she said. Mary stared down at her
soggy Kleenex. "A regular tiger," she said softly.

"Well," said Jill, arranging the covers, "the important
thing now is to try not to get upset. I'm going to order
some routine tests, and when the results come back, I'm
sure whatever it is has nothing to do with the pregnancy."

"You're very sweet," said Mary Hollins.

Jill gathered up her chart and prepared to leave. "I'll
send the nurse down with some aspirin," she said, stopping in the doorway. "And promise me," she said, shaking her finger, "no worrying allowed."

From her bed Mary Hollins smiled softly. "I'll try,"
she said.

Jill walked briskly back to the nurses' station. Gladys
Hemendinger and another older R.N. were busily explain-
ing the contents of a Rolodex to the two student nurses.
On the counter top were several new flower arrangements,
awaiting delivery.

Jill loudly clapped the Hollins chart on the counter top,
startling the group.

"Would you pick up these orders for Mrs. Hollins in
824?" Jill looked directly at the head nurse. "The lab tests
are to go out stat. Also, check patient's vital signs Q4h
and give aspirin, ten grains, Q4h prn, temp over 101. The
aspirin order is also stat."

"Aspirin, certainly," said Hemendinger. There was a
ringing sound, and she added: "Just as soon as I answer
the telephone."

"Now, please," Jill said.

The head nurse's hand stopped in midair above the
phone. Jill saw Hemendinger hesitate, mutter something,
and reach for the Hollins chart. Jill looked at her watch,

startled, and checked with the wall clock. There must be some mistake.

It was 10:40. She was already ten minutes late for her clinic duty downstairs. *Damn,* she thought. By the time she got there, because of the slow elevators and long corridors connecting the new part of the hospital with the old, she would be nearly twenty minutes late.

She rushed toward the bank of elevators, pressed the button and glanced nervously at the waiting people. Some were house staff, some relatives of patients.

While she waited she pulled out her small black notebook from a waist pocket. It was her special organizer, the one in which she jotted important memos to herself. She wrote, then twice underlined: "Follow closely case of Maria Hollins." Overhead the elevator dinged its arrival, and the crowd pressed forward, but Jill was only dimly aware of their movement.

She stood, blinking down at the mistake she had just written, and suddenly felt cold.

5

"GOD, WHAT A MORNING," Jill heard David Levine say to Sam MacIntyre. "One amnio job that's not looking too good and one maternal death. Complete blitz. Just like that."

She stood unobtrusively behind him in line in the noisy cafeteria. It was 12:35. At one o'clock a vitally important conference was scheduled, so it wasn't surprising that nearly everyone in the department plus what looked like half of the hospital had converged on the cafeteria.

Jill slid her tray along, watching MacIntyre stuff an unpaid for roll into his mouth.

"And a stillborn for me!" MacIntyre hollered. "Healthiest pregnancy you ever saw—and bang! Patient's brought in in premature hard labor and out comes this dead . . ." He brushed his hand through his hair, looking down. "Jeez, David, the tomatoes look like plasma."

Levine frowned. "Which patient had the stillborn?" he asked.

"Burke," said MacIntyre. "Remember nice Mrs. Burke? Chrissakes, what *is* it around here—something in the *water*?" He shook his head. Levine reached halfheartedly for a plate of something steaming. MacIntyre glanced past David to Jill. "Oh, 'lo Jill."

"Hi," she said, wishing she were somewhere else in line. All this talk was unnerving. The ninety minutes spent in the outpatient gyn clinic had been blessedly undramatic. Time to clear the mind. All routine, almost boring.

Now she was back in the eye of the storm as the two residents rehashed the morning's casualties. And it wasn't only them. It was all of them. All through the cafeteria anxious knots of people were comparing notes. Faces were tense, and the undercurrent of strain was palpable.

Jill took a curling ham and cheese sandwich, thought better of it, and settled for a plate of beef stew.

"Bad day," she said to Tricia Donovan, who stood in line behind her.

"The worst," Tricia said. "I heard about the Moran case. Awful, awful . . ." Tricia eyed a pyramid of grinders. Jill moved further along. "By the way," Tricia called, "did you hear about the eclampsia case?"

"What?" said Jill, signaling that she couldn't hear over the noise.

Jill looked away. She had the sudden beginning of a headache, and the feeling of depression she'd had earlier was beginning to creep back. Ahead, farther down, she saw Levine, listening and nodding with grave, thoughtful eyes as MacIntyre yammered on. Levine was leaning with both elbows on the steel counter as if he wished it were a bed. Jill had to admit, even leaning over, shoulders hunched, his straight brown hair falling into his face, he was remarkably good-looking. At about six foot one he was perhaps an inch taller than MacIntyre, who, in his own sandy-haired way, wasn't exactly bad-looking either. That is, if one managed to overlook the irascible temper, the white jacket that always looked slept in and the eating manners of a timberwolf. They had reached the cashier. Levine, straightening, must have sensed Jill behind him because he abruptly turned and found her standing by his shoulder. He smiled, looking at her. She felt her face go crimson.

MacIntyre, meanwhile, was paying for his lunch and loudly berating himself for having perhaps used the wrong medications on the eclampsia patient. Or the right medications in the wrong order.

Levine turned back to the second-year resident. "You did fine," Jill heard him say. "Only next time, if it's that far gone, give the Lasix and Mag Sulfate *simultaneously*. And give the Mag Sulfate deep IM . . ."

Jill didn't hear the rest because the two residents headed off to find a table. Jill, Tricia Donovan and an intern named Charlie Ortega carried their trays to a favorite table, far enough from the noise yet close enough to the house phones in case they were paged.

They sat down. Tricia and Charlie were still discussing the morning's abruptio, eclampsia, and stillborn cases in low voices. Jill, listening, stared at her food. She felt Tricia's eyes on her.

"Something wrong, Jill?"

Jill shrugged. Toying with her fork, she said, "This morning really threw me. You know"—she looked up—"when I finished medical school, I thought I was going to save everybody."

Tricia shook her head and sighed. "Didn't we all?"

Jill leaned forward and began to eat. "And I guess I thought OB was going to be a happier place."

"Oh." Tricia frowned and glanced around. "Well, today certainly *has* been horrendous, no denying that."

There was a loud scraping of chairs and three more interns arrived. Gary ("Motormouth") Phipps, from California via Yale, horse-faced Carole Shelton from Minneapolis, and Ramu Chitkara, born in New Delhi and educated at Oxford. With comic primness, Ramu placed his plate of grinders distastefully on the table.

Jill smiled at him, then said to Tricia, "Tell me about the eclampsia."

Tricia straightened her glasses and whistled. She took another bite and gestured toward Ramu and Charlie Ortega. "We were all there, helping MacIntyre," she said. The others nodded.

"It was bad. Poor MacIntyre. Would you believe it came in only thirty minutes after that stillbirth?" Tricia's hand clenched into a fist. "By the time we got her into treatment, the woman's BP was already 260 over 140. It was rough, but we got her pretty stabilized. I mean, her vital signs are doing better and she's not having convulsions any more."

Tricia took another mouthful. "Now here's the *weird* part. Eclampsia, as we know, usually happens to overweight women with elevated blood pressure, high salt intake and albumin in the urine. For weeks and even *months* they have these symptoms that slowly get worse— plenty of warning, plenty of time to treat it, right?"

Jill nodded.

"Well, get this. Today's eclampsia patient arrives, a slender young woman obsessive about her salt intake, and—as of her last week's prenatal visit—BP okay and no albumin in the urine." Tricia paused. "So that's it! Absolutely no antecedent toxemia symptoms at all. And this morning—Bang! Not normal, I tell you. Mo-o-st peculiar."

Jill stared at her. Slowly her eyes moved from Tricia to the others at the table. "You know," she said, "for a supposedly world-renowned medical center, this place has had one helluva bad morning."

Carole Shelton looked at Jill sharply. "What do you mean, '*supposedly* world-renowned medical center?'"

"She means," Charlie Ortega said, "that this morning's

been worse than most, and I couldn't agree more." Charlie glanced at his watch. "Nine minutes till show time."

Ramu Chitkara spoke up. "Jill," he said, "remember that Madison is a magnet for the toughest cases. The high-risk private patients. The ones who get sick in the *street* and might be turned away by other hospitals. Every ambulance driver knows that. No doubt that's how your abruptio case wound up here—"

"Hear! Hear!" Carole Shelton said. "And all of *that*"— she tapped a forefinger on the formica table top—"is what makes this hospital the unsurpassed teaching institution that it is!"

Gary Phipps broke the tension by making a vulgar sound. He rose noisily, tossing his plastic plates onto his tray like Frisbees. "Hospital knows what it's doing," he said. "We'd better get going if we want good seats."

"Or *any* seats," said Ramu, also rising. "Come on, ladies," he said. "This conference is supposed to be one of the biggies."

Jill Raney looked at Carole Shelton. "We'll see how the afternoon goes," she said quietly.

The women stood up, deposited their trays on the rack and headed toward the elevators. Jill and Tricia walked behind the rest. Tricia said in a low voice, "I'm going to research that eclampsia case on my own. Dammit, there's *got* to be more to it."

Jill nodded. "Same here. The abruptio, I mean. Strictly on the *q.t.*, right?"

"God yes." Tricia frowned. "But when are we going to find the *time?*"

"We'll find it. And then we'll compare notes."

"You're on."

Carole Shelton dropped back to join them. "I mean, really," she said. "What *actually* happened this morning? Two unfortunate tragedies that have absolutely no connection, and a case of eclampsia that is in the process of being corrected."

"The eclampsia might still abort," said Tricia.

"Well, even *so*," persisted Carole Shelton. "There's

still absolutely no common clinical causation between abruptio placentae, stillbirth and eclampsia, and frankly"—she looked directly at Jill—"I think it's irresponsible to go around detracting from the institution because a few unrelated events happen to occur within the same period."

Jill didn't respond, but made a mental note to spend the rest of the year ignoring Carole Shelton. They reached the vestibule, filled with house staff waiting for the elevator. Jill was glad to see Woody Greenberg there, although there was no sign of Levine or MacIntyre.

Woody was joking loudly with another resident about an incident yesterday in the clinic. A fourteen-year-old had shown up requesting birth control. Woody told her that she was underage, and that she would have to return with a parent or guardian. The girl asked if her aunt would do; her parents were away. Woody said yes, the aunt would be okay; so a few hours later they both showed up—and the aunt was twelve years old.

Jill laughed along with everyone else.

"Well?" she heard from behind her.

"Well, what?" said Jill, turning.

Carole Shelton's voice dropped to a whisper. "*Do* you agree that there's no connection between these events we've discussed. I mean, even implying . . ."

Jill realized that she wasn't talking to a person but to the institution itself, fiercely uptight about its image.

"Listen, dammit," she said, coloring. "I never said those things were related. How *could* they be?" She paused. As she heard her own words she felt vaguely uneasy.

Jill looked at Shelton steadily. "It's just kind of a pity those things seem to be *happening* here, isn't it?"

The elevator doors opened and Jill followed the crowd in. Carole Shelton, still arguing, followed after her.

$$\overline{6}$$

THE PLANET WAS violet and floated lazily in a brilliant orange sea. Whitish specks dotted the planet in odd-shaped clusters, some crowded, some sparse, suggesting civilizations of greater or lesser density—and who knew what inhabitants?—on this awesome sphere being viewed for the first time.

A voice, electronically amplified, floated out over the gloom of the amphitheater; penlights switched on like a sudden constellation, and the sound of furious note-taking accompanied the murmur of awe that ran through the tiers of students.

"What you are seeing," intoned the voice of Dr. William Stryker, "is, I promise you, not Star Wars."

Appreciative laughter broke out from the rows of seats. Tension dissolved and the audience was reminded that this was, after all, a Grand Rounds conference like any other. Well, almost any other. Many had arrived whispering that its title, "Latest Advances in Human Reproductive Technology," sounded *creepy*, but such feelings only heightened the anticipation and pulled people closer to the edge of their seats.

Dr. William Stryker, chief of Madison's Obstetrics and Gynecology Department, stood off to one side of the elevated podium, leaning on a dimly illuminated lectern. The violet light from the screen gave his tall, silver-haired figure a reddish cast. Jill Raney, sitting with Tricia

Donovan in the fourth row, saw his face half in shadow: a crimson mask from some ancient play.

"Nor is this a slide of outer space at all," Stryker went on. "It is, rather, a picture of inner space: an *in vitro*–fertilized mouse egg, magnified three hundred times and stained for the purposes of photography. We can't, of course, do that with a human egg."

With a flourish Stryker flicked on a flashlight with an arrow beam and pointed it at the screen. "That exotic-looking sky," he said, "is the culture medium that nourishes the egg. It contains enough amino acids and glucose to nurture a mammalian egg *at least* to the blastocyst stage."

The flashlight arrow zoomed around in the orange broth and then flicked off. Most of the students underlined what the doctor had emphasized.

Still leaning on the lectern, Stryker spoke briefly about the hospital's two main methods of treating infertility. Depending on its cause, he said, a couple may now choose to achieve pregnancy through artificial insemination or *in vitro* fertilization, "which is still commonly called a 'test tube baby,' although the term is erroneous."

In vitro fertilization, he declared, was the most spectacular development of all. Using a laparoscope, doctors removed the woman's egg from her ovary, united it with her husband's sperm in a Petri dish, and implanted the resulting fertilized embryo in the wife's womb. It was a procedure, he said, usually done to bypass damaged Fallopian tubes.

"But I understand the fear," he went on solemnly, beginning to pace. "Like many discoveries, the technique has opened up frontiers undreamed of in science. It has revolutionized the classic concept of genetics, has enabled us to treat genetic disorders in the newborn, and"—his voice became stiff—"has opened a Pandora's box of controversy. It's knowing too much, you see, that creates dilemmas. May I have the second slide, please?"

Jill saw the light beam click again, and looked up at a human egg, magnified two hundred times, watery, pale and

mucoid. In the slide it was surrounded by hundreds of
iridescent sperm that almost seemed to be moving. "Only
one sperm will penetrate the egg," Stryker was now saying,
"and fertilization will occur *not* in the female's body, but
in a glass Petri dish, a humble little saucer, four inches
across and one-half inch deep. Nature, always indifferent,
does not *care* where fertilization takes place: given the
right temperature, the right egg and the right sperm will
mate in a teaspoon!"

Stryker leaned on his wooden pointer, allowing a momemt
for the scribblers to catch up. In her notebook, Jill Raney
wrote "life in a dish," and underlined it several times.

Stryker walked a few steps away from the lectern and
tapped the screen with his pointer. "I'm now going to
show you a series of slides showing conception and the
cleavage divisions—the beginning of life—of this egg as it
sits and is nourished in its dish."

He showed the egg twelve hours after fertilization, when
it began to rearrange itself. "Examine now for defects," he
said, moving his pointer across the screen. He told them to
look for injury to the cell wall; deterioration of the nucleus; disintegration of any cellular details. "Next!" he
called out to the projectionist, and then "Next!" again.
They saw the luminous, almost stroboscopic stages of a
single cell as it split into two cells, which in turn split, a
day later, into four cells; big enough now to be reimplanted
in the mother.

"And so," concluded Stryker, turning to face his audience, "to the joy or dismay of many, we have . . . created
life in the lab." He walked back to the lectern, placed his
hands on each side, and said: "May I have the lights back
on, please?"

The recessed lights came on and for a moment the
crowd of students sat, dazed and blinking. There was an
excited buzz. Dr. Stryker stepped down from the podium
to confer with a group of older doctors in the front row.
Jill Raney guessed they were members of Madison's genetic counseling team, and wondered about them, until she
suddenly felt Tricia's eyes on her.

Jill turned. Tricia leaned over and said in a lecherous whisper, "I was conceived in a Packard."

Jill laughed loud in spite of herself, and covered her mouth quickly. She saw David Levine, in the second row by the aisle, turn back and frown. The lights dimmed, and Dr. Stryker was back at the lectern, waiting. When the audience grew quiet, he cleared his throat.

"Many of you are new to the hospital, and that being the case, I would like to introduce you to our vice-chairman of the Genetic Counseling Committee, Dr. Clifford Arnett. Dr. Arnett is deeply involved in reproductive endocrinology and infertility research; however, he gives most generously of his time to our clinics and the practice of medicine. He is an invaluable member of this highly-advanced obstetrical teaching program of which you are all privileged participants. I give you, therefore, Dr. Clifford Arnett."

A ripple of applause had already begun as a large, white-coated figure mounted the podium. Clifford Arnett had ginger hair, a broad, toothy smile, and wore an open-collared sportshirt under his lab coat. Jill had admired him since medical school. He was volatile, but popular and approachable as a teacher, and was almost as big a medical celebrity as Stryker. For two years Jill had dreamed of one day being invited to join Arnett's research team, although you had to be *very* high up the ladder to qualify for that.

I should be so lucky, she thought.

Arnett waved a sheaf of papers. "Last week, friends, I prepared a wonderful and highly technical lecture to give to you. But alas, medicine is changing so fast that everything in my speech is already obsolete!"

Loud laughter. Arnett held up his hands in a helpless gesture and waited patiently. Then he stated his real business.

"I'm here to talk about DNA," he said. "DNA, or deoxyribose nucleic acid, with its miraculous double helix, is the secret of life itself: the microscopic coils containing the genetic blueprint for every living thing. Discovered by James Watson and Francis Crick in 1953, it had by 1980 opened the way for the unheard of—and previously unimaginable—concept of genetic engineering.

"*Aw*ful expression, isn't it?" Arnett continued. "For that reason, please, let's use the term only in connection with agriculture and the pharmaceutical industry." He paused, scanning his audience. "Most scientists feel that not enough research has even been done on animals to make these concepts applicable to human beings. That is certainly the position of the National Institutes of Health—and *they* are regular fuddy-duddies when it comes to overseeing our research and handing out grants."

Taking pleasure at the expected laughter, Arnett glanced away from the audience to the white screen behind him, then looked back.

"So. What I'm going to show you are some marvelous slides. Technicolor DNA molecules taken from the cells of a variety of lower organisms . . ."

A sudden, beeping noise filled the room. All eyes looked up to a flashing red light and, below it, an illuminated TV screen, as the digital figures of a code marched across the screen: "117-99-Ch8."

"Hell," muttered David Levine, up as soon as he saw the message. David's call number was 117; the rest of the code meant emergency in Obstetrics, Chapin Eight.

Heads turned as interns Raney and Donovan fell in behind him, looking pained as they glanced back over their shoulders toward the podium. Ortega joined them higher up in the aisle, just as the lights went out.

In the darkness Arnett's voice could be heard as the first dazzling slide hit the screen.

"Attempts to insert DNA into the in vitro–fertilized embryos of lower organisms have met with problematical but highly photogenic results, as you'll see here."

Ortega and the others were already out the door. Hesitating, Jill clutched at her notebook and stared at the brilliantly lit screen. She saw, as if they were floating, two tall, intertwined spirals jammed with hundreds of multicolored balls.

DNA. The miraculous double helix. One could hallucinate looking at something like that . . .

She felt a hand on her arm.

She turned. "Don't want to go," she told Levine.

"I'm afraid we have to." Reluctantly, Jill followed him out the door and into the foyer, leaving behind the darkened room with its entranced students, all of them immensely relieved that it hadn't been they who had been called.

7

LEVINE TOOK THE stairs two at a time; not even Ortega could keep up.

"Hey, that lecture," Tricia huffed a few steps behind Jill. "We missed the DNA part, *the important part!*"

"Yes. Well, rotten luck," Jill breathed, rounding a polished mahogany landing. She continued running.

Tricia, perspiring, inhaled then hurtled after Jill. "When *I* have a child," she called down, "I'm going to write its whole genetic code. It will have blue eyes and black hair, like my grandfather, who was handsome but not smart, and it should have an IQ of 150 like my uncle, who is smart but *really* ugly, and . . ."

Jill glanced back at Tricia. "Do you think it will ever come to that? Procreative technology?" They had reached the marble floor of the first floor foyer.

There was a loud clang as Levine opened the heavy door that led down the steps to the tunnel. The decrepit tunnel was the only inside communication link between the old med school building and the complex of structures, four blocks long, that made up the modern city within a city that was Madison Hospital.

Ortega sprinted ahead as Levine held the door for the two women. "Gotta get you two running shoes," he said; then they all ran toward the main bank of elevators. Moments later they were tearing down the eighth-floor corridor to Delivery Room Number 3.

Outside, an obstetrical nurse was wheeling away a table loaded with instruments. They saw the look on the nurse's face and stopped abruptly.

Levine stared at her. "Unbelievable," said the nurse, shaking her head.

"What *happened?*" Levine asked. She continued to shake her head.

"Go see."

Ortega and Donovan went through the swinging doors as Jill Raney and Levine ducked into the anteroom for a quick scrub. As they entered the delivery room they found two nurses and Sam MacIntyre, his gown blood-spattered, struggling with a suction tube to resuscitate a cyanotic infant. The newborn appeared to be of about twenty-one weeks' gestation, and could not have weighed more than two pounds.

"Broke our necks to get here . . ." began Levine, his voice muffled as one of the nurses tied on his surgical mask. Then he looked down at the newborn on the table and stopped in midsentence.

The tiny infant was turning bluer by the second and making sucking sounds at the rate of about seventy respirations per minute. In an adult, twenty was normal. Levine, stunned, approached the draped table where the two pounder lay struggling for life. Jill came forward and stood next to him. The young mother was groggy from medication and moaned. Ortega and Donovan, on the other side of the table, stared slack-faced down at her until they heard MacIntyre's voice.

"Respiration sixty at birth, nine minutes ago," he said from behind his mask. "Respiration now almost"—He looked up at them—"It's up to eighty per minute." He glanced toward the head of the delivery table, where one of the two nurses was sorting out IV tubes which fed into the mother's arm. Then he looked back to Levine, ignoring the interns.

"It's Mrs. Sayers. Remember her?" MacIntyre shook his head. "She was going to name this one Christopher, if it was a boy."

"Christopher," echoed Levine, for no reason at all. Over his shoulder he said, "Nurse, get more sterile towels, medium, and an incubator. Stat!"

MacIntyre stopped his attempts at suctioning the child and stepped back. Levine moved closer and his gloved hands went to work. With his left hand he lifted the baby's rump and tilted him headdown to promote faster drainage from the trachea. His right hand reached for MacIntyre's rubber suction bulb; with both elbows up he tried to clear the infant's breathing passages.

The baby coughed; everybody cheered.

"No, not yet . . ." said Levine in a low voice. "I don't know . . ." He was breathing rapidly. His hands were shaking.

Forgetting sterile procedure, Jill raised one of her gloved hands to her mouth and pressed hard, trying not to be ill.

"*Can't* be Thalidomide—nobody's used that in twenty years!" Levine was saying.

"Then what?" MacIntyre's voice was dull.

"God only knows." Levine's hands were working furiously, and his voice suddenly rose. "Oh, Christ. The kid's retracting. Look at his ribs. Oh, Jesus—"

Jill Raney and Tricia Donovan stood looking stricken as Levine and MacIntyre bent over the child. Through the swinging doors the second nurse arrived pushing a preemie incubator.

Jill helped push the incubator into place. The infant's form was darkening rapidly; his almost inaudible gasps were now coming faster and more shallowly. The infant's features were indistinct—at two pounds it was like a tiny doll, a doll with four little stubs where there should have been arms and legs. Like a baby seal, Jill thought. Overcome, she looked away.

She steadied herself by staring at the sweeping second hand of the wall clock. "David," she said softly, "it *has* to be drugs, doesn't it? The mother took drugs?"

Levine glanced back at her as MacIntyre and the nurse moved the resuscitator into place.

"Mother is a Ph.D. candidate in anthropology," he said. "Straight-arrow as they come."

Turning his back to them Levine and the nurse went to lift the gasping bundle into the incubator.

It was Levine who was holding the infant when all activity in the room ceased—abruptly, noiselessly, like a freeze frame in a screening room.

"Forget it," he said. "Kid's had it." He looked down at the infant he cradled, no bigger than a newborn puppy.

The infant's respiration had stopped. The tiny lips and eyelids were blue, the miniscule nostrils which only seconds before had been flaring desperately were now still.

It must have been fourteen minutes before Christopher Sayers died.

Fourteen whole minutes on earth.

Faces fell and there was silence. Gently the baby with stubs instead of arms and legs was placed on a gurney. Jill Raney backed slowly away, feeling tears well up painfully.

No, she decided, Obstetrics was definitely not a happy place.

8

JILL WAS EXHAUSTED.

From the stairwell on the eighth-floor landing, she looked out at First Avenue and beyond; the tenements shrouded in haze, the office buildings, the snarled traffic. There was a sullen darkness, as if a storm threatened. Trudging people were going home, heading for subway holes, crowding into buses.

For them, Jill thought, the day was finished.

Glancing at her watch, she saw that it was six o'clock. Four hours since the death of Christopher Sayers, nine hours since the Moran tragedy, and at least three hours until she could fall into a bed somewhere. Anywhere. The on-call room maybe, or back in her apartment on East Twenty-first Street.

She decided against "home"; she was too depressed to sleep in a lonely third floor walkup.

Outside was getting so dark that the glaring bulb in the stairwell cast her scrub-suited reflection on the glass. Her image looked ill. Something else on the glass suddenly moved, and she turned around.

"It's called phocomelia, Jill."

Her green eyes fixed on him.

David Levine, back in white jacket and pants, leaned against the door, holding a tape recorder in one hand, a microphone in the other. He held up the recorder. "The Sayers case," he said. "Pretty bizarre. Want to hear about it?"

She nodded. "Please." She was too drained to say more. She couldn't admit to him, to herself, how devastated she felt, how insecure about the world of medicine. Suddenly it occurred to her she hadn't told anyone where she could be paged.

"How did you know where I was?"

He came to stand by her, and gazed out at the view. "It's where I used to come," he said, "when things got bad."

"Oh . . ."

He had said it so simply, and yet his words had spoken volumes. He had *been* here before: same place, same pain. Three or four years ago, perhaps, but still—it was hard to think of him as having ever been as vulnerable as she felt now. Jill studied his features. His face showed stamina— the trademark of most residents. How do they *get* that way? she thought. But his eyes . . . he looks so tired.

As if reading her thoughts, Levine went to sit on the stairs, placing the recorder between his feet on the lower step. He drew a breath.

"Phocomelia's one of the rarest obstetrical aberrations," he said softly. "Fact is, today's was the first case I've ever seen."

Jill folded her arms and leaned with her back to the window. "I remember the term," she said. "It's only supposed to happen in textbooks."

"Right." He grimaced, and fiddled with the microphone. In a monotone he described the fetal growth disorder which, for reasons unknown, suppresses the development of limbs in the unborn. "The whole place is upside-down over that Sayers case," he went on. "They're calling it the Thalidomide baby for some damned reason. Pretty stupid since the mother has no history of having taken Thalidomide, or any drug for that matter. I've been over her chart a hundred times."

"How is she?" Jill asked.

"Sedated. I'll be checking in on her later . . . hold her hand or something." He shrugged. "Poor kid."

Jill watched him. It occurred to her that she liked him,

liked him in a warm and comforting way. She liked the
way he talked, his lack of pretense, and the way those dark
blue eyes looked right at her. She looked down. She had
misjudged him. It seemed as though their fight had happened a long time ago. Had it only been that morning,
when he had humiliated her before a patient?

"Want to get out of here?" he said suddenly.

She looked up in surprise. "What?"

He strode to the heavy swinging door and held it open
for her.

"Come on," he coaxed. "Wouldn't you like to get
some fresh air for a few minutes? A sandwich someplace
near, instead of dinner at the Cafe Claustrophobia?"

She stared at him, tongue-tied.

"My arm is getting *tired*, Jill."

She gestured toward the window, at hazy First Avenue.
"You call that fresh air?"

"I call it outside. Will you come?"

"Okay," she said, and smiled.

She followed him through the door and then down the
crowded corridor. It was dinner time on the ward. They
walked past wheeled, multitiered carts loaded with steaming trays. "Got your squawk box?" he asked her, halfway
to the nurses' station.

She patted a side pocket of her scrub pants. Her beeper
was there.

"Good," he said. "We'll tell them to put us on page."

At the main desk he left his recorder with orders for the
reports to be sent down for typing. Then they dashed for
the crowded elevator, and moments later emerged from the
building by the front entrance.

They stood under the portico for a moment, David
eyeing the darkening sky and Jill watching a paper cup
tumble along the walk. She looked up at him in wonder.
"I had forgotten what air that *moved* was like," she said.

He laughed. They walked down the hospital drive and
turned south onto First Avenue. The air was hot and steamy
and smelled like tar, but Jill took a deep breath and
had to admit it felt great to be out. They passed the

Madison Bookseller on the corner, and crossed Twenty-first Street. On the next block they passed a florist and a dry cleaners. "You spent the afternoon in the clinic?" David asked.

"Most of it."

"Well," he said, "while you were gone we had two deliveries. Both terrific. Completely normal."

Jill looked at him. "Gee," she said.

He ignored that. She followed him across Twentieth Street. Halfway down the block they turned into the Madison Delicatessen, and headed for a booth in the corner. The windows were open and a breeze moved the red and white checked curtains. A country and western song was playing.

Jill looked around, savoring the hominess of the place. An exuberant sign over the front counter read EGG ROLLS AND PIROGIES TO GO. A bearded young man at the next table was sketching.

Jill sighed and leaned her cheek on her hand. "It's just so good to be out."

He watched her pensively. "Pretty bad, huh?"

"Bad? Today was *worse* than bad, David. It was traumatic. For the whole department . . . don't you agree?" She searched his face.

He was twirling the tassel on his menu. "Of course I agree," he said.

"Well?"

"Well, what?"

She gestured. "Listen. I realize I've been an intern for all of eleven days—big deal, right?—and I also realize that Madison is gigantic, so it's going to get a lot of emergencies—"

"Twenty in an hour isn't unusual—"

"—and I'm taking its size into account. But today was . . . well . . . today was *disproportionate*." He stopped toying with the tassel. She leaned forward. "Too many things in one day, David, even for a place this size!"

There was a silence. Then he nodded. "It's called the cluster syndrome," he said.

"The what?"

A waiter came and poured coffee. They hurriedly gave their orders and the waiter left.

"Custer?" she said. "As in George Armstrong Custer?"

"Don't be cute. Do you take sugar?"

"Please." She watched in surprise as he tore open a sugar packet and poured it into her cup. Then, to her greater surprise, he reached for her spoon and began to stir.

She leaned back in the booth. "I know what you're saying, David. But it's still bothering me."

He put down the spoon and looked at her. "Tell," he said.

She ticked off the items on her fingers one by one. "Abruptio placentae, phocomelia, eclampsia and MacIntyre's stillborn. These—certainly the first two—should be exceedingly rare. And yet they happened, and *on the same day,* mixed in with what I consider a disproportionate number of regular emergencies."

"You consider?"

She felt embarrassed yet determined, and plunged ahead. "Those tragedies today . . . do you suppose . . . I mean . . . is there *any* way they could be potentially related?"

Levine looked at her as if he hadn't heard right. He put his elbows on the table, and was about to answer when the waiter arrived with their Cokes and cheeseburgers. David was distracted momentarily. When the waiter left, Jill said, "Well? Were you listening?"

He was pounding an upturned ketchup bottle. "Were you serious?"

She nodded.

"You mean, *related* related, like common etiology and all that?"

She shrugged and nodded again.

"Eat your cheeseburger."

Jill stared down at her plate. She hadn't eaten much all day, but still didn't feel hungry. There was a rumble of thunder outside and she shivered.

They ate silently for a few moments. Levine looked

thoughtful. "Jill," he said finally. "The thing you have
to learn at a place like Madison is, the only rule is the
exception. Words like 'disproportionate' just don't apply,
and as far as those tragedies being related . . ." He shook
his head. "I just don't believe you *mean* that. Nothing
today had any common symptoms. Not one. Those women
all had different doctors, different backgrounds and different case histories. Abruptio and phocomelia are *poles*
apart medically." He paused and his voice grew more
gentle. "They were just isolated tragedies, that's all. The
only freaky thing is that they happened on the same day,
but . . ."

"I know," Jill said. "Cluster syndrome. Words like 'disproportionate' don't apply. The only rule is the exception."

Levine looked at her and frowned.

Just then his beeper went off.

"Shit!" David got up and stormed over to a pay phone
on the far wall. Jill watched him dial, speak briefly, and
slam down the phone.

"What's up?" she asked when he returned.

"Plenty. I've got to run back." He glanced at the plates
on the table. "You stay," he said. "Do me a favor. Eat
for two."

She shook her head. "I'm coming."

David paid and they tore out the door. Outside, the first
fat drops of rain fell as they began to run back. Levine was
fast, but Jill kept up pretty well as far as the Madison
Bookseller. She saw him pull ahead with a hoot and sprint
up the drive toward the portico.

"Hey, David! Wait up!"

On the sidewalk outside the overhang he stopped and
waited, grinning like a kid, his hands jammed into his
jacket pockets. The rain was heavier now and a breeze was
gusting strongly. His face, like hers, was wet from the
downpour. His dark hair blew wildly about, but in the
manner of a man used to the outdoors he made no move to
push it out of his eyes.

Heart hammering, Jill only half pretended to collapse into
his arms. He caught her, laughing, and they looked into

each other's eyes. His smile faded. He brushed aside a strand of her long, wet hair. "Are you going to be on call tonight?"

Still puffing, she said, "Yes. And you?"

He shrugged. "Same." He let go of her.

He noticed that her scrub suit was so wet that it clung to the curves of her body. He felt a terrible ache. He pulled off his white jacket.

"Put this on," he said. "Don't walk through Emergency like that."

"What?" Then she understood, and lowered her eyes to hide her embarrassment.

She put on the jacket.

He smiled. He stepped forward and kissed her on the cheek. "You're too much," he said.

They went inside together. As she looked at the throng in the main entrance, Jill said suddenly, "Are you going to go see that Mrs. Sayers? The phocomelia case?"

"Yes," he said. "Later. If she's awake." He held up his watch. "Oops. Gotta run." He smiled at her, and then was off.

"Maybe I will too!" Jill called after him, then realized he hadn't heard. Big-shouldered and lean, he was moving fast, like an athlete, across the teeming entrance hall, and in a moment he had disappeared from sight.

9

SHE TOOK THE elevator up, and for once didn't mind the press of the crowd or the fact that half of them were visitors in soggy raincoats. Her earlier depression had receded and her mind was clearing, sharpening, replaying her noontime conversation with Tricia.

Getting off at the eighth floor, she walked briskly up the hall, stopping midway to peer in at the nursery. The sound of squalling was muted by the glass window. Three nurses wearing masks moved among the rows of isolettes—the babies up front could be seen squirming or sleeping or screaming. Jill looked closer, a smile flickering across her face. Then she remembered the day's events, and the smile vanished abruptly. She turned and continued walking.

In the women doctors' lounge she changed into a dry scrub suit and threw her wet things and David's jacket into the hamper. She left the lounge and walked to the nurses' station. Nonchalantly she said to the nurse on duty, "I'm taking the Sayers chart." The woman looked up, smiled vacantly, and went back to her pile of order sheets. Jill rummaged, pulled out the chart she wanted, and carried it across the corridor to the male doctors' lounge.

Twice the size of the other, the front sitting room served as a general gathering area. She could hear someone in the shower around the corner, but the vinyl chairs in the front room were empty and the low table was covered with half-filled mugs of cold coffee. Jill recognized Tricia Donovan's bright red one; Woody Greenberg's with the painted rabbits; somebody else's with the words, "Oh, screw it!" hand-painted in a dozen languages. On the wall over the sagging couch was a lavish, 1940s-type poster welcoming the visitor to the Stork Club.

Jill pushed aside the mugs and sat by the table. She opened the chart and looked at the wall clock. It was 7:40.

SAYERS, MARY JO, read the label on top. The patient had been in the hospital only six hours and her chart was already thick. That was common for cases that turned out badly: the number of consults and lab tests alone was prodigious.

Jill began flipping pages, skipping until she came to "Delivery Report." The white sheet was covered with David's scrawl. With a navy-colored pen he had written the date and time at the top and then, in large, shaky handwriting, had described the case. The patient had gone into premature labor at an estimated twenty-two weeks' gestation. The first stage of labor, beginning with the initial contraction, had lasted three hours. Duration of the second stage was thirty-five minutes, culminating in a shoulder presentation accompanied by meconium-stained fluid and signs of fetal distress. Five more minutes elapsed until the third stage of labor—delivery of the placenta—at which point an umbilical vein blood specimen was taken and rushed to the lab.

A long, navy line was drawn under the last sentence. Next came a new paragraph, followed by more terse language detailing the physician's findings. The newborn, weighing two and one-half pounds at birth, was grossly abnormal with vestigial limb buds. Diagnosis: phocomelia. Apgar rating 1. Infant tachypneic—rapid, shallow breathing —with a respiratory rate of 70. Infant succumbed at 14 minutes despite intensive efforts to resuscitate.

Jill began to turn pages again. She had no idea what she was looking for—what *could* she be looking for?—but some impulse prevented her from closing the chart. The shower in the other room had been turned off, and a man's humming could be heard as well as much slamming of locker room doors. It was hard to concentrate in here; Jill regretted she hadn't gone back to the women doctors' lounge, where it was quieter, less frequented.

She continued reading. Let's see . . . progress notes, nurses' notes, more lab results, a history and physical done several months ago. . . .

She stopped, staring. Her eyes moved up to the top of the page, and then she stared again.

Mary Jo Sayers had had a routine gynecological examination on January 27, at Madison Hospital. Today was July 11; Mary Jo had delivered her premature child at twenty-two weeks' gestation, or five and one-half months. Jill counted on her fingers to make sure her addition was correct. Then she looked up at the darkened, rain-streaked window.

January 27 was exactly five and a half months ago.

I didn't see that, Jill thought. She frowned, puzzled. So what did it prove? A fantastic coincidence, that's all. Probably whoever did the exam was one of the hospital's better-looking residents, and afterward Mary Jo got all steamed up and ran home to her husband.

Jill looked down at the GYN report again. It was only one page. A routine exam on a healthy young woman. Handwriting she didn't recognize. But who was the examining doctor? And why hadn't the guy signed his note? The only identification was the sheet of paper itself; the letters at the top read Madison Hospital Gynecology Clinic.

Jill hunched her shoulders in concentration. David had said in the delivery room that the patient was a Ph.D. candidate. That often meant poor, Jill thought. Many students came to the outpatient GYN clinic because it was free.

She shook her head. She told herself she was being silly—unprofessional, in fact. She remembered that even with today's speedier BioCep G blood tests, pregnancy still could not be detected for two or three days, sometimes even four, after conception. That meant that Mary Jo Sayers could have conceived several nights before her exam, and still have tested negative on the pregnancy test. She could even have conceived *after* the exam, couldn't she? Levine's report had described the infant as of *approximately* twenty-two weeks' gestation . . .

Jill flipped back to the delivery report.

"Hey there! How're you doing?" George Mackey came out of the shower room in a fresh scrub suit and headed for the door.

"Yes," Jill said absentmindedly.

"That's good!" Mackey called back just as absently over his shoulder, and hurried out.

She got up, her eyes scanning Mary Jo Sayers' history and physical exam. She was a white, twenty-eight-year-old female without a history of serious medical problems. She didn't use drugs or medications regularly, didn't smoke, rarely drank, had no allergies. There were no serious illnesses in her family history. Her job did not bring her into contact with chemicals or pollutants.

Reading on, Jill walked toward the door. The review of Sayers' systems was negative; her ob-gyn history contained no menstrual irregularities, no previous pregnancies. Her last menstrual period was January 14. The lab tests ordered were routine: Pap, urine, cervical mucous, hemoglobin.

Jill stopped in the doorway. She reread the list of lab tests. *Was* the cervical mucous test routine? Usually it was considered a prepregnancy test, to determine if a woman was ovulating—or to ascertain if her cervical mucous was hostile to her husband's sperm. Jill rubbed her chin. Well, there were probably other reasons why the test was administered. *All* doctors gave too many tests these days. The public had become so malpractice-crazy that doctors were afraid not to give patients the full barrage of tests, even if they were unnecessary.

Her eyes went back to the page, to the only thing that really bothered her: the date. It was odd, she thought; a bizarre coincidence that the only thing in any way related to the eventual tragedy was the *exact date* on which the exam was given.

She walked back to the nurses' station. The corridor was now crowded with visitors. She struggled to remember something that was nagging at her from this morning. They were down in Emergency. The Moran crisis. Woody Greenberg, agitated, speaking rapidly, telling Levine something. Something important. She racked her brain to remember what he had said.

At the desk she handed the Sayers chart back to the nurse and reminded her that she was still reachable on page. Then, crossing the foyer, she approached the elevators and pressed the down button.

This is ridiculous, she told herself. Go back, get an hour's sleep. You could get called any minute.

But I told Tricia I'd find the time.

The elevator arrived. Jill squeezed in, glancing at her watch—8:20.

On the third floor the doors opened again to admit a young couple and an elderly woman, who looked as if she had been crying.'

Crying. *That was it.* The sight triggered the association she had been seeking. Woody Greenberg had told Levine that a weeping and barely coherent Maria Moran had begged the ambulance to bring her here. Why? There was only one reason. Moran had *been* here before, felt more comfortable in familiar surroundings. There was nothing random in the fact that the dying Maria Moran had been brought to Madison Hospital.

At the ground floor Jill got off, crossed the main entrance and headed down the busy hallway leading to the emergency room. Rounding the corner she approached a nurse at the desk.

"Do you still have the chart of a Mrs. Maria Moran?" she asked. "The patient was admitted this morning."

The middle-aged nurse smiled pleasantly and bent to look. "Moran . . . Moran," she echoed, her fingertips moving down the file beneath the counter. Jill peered over to watch, then pulled back as the nurse straightened and shook her head.

"No, no Moran. Sorry." She smiled again.

A clerk wearing horn-rimmed glasses looked over to her. "Moran? I remember that name. Look in the outbasket."

The nurse did. Tilting her head and reading sideways, she said, "Aha!" and pulled a chart out of a pile that looked ready to topple. She handed it to Jill.

Jill thanked her. "Busy day, huh?" she said absently, already flipping open the cover.

"Busy!" exclaimed the nurse. "You wouldn't believe the backlog. You were lucky to find that chart. Another five minutes and it would've been on its way down to the record room. When you're finished, just put it on top of the stack, okay?"

"Sure," said Jill. The nurse went back to stuffing cards onto a Rolodex file. Jill turned the Moran pages rapidly, skipping past several pastel sheets until she came to a cream-colored one near the bottom.

The color was the giveaway. At the top were printed block letters: MADISON HOSPITAL GYNECOLOGICAL CLINIC. To the right, in neatly typed letters, were the patient's name and the heading "annual GYN exam." And to the left the date of the exam: January 3.

Jill looked up, her heart thudding. About twenty feet away from her, the large, swinging doors leading to the ambulance bay were open, exposing the glistening night. Two policemen and an orderly were struggling with a laden stretcher; somebody shouted that another stretcher was coming, and the wind suddenly strengthened, sending a blasting sheet of rain into the vestibule.

Jill went back to the Moran chart, trying to concentrate. Moran's exam date had been January third. On the pathology page her pregnancy was estimated at twenty-five weeks. Simple arithmetic.

Jill closed her eyes. January third plus twenty-five weeks brings us right up to now. Today. . . .

She opened her eyes. Double-checking, she flipped back to the gynecology report made in January. There it was: the onset of Moran's last menstrual period was December 20. That made the exam date the same day as Moran's ovulation time.

Two coincidences?

Jill shakily pulled her black notebook from her pocket

and jotted down the facts from the Moran chart, plus those from the Sayers chart which she still remembered.

Gently, she closed the chart, the gesture itself a reminder of a young life that was over. Her hands trembled badly. In a sick wave of memory she recalled that the hospital morgue, in the basement, was just below her feet. *They must still be there,* she realized: tiny Christopher Sayers and Maria Moran, her body in death still cradling her never-to-be-born child. Jill shivered, but she knew it was not from the chill coming in through the open door.

Outside, the sky lit up and thunder crashed.

Shortly after nine o'clock, during the lull after visiting hours, Tricia Donovan went to the nurses' station looking for the eclampsia chart. She couldn't find it. She couldn't find the nurse either, but knowing that charts couldn't wander too far she went to the doctors' lounge, where she found Gary Phipps and Charlie Ortega sitting at the coffee table, hunched over the very chart she was looking for.

She peered over Gary's shoulder. "Is that the Prewitt chart?"

"Ah, yeah," he said, looking up. "Charlie and I have been going over this case. I've decided I'm bothered by it after all."

"Thought you said the hospital knew what it was doing?" Tricia challenged.

Phipps glanced uncomfortably at Ortega, who was scanning a lab sheet. "Well," he said, "it may be that the hospital knows what it's doing, but *I* sure as hell wouldn't have known what to do if a sudden idiopathic eclampsia came in." He shrugged. "I guess you were right. This one *is* weird."

Ortega looked up, serious-faced. "I reminded him that a case like Prewitt here"—he tapped fingers on the chart—"just doesn't happen in a hospital with *class.* Maybe at Backwater General, staffed by ninety-year-old G.P.'s, but not *here,* for God's sake."

Tricia pulled up a chair and sat down. "Count me in."

They slid the chart down the table in front of Phipps,

who sat in the middle, and all three began to discuss and shake their heads over the patient's history and lab notes.

Moments later Ramu Chitkara appeared at the door, looking frustrated.

"I say," he greeted them. "Have any of you seen the Prewitt chart?"

10

THE STURDEVANDT RESEARCH wing was the pride of the medical center. Only four stories high, it extended perpendicularly from the main hospital complex to a group of older buildings on the other side. Logically, it should have served as a connector between the new and old parts of the medical center, but it did not. House staff members could use the tunnels or cross the parking lot to get to other sections, but the research building, for reasons never specified, was off limits to general traffic.

Jill Raney was tense. Having bolted down an early breakfast, she and the other interns had rushed along hallways, stepped into a designated elevator, and were now being carried to the fourth floor of the one place they had never been. All carried notebooks. All stared at Jill, as if trying to register what she was saying.

"*Both* women?" said Tricia. "*Both* exams at ovulation time?"

"It's in their charts?" Phipps asked.

"In black and white," Jill said. "See for yourself."

Charlie Ortega eyed his watch. "We spent time on charts last night, too. Prewitt and Burke."

"Burke?" Jill asked.

"MacIntyre's stillborn."

Ramu Chitkara quickly described the oddities they had found in both cases.

Now it was Jill's turn to stare.

The elevator doors opened and the group stepped out into a brightly lit foyer. Across from them was a sign with an arrow reading: FERTILITY AND GENETIC COUNSELING CLINIC.

They turned right and hurried down the hallway lined on both sides with closed office doors, their footsteps echoing. They stopped at a door which announced: Department of Obstetrics and Gynecology, Professor W. T. Stryker, M.D., Ph.D.

Chitkara raised his hand and knocked. There was no answer. Phipps muttered, "Do you think we need a password?" The interns broke into nervous laughter, then froze to attention as the door opened. Dr. William Stryker, thin and stern, looked out.

"You may come in," he said tersely, then turned, leaving the door open. Exchanging glances, they followed him through a large anteroom full of secretarial desks and chairs. Off to the right was a closed mahogany door which Jill guessed was Stryker's inner office. To the left, down a short, narrow corridor, was another door which Stryker threw open.

"The laboratory of laboratories," he said, stepping inside.

The interns followed him in and looked about.

The room was large and sunny. The rain of the night before had stopped, and a hot, muggy brightness poured in through the east window. Three white counter tops ran nearly the length of the lab, and were crowded with sinks, gas jets, and microscopes. Shelves full of laboratory glassware were mounted over each of the counter tops, creating the feeling of separate alleys dividing the room.

Stryker led the interns down the center aisle and stopped by a metal box with protruding wires. Placing his hand on the box he said, "I always make it a point to personally conduct new interns around the research department, and this seems as good a place as any to begin." Folding his arms, he raised his chin and leaned against the counter, a lordly figure with silver hair, a hawk nose, and the manner of a man accustomed to command.

"The fame of this hospital," he went on, "lies not just in the superb care extended to its patients, but also in the advanced research which is done in this room, and on this floor." His eyes probed every face as he spoke. "Madison Hospital Medical Center has pioneered techniques which are now used worldwide: in helping human infertility; in the early diagnosis and treatment of birth defects and inherited disease; and in improved methods designed to manage the high-risk pregnancy and insure fetal well-being." He glanced significantly around. "The work never stops, of course. Consider this metal box."

They considered it.

"This is our embryo bank," he said, patting it affectionately. "Oh, not human embryos. Look here." Opening the incubator he showed them row after row of numbered flasks. "Higher vertebrates," he called over his shoulder, as everyone pressed closer. "Healthy, growing embryos of two chimps, three dogs, several rabbits, and . . . mice. Many mice."

He straightened. "All have been in vitro fertilized. That's the easy part: bringing sperm and egg together in a dish. The hard part involves the embryo transfer: that is, successfully implanting the embryo into the female's uterus. Our success rate with human embryo transfer is forty percent. We'd like to make it higher. Hence our experiments using animals as research subjects."

Dr. Stryker allowed the interns a last look into the incubator, then shut the door. He pointed to where a team of third-year residents was running hormone assays on women who were habitual aborters; then indicated another counter just opposite, lined with bottles of whiskey, packs of cigarettes, a bin full of sleeping pills and tranquilizers, and stacked cages of white mice—all research material to study the causes of defective ovulation.

"Other projects are over here," he said, leading the

way across an intersecting aisle and past an array of con-
densers and distillation chambers, liquid nitrogen containers and more cages of mice. Jill Raney stopped to look.
Some of the mice were painted blue. Control groups with
stripes of green or purple or orange running down their
backs scratched around in adjoining cages.

She rejoined the group. Stryker had stopped by a work
table and waved his hand dramatically. "This," he said,
"is one of the most important studies going on. It involves
DNA research. It is the work of Thomas Gacey."

At the mention of Gacey, Jill and Tricia exchanged
glances. Thomas Gacey was notorious as the hospital nasty.
Having played his politics well, he had intrigued his way
to the top—the position of fourth-year chief resident of
Obstetrics and Gynecology. The interns felt that Gacey
was as obnoxious a medical ego as ever swung a stethoscope. People called him Stryker's deputy. Stryker's spy.
Stryker's hatchet man. . . .

". . . remarkable, astonishing observations on rabbit ex
utero embryo survival," Stryker was saying, using both
hands as if to embrace Gacey's cluttered table. Jill looked
at Gacey's open notebook, its handwriting illegible and
full of wild thrusts.

"Nine days!" trumpeted Stryker. "He kept a rabbit
embryo alive ex utero for nine days! The mother had
scoliosis. If Tom had had one more day to examine the
chromosome structure of the offspring, he might have . . ."

Stryker stopped in midsentence. "Well," he said. "Next
time."

Charlie Ortega asked, "You mean, sir, that the rabbit
died?"

Stryker stared at him. "You might call it that," he said.

He looked at his watch. "Getting late," he muttered,
ushering them out into the corridor. It was now 7:25 A.M.
The interns followed after him. Jill Raney brought up the
rear as she took one last look around the lab. She was
more than impressed, but also a little frightened. They're
all vying for the Nobel, she thought: Gacey, Stryker, the

others who work here . . . they're all more interested in research than in patients.

I'll bet they'd love to put real women into those cages.

The thought was jarring to her, and she hurried to catch up.

David Levine was pacing nervously in front of the nurses' station on Chapin 8, looking at his watch every twenty seconds.

"So where are they?" he demanded out loud. "We have to start rounds in a minute."

A petite nurse behind the counter, watching him, looked up at the wall clock and shrugged. "Stryker's got them," she said, as if that were explanation enough. She smiled but he missed it; he was too busy scowling at the chart rack before him. So many patients to see and no time to do it!

Woody Greenberg came hurrying through the morning commotion and David called to him.

"Listen, will you start rounds for me? We're behind."

Woody looked down at the charts in the rack and made a face. "Can't. Mackey's doing a Fallopian reconstruction and I gotta scrub in for it."

"Mackey . . . *what? Now?* It was scheduled for nine!"

"Time's been moved up."

"Oh, shit. I wanted them to see *that*, too."

Woody looked at his watch. "I've got about twelve and a half minutes . . . well, I can take three of these off your hands." He reached in and pulled out three charts.

"I appreciate that, Woody."

Woody muttered something like *c'est la guerre* and hurried off. Levine shoved his hands in his pockets and turned back to face the nurse.

She looked up from something she was writing. "Not back yet, huh?"

"Nope." He paced a few steps. "Well, I hope they're minding their manners, at least."

"Hah!" she said. *"Interns?* You kidding?"

*   *   *

Stryker led the group around the rest of the floor, showing them the sonography room, where a woman lying on a table could see an image of her fetus on a sonogram. "Ultrasound!" said Stryker. "Instead of harmful X rays! Extraordinary advance in prenatal diagnosis!"

They followed him to the Special Procedures Room—identical to the one on the obstetrical floor—where amniocentesis, artificial insemination, and laparoscopies were routinely performed. "And this," said Stryker, throwing open another door, "is a lab devoted exclusively to in vitro research in humans."

The equipment was familiar; the room was near the main lab where they had started.

"Human eggs?" blurted Jill suddenly. "You keep *human* eggs in here?"

Stryker looked at her. "We do not *keep* human eggs," he said.

"But what do you do with the *extras?"* she persisted. "These infertility cases—you give the women *fertility drugs,* don't you? And that produces extra eggs at ovulation time which you suction out with a laparoscope—"

"All eggs are fertilized and reimplanted in the mother," said Stryker. "That increases the chances of at least *one* conception. It also increases the chance of multiple births. You heard about our quadruplets last May?"

Abruptly he moved away, stood in the center of the hall, and began pointing out the offices of the other members of the Genetic Counseling Committee. "Doctors Simpson and Rosenberg are *there,"* he said, pointing to their marked doors across from the main lab. "And Dr. Arnett is *there,* two doors down from my own office. All of these men will be glad to answer your questions. All have their own independent labs, and together they combine expertise in the areas of perinatology, ultrasonography, high risk obstetrics, epidemiology, and genetics. I truly doubt if you would find a better research faculty in the country." He paused. "Now. Are there any more questions?"

There was a long silence. Jill decided not to jump in first.

"About yesterday . . ." said Phipps.

"We were concerned about some cases," said Ortega.

"*Strange* cases," said Tricia.

"The eclampsia, for one," said Chitkara. "That Prewitt case didn't present *at all* like eclampsia . . ."

Stryker's body seemed to stiffen. "Of course it didn't," he said.

They looked at him.

He folded his arms. "We had a near tragedy because some *fool* of a student nurse gave the patient the wrong medication. Prewitt had been getting penicillin for an ear infection. The nurse injected her with norepinephrine by mistake—sent her blood pressure through the roof."

They stared at him, unable to believe what they were hearing.

"The girl denies it, of course," he went on. "The nursing supervisor is dealing with *her*. And *we* didn't have the answers until eleven last night, when our review committee finally sorted out what had happened."

"Review . . . committee?" Tricia looked at him with wide eyes.

"Yes." He turned to her, pointing a finger. "And you should have enough *faith* in this hospital to *know* that cases like this automatically come under the most serious scrutiny." He frowned at her. "You said, 'cases,' I believe. Was there something else?"

Phipps said, "The Burke infant. That baby *should* have made it because he was full term and *seemed* normal—"

"He wasn't," Stryker snapped. "The child had a heart defect. I received results of the post last night."

"Who did the post?" Ortega asked belligerently.

Stryker glared at him. "That is *quite* enough!" He glared at all of them. "Doctors," he said coldly. "I appreciate your concern, but I must remind you that minds more highly trained than yours have the responsibility for dealing with these things. Your responsibility is to *learn*, not to question a system more advanced than your thinking."

The interns looked humiliated, embarrassed. Jill Raney was the only one who met Stryker's gaze.

"Why, Doctor Raney, you've been so *quiet*. Your friends seem to be such experts. Tell me, do *you* have something on your mind, too? Some terrible instance of bad medicine and misdiagnosis which *you* have uncovered?"

Jill felt her palms become sweaty. She saw Tricia's eyes sending out frantic messages of "No! Save it!" and she took a deep gulp of air.

"As a matter of fact," she said, surprised at her own voice, "among your patients, Dr. Stryker, were there ever two women by the names of Sayers and Moran? They were treated in the clinic, I realize. But since every doctor on the staff puts in clinic time—that *is* the policy, isn't it?—I was wondering if you had ever seen them. Or if *anyone* here in the research group had ever treated them."

Stryker's pale eyes narrowed at her. "And why would you wonder such a thing?"

Jill's heart raced. "I was reading their charts last night. I noticed something . . . alarming . . . and I feel that perhaps it should be discussed."

Tricia Donovan tugged at Jill's arm. "Come on," she said, "it's getting late." But Jill pulled away and stood stubbornly facing Stryker.

"It is now 7:36," he announced calmly. "The rest of you may continue on to your ward duties. I will have a talk with Dr. Raney."

The other interns stood watching him uncertainly. Gary Phipps said, "We can wait, sir. It's really all right if we're a little late. Dr. Levine knows—"

"Now, please," said Stryker.

At a loss they turned, and Jill uneasily watched them straggle to the fire door. As the door closed behind them she turned back to Stryker and found him studying her.

"Well, now," he said. "Suppose you tell me about this alarming discovery missed by the greatest minds in medicine and made by an intern barely into training!"

Jill fumbled in her pocket and pulled out her black notebook. Carefully she said, "I copied down some rather curious information from the Sayers and Moran charts, sir."

"And?"

"When these two women arrived at the hospital yesterday, it was the initial impression of the doctors treating
them that they had been brought in off the street, as it
were. This was because there were no records of their
having received prenatal care here."

"Continue," Stryker said, watching her.

"Well, because these cases seemed so bizarre I felt
impelled to do a little research into their backgrounds.
Neither was a stranger to this hospital. In fact, each woman
was here five or six months ago respectively for a routine
Gyn checkup. A little arithmetic, Dr. Stryker. The time
that each had her checkup coincides *exactly* with the time
that she conceived. And each pregnancy ended in tragedy.
I've written it all down if you'd care to check their ovulation dates with the time of their deliveries." She held up
the open notebook.

Stryker ignored it. "Is that all?" he said.

She stared at him. "Is that all! Dr. Stryker, you can't
mean that! Two ill-fated, horrendous pregnancies almost
look as if they got *started* in this hospital, and you dismiss
it just like that? I just can't believe there wouldn't be at
least some curiosity about this . . . this coincidence. Or
some investigation launched or—"

"Doctor Raney," said Stryker cutting her off. "You are
to be commended for having the beginning—note, I said
beginning—of a research mind. You have found a common
denominator between two vastly different obstetrical mishaps, and that is impressive. However, to have the audac-
ity to stand here demanding an investigation, or 'at least
some curiosity,' as you so offensively put it, is both
irresponsible and intolerable on your part."

"But—"

"No buts!" Stryker shouted. Jill stepped back, startled,
and he abruptly lowered his voice.

"It is in your *interest* that I'm telling you this, so listen
and listen carefully. First, it is common nowadays for
women to update their Gyn status before initiating a pregnancy; you'll find *plenty* of babies born nine months and a

few days after their mothers' exams. Second, you have the privilege of training in a superior institution, so"—he looked very grave—"be sensible, and know your place. I would certainly hate to see you jeopardize your position here."

Jill felt confused. "I . . . I only wanted to help . . . Those poor women . . ." She backed away, her eyes still on his rigid face. Without another word, Stryker marched into his office and closed the door.

Jill turned and headed for the stairwell, her cheeks aflame with anger and humiliation. She pushed open the heavy door, took a deep breath, and tried to control the tears that threatened.

11

LEVINE LOOKED UP at her as she approached. "Still in one piece?" he asked, offering her a box of Kleenex.

Jill gave him a stony look. "I don't need that," she said. She slammed her notebook down on the chart rack. "There's something rotten around here. Bossman Stryker is a cold fish. He treats the interns like three-year-olds. He blames everything on the *nurses!* He has pat answers for the most appalling cases. I don't buy it!"

"Yeah," David said. "He's a real charmer. Come on."

They hurried along the crowded corridor. Sullen-eyed, Jill forced herself to listen as Levine ran down the morning schedule. "You're not really late for rounds. Greenberg held the fort," he said. "He just took the rest of the interns to observe some surgery. At 9:15 in the eleventh-floor conference room, Cliff Arnett is going to repeat the end of yesterday's lecture. Too many people missed it. The DNA part, remember? I've already told Tricia and the others. It's important. *Be* there.''

Jill realized that his look of last night was gone. That small smile, the gaze she had shyly returned. Was this the same man? He was talking so rapidly, an exhausted man going on his nerves and probably having a hard enough time concentrating on the business at hand.

Now, she decided, was not the time to tell him about her confrontation with Stryker.

But she was still burning with such anger that an odd question popped into her head.

"David, I've heard people around here say you're a crack shot. Is that true?''

He kept pushing the rack. "Oh, sort of.''

"How sort of?''

He looked at her, looked away again. "Well,'' he said, "I'm from Denver, and out there they give prizes to kids for marksmanship. That's how it started, anyway. Then when I was sixteen my folks sent me to an Israeli kibbutz—you know—a summer camp sort of thing to toughen up spoiled kids?''

She nodded.

He grinned. "Well, everyone *else* picked grapefruit all day. I found an army base nearby. Spent the whole time over *there* doing target practice.''

She looked at him thoughtfully. "You're still in practice?''

They were standing outside room 808. David got out the chart. "Once,'' he said, "back home I was camping out with friends in the mountains. I shot off a rattler's head at forty feet.''

"Mm,'' Jill said. "No wonder you think Madison is so tame.''

He gave her a quizzical look. He flipped open the chart, tilted his head toward the room and said, "Shall we?''

Fidgeting, Jill watched as David became all business. Chart in hand, he greeted Mrs. somebody Edwards. He asked the patient how she felt. He did the physical, check-

ing the pulse and blood pressure; then felt the belly to
make sure the uterus was contracting down, which it wasn't,
not fast enough, anyway, so he wrote an order for some
Ergotrate (light green sheet), and then snap-clamped it to
the outside of the chart.

And all the while, as his eyes scanned the lab reports
that had come back, he cracked jokes with the patient.
Told her she had been a real tiger in the delivery room;
promised her a bullet to chew on for next time; said, "Oh?
Factory closed?" when the patient said there wasn't going
to *be* a next time. Mrs. Edwards smiled at Jill. Jill smiled
back.

They left. They did the rest of the even numbers, and
most of the patients were easy. They crossed the hall at the
far end, and stood together writing notes on progress
sheets before beginning the odd numbers.

Outside room 819, David looked up and frowned.

"Hey," he said quietly. "This is the Sayers room."

"Sayers? You mean Mary Jo Sayers?"

"The same." He pulled out the Sayers chart and began
reading rapidly as Jill craned her neck and tried to see into
the room.

The door was open a crack. It was dark inside.

"Awfully quiet in there," she whispered.

Still reading, Levine shook his head. "She was only
slightly sedated last night. Listen to this: 'Patient spent the
night exhibiting borderline hysteria. Seems delusional with
some paranoid tinge. Should be closely observed for signs
of psychotic behavior.' "

He looked up again, toward the door, and Jill saw that
he was astonished. "They've knocked her *out*," he said.
"Fifty milligrams of Thorazine at six this morning."

Jill looked at her watch: 8:20. The effects of Thorazine
lasted from between four to six hours. Jill's brow creased.
She had wanted to see Sayers, to talk to her. She looked at
Levine. "Who signed the note?"

"Gacey," he said, and there was anger in his eyes.
"Guess Thomas Gacey doesn't like people to grieve too
loudly." He flung the chart back onto the rack.

Eyeing the chart Jill asked, "Did you see her during the night?"

"Yeah. Between the Edwards and Dolan deliveries. She seemed okay. Upset but"—he glanced back toward the door—"definitely not delusional." He frowned. "Of course, I saw her around 1:00 A.M. Maybe later she got worse . . . who knows . . ." He gave the rack an exasperated shove and moved on.

The moment was now.

"David," Jill called out, hurrying after him. The morning rush had thinned out at this end of the hall. "There's something I want to tell you," she said, reaching him. "Something important. Last night I—"

A nurse popped out of 813 and hurried over to Levine. "Oh, doctor," she said. "The hemoglobin and hematocrit you ordered for 810 are back. Shall I send them down?"

He did not break stride. "Yes and stat, please. Dolan lost a lot of blood."

The nurse hurried off. For a moment Jill wondered at Levine's ability to remember patients' names. These women were in and out in a matter of days, but they never seemed to be only room numbers to him. *Well*, she thought: *all the more reason for him to be interested in what I have to tell him*.

She was ready to speak when they heard his name paged. "Doctor Levine, Doctor Levine. Extension 214."

He stopped, irritated. "That's the record room! Hell, they've probably gotten everything screwed up again!"

Furiously shoving charts back into the rack he said, "Finish this, will you, Jill? There's only a few left. Oh, was there something you wanted to tell me?"

"No, it's okay," she said ruefully.

He studied her and frowned. "Hey, is something really going on with you?"

She shook her head. "It'll wait."

He smiled. "Will it wait until tonight? We'll both be off. How about dinner out. Would you like that?"

She felt her color rise. "David, I'd love to, but you didn't sleep at all last night. You can't go two nights—"

"And how much did you sleep? Three hours? Two? Listen, there's a great little French restaurant nearby with music, and it's quiet. We could stay there for a couple of hours and still be back early. Come on. What do you say?"

Her cheeks burned. Suddenly they were no longer subordinate and academic superior. They were actually discussing a date like normal people.

He bent slightly and she found him peering mischievously into her face. "You're blushing," he said. "That means yes."

"David, I'll kill you," she said hoarsely.

He grinned, straightening. "So tonight it is!" Then, overhead, the page again. As if he hadn't heard it, he reached out and touched her cheek. "Don't forget that 9:15 lecture," he said softly. Then he turned and disappeared down the hallway.

Jill stood, watching him go. Slowly, she looked back over her shoulder at the almost closed door of room 819. She calculated: fifty milligrams of Thorazine doesn't always knock a person out completely. Especially if the patient is highly agitated to begin with; at best, the drug would only induce heavy grogginess.

And maybe the patient could *talk* . . .

Jill reached down and counted the odd-number charts remaining. Five. She had more than enough time to complete rounds, then stop in the doctors' lounge for coffee, which is what the others usually did.

On the other hand . . .

She told herself she would only peek. The patient was probably asleep, or if awake, then barely so. Jill could not shake the compulsion of wanting to see her.

She snapped up the Sayers chart and headed back toward the end of the hall. As she walked she read through the notes and saw Gacey's firm instructions: the patient was not to be disturbed. By whom? Jill thought. Relatives? Visitors? Eighteen hours in the hospital had produced no sign of either. Flipping back to the face sheet, Jill noticed that on the lines designating marital status and next of kin were written, "divorced" and "none."

The stillness of 819 was almost frightening. Glancing briefly over her shoulder, Jill knocked very gently and went inside.

$$\overline{\underline{12}}$$

THE YOUNG WOMAN was pale, with long, dark hair that spread across the pillow. Her swollen eyes were closed.

Jill stood by the bed and in the gloom checked her watch and the medication sheet she carried. It was 8:34; the Thorazine had been administered two and a half hours ago. It's working full strength now, Jill thought. Patient's probably out cold.

She turned a page in the chart. It was while she was squinting at some lab reports that she felt eyes on her. She looked up. Mary Jo Sayers was staring at her. The expression in her eyes was not sleepy at all. It was sharp and full of hate.

"Mrs. Sayers?" Jill's feeling of sorrow for the woman deepened. Her face—so full of agitation and fury, fighting the medication as if it were an assault . . .

Jill's hands fell to her sides. "It's okay," she said softly. "Please trust me. I'm a friend."

The patient continued to watch her. Another thirty seconds passed, and then the body—those white-knuckled fists and rigid arms outside the covers—went limp.

"Go . . . away," she whispered.

"I will if you want me to," Jill said. But she did not go

away. She remained staring sadly at the name bracelet on the patient's wrist, allowing the silence to stretch between them.

"I want to die," Mary Jo Sayers said. Quietly and calmly, no hint of hysteria. Profoundly depressed, yes; but . . . delusional? So far, nothing.

Jill inhaled. "I don't believe you mean that," she said gently, eyeing the raised siderails, groping for words. She made a helpless gesture.

"Mrs. Sayers, I'm not a psychiatrist and I'm not even a full-fledged doctor. I'm an intern, and I came here because I . . . cared, I was in the delivery room with you and . . . oh, Mary Jo, I just wish I could help in some way."

Surprise registered on the patient's face. A moment passed. Then Mary Jo Sayers managed in a trembling voice, "But you can't help me, can you?" She closed her eyes. "Nobody can."

"We can talk," Jill said with sudden firmness. She went to the window and pulled up the blinds. Morning sunlight poured in. The room was a typical private: small, the floor covered with worn linoleum, one window overlooking the parking lot.

And then she saw that Mary Jo Sayers had begun to weep, quietly and defeatedly, crossing her arms tightly across her chest.

"Oh, God!" Jill rushed to lower the siderails. Tears came streaming down Mary Jo Sayers' face and her shoulders were heaving. "Oh, poor kid"—Jill tried to soothe —"go ahead and cry. It's good." She wiped the young woman's cheeks with Kleenex and smoothed her hair.

After a while the tears began to slow.

Haltingly, Mary Jo said, "You know, it wasn't *supposed* to turn out like this." She raised her glistening face to Jill. "I was *promised* that everything would be perfect, and now the baby's dead and . . ."

She broke into sobs again.

Jill felt herself stiffen. "You were . . . promised?" She looked down at Mary Jo's hands. They held a crumpled wad of Kleenex and they were picking, picking, tearing the tissue into ragged pieces.

"Who promised you, Mary Jo?" Jill's voice was even.

The fingers stopped. Mary Jo Sayers looked up suspiciously from her pillow.

"Why should you believe me? No one else around here does."

"Try me." The eyes that met Mary Jo Sayers were clear, intense, honest. The two gazes locked, and something flickered in the depths of Sayers' eyes. She looked away and gazed down at the soggy shreds on the blanket. Then she began to speak, the words coming out like a long sigh of relief.

The phone shrilled on the main desk of the psychiatric floor. Head nurse Vera Crowley, looking harassed, put her own call to Pharmacy on hold, and looked around frantically for someone else to take the call. There was no one. The floor nurses were scattered, and there was no sign of the ward clerk. Vera Crowley hated working alone. This caller could not have picked a worse moment.

After five rings she sighed and pressed the flashing phone button. "Psychiatry," she said.

What she heard on the other end caused her to frown. A gruff male voice, identifying himself as Dr. Mackey, was ordering the immediate transfer of a patient from obstetrics to the psychiatric ward.

Vera Crowley did not know any Dr. Mackey, but his voice sounded very authoritative.

"But doctor," she said, puzzled. "Any transfer would have to be okayed by our psychiatric resident, Dr. Downey, and I'm afraid he's stepped away for a moment—"

"Downey's already okayed the transfer!" barked the voice. "Listen. This patient is creating havoc down here. You get her off my floor within ten minutes or I'll have your name before the hospital administration. Do you understand?"

Vera Crowley saw the other phone button go dark, and realized that Pharmacy had hung up.

"But doctor," she persisted. "We have to have the transfer order *here* before we—"

The voice at the other end was threatening. "The paperwork is being done right now. It will be sent up as soon as it's ready. In the meantime, this is urgent. Do you *understand*, dammit?"

The receiver was slammed down.

Shaken, Vera Crowley hung up and stared out the window, thinking how, after sixteen years, she really ought to be used to this type of call. Only psychiatrists were soft-spoken; all the other doctors *yelled*. She was certainly glad she didn't have to work with *them* all the time.

She shrugged. Well, one mustn't take these things too personally, she thought. With that she leaned forward and pressed a buzzer on her desk.

"During the night, I *tried* to tell, but I couldn't, not everything, because of a . . . a . . ."

"A promise?" Jill urged her on.

A long silence, then: "Yes." Sayers looked up at her, looked down, continued in a stronger voice. "I'm writing a thesis, you see . . ."

"Oh, yes, anthropology. I was told you were a Ph.D. candidate in anthro—"

"*Paleo*anthropology," said Sayers. "I work at the Madison Museum, right up the street."

"Oh," said Jill; and she thought: sharp as a tack.

Sayers meandered for some moments on the rigors of fossil study and her thoughts on evolution. "Anyway," she went on, "I wanted a child at the same time, and with all my heart . . . but I'm divorced, you see, and then it was while I was doing my research that I—"

There was a noise in the hall, and the door banged open. Two orderlies—one tall and bull-shouldered, the other swarthy with dog eyes—came in pulling a gurney. They looked like furniture movers.

Jill stared—and froze.

"We got orders to transfer dis patient," the bigger one said. In his left hand he carried a thick restraining strap.

"What?" cried Jill, recognizing the uniforms of psychiatric orderlies. Mary Jo Sayers sat up in bed, blinking, comprehension dawning fast as her face too became shocked, then terrified. Her wide staring eyes looked up to Jill, who rallied, and bolted around the bed toward the men.

"Just what in *hell* do you think you're doing?" Jill saw the tall one gesture to the swarthy one, who left the room. Bull shoulders held up a white paper.

"Orders," he rasped. Furious, Jill snatched the paper from his hand and scanned it quickly.

She looked up. "Get out," she said, her voice more charged with fury than she had ever heard it. "This paper isn't even signed. How *dare* you frighten this patient?"

Bull shoulders' features contorted. "Listen, doc, don't look at *me!* We was told to come get this patient, and see? *Dere."* He pointed. "It *says* Dr. Downey already okayed the transfer. So if you don't mind . . ."

Dog-eyes reappeared with a nurse who was holding a syringe. Seeing it, Mary Jo Sayers cried out in anguish. In a scolding voice Jill intercepted the nurse, who looked up at her with sorrowful eyes. The syringe glinted.

"Yes, I know. So sad. But Dr. Gacey's orders said Thorazine as needed, and since the patient's resisting—"

A thrashing noise. Jill looked. Mary Jo Sayers, whimpering in horror, was trying to climb out of bed.

"See?" bellowed bull shoulders. "Resisting!"

There was a daze, a swirling of images. Jill hearing her own protesting voice as dog-eyes lunged and swung Mary Jo Sayers, crying, back onto the bed; as bull shoulders, forcing her down, began attaching straps, here, there; and the nurse, all bristling efficiency, leaned over the hysterical young woman and delivered her split-second injection. "One hundred milligrams! That ought to do it! Sorry for your trouble, boys."

Incredulous, Jill watched helplessly. Mary Jo Sayers' body grew limp. Her eyes struggled to stay open but failed. Her lips worked slowly.

"Help . . . me . . ."

In a rage Jill pushed past and gripped the siderails of the

bed. "Don't worry, Mary Jo!" she cried. "I'll come for you! I'll help you!"

Mary Jo's eyelids fluttered open; saw Jill; believed.

One of the orderlies was still tightly gripping the patient's arm.

Unnecessary. Mary Jo Sayers' head fell to one side, and then she was still.

Muffling tears of fury, Jill ran from the room.

13

"JESUS, WHAT IN *hell* is going on in there?"

Sam MacIntyre had heard the noise and rushed down to investigate. He ran headlong into Jill outside 819, and was now staring beyond her toward the open door.

In a highly emotional state, she told him what had happened.

They could hear the sound of activity from inside. A gurney was being maneuvered toward the door. Slightly behind them in the hall a group of people stood: two nurses, staring gape-mouthed; several wide-eyed patients in pastel robes. Jill was repelled. Their faces reminded her of people who rush to see a building on fire.

"Transfer order?" MacIntyre said crossly. "I don't know anything about any transfer order."

Jill held up the paper she had snatched from the orderly. "It's not even *signed!*" Her chest was still heaving.

"Give me that." He took the paper and frowned, reading. "There's got to be some—"

At the sound of wheels they both looked up. The unconscious strapped-down body of Mary Jo Sayers was pushed past them. The sight made Jill's stomach turn. The swarthy orderly stopped and regarded her peevishly.

"We gotta have that paper back," he said.

"Drop dead!" she said. It came out more stridently than she had intended. Down the corridor, doors with other stenciled numbers opened; heads craned out questioningly.

"Lower your voice," MacIntyre said.

"The hell I will! Do you know what happened in there?" Jill pointed. "A travesty, that's what! A lousy, rotten *mistake*, and this poor patient has to pay by being manhandled and traumatized . . ."

MacIntyre scowled and then held up both hands, as if in surrender. He turned to the orderlies. "Okay, beat it," he told them. "If there's an error, we'll straighten it out."

They left, pushing their tragic cargo. People whispered and watched with avid curiosity as they passed by. The syringe-nurse came briskly out of 819 carrying some linen; she joined the other two nurses who stood watching, and the three turned, staring at Jill.

"This better be good, Jill." MacIntyre said.

She turned back to him. "*What*?"

Frowning, MacIntyre straightened and put his hands on his hips. "So you got an unsigned transfer order," he said. "It's sloppy, but it happens all the time. Somebody made a *mistake*, that's all. What gives you the right to go off half-cocked and stir up the whole damn floor?"

"Half-cocked! Listen. Signed or unsigned, that patient was as normal as we are. Well, me, anyway. And we don't even know who *gave* that order. This so-called transfer hasn't exactly followed hospital regula—"

"I'll find *out*," MacIntyre's face was getting red. "I'll go through the proper channels and—"

"Proper channels! And how long will that take? Days?"

"—and the hospital hierarchy will see to it that—"

"The hospital hierarchy stinks, too!" Jill stopped to catch her breath. She felt drained. "Sam, that patient was starting to tell me something. And you know what I think? I think someone is trying to *hide* that phocomelia case, that's what! That explains the rush to hustle her off the floor. That explains—''

She stopped, sensing someone watching her, and turned to see Thomas Gacey, standing with arms folded, about eight feet away. Gacey was looking at her the way he might look at one of his wriggling lab animals.

"Having a little trouble, Sam?" he asked.

Jill turned white.

Gacey was a thin-faced man with a receding hairline and the eyes of a Doberman. It was said he had a range of human feelings that stretched from remote to outright vicious. He looked older than a fourth-year resident.

MacIntyre shoved his hands in his pockets and switched expressions with remarkable speed. "No-o," he said with studied casualness. "Just a typical morning."

Gacey sneered. "Well, now. Judging from what I just heard, your typical morning sounds like a soap opera. Lousy medicine, of course, but maybe that's because certain individuals around here"—he looked directly at Jill— "have overactive imaginations. *And* personalities detrimental to the running of a hospital. What would you say to that, *Doctor* Raney?"

She glowered at him. "You ordered that transfer, didn't you? Anyone who makes you or your department look bad—"

Gacey took a menacing step forward. "That's enough!" he said. He shook his finger at her. "You're an interfering female sticking your nose where it doesn't belong! I *distinctly* said on the night note that that patient was not to be disturbed. You disobeyed! I could get you thrown out for this!"

MacIntyre cleared his throat. "She was acting on the patient's behalf, Tom."

"Disobeyed!" Gacey repeated. "And how dare you pull a scene like that in a hospital corridor?" His eyes fell to the Sayers chart that Jill was still holding. "Give me that chart."

Jill hesitated, and looked at Sam, who shrugged. Reluctantly, she handed Gacey the chart. Her hands were ice cold, but her face appeared calm. She lifted her chin. I know what I'm dealing with, she thought.

"Now," said Gacey, thrusting the chart under his arm with the face sheet toward his body. "I want you to tell me exactly what nonsense the patient told you." His manner became silky. "For our psychiatric evaluation, of course."

Jill remained silent.

"Don't be so damned cool! I heard you tell MacIntyre that she started to say something."

"Only started," said MacIntyre. "She didn't get the chance to say much."

Gacey wheeled on him, pointing to Jill. "What is she, your wooden dummy?" He turned to Jill. "You know that with this noncooperation I'll have no option but to report you? You *know* that, don't you?"

She looked at him blankly.

Gacey stood motionless except for a slight leaning back on his heels. "I think," he said, "I'm going to send this intern to the Administration Office. Let her spend a few hours down *there* cooling her heels, seeing what probation would be like. *That* will teach her how to obey—" He stopped. MacIntyre was studying the ceiling tiles and slowly shaking his head.

" 'Fraid you're overruled," MacIntyre said mildly. "Arnett has dibs on her first." Sam held up his watch. "Fact is, Jill, you're late. I'll bet ol' Cliff is up there alone with his projector and feeling like a wallflower." Jill blinked at MacIntyre, who smiled winningly at Gacey. "Cliff Arnett would be *very* upset if certain interns don't show up for something he's prepared for them."

Jill stared at MacIntyre as if she was seeing him for the first time. He looked back at her and cocked his head imperceptibly. "Better hurry," he said.

She looked over at Gacey, who stood silently, hostile, watching her. "There are other ways to handle this," he snarled.

Without a word, she turned and walked away. She glanced up at a wall clock. Not really late, she thought.

That Sam, bless him. She estimated how long Arnett's lecture would take. *Good, there would be time*. She knew what she was going to do.

She opened the door to the stairwell that would take her to her 9:15 lecture. There she breathed at last, and in a burst of resolve began to run up the stairs.

14

IT WAS 9:18 when a man in a blue Buick pulled into the receiving area of Madison Hospital. There were already three ambulances parked by the platform; a police car, empty, was parked off to one side. Slowing down, the Buick slid into place next to the last ambulance, and the young man, well-dressed, got out and began walking toward the emergency entrance.

"Hey, mister!"

The young man turned, and blinding bright July sun flashed on his sunglasses.

A middle-aged security guard approached him. "You going to be there long? You're not supposed to park there, you know."

The young man hesitated. He was gaunt-faced, and wore khaki pants and a button-down shirt. "Oh, I won't be long," he said. "I'm picking up someone in a wheelchair. Our doctor said it would be okay." He smiled the convincing smile of an anxious relative.

The guard hesitated. "Well, all right, in that case," he said. He relaxed his posture and rested one hand on the walkie-talkie that was hooked to his belt. He did not see the young man's eyes, behind the sunglasses, dart to the gun which hung from the other side of his belt.

The security guard's features became friendly. "Listen, if you need a hand, just give a holler when you get back. Emergency has plenty of attendants who can help you with the chair."

The young man looked grateful. "That's very kind of you," he said. "We probably will be needing a little help."

With that he turned and leaped up onto the platform with a familiarity that surprised the guard. Looking neither right nor left, he entered Emergency through the automatic sliding doors.

15

WHEN JILL RANEY entered the faculty room of Chapin North, Clifford Arnett was busy shoving his carousel onto the projector and sharing repartee with his audience. "Don't feel too bad," he said, "the only people who made it to the end of yesterday's lecture were the med students." It was an old joke: interns and residents were constantly getting called away from conferences. But everyone laughed, just the same.

Jill sat down next to Tricia Donovan, who looked up and smiled brightly. Jill smiled grimly back. More members of the house staff filed in after Jill; and by 9:20, all seats were taken and several people had to stand.

Arnett, typically, was late in starting, and made much fuss as he fumbled with an electrical cord. Tricia watched him, amused, until her glance brushed over Jill, who was sitting, oddly quiet, staring down at a folded paper she held in her lap.

Leaning over, Tricia whispered, "What's the paper?"

"Trouble," Jill said, without looking up.

"Still upset about this morning? Stryker sure shot us all down, didn't he?"

"No . . . yes, but . . ." Tricia's question had forced Jill's mind to switch tracks, and she frowned.

"You know," she said in a low voice, shaking her head, "I really thought I had found some weird link between those two tragedies, Sayers and Moran." She mimicked Stryker's voice angrily: " 'Many women update their Gyn status before initiating a pregnancy.' "

Tricia cocked her head to one side in thought. "But Jill," she said, "we don't know that either of them *wanted* to get pregnant, do we?"

Jill stared at her.

"Lights please," called Arnett, and the room went dark. There was a clicking sound, a hum, and suddenly a beam burst forth to cover the screen with spangles. Arnett focused, and an image of a corkscrewed ladder densely studded with glowing balls came into view.

"The secret of life," Arnett said simply.

Firefly penlights began moving across notebooks.

He reviewed his material: how DNA, the microscopic coils containing the genetic blueprint of every living organism, had been discovered in England by James Watson and Francis Crick in 1953. He explained how, by 1980, DNA technology had opened the way for the astonishing concept of genetic engineering. He told about the "knowledge explosion": the fact that things were happening so fast in science that nobody could keep up; and that, most astonishingly, the new field of recombinant technology was probably still in its infancy.

"Although," he continued, "it has already greatly affected the course of human history. Consider this next slide."

There was a click and the narrow beam flickered amber. Clifford Arnett cleared his throat.

"An ear of corn," he announced. "Or rather, the genetic master molecule of a super new mutant."

Jill Raney lifted a brooding glance to the screen. *Corn?*

". . . only about eight years that scientists have known how to use recombinant DNA techniques," Arnett was saying. "The procedure is called 'gene splicing'; that is, scientists have learned to biochemically snip off lengths of genetic material—*desirable* genetic material—from any plant or animal, then splice it together with the DNA of an entirely different organism. What results is a man-made combination of genes never before encountered in nature." He began to pace. "Scientists next insert these recombined genes into a selected organism, and lo! A new life form on earth. A *better* life form. This corn, for example."

They looked at the screen. The plump, pale-yellow-to-brown atoms crowding the molecule looked as complex as those of any higher organism.

Arnett snapped on a small lamp next to the projector and began reading from a report written by Dr. Hubert Crump, a leading agricultural geneticist. "Crump says that we've got to produce as much food in the next twenty-five years as we have in the past ten thousand!" Arnett read on, describing how the world population would probably double by the year 2000. How the fertilizer-demanding strains of wheat and rice and corn, planted around the world in the 1960s, were now dying out; soaring prices had pushed the cost of petrochemical fertilizers out of the reach of poor countries. Arnett described how exotic new plant diseases had proliferated; why the world's water was in short supply. "And the United States alone loses four million acres of farmland—a year!—to erosion and increasing urban development. I could go on," he sighed, putting down the report, "but it's too damn depressing." He snapped off the light and with a rustling sound the audience turned back to the screen.

Tricia leaned over to Jill. "I'm hungry," she whispered.

Jill found herself still in an angry daze. She had tried to

be diligent, taking notes like the others. Yet the events of half an hour ago still preyed on her mind. She flicked on the tiny light in her digital watch: 9:41. She sighed impatiently.

Arnett's voice was jolting. "Pretty amazing," he was saying. "This corn"—he tapped the screen with his pointer—"has had its genetic makeup manipulated until it's become nothing short of miraculous. It has received nitrogen-fixing DNA from soybeans—*here*: see this molecule?—and now can manufacture its own fertilizer. From plants highly resistant to disease, it has received toxins to drive off pests—this molecule down here. Pretty color, isn't it? In another two years of research, I'm told, it will be able to live in salty or akaline soil. A-a-and," he inhaled, "live for *weeks* at a time without water."

People shifted in their seats, leaning forward in fascination. Arnett waited for the hushed exclamations to subside, then continued.

"Now, how does all this concern us?" he asked rhetorically. He walked back to the projector, and then his voice went up like a man shouting "fire."

"Human genetic therapy!" he exclaimed. "Just think of the possibilities. And compare. A plant has frailties imposed on it by an indifferent nature. And so we snip them out, just like that. *Imagine* what it would be if, someday, in the same revolutionary way, we could eliminate birth defects and genetic disease . . . which every year affect ninety thousand live births. Got that? Ninety thousand children a year! Imagine! Hemophilia, gone. Cystic fibrosis, muscular dystrophy, Tay Sachs, sickle cell disease . . ." He shuffled back and forth. "Why, do you know there are *hundreds* of genetic disorders which will someday be as extinct as . . . smallpox? Tyrannosaurus rex?" He cleared his throat with effort. He was growing hoarse.

"More research is needed. *Lots* more research. Which is why we all work the insane hours that we do, right? Okay, next slide."

A third film flicked onto the screen.

Jill Raney turned, saw Arnett wipe spittle from the

corners of his mouth with a handkerchief. He looked up
suddenly; the light from the new slide illuminated the
room, and he saw her looking at him.

"Dr. Raney," he said. "Suppose you tell us about this
next slide. My voice isn't what it used to be."

Jill tensed, dreading a display of ignorance. Looking
back toward the screen, she caught her breath. She had the
eerie feeling that she was inside an old cathedral. And
floating above her, glowing light surrounded by darkness,
was the most exquisite stained-glass window she had ever
seen. Ten points, like a rounded star. Medieval reds and
blues and greens. Golden filaments instead of lead panes,
graceful and fragile, geometrically perfect.

Jill stared for a long moment, mesmerized by the technical perfection of the slide. "Yes," she said finally. "That's
a DNA molecule, sliced transversely, rendered by computer in cross section."

Arnett was delighted. "Very *good*," he said. He looked
around his audience. "It's nice to know that *some* of you
have been over this in medical school." He reached for his
wooden pointer, strode to the front of the room and stood
by the screen. Returning his attention to Jill, he raised the
pointer to the screen, lightly touching a red, glinting area
on one of the star's "tips."

"Do you know what this is?"

Jill moved to the edge of her chair, concentrating. "I
believe it's, um, one of the atoms of a ribose molecule,"
she said. She did not breathe.

"Excellent," snapped Arnett. "And this?" The pointer
moved to a pin of light, strongly green.

Jill shifted in her chair. Squinted. Inhaled. "Well . . .
that's probably an atom belonging to a nucleic acid molecule"
—she exhaled—"yes, that's it . . . assuming the sequence
of chemical base pairs runs in the same—"

"Bingo again!" exulted Arnett. He scraped the pointer
clear across the stained glass star and stopped at another
area of light. Very pretty. Rose-colored.

"What's this?" he demanded.

Jill looked. She frowned. "I . . ." she began. She

stared hard and ransacked her brain. Nothing. She looked in Arnett's direction and shook her head. "I don't know."

Arnett, still holding the pointer, was silent for several seconds, as if letting the awfulness of not knowing sink in. He continued to gaze at the unnamed, rose-colored area.

"Sequence of CAT," he said. "You see here," he tapped the screen, "we have the cytosine-guanine pair, followed by adenine-thymine, followed by thymine-adenine. Now, this particular sequence of these three pairs constitutes a gene which . . ." he turned to face his audience, ". . . will dictate for this patient an existence of painful transfusions and shortened life expectancy." He inhaled, leaned on his pointer. "Hemophilia," he said crisply.

Everyone stopped scribbling, frozen.

For Jill Raney the glowing on the screen ceased to be stained glass.

"And by the way," said Arnett, as if just remembering something. "This particular patient has an important date in store for him in six weeks. Can anyone guess what it is?"

The interns waited expectantly.

Arnett's tone was flat, expressionless. "He will be born," he said. "May we have the lights back on, please?"

The fluorescents buzzed on. Arnett shut off the projector, circled the room, then leaned against one wall, his arms folded. "Time to wind up," he said. "But first, a quick rundown of prenatal testing and diagnosis techniques. Let's start with chromosome mapping." Abruptly he thrust forth his pointer as if to skewer one of the interns.

"Billings," he said. "Say you suspect a problem. Where do you begin?"

The intern named Gus Billings straightened in his chair. "Amniocentesis, sir. Always amniocentesis. For anything."

"Good," said Arnett. "And by the way, I think *younger* than 35, say 32 or 33, should be the recommended maternal age for amniocentesis. My colleagues don't all agree with me. Not *yet*, anyway." He paused self-importantly. "Now, gross chromosome mapping. What about that, Ortega?"

Charlie Ortega, standing in the rear, answered promptly. "Still used for diagnosing Down's and Klinefelter's syndromes," he said. "Otherwise, limited."

"Right," said Arnett. "Because now we've learned how to go *inside* the chromosomes and seek out errors in genes, which are the *true* genetic disorders . . . so . . ." He pointed to a resident. "What comes next?"

A tense monotone. "You isolate fetal cellular material floating in the amniotic fluid."

"Good. And?" Arnett pointed to Tricia Donovan. "What next?"

Tricia was ready. "From the fetal cellular material you grow out more cells in tissue culture—"

"You realize this is cellular cloning," Arnett cut in.

"Yes. Then when you get enough cells you examine them for genetic deformity . . ." She hesitated, looked around. "You have to use an electron microscope," she added helpfully.

Arnett, raising a comic eyebrow, said, "Well I should *hope* so." The audience, grateful, laughed.

"So!" Arnett continued to probe. "Suppose you do find some genetic deformity. What next? Jill Raney?"

Her hands were fumbling in her lap, turning over and over again the folded, unsigned order transferring Mary Jo Sayers. Peripherally, she had been following the discussion. She had studied enough to know that Arnett's barrage of questions had reached the end of the line.

She glanced up, thinking. What *do* you do if you find a genetic deformity? She bit her lip.

"You . . . hope, I guess," she said. "At this point so much of genetic therapy is still in the research stage. So little is known—"

"But theoretically," Arnett interjected. "And *please,* try to sound a little more positive."

She smiled faintly. "Okay. Well, you locate the gene deformity and you, well, you cut it out with a . . . restriction enzyme, I believe they're called." She licked her lips, saw him nodding approval. "Then you incubate the defective material with a . . . 'soup' of correct genetic material, along with a ligase enzyme . . . works like glue . . . to seal the transplanted gene back into its DNA chain. Then you get all this . . . stuff . . . back into the fetus . . . I don't know how . . .''

"It's done surgically. You find a blood vessel in the fetus and inject your corrected material . . .'' Arnett waited for her to finish.

Her brow furrowed, she turned a ballpoint in her hands. "Yes, well, so you inject it in and you . . . you *hope* that the corrected genes will multiply and crowd out the defective ones.''

She was aware of many eyes on her, including Arnett's, who studied her for a long moment.

"Bravo,'' he said quietly. "At this rate, my dear, you'll be a research fellow before you reach your first year of residency.''

He gestured sweepingly. "Well, I guess we've about covered everything. Any questions? If so, don't ask. Go home. Hit the books instead.'' He looked back. "Jill, I'd like a word with you, please.''

The rest gathered up their things, murmured thanks to Arnett, and filed out of the room. In the doorway Tricia turned, mouthing something which Jill didn't understand. Tricia disappeared.

Jill approached Arnett, wondering what he wanted with her.

Without looking up, he said, "You're very advanced, Jill. You're obviously interested in research, aren't you?''

He hoisted the heavy projector off the table and up into a cabinet. "Yes,'' she answered to his back. "I've been doing a lot of reading . . .''

He turned, red-faced from exertion. "You mean, before you were *forced* to? Hah! Now *that's* something. Well I just wanted you to know I'm impressed. Continue with your enthusiasm, and . . .'' He hesitated.

She looked questioningly at him.

He lowered his voice. "Play your cards right.''

She frowned. "Sir?''

He smiled paternally. "Oh, you know. Hospital politics. If you want the top, or feel headed for research, being brilliant is not enough. You have to be . . . smart, too. The favoritism system around here is downright feudal." He pursed his lips, appraising her.

"Don't step on the wrong toes, Jill. I got one hell of an angry phone call from Stryker this morning. I think he called others, too. So for God's sake, act like an intern and stay out of trouble."

She flushed, at a loss for words.

"Of course, I'm telling you this for selfish reasons. I'm always on the lookout for promising research assistants, and if you're this brilliant this early . . . Well! Don't throw away your chances by being overemotional and underinformed. Will you promise me that?"

Her heart was pounding. "I appreciate your concern, Dr. Arnett."

He patted her arm. "And stop by any time at my lab. If you want to talk, or observe, or whatever." He gathered up his papers. "I've got some pretty fascinating research in the works by the way. Even the *failures* are fascinating."

"I certainly will," she said. "Thank you for the invitation."

"You'd better hurry along. I know how life is for you interns." He smiled.

"Yes, thank you, sir," she said, shook his hand, and then went out.

16

TRICIA WAS WAITING in the hall. Jill walked purposefully, Tricia following, still excited over the lecture. They rounded a corner and headed down a wider, empty corridor.

Tricia looked around, puzzled. "What are we doing in the psychiatric wing?"

Jill pointed. "You see that elevator?"

Tricia peered down the corridor. Looking alarmed, she turned back to Jill. "Yeah, I see the elevator. Come on, let's get out of here. Psychiatric wards give me the creeps!"

Jill shook her head and continued walking. "It's only the outpatient, silly. See the lights? They're on. Everyone's inside—having their forty-five minutes. Say, what kind of a doctor *are* you, anyway?"

Tricia stared belligerently at the line of red lights outside each door, which meant that psychotherapy was in session and the doctor was not to be disturbed.

"Okay." She caught up to Jill. "So what gives?"

Jill was silent until they reached the twin metal doors of the elevator. She did not press the button. Instead she turned, told Tricia about Sayers' mysterious, unsigned transfer order, described the young woman's high intelligence, and the sudden brutal scene with the orderlies.

"Not even so much as a provisional diagnosis!" Jill finished, her voice rising.

Tricia's face showed disbelief. "Oh, my God," she whispered, "so they've got her up there?"

"Not for long."

Jill punched the button.

Tricia stared. "You don't mean you're going *up* there? You *can't* . . . look, I don't think the elevator even *stops* on this floor. It's programmed to go straight up until . . ."

"It stops," Jill said. "Don't worry. No more confrontations with superiors. I'm going to do this quietly and carefully. Just give hospital paperwork a little shove, that's all."

Tricia's face screwed up. "Wait! There's *got* to be an explanation for all this. Besides . . ." She rubbed her temple, groping for a thought. "There's a *reason* you can't get there from here," she said. "I mean, even if the damn thing stops there's a . . ."

They heard a humming sound. Then a thumping and clanking as the cables pulled the car upward. A bell dinged. The doors slid open, and Jill got on.

She looked out resolutely. "I have to do this, Tricia."

"Stop!" pleaded Tricia. "Wait a second. You can't because—"

The doors lurched; and then, almost soundlessly, began to close.

"Omigod!" cried Tricia. "I just remembered. You can't get in there without a *pass!* It's a magnetic plastic card and—"

Thump.

The doors slid closed. There was a whining, mechanical sound as the car inside began to rise in its shaft. Tricia stared helplessly ahead at the shiny metal, took her glasses off, put them on, took them off—a nervous habit since her teenage years. The tension in her face turned to all-out dismay. "Oh, Jill," she said out loud. "What now?"

17

THE ELEVATOR WAS actually *padded*.

Jill stared at the heavily quilted green padding and looked at the control panel. The elevator was programmed to stop at only three places: first floor emergency, eleventh floor outpatient, and fourteenth floor psychiatric inpatient, where she was headed. The corresponding buttons were painted blue. All the rest were inked out.

It occurred to Jill that she couldn't get off now even if she wanted to.

The car jerked to a stop and the doors opened.

Jill found herself in a darkly gleaming vestibule without windows. The floor shone. There was a wide, stainless steel door directly across from her, but there were no knobs; no visible means of opening it. Confused, she looked around, then heard a female voice evenly announce: "For admittance, please place staff card in slot indicated. Thank you."

Staff card? So that's what Tricia was shouting before the doors closed. Jill fingered the name tag on her lapel. That was her staff identification, wasn't it? That's all anybody ever . . .

"Anybody here?" she called out, feeling foolish.

"For admittance, please place . . ."

Jill cursed silently. It was a recording. Psychiatric personnel were apparently issued special cards which one inserted . . . someplace, and that activated the mechanism which opened the door. Simple, Jill thought. Except that she didn't have a card, and she didn't know how the damned thing worked.

Anger took over. Abruptly Jill stepped forward, raising her clenched fist as if to pound on the metal door.

The sound of a bell ringing made her jump.

Turning, she saw the elevator doors open and a pair of orderlies coming toward her, eyeing her suspiciously.

"Looking for something?" one said. It was not a friendly voice. His face was badly pockmarked.

Jill's mind raced. She made a gesture of feminine despair and said, "Oh, I'm afraid you can't help me. You see, I was sent here by Obstetrics for a followup on a patient, but they never told me you need a pass. I guess they forgot. Now I have to go all the way back down—"

"For admittance, please place staff card in slot—"

The orderly glanced up angrily. "Aw, shaddup!" he growled, stepping forward to yank a concealed wall switch into the "down" position. The recording stopped with a metallic screech. The second orderly extracted something that looked like a credit card from his pocket and pushed it into a slot to the left of the door.

"Nobody ever tells nobody *nothin'* around here," he said.

They stepped back.

Noiselessly the metal door slid open.

Jill found herself facing a wide, brightly lit hallway. An administration desk, in the center of the foyer, was staffed by two nurses and a heavyset clerk, all of whom looked up questioningly as Jill followed the orderlies into the area.

She felt elated. Moving forward briskly, pulling the Sayers transfer document from her clipboard, her mind ran over the correct procedure: Introduce yourself as the patient's doctor, show the unsigned transfer order and say that a mistake had been made. Send the patient back. Simple. And what if, in the meantime, a *signed* order had arrived at their end? Easy. Demand the doctor's name who signed the order. Say that the entire obstetrical staff thinks that *he's* crazy.

Send the patient back.

The orderlies headed off into one of the side corridors, and a fortyish nurse wearing glasses smiled attentively as Jill told her story.

"Sayers . . . Sayers," the nurse repeated. She flipped through the patient log, and moved her index finger down the page marked R-S-T.

She looked up. "I'm sorry," she said. "We have no such patient listed on this floor."

Jill stared stupidly. "That's ridiculous," she said.

The nurse appeared at a loss, glanced again at her log and said hopefully: "We have a Mr. *Jesse* Sayers in Section Four. He's an acute alcoholic with neurological—"

"Let me see that." Jill moved around the desk and inside the nurses' area before the woman had finished. She grasped the wide notebook and scanned it quickly. Her eyes reached the bottom of the page. She straightened slowly.

"Listen," she said. "At precisely 8:50 this morning two of your orderlies came for this patient. That means she was admitted here a little after 9:00. It is now 14 minutes past 10. So exactly how—"

"May I help you?"

Jill turned toward the voice. Facing her was a large-bosomed, gray-haired woman. The black double stripe on the woman's cap designated her as head nurse.

Frowning, Jill said: "I certainly hope so. Your department seems to have lost one of our patients. The last name is Sayers."

"I beg your pardon?" the woman said coolly. She wore a name tag that identified her as "Mrs. Vera Crowley."

Jill pointed to the patient log and again waved the unsigned transfer order.

"Is this your handwriting?" Jill asked, pointing. "It says here that your psychiatric resident okayed the transfer *verbally,* which isn't—"

"No," replied the woman acidly. "I was *told* on the telephone that Dr. Downey had okayed the order. Someone on your floor wanted the patient out immediately." Vera Crowley became defensive. "He sounded *very* angry," she said.

"Well, *who*, for God's sake?" Jill was suddenly aware of the heavyset clerk, who had stopped sorting papers and was eyeing her steadily.

"I do not *recall* the name of the caller," Nurse Crowley said, "and in any event, it no longer matters *who* it was." She lifted her chin with a self-satisfied air. "You see, moments after Mrs. Sayers was brought in, her husband came for her. A *wonderful* young man. So concerned. He wanted her to be in some fine place in the country."

Jill was stunned. "Mary Jo Sayers was divorced," she said tonelessly.

"Doctor, I saw her husband with my own eyes!"

"You saw!" Jill burst out. "You mean any idiot can walk in off the street and call himself a husband? Take a patient away, just like that? Do you have any idea what you've *done*?"

Crowley, aghast, took a step backward. A patient in blue pajamas came shuffling out of the nearest ward, and then another. The floor resident came hurrying down the hall and waved a tense hand.

"What's all this about?" he demanded angrily. Jill looked at his name tag—the mysterious Dr. Downey at last. He looked to be in his early thirties; he was overweight and had an eye tic and his complexion was sallow.

Breathing rapidly, Jill began her story again, but he cut her off by turning to Crowley and saying, "You've told her the patient's been discharged?"

"Yes, but she refused to—"

"Excellent," he snapped. He turned to Jill.

"Listen," he said. "You don't just come barging in like this. It's not done. You've disrupted my ward."

She glared at him. "And you," she shot back, "have abetted a kidnapping!"

"A *what*?" Downey's eye tic speeded up. Jill spun on her heel before he could say more and headed for the vestibule and the elevator. She heard angry footsteps at her heels, but did not turn back. Punching the button, she waited, her mind still reeling.

From behind she heard his voice, once again the low,

controlled tones of a psychiatrist. "I could g-get you thrown out f-for this. One c-c-call to administration, and you'd be . . ."

Jill looked at the closed elevator doors. *Stutters too?*

She turned to face him. "I know an excellent speech therapist."

His eyes blazed fury.

"Me! Me-e-e!" she heard suddenly. Glancing to the right, she saw a female patient shuffling toward her. The woman, in a dingy nightgown, had pinched, pathetic features under straw hair with three-inch dark roots. She was gazing at the elevator in childish rapture. "I'm goin' down too!" she cried. "Gettin' outta here!"

Jill saw the open sores of terminal syphilis about the woman's face and neck; saw Downey intercept the woman, who began to struggle, and then heard Downey yell for the orderlies.

They came. Jill stared. It was the same pair who had carried off Mary Jo Sayers. The smaller, darker one threw Jill a look of pure malice. A nurse arrived, proffering the inevitable syringe.

"Close the d-d-damn door, will you!" Downey yelled, hauling the patient clear of the still-open steel door. Behind her, Jill heard sounds of the elevator approaching. She took one last, incredulous look at the bedlam before her, and then the steel door whumped closed and blocked her view.

She was trembling badly. She turned, and when the car arrived and the metal doors hissed open, she got in.

So fast, was all she could think. So *fast*.

Still shaking, Jill sat on a bench on the eleventh floor. Minutes passed while she concentrated on nothing more than slowing her heart rate and getting her mind to stop running in frantic circles. It was difficult. Her problem lay in absorbing this latest turn of events.

Coincidence? The two most bizarre obstetrical cases in the hospital's recent past, and both women were *gone?* Moran dead. Sayers—presto, now you see her, now you don't.

Concentrate, she thought. Try . . .

She stared into space, seeing nothing, seeing Maria Moran bleeding to death. She shook her head, blinking away the terrible sight. Saw now Mary Jo Sayers begging hysterically for help. Then disappearing.

Head nurse Vera Crowley: "Her husband came for her. A *wonderful* young man."

Mary Jo Sayers, rambling on about her career: "I wanted a child with all my heart, but I'm divorced, you see . . ."

And Sayers had written "Divorced" on the top of her Admissions sheet, which the fools would have read if the chart had ever been sent . . .

Jill stared numbly down at her hands in her lap. What if she was wrong? Had she gone paranoid because of a couple of shocking cases? The sort of thing that experienced doctors took in their stride? She imagined her humiliation if Sayers really was married, or even separated. Estranged spouses often became concerned in times of crisis. Jill rubbed her eyes; conceded to herself that the mentally ill can sometimes appear deceptively lucid; can "flip in and flip out," as doctors often put it to each other.

The older doctors were so casual. That was what she lacked. The cool detachment of a real pro. Emote, and you'll be no good for the next patient. How many times had she heard that at med school?

And then a devastating thought occurred to her.

She jumped to her feet.

"You're an idiot," she said out loud.

She ran to a wall phone and dialed an extension number. While she waited she looked at her watch. It was 10:49. The so-called husband of Mary Jo Sayers had signed her out more than an hour ago.

"Morgue," a voice answered.

Jill identified herself. "Listen," she said. "I want you to look up an infant who succumbed yesterday. Around 2:00 P.M. The name is Christopher Sayers."

The voice told her to wait and then was back in a minute. "Yes, number fifty-eight in our log. He's here."

"Have there been any . . . arrangements made for him?

Have you been contacted by the family, or a funeral service?'' Her voice rose. "Any calls at *all?*''

"No, nothing. Fact is, we were beginning to wonder . . .''

"Yes, it *is* unusual, isn't it?'' Another thought rushed into Jill's mind.

"Maria Moran,'' she said. "Succumbed around nine yesterday morning. Do you still have her?''

"Just a sec.'' There was a clunking noise at the other end, and Jill had time to think before the answer came back. She calculated—Maria Moran had been dead only twenty-six hours; funeral homes often did not pick up the deceased for two or three days.

The voice at the other end returned. "Yes, she's here too. Let's see . . . according to our records, she's scheduled to be picked up at eleven today. Any minute. There's going to be a wake and the funeral director called to say that—''

"I'll be right down.'' Jill slammed down the phone.

As she ran down the corridor, she heard herself paged. "Dr. Raney. Dr. Jill Raney. Extension 204, please.''

Damn, she thought. The clinic. I'm late. Well, they'll just have to wait.

On her way down she sprinted into Pathology, on the tenth floor. The lab was full of interns and residents.

"Specimen jars,'' she breathed to a Path resident. "I need two small ones.''

He gestured with his head. "Supplies over there,'' he said, indicating a long counter with cabinets above and below. He bent over his microscope again.

Jill went to the counter and found the glass containers she needed. They were the shape of baby food jars, only smaller. She took two. Then she found the other thing she needed. Carefully she poured a small amount of isotonic saline solution into each jar. She straightened, pondering her next problem. The two jars had to be transported correctly, maintained at body temperature. To go out wheeling an incubator would attract attention. No. She'd have to find another way.

A minute later she was in a supply closet in the hallway, stuffing the tiny containers into her bra.

And four minutes later she was emerging from the elevator into the basement tunnel. Directly across was a sign that read: MORGUE: FOLLOW RED LINE.

She had been here once before during the two day orientation tour held for the interns, and the place had unnerved her. She hurried, pushing down her fear of the century-old stone passageway. It was painted the color of mustard and was dimly lit. The morgue's red line ran ahead along the middle of the wall, turned sharply where the corridor turned, and snaked its way down a curious grade. Place is like a crypt, Jill thought. Even the air seemed danker and smelled of decay.

Jill stood before the double swinging doors which led into the morgue. Be calm, she told herself.

She pushed open the doors, and instantly was overwhelmed by the smell of formaldehyde. Straight ahead in the gloom were four stainless steel tables, with slanting tops and drains at their lower end. The floor was a dingy cement with stains here, there, that made her feel queasy. Ancient tiles lined the wall, and hooded lights hung over the work areas. Only two lights shone, their beams so narrow that they left the rest of the room in shadow. Jill looked toward the far end and saw the drawers. Tier upon tier of metal-fronted refrigerated drawers.

She started to move in that direction, trying to ignore the gooseflesh on the back of her neck as she walked slowly toward the right, picking her way around the last of the steel tables. This side of the room was cast in deeper shadow, but it had its compensations. It was farthest away from the shrouded form she had seen on the first table, and the array of knives and cutting instruments placed haphazardly on top of the gray sheet.

A liquid, sucking noise made her spin around in terror.

"Oh!" said a male voice. "Did I frighten you? Guess you didn't see me come in."

Jill's breath stopped. Staring wide-eyed across the room she saw an examining lamp flicked on, then the beefy figure of a man in a long rubber apron fiddling with faucets, directing the flow of water that ran down the table toward the drain.

"You an intern?" he said casually, glancing at her short, white jacket. He had picked up a knife and was testing its edge with his thumb.

"Yes," she murmured. "Here for some . . . followups."

"Ah!" he said, throwing back the gray shroud to reveal a body riddled with bullet holes. Jill shuddered. "Well," he continued, "you're on your own, unfortunately." With his knife he gestured toward a desk illuminated by a gooseneck lamp. "Attendant seems to have stepped away."

"I can manage," she said. "Thank you." She hurried over to the desk and found the morgue file—a worn, looseleaf notebook. She easily located the correct drawer numbers. Christopher Sayers: fifty-eight. Maria Moran: twenty-one.

She went to fifty-eight first, the closer of the two. Second tier up, just behind the desk chair. After glancing nervously over her shoulder she pulled out the drawer. Halfway was enough: the porcelain, doll-like remains of Christopher Sayers were so tiny that he could have fit in a shoe box.

She looked at her watch. Seven past eleven. She had to hurry.

She turned her back to the pathology resident, who was busily slicing away. He was, she realized, *humming*. In the semi-darkness, Jill rummaged beneath her blouse, and withdrew the first of the specimen jars. Opening it, she placed it in the cool drawer, next to the child. That wasn't good, she realized: the temperature was too cool in there.

Her fingers were deft. Extracting a small scalpel from her left pocket, she reached in, gently flipped the chilled body on its side and, from under the armpit of the stub that should have been an arm, excised a small segment of skin. Then, hands shaking, she tapped the scalpel's contents into the jar, closed it, got it back inside her bra, and closed the drawer. She looked at her watch. Nine seconds had elapsed.

Self-consciously, she glanced over her shoulder at the busy resident. He was lifting out a gleaming, enlarged liver and plopping it into a scale. Now humming, "The Stars and Stripes Forever."

Jill shook her head.

Turning back, she checked her watch. Nine past eleven. She hurried to drawer twenty-one, remembering what the morgue attendant had told her over the phone; the remains of Maria Moran were to be picked up by the funeral service at eleven. Good thing they're late, she thought.

At that moment they arrived.

She had just located the right drawer, first tier close to the floor, and was kneeling to open it when she heard a peculiar scraping noise. She looked up. Along the far wall there was a ramp leading up into total darkness, which suddenly became a widening bar of sunlight as the door at the top was pulled open. Two men pushing a stretcher were heading down the ramp. Behind them the door swung closed with a heavy, groaning sound, and the ramp was again plunged into darkness.

"Jesus, I hate this place," said one man as he reached the floor.

"Yeah. Me too," said the other. Both were wearing green uniforms.

On her knees, Jill thought: Oh, no.

The first man, pivoting the stretcher around, looked over to the pathology resident. "Hey doc, ya know where we can find a Mrs. Moran? We're from the Greenwillow Funeral Home."

The beefy resident kept his chin tucked in an attitude of concentration, and glanced up with his eyes only. "File's on the desk," he said.

"Thanks," said the man, and began heading in Jill's direction.

The second man lingered a moment, his eyes suddenly wide. "Hey Frankie," he called. "Look at *that*."

The first man stopped and followed his companion's gaze.

Open-mouthed, they watched the resident pick up a rotary saw and prepare to cut into the chest cavity.

"Jesus Christ, you gonna *use* that?"

Looking annoyed, the resident flicked on the high, screeching machine. The men, like fascinated children, came closer to watch. Jill thought: Now!

Still on her knees, Jill pulled open the drawer and for a horrible instant gazed at Maria Moran's lifeless features. Then, quickly, she placed the open specimen jar on the corpse's chest and readied her scapel. Raising the stiff left hand, she cut a sliver of skin from under the small finger, rushed the specimen into the jar, clapped the top back on, and shoved closed the drawer.

Straightening, Jill looked at her watch. Ten seconds—not bad.

The resident turned off the saw.

"Gawd," she heard one of the funeral men say. "Hey, I got a Black and Decker can cut through a drainpipe!"

"That's nice," the resident said.

Jill turned her back to transfer the jar from her sweating palm to the inside of her bra.

She turned, marveling at the timing, because just then the two men began pushing their stretcher toward her. She smoothed her hair, walking past them. "Moran's in twenty-one," she told them casually as she headed for the door.

"Leaving so soon?" asked the resident. He looked up from the pile of bullets he was counting.

She stopped by the door. Her heart was still racing, but she managed a smile. "Yes. Thanks for . . . the company."

"Thank *you*," he said. He smiled back. "Say, you know anybody going up to microscopic pathology? I've got some slides to send up."

Yeah, me, she thought. She said, "Better ring for an orderly. They're fast."

"But not as pretty," he said ruefully. "Oh, well." He reached above his suspended microphone and pressed a button. "Good luck with your followups," he said.

"Thanks," she said. "I'll need it." She turned and hurried out.

18

WHEN JILL OPENED the door marked Pathology, she had the eerie feeling that she was bringing Maria Moran and the Sayers infant back to life.

The room was nearly empty. Only two older-looking residents were there, working separately. One, Peter Gregson, Jill knew vaguely. She decided to try her luck and ask for his help.

"Hello, Peter."

He looked up from the slides he was staining, and grinned.

"Well! Well!" he said. "What brings you here, Jill?"

She came closer, clutching the two specimen jars she had already taken from her blouse.

"Peter," she said, "would you have time to teach me how to grow out a tissue culture?"

He shrugged as if she had asked for nothing. "Have a seat," he said, indicating the stool next to him. "It's easy."

She sat, handed him the two labeled jars, and nodded as he began to explain. She understood the basic concept—that for as long as two days after death, a person's skin cells continue to be viable. She knew this from medical school. A man could die clean-shaven, then later be examined and found to have sprouted several days' growth of beard. This, she knew, was because hair, nails, and beards were all skin organs; and skin cells, unlike brain cells, required little oxygen.

Gregson was saying, "You'll have to grind out a homolysate, you know."

"A what?"

"A homolysate. We've got to make some mush. Here's how."

He stood up and reached for what looked like a miniature food blender, complete with beaters and a 30 cc stainless steel flask. He eyed it affectionately. "We call it a milkshake maker for elves."

"That's cute," she said. And she thought: *please* hurry.

"Well." With a flourish he sat again, pushed a jungle of glassware out of the way, and positioned the homolyser. Removing the lid, he dumped in the contents of the first jar, flicked a switch and watched the beaters churn the specimen until it was frothy.

"It has to be pulverized like this," he said. "It's the only way to free the cells from their intercellular connections."

Jill glanced at her watch and her stomach knotted—she was way behind schedule.

Above the whir of the machine she asked: "How long will it take to grow them out?"

Gregson turned it off. "Actually," he said, "you'll get your first cellular divisions in a few hours." Using a pipette he placed some of the soupy material on a slide which he put under his microscope. "But to be safe," he added, peering in, "you'd better give it a couple of days."

Damn! Jill thought. How could she possibly wait that long?

Using a micropipette, Gregson explained how he was teasing out some of the cells into discrete particles. "Nice crop," he murmured. "Very nice."

Jill watched as he transplanted the separated cells from the slide onto a Petri dish, its amber culture medium loaded with nutrients and antibiotics, the latter to suppress bacterial growth. The Petri dish disappeared into a nearby incubator, and then Gregson slammed the door.

"Want to do the next one?" he asked.

Thomas Gacey paced the first-floor foyer of the Gyn Clinic. "Goddammit!" he bellowed. "Where's Raney?"

His outburst was met with startled looks. A nurse scuttled away, and one of the interns nearly dropped the tray of instruments he was carrying. Patients—rows of them sitting on dingy wooden pews in the adjoining waiting room—turned their anxious gazes in his direction.

Tricia Donovan poked her head out one of the examining rooms. "Jill's coming," she said carefully, not wanting to further enrage the chief resident.

Gacey glared as he approached her. "Jill's coming," he echoed sarcastically. "What do you women think this is, a goddamn country club?" He held up a green schedule sheet and pointed back toward the waiting room.

"We've got patients lined up to the *door* out there because one of the interns is probably shaving her legs. She's an hour late, for Chrissakes! Now just where in the hell . . ."

"I *said,* she's coming." Tricia stood in the doorway staring him down. Unaware of Jill's run-in with Gacey that morning, Tricia groped for a safe answer.

"As a matter of fact, I believe Jill's involved in a followup."

Gacey's eyes narrowed. "Followup? What followup?"

He stepped through the door. Tricia had to back up into the examining room, where a patient, naked except for a flimsy paper gown, looked very startled. Gacey ignored her. "Which followup?" he demanded, his voice low.

Tricia realized her mistake and swallowed. "Why . . . Dolan," she said. "Dolan lost a lot of blood, and this morning her hematocrit—"

She never got the chance to finish.

Gacey turned, walked swiftly back down the corridor, and into the office behind the nurses' station. He closed the door carefully, picked up the phone and began to dial.

The idea of doing "cell autopsies" had first occurred to Jill during her phone conversation with the morgue attendant.

She still found it mind-boggling: that specimens from cadavers in the morgue could be grown out, multiplied and studied—as easily as if they had come from living patients. The cells, Jill thought, might have something to say about what had gone wrong with each pregnancy. And more compelling—although Jill told herself this was far-fetched—the cells might reveal if these two vastly dissimilar cases were somehow related.

She was frowning as she left Pathology and walked toward the tenth floor elevators. The more she thought about the last twenty-four hours, the more her rational self lost ground. Gaining hold instead was a feeling that the cases *were* somehow connected, that someone wanted Mary Jo Sayers out of the way, that her infant's body held secrets, that something was very wrong at Madison Hospital.

A group of medical students were waiting in the elevator foyer, but Jill barely noticed them. The Sayers baby, she was thinking, would be easier; his problem had probably been genetic, and the answer would be easy to find.

But what about Moran?

The elevator arrived, and Jill followed the med students in. Moran's family had forbidden an autopsy or removal of the unborn fetus for examination. Ironic, Jill thought, that the nature of the woman's death made all that unnecessary. She had died of abruptio placentae. This meant that, after the initial catastrophic rupture, amniotic fluid *containing fetal cells* had surged through the maternal circulation via the large uterine vessels, then had "seeded out" everywhere throughout the mother's body. Moran's skin cells had then stayed alive, and plenty of those cells, Jill suspected, would carry a dose of fetal hemoglobin "marker."

So there it was. The clue—if there was one—would be found in two tiny skin tabs.

On the first floor she got off and turned left, heading down the gray corridor. She passed crowds of indigents, milling about or waiting in passive lines. Her eyes were preoccupied; she was reviewing the facts in her mind again.

Yesterday, a run of obstetrical disasters.

No connection, said the experts.

Last night, a link discovered between Sayers and Moran.

They had both *been* here, in the Gyn clinic. Both at ovulation time.

Today, Sayers mysteriously yanked off the OB floor, signed out by a man probably not her husband, and the infant apparently forgotten. . . .

What else? Jill stopped in the busy corridor, heedless of the stream of people jostling her. She looked up at the ceiling, as if she could see through it all the way to Obstetrics. She wondered what else had gone wrong there: before her internship had begun; last month; last year. Mishaps perhaps not so rare and dramatic as those of Sayers and Moran; but still, trouble . . . some of it so subtle as to be missed by anyone not actually looking for it. . . .

She shook her head. Her mind returned to the two little jars in the incubator on the tenth floor. Somehow, she knew, her answers would come from there.

She glanced at her watch, catching her breath in dismay. Eleven twenty-five, and Gacey was clinic head for today. Rotten luck. Steeling herself, she pushed open the heavy, wooden doors, and entered the tumult of the area beyond.

"Hold it."

He caught her by the wrist as she was rushing between her twentieth and twenty-first patient. It was 1:09, and by skipping lunch she had whipped through twenty routine prenatal exams; no frills, no conversation, just do it right and catch up quick.

Except that here was David Levine suddenly blocking the way.

"Let go!" she complained. "What are you doing?"

"Have to talk to you," he said.

"But I've got five more patients—"

"Woody'll do them." David turned. "Won't you, Woody?"

Jill looked and saw Woody Greenberg bringing up the rear, carrying a pile of charts.

"Why sure," said Woody jovially. Without hesitating

he turned into the next examination room, chirped a greeting to the patient, and closed the door.

Jill turned angrily back to Levine. "What's going on, David?"

He pulled her into a free examining room, closed the door, and sat her down.

"Funny," he said, leaning over her. "I was about to ask you the same question. Listen. Do you have any *idea* of how much hot water you're in? Stryker's office has been besieged by angry calls. You shook up the whole Psychiatry floor. You didn't answer your page. You were late *here*. Tom Gacey went up to Stryker's office personally to complain about you. My God, Jill, whatever could have *possessed* you to go off the rails like that?"

She regarded him stonily. "Go off the rails?"

"You heard me. Now I want to hear your side of what happened. You want to start at the beginning?"

She studied his face. He was not being condescending; he seemed actually to want to hear what she had to say. She relaxed somewhat and drew a breath.

She recounted what had happened since last night: the uneasy feeling that persisted after yesterday's OB casualties; the charts in Emergency where she found a link between the Sayers and Moran tragedies . . .

"This was after I saw you?" he asked.

"Yes." Jill began to speak more rapidly. "Bizarre, isn't it, David? Both women were here for exams just at the time of their last prepregnancy ovulation. Neither exam report was signed, which is unusual . . ."

"Not as unusual as you think. People get busy, absent-minded—"

"But some *coincidence*, wouldn't you say?"

Levine looked at her and frowned. "Yeah, some coincidence. But I've seen stranger things in this place. You learn not to react so dramatically every time the impossible happens."

"And what about the Sayers kidnapping?" she challenged.

"The *what*?" He looked at her as if he had not heard

correctly. "Her husband comes for her and that makes it a kidnapping?"

"He *wasn't* her husband."

David waved a hand. "I saw the chart. Sayers told the admissions clerk she was divorced. Well . . . so maybe the guy was her divorced husband. Or a lover. Jill, I called Psychiatry, and the nurse said he looked pretty damned concerned, so apparently he was *someone* who cares . . ."

"They left the baby," Jill said tonelessly.

Levine stared at her for a moment. "We don't know that they've left the baby," he said uncertainly. "After all, it's only been since yesterday. Presumably he needs time to . . . get her settled . . . and then . . ." David shrugged. "Well, I'm sure he's at least called the morgue."

"No." Jill shook her head. "No calls. Find out for yourself."

Levine continued to look at her, an expression of confusion crossing his face. Then he looked away.

"Jill, this whole conversation is absurd. You're over-reacting because these are your first . . . unusual trage-dies." His voice became low. "God knows, most of us never get used to the things we see. But we don't turn the place into total chaos, either."

Jill stiffly rose. "And you don't have the slightest feel-ing that anything peculiar is going on in this hospital?"

"Of *course* not." He gave her an exasperated look. "Notions like that are the exclusive domain of new interns."

Jill, looking tense and angry, began to head for the door. As she marched past him, he reached out and pulled her back. "Listen," he said, his face coloring. "I want you to play it very cool from now on. Don't buck the hierarchy! Not yet. *Later* you can be Joan of Arc. When you're higher up the totem pole!"

She smiled in spite of herself. Why, she thought, he's funny when he's upset. "You're mixing metaphors," she said in a sweet voice.

Levine stepped back to look at her. He was surprised at the delight he felt in seeing her smile. "Hey," he said softly. "That's more like it." For an instant he glanced down at the gentle rise and fall of her bosom under the white jacket.

"Ahem," he coughed. "Do we still have a date for tonight?"

Jill hesitated, then shrugged and nodded. "Sure. Provided I'm not thrown out by then."

"You won't be. You haven't received any blistering phone calls?"

She shook her head. "But I'm still waiting for the ax to fall."

"Maybe it won't. They complained to me." He grinned. "If anyone asks, say I flogged you. Is seven okay? I'll stop by your on-call room."

He opened the door and they went out to the corridor.

"David, I appreciate your trying to help," she said.

He shrugged. "I'm not sure if I have, yet."

She smiled and walked away, leaving Levine staring after her, looking worried again.

19

SHE WAS NOT surprised to receive the summons. At 5:20 she had been returning from the X ray department when Stryker's secretary paged her. Hanging up, Jill realized she had been rehearsing all afternoon what she was going to say. She would be cool and professional; she would present her point of view about the Sayers case and the actions she had taken. She continued to feel confident until the moment she entered the conference room—and saw the expressions on the four men who awaited her.

"Sit down," said William Stryker, indicating the chair at the far end of the table.

Jill tensed. She hesitated, then dropped into the chair and felt even more vulnerable. Her end of the long table was all empty seats; the four grim faces watching her—Stryker, Simpson, Arnett and Rosenberg—seemed to be staring across a gulf.

God give me strength, she thought.

Stryker leaned forward, his expression solemn. "Dr. Raney, I'm going to make this brief and to the point. The list of your infractions today is very serious. You have jeopardized the smooth functioning of the obstetrical department, and you have disrupted other parts of the hospital as well." His eyes seemed to bore into her. "I have, frankly, called this meeting to discuss the feasibility of retaining your tenure. Do you have anything to say?"

Jill felt stubborn anger well up. Carefully she said, "I was acting in the best interest of the patient."

Dr. Willard Simpson, whose field was human genetics, snorted. "And *not* of the hospital!"

Jill looked hard at him. She squared her shoulders and struggled to keep her voice steady. "You all know the circumstances, I presume. In my judgment, Mrs. Sayers was perfectly sane and lucid. There was no reason for the medications ordered for her, and the mere fact that the transfer order was not signed—"

"The entire matter is already under investigation," Stryker snapped. "And by the correct authorities, which you certainly are not." He pointed his finger at her. "You had no right whatsoever to leave your floor and act as you did!"

Jill eyed him levelly. "An innocent person was cruelly manhandled, and you talk about rights?"

Stryker's spectacles reflected the glaring light from outside. "You are being very foolish, Dr. Raney. You have been given the opportunity to work under the most eminent teachers of human fertility in the country. You are ruining your career before it has even begun, and worse, you are ruining the chances of others. Are you aware of that?"

Jill felt herself go cold. Ruining the chances of others? What was he talking about?

Stryker said sharply, "You have by now spoken with Dr. Levine?"

Swallowing, she nodded.

"Well then, I'm sure Levine has told you that he is being held responsible for today's troubles. This is of course standard procedure. A senior resident loses control of his floor, and the blame is on his head." Stryker paused. "Now, it so happens that Levine for some time has been first choice for Tom Gacey's position next year. Levine knows this. Unfortunately"—his voice roughened— "sabotage like today's could severely undermine his chances."

"Sabotage!" Jill was dumbstruck. The bastard, she thought. The absolute conniving, manipulating bastard. She was flooded with guilt. No, she thought, David said nothing about his own career being in danger . . .

Her eyes went to the three other doctors. Arnett was somber. Simpson and Rosenberg, an epidemiologist, looked at her with distaste.

"I . . . I had no idea my . . . concerns would involve others in any way." Her voice shook. She hated that they could see her losing control.

"Well now, hang on there a second." Clifford Arnett broke the silence.

Jill looked up.

Arnett glanced over at Stryker, who nodded imperceptibly. He turned back to Jill.

"Dr. Raney," he said. "Surely you realize where our intense concern is coming from. For months our work has been bogged down by so-called ethical controversy. We cure birth defects—in utero, yet!—and the morons call it tampering with nature. The in vitro program alone attracts picket signs by the busload." He shook his head.

"You couldn't have picked a worse time to be stirring up trouble," Simpson said.

"To put it mildly," Rosenberg said. "Now, something like the Sayers case is an isolated tragedy of unknown causes. But the fact that it occurred in this hospital . . . well, people seize on this sort of thing. Make all sorts of ugly allegations.''

''And we don't need you,'' snorted Simpson, ''running around calling *attention* to the problem. More qualified— and, if I may say—more loyal people than you are already studying the Sayers case.''

''Quietly,'' said Rosenberg.

Jill stared at them. ''I understand,'' she said. ''The reputation of the hospital is at stake.''

''Exactly,'' said Simpson.

She watched them, studying their smug faces, feeling her guilt turn into boiling resentment. ''And that is why the whereabouts of Mary Jo Sayers is classified information?'' she asked. She stopped struggling to keep calm. ''Or, if it's true that the Sayers case is already under investigation, why don't you just *call* her place of employment—the Madison Museum, which you know, of course—it was on her admissions sheet. *Ask* them if she was really married! And if she wasn't, dear God! You can add a *kidnapping* to your stillbirths, fetal abnormalities, a maternal death—''

Stryker banged his fist on the table. ''That's it!'' he shouted. ''She's out. This is intolerable.''

The others reacted similarly until Arnett stood and held his hands up, palms outward, in a gesture of conciliation. ''I have an alternate idea, if I may.'' No one stopped him, and his expression, unlike the others, was one of sadness, like a teacher who had expected better things from a student.

''I suggest we start over on a new footing,'' he said. ''Dr Raney, I hope, will rethink her attitudes and promise to behave hereafter as an intern should. After all''—he glanced back at Stryker with a subtle look—''a dismissed intern becomes an adversary, and what we need at this time is support, isn't that right?''

Stryker continued to glower at Jill. He said nothing.

''I might add,'' Arnett said with emphasis, ''that Dr. Raney is a person of extraordinary research potential.''

Jill stole a glance at Stryker. Oddly quiet, he seemed to be pondering something, peering through his spectacles as though from a place far away.

"You will be watched very carefully," Stryker said at last in a deadly calm voice. "Every move you make will be scrutinized, and will reflect directly on your superiors."

Jill held her breath. Stryker locked his gaze on hers and continued.

"I have another stipulation to retaining you as an intern," he said. "Sometime tomorrow, I want you to visit the Infant School."

Jill stared. "The Infant School?"

"You are familiar with it?"

"Yes. It's on the third floor of Chapin. We sometimes see the mothers bringing their babies—"

"The infants you will see there," interrupted Stryker, his voice cold, "are the children of habitual aborters; of couples pronounced incurably infertile. They are children who would have had a host of birth defects, were it not for the prenatal diagnosis and treatment received at this hospital."

"Yes, I realize, but—"

"When you see those children, I want you to remember that they represent medical advances *unthinkable* even five years ago. Perhaps *then* you will exhibit some of the respect which is due this institution!"

His words stung. "I'll go," she said heavily.

She stood. Not another word was said as she gathered her things together and turned to go.

At the door she wrestled briefly between impulse and restraint, and then turned back. The words came tumbling out by themselves.

"If that man *wasn't* Sayers' husband, will you be calling the police?"

The faces of all four men changed. As if by signal, something new and guarded crept into their expressions. No one answered Jill's question. She stood watching them for a moment, then opened the door and went out.

_20_

RUINING THE CHANCES of others, the man said . . .

On the obstetrical floor, Jill reached a wall phone, removed the receiver and looked bleakly at her watch.

Six-fourteen. Time enough to cut my throat.

The operator answered. With an ache, Jill slowly recited her message: "Please tell Dr. David Levine that Dr. Raney will be unable to keep tonight's appointment." She hesitated. "Tell him I'm sorry." She signed out for the night and hung up.

The elevator arrived, and a group of husbands came rushing out carrying flowers. Jill entered, staring dejectedly down until the car reached the main floor.

She looked straight ahead as she made her way through the throng. Overhead, she heard the page system come alive to page Dr. David Levine. That was her call, she realized, and her heart turned over.

By the entrance she tore off her white jacket, balled it and tossed it onto a stand for cigarette butts.

She pushed through the heavy glass door and went out. "Sabotage," she hissed to herself, and kicked savagely at a beer can as she walked down the driveway. She felt wretched and depressed. She reached First Avenue and began to cross.

She had done right to cancel with David, she thought. She had already caused him enough trouble. If word got around that he was dating her, things would get even worse for him. Jill tugged uncomfortably at the collar of her blouse. The evening was sultry.

A truck honked and brakes squealed. "For God's sake, lady," a man leaned out and yelled.

She reached the other side and headed west on Twenty-first Street. At the steps of her brownstone she paused, thinking: How shabby and neglected it looks. Sighing, she mounted the steps, pushed open the heavy door that never locked, and went in. The vestibule smelled of sour cooking odors. A weak light shone through the translucent glass in the door behind her, illuminating a baby carriage pushed up against a wall.

Jill closed her eyes and thought, if I see another baby thing today I'll have a psychotic break.

She opened her eyes and walked slowly up the stairs. The first landing was dimly lit. She rounded the corner and trudged up the second flight.

Lost in her thoughts, she reached the next landing. She did not hear the door open below her; did not hear the footsteps coming up the first flight, the second, until a floorboard creaking loudly behind her caused her to wheel in terror.

In a blur she saw a darkened figure in blue shirt and blue jeans coming toward her; suffered a moment of blinding panic before she recognized the face and felt her body go limp.

"David!" she cried. "Oh, David!"

Unsmiling, Levine took her in his arms as she crumpled, sobbing, to his chest. "It's all right," he whispered as he patted her back. "It's going to be okay." He held her, feeling the hot tears soaking through his shirt, and then he looked up, studying the two facing doors on the landing above. "Let's get inside," he said.

David pushed the door closed and reached up to flip the slide bolt. Then he turned. For a long moment they stared at each other. "Jill," he said softly. The apartment seemed bathed in bronze. From a window overlooking the street, the setting sun angled a beam of light across the fading carpet, an old couch. Through a narrow door, he could see the bed.

She took a step toward him. Her arms went around his neck as he pulled her to him, folding her tight into his arms. She gasped as he kissed her. Desire hit them both like a tidal wave.

Later, she would not remember if he had carried her to the bed, or if they walked. That part was a blur. The magic that she did recall was the sudden heaviness of him, of his strong, lean arm sliding under her naked waist like a ring of fire, sending a shudder of pleasure through her. She felt her mind reeling, felt her heart would burst. Again and again she called out his name as the ecstasy mounted, as he kissed her and put his stubbly cheek into the softness of her shoulder, in his driving passion clinging to her as if he would never let her go.

When it was dark, and they lay there, spent and whispering, David said: "Do you remember what you told me?"

She was stroking his chest. "Told you?" she said. "When?"

"The second time."

"Oh." She looked into his solemn, dark blue eyes. "I'm embarrassed," she said.

He shifted on an elbow and looked down at her. "Please? I don't want to think I'm imagining things."

He put his hand over hers. His hand, she saw, was lean and muscular, with red knuckles, like an athlete's. There were also a couple of long scars near his thumb and forefinger; for no reason Jill thought of a fourteen-year-old, experimenting with his jackknife. She smiled softly.

"I told you I love you," she murmered, "but that's crazy isn't it? It's too fast."

He smiled. "Not as fast as I fell for you."

Her eyes searched his. "Fell for me? You? When?"

"Yesterday morning. In the supply closet. When you were screaming at me."

Now it was her turn to twist around and look at him. "Oh, David. I was so awful to you yesterday. I'm so sorry—"

His smile was sleepy. "Forget it," he said, pulling her down, kissing her forehead. "Yesterday was ages ago."

And thinking about it, thirty minutes later as she lay under his arm, listening to his heavy, exhausted breathing, she realized that he was right. Yesterday did seem like ages ago.

There were hundreds of them and they walked across a wide and barren landscape, carrying their babies. Maria Moran was near the head of the line, her eyes unfocused, and she did not hear when Jill cried out to her. Desperately Jill tried to force her way through the underbrush. "Maria don't go!" she shouted, but the women continued to trudge toward a low gray building. Feverishly Jill disentangled her clothes from some briars and began to run. Toward the women, toward the squat building. Over the entrance were the words INFANT SCHOOL. Workers in overalls stood before the entrance and smiled reassuringly as they took the babies, one by one, from their mothers. "Follow the red arrow," said the head worker, gesturing with more smiles toward a path that led to a river. The noise of the rushing water was loud. Gasping, Jill recognized the red arrow, ran faster and caught up to Maria Moran. The earth before the river split open and Moran slid down into it. Jill screamed "No!" but the roaring water drowned out her voice and she woke up, lying perspiring and shivering, in her bed in her room.

She lay on her back, still hearing water. She realized it had been a dream. Blinking, she pulled the covers over her, and lay and thought. The sound of water turned off. David. In the shower. She ached from lovemaking and squirmed to get more comfortable. She stared up at the window, feeling dread begin to creep in. Stryker. Moran. Sayers. Thirteenth day of internship. Stryker again.

"Rise and shine, babe." David stood over her now, dressed and looking unforgivably morning fresh.

Jill groaned and threw the pillow over her face.

David sat on the bed and spoke to the pillow. "Anything broken?"

He heard a muffled, miserable voice. "You will be watched very carefully," Jill mimicked. "Dammit, I *hate* that place!"

Gently he pulled away the pillow and pulled her up and looked at her, amazed that even in the harsh light of morning she was beautiful. The sheet she clung to only half-covered her nakedness. Her skin was the color of cream; her honey-colored hair fell past her shoulders.

He held her in his arms. "It's happened to others," he said softly. "They just *love* to intimidate interns. Give it time and it will pass."

"Sure," she whispered fiercely. "It'll pass. If I'm a good little intern and walk the straight and narrow and don't go rushing to help patients with mysterious ailments and even more mysterious treatment . . . Oh, God . . . do you *realize* if it weren't for Arnett I'd be on probation, maybe even thrown out by now?"

"Well," he said, stroking her hair. "Unfortunately, the assumption is always that interns are undertrained and overreact. It's bad enough if you play it straight. The fatigue and the stress are killers."

She said nothing, knowing what was coming.

"Jill, you really had me worried yesterday. Please . . . watch yourself today. I mean it. If *anything* doesn't seem right, talk it over with me before you . . ."

"I know. Go running around half-cocked."

He hesitated. "Yes."

She nodded, but her mind was boiling with conflict. If only he would stay here, she thought. If only I didn't have to face the day. The lean power of his body was so reassuring, and she realized how much she preferred him like this: in blue jeans and an ordinary blue shirt, his dark hair falling over his brow. It was unbearable to think of him walking into the hospital in a few minutes, changing into his whites, becoming crisp and impersonal again. She put her arms around his waist. She wanted this moment to last forever.

"I have to go," he said quietly.

She looked at him plaintively. "Six-thirty in the morning! You can't stay a second longer?"

He stood up. "Nope. Got to get a head start today. The morning's going to be practically nonstop surgery."

Clutching her sheet, she hopped off the bed and followed him out of the room. "But David—"

At the door he turned and drew her to him. "And *you* be on your best today. Stryker will probably have Gacey spying on you every minute!"

Jill began to twist a corner of the sheet. "David," she said hesitantly, "that Sayers case still rankles. If only I could find out more about that poor girl, maybe then I could get rid of this bad feeling I have. About the hospital. Everything."

She caught his look, but plunged on. "Listen. Even if it *does* turn out to be a kidnapping, the hospital isn't going to do a damn thing about it! They'll just hand it over to the police, where it will disappear among all the *other* kidnapping and missing persons cases. God, there must be thousands—"

"Jill—"

"No, wait. Sayers worked at the museum just up the block. I could go there on my free time, couldn't I? Ask a few questions? What's wrong with that?"

David looked dubious. "Well . . ." His hand was on the doorknob.

"On my *free time!* I have some late this afternoon, and . . . I promise to be super sharp in the hospital . . ."

He put his head to one side, considering. "I suppose what you do with your free time is your business," he said. "And if it will get this thing off your mind . . ."

"And get me back on the track. I'll be a normal intern again!"

Levine looked at her uneasily. "Why do I have the feeling I shouldn't let you out of my sight?"

She smiled. "Please don't."

He bent and kissed her. "I don't plan to," he said.

Jill Raney looked at herself in the mirror and thought: Now I change from wanton back into doctor.

Her hair, she decided, looked not so much messy as

. . . well, loved in. She leaned closer to the glass and rubbed her cheeks. They were sore: red in places from being sandpapered by David's beard. I'll have to speak to him about that, she thought, and caught herself smiling. The image in the mirror smiled back.

Suddenly, the smile vanished. She remembered that Stryker would go through the roof if he knew David was seeing her. They had better be careful, she thought, but maybe it's just as well. It will keep a serious look on my face. They give brownie points over there for grim expressions.

She showered and dressed in a white skirt and pink blouse. She brushed her long hair back and clasped it with a tortoise-shell barrette, put on sensible shoes and then turned to look at herself in the mirror.

There, she thought. Spic and span and sexless. Ready for another day at Madison.

She picked up her keys and from the bedside table the black notebook that went with her everywhere. Lord, she thought, if I forget that, I'm dead. The book was her brain, her organizer, no matter how trivial the notations. She slipped it into her skirt pocket, then grabbed her things and left the apartment.

In the street Jill was buoyant with the memory of the night. She passed the shabby brownstones, the same garbage and dog feces and litter. None of it depressed her, as it had the evening before.

Except for the dark, insistent feeling that she had to find out more about Mary Jo Sayers. Maybe Maria Moran, too. And David himself had conceded that what she did in her free time was her own business. Nobody in the hospital could argue with that.

She checked her watch: 7:20; good timing.

Waiting to cross at First Avenue and Twenty-first Street, she stepped off the curb before the light changed to see if she could see the museum. It was only four blocks north and she squinted—but no museum. The building once considered quite grand a hundred years ago was now obscured by the towers of the hospital.

Figures, Jill thought. Seeing a car bearing down on her she stepped back onto the curb and decided to think about the museum later. Between then and now was another grinding day at the hospital. The thought made her go pale.

21

"READY TO POP," somebody said, and Jill in her surgical mask glanced up from the screen of the fetal monitor.

They had barely made it to the delivery room. The patient had been brought to the hospital only twenty-eight minutes before. In the labor room Jill had to rush the history and physical, assess the labor and check the degree of cervical dilatation.

At 10:22, Tricia Donovan, a nurse and Jill had wheeled the bed from the labor room into delivery. There a second nurse helped Woody Greenberg, already scrubbed, into his surgical gown, while the other three, babbling orders to each other, hoisted the moaning woman onto the table.

Now, at 10:41, dilatation was a full ten centimeters. In an opening a bit larger than a silver dollar, they could see the miracle of wrinkled scalp and wet, flattened hair.

Woody was excited. "Okay, a couple more good pushes and you'll have a baby!"

Tricia echoed Woody. "Hey, looks like a little blondie!"

The response of the mother was a horrendous cry, followed by sharp panting and then another cry.

One minute later Woody with a hoot delivered an eight pound, one ounce baby girl and placed the howling newcomer across its mother's belly.

Jill beamed like everyone else. A normal birth was always a joy to behold. And—secondarily of course—the labor and delivery had come off with unusual speed.

Getting called in to help had gotten Jill excused from morning clinic duty.

She now had an unexpected chunk of free time.

It was not, she decided as she left the delivery area, enough time to leave the hospital for any errand. It wasn't even enough time to change out of her scrub suit. But there were other things on the premises that had to be done. Jill stopped in the hallway to consult her black memo book, and nodded to herself. She had nearly forgotten Stryker's demand. Odd request, but one had to humor him.

Jill calculated exactly how much time she had. Then she turned and headed for the elevators.

She got off on the third floor and turned to the right. She passed the radiation therapy suite, on her left, and the radioisotope, hematology and chemistry labs, all on the right. Next, after the chem lab, came a long stretch of blank wall, followed by a rectangular glass window and the muffled sound of baby noises. When she saw Kermit the frog peeping out at her from the last door on the right, she knew she was in the right place. Below Kermit were the words: "Infant School of Madison Hospital Medical Center, Division of Perinatology Department."

Infant School indeed, Jill thought, frowning. Stryker thinks sending me down to look at a bunch of well babies is going to have me cooing his praises again.

Turning the doorknob, she stepped uncertainly inside.

"Well, Hello there!"

Above the baby babble and the tinny sound of nursery school records, a shrill voice rose to greet her.

Turning, she saw a middle-aged woman moving rapidly toward her: *too* rapidly, Jill thought, as though the woman were in the habit of watching the door.

"I'm Corrine Dewitt." The woman's blondish, angular face smiled broadly as she extended a hand. "Doctor

Stryker called to say you might be stopping by.'' She smiled again, her teeth large and glinting. ''He described you *well!* So you're the young doctor who is so interested in our superkids. Well, here they are!'' she said leading Jill deeper into the room.

The walls were painted with bright reds, yellow and blues. The red carpeting was lush, strewn with every conceivable toy. Sweet-voiced attendants hunched individually over each baby and talked, smiled a lot, punched buttons on toys and gesticulated. There seemed to be about fifteen babies, although it was hard to tell: they were all over the place. Crawling, squirming, climbing, sitting—so what was the big deal, Jill wondered, looking around. They were acting like babies were supposed to act.

And then she took another look.

Near her feet was a golden-haired eight- or nine-month-old, lying on his back and operating a pulley. A ''teacher,'' dressed in a bright purple sweater, kneeled over him and smiled extravagantly as her trilling voice called out: ''Pull down the red donut, no sweetheart, *not* the yellow donut, the red donut, *that's* right. Now make the blue ball go *up* at the other end, oh *yes,* and *hit* that funny little clown in the orange hat. Ye-e-s, just like that! Oooh, isn't that funny?''

Jill stared.

Each time the clown took his comic little dive, the infant would chortle with delight and rebegin the process.

''Stryker's children,'' Corrine Dewitt said proudly. ''Every single one of them.'' She pointed to several. *''That* baby would have been born with hydrocephaly, were it not for the fetal surgery performed by Dr. Stryker. And *that* baby would have had heart problems, and *that* baby's father's sperm count was too low, so artificial insemination was used . . .''

Jill's attention was captured by another sound.

''Cow . . . cow . . . cow . . .'' An exquisite eleven-month-old girl with Oriental features was listening to a mechanical voice repeat the word ''cow'' while an image of a grinning Guernsey flashed before her on a foot-square screen. With her pink barrette secured in her scanty hair, the tot's face was the picture of concentration as she studied the cow.

Jill knelt and watched her. Then she looked up to Corrine Dewitt. "Does this thing get any other channels?" she asked.

"Indeed it does!" Dewitt exclaimed. "There are at least thirty other animals and the child is *supposed* to learn them all!" She bent at the waist and in a stern tone usually delivered to twelve-year-olds said, "I do believe you've seen enough of your cow, Melissa. How about looking at that nice Mr. Horse for a while?"

With that Corrine Dewitt reached down to a row of brightly colored buttons, pressed the yellow one marked "forward," and advanced the picture to the image of a horse.

"Naw! Naw! Naw!" Melissa protested. Angrily, she reached out and punched a blue button, marked "reverse."

As the image of her cow reappeared on the screen, Melissa popped her thumb into her mouth and happily resumed watching.

Dewitt straightened, lips pursed. "I'm afraid they spoil her terribly at home. Her parents had been pronounced incurably infertile by other doctors. So they came to Dr. Stryker's fertilization clinic and—presto!"

"In vitro fertilization?" asked Jill.

"Yes." Dewitt gazed fondly at the child. "Just *think*," she said. "Melissa began in a dish."

Jill looked in amazement around the room. She could not exactly recall the month-by-month schedule of average infant development, but she had a rough idea; and in any case it was clear that these were hardly average infants.

She turned back toward the older woman, her eyes still on the babies. "I think I'm beginning to understand," she said. "These infants all started out as high-risk pregnancies. And because they turned out okay, their grateful parents bring them here."

"Exactly."

Jill looked bewildered. "But why? I mean, they're alive

and *well*. They're normal. Why do they have to be geniuses?''

Corrine Dewitt waved a hand. "*We* might call them geniuses," she said. "But the generation they're going to grow up in will not. Their world will be one of supercomplex technology. The higher their intelligence, the better they'll be able to cope with that world. And intelligence *can* be elevated—that is Dr. Stryker's firm belief. It all depends on how early you begin your, er . . ."

"Programming?" Jill said.

"Teaching," Corrine Dewitt corrected. "Just teaching. Why, do you know there's a study now in progress wherein babies are taught *in utero?* You play records, you see, loud enough so they can hear—"

Jill had seen enough and it was getting late.

"Thank you very much, Miss Dewitt," she said. "This really has been . . . fascinating. I must go now."

They were about to head for the door when Jill felt something tugging at the pants of her scrub suit. She looked down. A six-month-old with coffee-colored skin grinned toothlessly up at her. He was in a sitting position. Jill gaped in astonishment as he held out a red block to her. She bent and took it. "Thank you," she said.

"Yeeow!" he said.

She tried to remember. Most babies that age could sit up only a few seconds without support; would not begin to hand you things until—what age was it? Forty-eight weeks?

"That's Henry," said Corrine Dewitt. "His mother had a five year history of miscarriages before she came to Dr. Stryker."

Jill watched as Henry tried to *stack* the blocks. "His parents must think Stryker's pretty special," she murmured.

"Special!" echoed Dewitt. "Like the rest of us, they think he's a god! You realize, of course, that these children actually *exist* because of Dr. Stryker. Mind-boggling, wouldn't you say? And his theories about the right kind of early sensory stimulation could increase their intelligence"
—she gestured loftily—"who *knows* how much?"

"Time will tell," said Jill faintly. "Well, thanks again."

"Goodbye." Jill shook Dewitt's hand. It felt like warm crepe paper.

She turned and walked away. At the door she stopped and looked back. Dewitt still stood over Henry, watching her.

Jill gave a terse smile.

Dewitt smiled back broadly.

Henry waved.

Stryker's children, she thought. The expression definitely had an ominous ring to it.

While waiting for the third floor elevator, Jill pulled out her memo book and drew a line through "Infant School." That left two other items she wanted to squeeze into the day, but they would have to wait until later.

She looked up at the row of numbers above the elevator. One number—nine—was lit. Surgery, Jill thought. Surgical people should take lessons from OB people on how to get a gurney off an elevator in a hurry.

But it gave her time to think.

Those babies in the Infant School: every one a medical miracle, there was no denying that. And every one of their mothers coddled and monitored carefully throughout her nine months of pregnancy. Jill rubbed her chin. Such patient care must be dreadfully expensive, she thought. Which meant that those children probably came from upper-class families.

Such services would be out of reach for the Maria Morans and the Mary Jo Sayers of this world.

But they were never high-risk patients in the first place.

Although the same doctors treated both groups.

Jill frowned. My mind is going around in circles, she thought.

The elevator arrived, and she got on.

22

"MAH EARL'S GONNA kill you," Bonnie Lee Gaines, aged sixteen, said as she sat on the examining table, eyeing Sam MacIntyre belligerently.

He glared back at her. "Look. No abortion under *any* circumstances. That's a five month viable fetus you're carrying! Now, I calculate the birth around mid-November. The wards here are as good medicine as you'll find any—"

"You mean, *have* it?" Bonnie Lee Gaines screwed up her pimply face. "Confound it, I wanna have it fixed."

"*Fixed?*" Sam MacIntyre said angrily. "*That's* what you call it?"

The girl tried one last, wicked glare and saw that she was getting nowhere.

"Mah Earl's gonna be *furious*!" She slid off the table and pulled a loose-fitting dress over her head. "An' ah thought you were goin' to hep me! Jesus! Some doctor!"

MacIntyre stepped back in revulsion as the girl ran out. He could hear her yelling obscenities all the way down the hall.

Bonnie Lee Gaines stormed out of the building and walked past the entrance of the geriatric clinic, next door. She quickened her pace. Bonnie Lee hated old people. There was a group of them standing there now, in front of the entrance, with their aluminum walkers and thick-lensed glasses and no place to go. Just standing there. Staring.

She gave them wide berth as she passed. She reached the corner and crossed at the intersection.

She moved as quickly as her bulk would allow. She was still fighting mad, and wanted to get out of the hospital neighborhood in a hurry.

She made her way to Nineteenth Street and headed west. Not until she was halfway down the block did she become aware of an odd, clicking sound behind her. She stopped, looked around. Her lip curled.

Nothing but some old guy, heading home the same way she was with his aluminum walker. Probably half blind, too; he was wearing dark glasses.

He saw her look at him and smiled crookedly. He gestured amiably and began to shuffle toward her.

"Aw, shee-it!" Bonnie Lee broke into an awkward, rolling trot, thinking, Hah. Maybe *this* will get rid of the baby. Nearing the end of the block, she slowed to a walk. She turned to look. The old coot was gone. Probably disappeared into one of those doorways she had just passed.

Good.

Bonnie Lee turned into an alley. It was a shortcut to Third Avenue and she knew it well. It was pretty shadowy, even by day, but it would get her home in half the time.

She moved past a stack of crates and the back door of a restaurant. Her eyes were not yet adjusted to the dim light, and she crashed loudly into a garbage bin. Cursing, she stopped to rub her knee. That was the trouble with this alley. You never knew where the restaurants were going to put their—

Two arms grabbed her about the middle and threw her to the ground. She screamed, then felt a medicinal smelling rag clamped over her nose and mouth, preventing her from screaming again, preventing her from . . .

Breathing?

She kicked wildly, tore at the arms that held her down. Her head began to spin, faster and faster. She felt the rag removed and hands take hold of her throat. The hands began to squeeze. She could kick no more. The hands squeezed harder, blackness closed in, and then all sensation was gone.

Which was probably just as well. Because the next sensation, of a four-inch needle being plunged into her abdomen, would have been unbearable if she had been awake to feel it.

Or, for that matter, alive to feel it.

23

JILL HAD FREE time and at a quarter past four she headed for the Pathology lab, where she found Peter Gregson bent over his microscope. His bland face smiled at her. "You came to see your skin cultures."

"I'm not disturbing you?"

"Hell no, I'm finished. You're doing me a favor. I need someone to wake me up."

She sat on the stool next to him while he stood to open his incubator. He peered inside.

"Here they are." Gregson grasped two of the circular glass dishes and brought them out. "Look at that!" he said, setting them down on the counter top. "Growing like Topsy!"

Jill stared down at the two specimens, and shivered.

Maria Moran and Christopher Sayers were dead. Yet here were cells from their bodies, growing and duplicating . . . *alive*.

Her heart was thumping rapidly.

Gregson stood with his hands on his hips. "Where do you want to start?" he asked.

"With the light microscope, I think. I'd like to see it under low power first."

"Light it is, then." Nodding, he reached for a microscope, removed an old slide and set it aside. He reached for a micropipette, saying, "You use this to draw up about .01 cc of the material. See? Like that. Then you put your stuff on the slide—no, not this slide. I'll show you a better one."

With his left hand he pulled out a box of thicker slides and withdrew one. He held it up and squinted. "This one's special for the needs of high magnification. See the square in the middle? Barely visible to the naked eye, but under the 'scope you'll see that it's got a crosshatched counting chamber. Very helpful when you get up to ten thousand power or thereabouts." He dropped the contents of the micropipette onto the slide, then replaced the two glass dishes in the incubator.

Jill asked, "Can you use that slide under an ordinary microscope?"

"For this purpose, yes. And it'll make switching easier." He looked at her. "Go ahead. Put it in and have a look."

Feeling a faint tremor in her hands, Jill leaned forward and placed the slide under the gleaming barrel. It was the sample from the dish marked number one—the skin cells of Maria Moran. Drawing a breath, Jill put her eye to the microscope and looked in.

"See anything?" asked Gregson.

"Yes. Teeming. Not enough detail, though."

"Let's go to one hundred power."

Gregson rotated the lenses while Jill continued to peer in. Moran's cells grew suddenly larger and brightly translucent. She could see cell walls and their nuclei and a few other features, but not well. It was as if someone were holding up a roadmap, but at too great a distance.

"One thousand power," said Gregson.

Her vision filled with a single cell nucleus. At the equator of the nucleus coiled a jumble of what looked like long, thin threads. She was beginning to get excited.

"I can see the chromosomes but they're indistinct. I'd like to go in deeper."

The light in her barrel of vision suddenly flicked off. "For that," said Peter Gregson, "we'll have to go to the electron microscope. Bring your slide."

She followed him the length of the long counter top. At the end stood a large console with a metal box on the top. "This EM is the RD model 400," he said. "It's the best. That box up there is an image intensifier, so you can project a picture of whatever the microscope is seeing." Gregson slid a white screen along its counter track until it was in front of the microscope. Then he took Jill's slide and inserted it into a metal housing. "We'll start at ten thousand power," he said. He clicked on the beam and adjusted some dials.

"Have a look," he said, focusing the beam.

Jill stared at the screen.

It was unbelievable.

In the time it had taken them to move from one microscope to the other, the cell Jill had been watching had entered a new phase of mitotic division. The chromosomes no longer looked like long, tangled threads; they had uncoiled from each other and were breaking up into fragments. Each fragment was in the shape of a knobby *x* with four distinct arms.

Jill caught her breath. "I've only seen this in photographs," she said. "*Look* at that. It's actually *happening*."

Gregson was silent for a moment. "Look normal to you?" he said.

She peered at the screen. "Seems to."

"Take another look."

She turned to Gregson. He was squinting and his lips were moving. She could tell he was counting. "There's an odd number," he said finally. "An extra chromosome. I'd have to cut them out and pair them to be sure, but it looks like a trisomy 14." He whistled. "That's incredible. I've never seen that before."

Jill's throat went dry. A fourth year resident in Pathology and he's never seen this before. God, what have I stumbled onto?

She said, "Should we go to fifty thousand power?"

He held up his hand. "No, wait. This is amazing. I think I see something else." He adjusted the beam to a tighter focus and stepped closer to the screen.

He pointed. "Look at that. Your patient has a transloca-tion, too. See this number twelve chromosome? It's miss-ing an arm."

Jill looked. He was right. Number twelve looked like a half-eaten starfish.

"And see here?" He pointed to a chromosome at the lower corner of the screen. "The missing arm is here. It's attached itself to chromosome seventeen. It's a 12–17 translocation. This is incredible."

He turned to her. "Who is this patient? Some victim of Hiroshima you're treating down there?"

Jill improvised. "As a matter of fact, we're looking into the possibility of radiation exposure." She swallowed. She disliked having to make up a story for Gregson. He was being very nice, and he was going out of his way to help. But like any good scientist he was seeing something ex-traordinary and was getting excited about it. His fascina-tion would lead him back to Obstetrics. They would discover that she had been snooping. That was all she needed.

She would only tell David, she decided.

Gregson was still looking puzzled. Then he shrugged. "We've got two Love Canal cases we're working on." He shook his head. "You should see *those* specimens."

She looked at the floor. "Awful, isn't it?"

"Yeah." He glanced at his watch. "Oh, I've got to leave. Listen, you can keep using the EM. Just flick off this switch when you're finished and put the cover back on."

She looked at him gratefully. "Peter, thanks a million for all your help. I really appreciate it."

He shrugged again. "Come any time. Pathology resi-dents get lonely for live company."

Smiling, she watched him head for the door. "Oh, and Peter," she called out. "Should I turn off the lights if I'm the last to leave?"

He made a face. "Don't be silly. No one's *ever* the last to leave."

He went out.

Jill sat for a long moment, absorbing the silence. Only now did the stab of discovery hit with full force. Her heart pounded hard as she thought: Maria Moran died of abruptio placentae, which was an accident, right? A freak of Nature. No tie-in at all with chromosomal abnormalities.

So where did *this* come from?

She looked up at the still-lighted screen. The chromosomes had straightened out again. Xs slid into long bars. They had divided into two groups, each group sliding along invisible tracks toward opposite cellular poles. In another few minutes the cell would divide. And then the two daughter cells would divide, and so on, each new generation replicating the same damaged chromosomal set.

Maria Moran had not been walking around all her life with that bomb in her cells. She would not have survived infancy.

It had to have started with her pregnancy. And the way she died. A ruptured placenta. Fetal cellular material had poured into the large uterine vessels, multiplied mitotically, and seeded out into every cell in the farthest reaches of her body.

So it must have come from the baby.

The baby.

Jill got up, removed the Moran slide and went back to the incubator for the other Petri dish. She pipetted out .01 cc of Christopher Sayers' growing skin cells, put the drop on an EM slide and hurried back to the console. She turned the dials and checked to see if the power was still at ten thousand.

It was. The light on the screen was very bright. She focused, sat back, waited and scarcely breathed as she watched the chromosomes sliding, coiling, uncoiling, pulling apart. The chromosomes fragmented; the screen was strewn with pulsating, odd-shaped little Xs. She left her seat and stepped forward. Her index finger made a trembling shadow as it traced across the screen, counting, counting . . . She stopped. There it was. The extra chromosome: trisomy 14.

"Dear God," she whispered. She tried desperately to count faster. *Damn*. The chromosomes were moving into their next stage. Hurry! Her finger stopped suddenly over a shape that looked like three mangled fingers, spread wide apart.

That was it.

The number 12 chromosome. Missing an arm.

And not far away, near the edge, was number 17. With five arms. Gregson's 12–17 translocation. The limbless Christopher Sayers had it, too.

Jill stepped back, her mind paralyzed.

Abruptio placentae. Phocomelia.

The two tragedies were poles apart.

What in God's name was going on?

$$24$$

IT WAS 5:09.

Jill, back in street clothes, stood at a pay phone in the main floor lobby.

The phone was answered on the third ring. "Madison Museum of Anthropology."

"Office of the curator, please."

"One moment."

There was a click and the sounds of circuits connecting.

A voice, liltingly British, came on.

"Margaret Haywood speaking."

"Mrs. Haywood?" Jill spoke rapidly. "I'm Dr. Raney, from Madison Hospital, and I'm calling to inquire about one of your students, a Mary Jo Sayers—"

"Mary Jo! Oh, I'm so glad you've called. Is there anything you can tell me? I've been terribly worried . . ."

Two minutes later Jill was racing up First Avenue to the Victorian mansion with its Gothic tower which was the Museum of Anthropology. Over the years the med center had expanded into the old mansion's land; then had bought the place; now appeared actually to be pushing it off hospital property. The worst offender was the Sturdevandt Research Wing. Four stories, mostly glass, it stretched from the tall new buildings to a point where it stood shoulder to shoulder with the museum. There was talk of pulling the old place down.

That's the hospital for you, Jill thought. If it's in the way, throw it out.

She hurried across the lawn, up the marble steps, and up a curved staircase to a second floor office.

"*Glad* you could come! So very, very glad." Margaret Haywood, with pale orange hair set as neatly as the Queen's, rushed forward to greet her.

Haywood re-seated herself behind a heavy, oaken desk, and Jill took the visitor's chair: a deeply carved affair with lion-head handrests. She leaned forward, still out of breath from running, and weighed her words carefully. "I should begin," she said, "by requesting that whatever is said in this room be held in strictest confidence."

Margaret Haywood clasped and unclasped her hands. "Not necessary to ask," she said. "I've known that something was wrong for the past forty-eight hours, since Monday. You see, Mary Jo and I had an appointment set for Monday morning, and Mary Jo *always* keeps appointments. My goodness, you could practically set your clocks by that girl." She shook her head. "One of our most dedicated graduate students. And her thesis almost finished, poor dear . . ."

"Monday," Jill prompted.

"Yes. Well. Over the phone she told me she was having terrible pains, and that instead of stopping by for her research material, as planned, she was going over to see her doctor." Mrs. Haywood waved a plump hand. "I don't know his name, but his office is just three blocks down, at the Medical Center.''

"Yes," said Jill. "She was a patient in the clinic."

"Well, Monday came and went. She never called. By that time I was concerned, so I called the hospital." Her face became flushed. "I got a run-around that was outright insulting! They told me that only next of kin were privy to information, and I told them Mary Jo didn't *have* any next of kin, so—"

Jill's hands clutched at the lion heads. "Mary Jo had no next of kin? Mrs. Haywood, was Mary Jo Sayers *married*?"

The older woman looked at her. "I should say not. A short-lived marriage ended badly about three years ago. To my knowledge, she hasn't seen the chap since. By the way, her parents are dead, and she has no family that I know of. None at all."

"Go on," Jill said softly.

Haywood related that on Tuesday—yesterday—she tried a different tactic. She called the hospital, said that she was Mary Jo's aunt, and demanded to be informed of her condition. She was told that the patient had gone home.

"Signed out by her *husband,* they told me! Of course, I couldn't very well say I didn't know of any husband after I had just said I was an aunt. Oh—I didn't know *what* to do."

"Did you consider calling the police?"

"Yes. And no." Margaret Haywood made a helpless gesture. "I felt, well, perhaps Mary Jo *did* have a boy-friend I didn't know about. And then *that* started to bother me. I believe I was on the verge of calling the police when you called."

Jill studied the older woman's features. Margaret Haywood seemed a person of sense and discretion. It was time to tell the whole story.

Jill bit her lip.

"Mrs. Haywood, on Monday around two o'clock, Mary Jo delivered a son four months prematurely. The child suffered from a serious developmental problem. He did not survive. On the following morning, Mary Jo, though grieving, was able to talk to me. Mary Jo said . . . things. Strange things, by anyone's reckoning. She was of course hysterical about losing the baby, but she somehow seemed to . . . *connect* the tragedy with the work she was doing. With her thesis.'' Jill looked at her hands and wiped them on her skirt. "Mary Jo used the terms 'they' and 'them,' and then would draw back and insist it was a secret and she couldn't divulge more. Anyhow"—Jill looked into the disbelieving face—"Mary Jo was convinced that she had been betrayed.''

The curator stared at Jill. She blinked, withdrew a silk handkerchief from her drawer, and turned her face away to dab at her eyes.

"I'm not surprised," Haywood said, looking back. "There had been trouble, you see."

"Trouble?"

"Yes." Margaret Haywood picked up a small jade elephant and began turning it pensively in her hands.

"The problem began when the university's anthropology department refused to okay her thesis subject. That was almost a year ago. It was felt that Mary Jo's hypothesis was too"—she waved a hand—"far out." Still holding the jade elephant, Mrs. Haywood gazed up at some faded angels painted on the ceiling.

"Mary Jo Sayers believed," she continued, "that we humans have come to an evolutionary dead end; that we're finished, as good as extinct, unless someone very soon figures out a way to speed up human evolution."

Jill stared at her in astonishment. "Speed up . . . evolution?"

"Yes. The interesting thing is that Mary Jo's hypothesis was grounded in reason. For example, adaptability, as I'm sure you know, is the primary factor determining whether or not a species survives. Mary Jo contended that we have so mucked up this planet that, within one or two generations the damage will have far outstripped our ability to adapt. We'll simply go the way of the dinosaurs!"

"Unless somebody . . . Well, how *do* you speed up human evolution?"

"Ah. But that was the crux of the problem. You see, Mary Jo consistently refused to divulge her sources. All she would say was that there was somebody out there—or perhaps some group or study program—and that 'they' were definitely working on a means to accelerate human evolution. However, you can't write a thesis and refuse to divulge your sources. It's simply not valid."

"But still she continued . . ."

"Yes. And became rather secretive. For example, she never even mentioned the pregnancy until a month ago. It didn't show."

Jill's heart was thumping. "Mrs. Haywood, do you have any idea at all who the father might have been?"

The older woman shook her head, put the elephant down. "No. For all I know she was artificially inseminated. That would *not* have been out of character."

Jill regarded her intently, then stood up. "You've been most helpful," she said.

Hayward rose too. "*Do* keep me informed, won't you? I care sincerely about that girl and—here, why don't I see you out? I say! It's already five past six."

They left the office and began walking down the curving stairway. Haywood mentioned that on Wednesdays the guard didn't close till 6:30 and suggested that Jill take a look around. "It's all really quite fascinating," she said, "and you *must* see our hominids."

"Hominids?"

"Yes. Apemen. Our earliest ancestors. You might say the hominid room was Mary Jo's world. It's in the basement, unfortunately. We're bursting at the seams in this old place, but the dioramas are recently built and well worth it. Are you interested in the art of Africa and Oceania?"

They had reached the marble floor of the vaulted entrance hall. To Jill's left the oaken entrance doors stood open, admitting the first faint breeze of evening.

"I go *that* way," said Margaret Haywood, indicating the street. "And you, if you're interested, go *that* way." To Jill's right, beyond the wide arch, stretched a gallery

that must have been one hundred feet long. The gallery
was empty of tourists, and beginning to fill with shadows.
Squinting, Jill could make out giant glass cases housing
humanlike figures.

"It does look intriguing," she said.

"Splendid!" said Margaret Haywood. "Remember, the
farther toward the rear you go, the farther back in time you
get. In fact, why don't you begin in the basement? The
hominid room. Sorry the lighting's so wretched down
there, but I believe they're still working. The stairs are
over there." She pointed. "You must catch them at it
before they go home."

"Who's they?" Jill asked.

"You'll see," said Margaret Haywood brightly.

With that she extended her hand, said something urgent
about staying in touch, and departed, leaving Jill staring
uneasily into the darkening gallery beyond.

25

I'LL MAKE IT quick, she thought. I'll dash downstairs and
see this hominid place and there'll be a few minutes to
spare for the first floor exhibits.

She found the door just past the arch, opened it and
looked down the stairs. It was dark and smelled musty.
She was about to close the door when she thought she
heard voices. She found a light switch on the side wall.
Flicking it on, she started down, thinking: so this was
Mary Jo's world.

It grew cooler as she descended. At the bottom a line of

bulbs illuminated a wide passageway lined with closed
doorways and, toward the rear, on the right, a single open
door from which emanated a wash of light and the hum of
working voices.

Approaching, she knocked on the door frame.

A man turned, and for a moment she forgot where she
was.

He was wearing a long white coat. He held a scalpel in
one hand and a pair of calipers in the other. The harsh
light from the studio fixtures flashed off his glasses.

"Come in! Come in!" he said.

She did, hesitantly. Around her stretched worktables
covered with paint and clay and plaster. The man's white
coat was smeared with plaster. So, too, were the aprons of
two male assistants sweeping up clumps of styrofoam. The
place smelled of bonding cement. Off to one side was a
table studded with bone fragments, a femur, several jaws,
miscellaneous bone pieces and skulls. Jill blinked in amazement at the skulls.

"Hominid fossils," the man said cheerfully. He wiped
his hands and approached her. One of the young assistants
glanced at her, then returned to his work. The other carried
a bag of styrofoam scraps out of the room. Removing his
glasses, the older man said, "I'm Henry Clark. I build
hominid reconstructions for the prehistory displays. May I
help you?"

Jill pulled her gaze away from a skull that looked like a
chimpanzee's, but was too large-brained.

She introduced herself, mentioning Mrs. Haywood's sug-
gestion to visit the studio. She looked around again. "It's
fascinating," she said.

Henry Clark smiled. "We have a joke down here," he
said. "We're not making history. We're resurrecting *pre*-
history." He gestured toward the fossil table. "Most of
these were only discovered eight or nine years ago."

Jill stared down at a fragment of female human pelvis.
"How old is this?" she asked.

"Oh, young," he said. "Only about a million years.
Are you interested in paleoanthropology?"

"Only indirectly. Actually I knew . . . I know Mary Jo Sayers. I was interested in seeing where she works."

"Mary Jo! Fantastic mind. Very dedicated." He walked to a glass cabinet and turned on the light. Inside was the head of an apelike human, its eyes expressive, its lips pulled back over yellowed simian teeth. *"Australopithecus afarensis,"* he said proudly. "Mary Jo and I worked on this together—well, Mary Jo did most of it." He paused. "It's a reconstruction of Lucy!" he said. "Do you know about Lucy?"

Jill thought for a moment. "Lucy . . . wasn't that the skeleton found recently in Africa—"

"Ethiopia."

"Right. Ethiopia. And her bone structure was closer to human than primate so it proved that she was the oldest example of any human ancestor ever found."

"And she lived three and a half million years ago."

"That much? No kidding."

"From that period dates the ascent of man." Henry Clark paused for significance. "Want to see more?" He went down a line of cabinets and began flicking on lights. *"Homo habilis* here—notice the smaller jaw and larger brain area; and *Homo erectus* here—brain even bigger, and this guy began to use tools; and here in this line is Java Man, Rhodesian Man, Peking Man . . . ah, Peking Man . . ."

Jill noticed that he was fiddling impatiently with a light inside the cabinet. It was either burned out or broken.

"Hey, Sonny!" he called. "Sonny Sears! You still there?"

The assistant appeared in the doorway carrying a card-board box full of wood shavings and scraps of animal skins. Jill turned back to admire the craftsmanship of Mary Jo Sayers' *Australopithecus afarensis.*

Henry Clark motioned to Sears. "Peking's light bulb is broken."

With a disgusted look Sonny set his box down in the doorway. He crossed the floor, flipped open Peking Man's glass door, and reached in to give the bulb a little twist. The light came on.

Without a word Sonny Sears crossed the room to the door. Picking up the box he said, "One last trip to the incinerator and then I'm clearing out. Jesus, it's twenty-five to seven!"

Jill heard him going up the steps at the end of the outside passageway, and then she heard the loud thud of a door. A moment later she heard more steps, and another loud thud. The second assistant leaving, she guessed.

Henry Clark put his hands in his pockets and shrugged. "Would you believe those two are an improvement over the *last* ones we had?"

She smiled. "I have to be going too," she said, then hesitated. "If you hear from Mary Jo, would you let me know? I'd really appreciate it." She wrote down her name and telephone number at the hospital.

Clark looked at it. "Oh," he said. "When you came you just said you were from the med center. I didn't realize you were an M.D."

With her address still in his hand he looked back to a full-sized hominid mannequin. Jill had already admired it. Anatomically, it was perfect—every bony ridge; every clay strand simulating bundles of muscle fibers; the skin; the styrofoam padding to represent fat deposits.

Jill turned back and smiled at him. "Perfection," she said. "Real as life."

He seemed very pleased.

"You know," he said, removing his white smock and hanging it up. "I'll bet people in my field know as much anatomy as any doctor."

"I can see that," she said. She walked with him through the door and stood out in the hall. "Where will the mannequins go when they're finished?" she asked.

He bent and locked the door. Straightening, he motioned across the corridor. "The other side, when it's restored, will be one continuous hominid gallery. Dioramas, special lighting, moss, everything. It'll need a lot of restoration, of course, and that front staircase will have to be fixed up. Then we'll have one of the best hominid study collections in the country."

Jill followed him up the cement stairs as they talked. On the landing, she gazed into the first-floor gallery. She could barely make out the exhibits.

"I had wanted to see that too," she said wistfully.

"Hmm," he said. "Our Ernest the caretaker. He's seventy-one and plenty spry, but he runs the place his own way." Clark looked back at Jill. "Well, he hasn't closed yet. Why don't you see what you can till he does?"

"I have to be back at the hospital by seven," she said.

"Suit yourself," Clark said. "But if you stay, just remember that Ernest is a little deaf. Keep your ears peeled for him, and when you hear those keys jangling in the doors it's time to scram." Henry Clark smiled at her. "I'd sure hate to see you get locked in for the night."

There's time, she decided. It's seventeen before seven, it only takes three minutes to run back.

She turned. Clark had left the back door behind her wedged open, providing some light. Only the middle of the gallery was lost in shadow. She went inside.

She stopped before an enormous glass case that had earlier caught her eye. When her eyes adjusted to the light, she saw that the diorama was the size of a small room. A plaque at eye level read: *Middle Pleistocene Period (1,000,000–500,000 years ago). Homo erectus: The First Man.*

Jill peered in. Mannequins with bodies more human than ape stood erect and used their hands industriously. They were shaping crude tools, skinning animals, making fire. The setting in which they lived looked like a cave. The figures had flat, sloping foreheads, no real chins and large, heavy brows. Their cranial capacity, Jill guessed, was about one thousand cubic centimeters. Pretty small, she thought. But the artistry of the mannequins was perfect. One of them stood close to the glass, holding his club aloft, and his eyes actually glared at Jill.

Involuntarily she drew back. Then something else caught her attention and she glanced over her shoulder. From somewhere she thought she heard an unseen door close, but she couldn't be sure.

She moved on.

The next diorama read: *Paleolithic campsite; 300,000 years old; found in 1966 in the South of France.*

Inside, more human-looking figures hunted and gathered food. Their tools were more sophisticated than those of their *Homo erectus* ancestors. They had learned how to build dwellings for themselves. An oval hut made of sticks stretched about thirty by fifteen feet. A child, his face pinched in concentration, squatted at the entrance to the hut, drawing a design in the ground with a pointed antler.

Jill stared at the child mannequin. For some reason it reminded her of little Melissa, the Chinese child in the Infant School. The intense concentration on the face—that was it, Jill realized. She was reminded of Henry Clark's "ascent of man" hypothesis, and pondered that too for a moment.

Did *he* know about Mary Jo Sayers's thesis? That mankind was coming to an evolutionary dead end? Jill thought of Corrine Dewitt and her superkids: *"We may consider them geniuses, but future generations will not."*

Jill looked back at the child with his pointed antler, and had a vague, insistent feeling that there was some sort of connection in this building. Something to do with Mary Jo, but—what?

Her puzzlement deepened.

A muffled noise caused her to look up suddenly. She listened. Was that the caretaker? No, it hadn't sounded like a caretaker: they were *noisy;* they stomped around and jangled their keys. The wind, no doubt. It was getting late. She would have to hurry.

She rounded the corner of a small side gallery and stared. *Art of Oceania,* read the lucite plaque on the wall. Above the plaque was an array of gruesome objects: grotesque funeral masks from New Guinea, elaborately carved shields, a dagger carved from a human rib, shrunken heads, several necklaces of human teeth.

The objects made Jill so nervous that when a floorboard

creaked behind her, she spun around. "Who's there?" she
cried.

Silence.

Definitely time to go, she thought. But she couldn't
move. A tall object in the corner had seized her attention
and demanded a closer look. It was, Jill thought, the most
breathtaking New Guinea funeral mask of all. Made of
woven straw, it covered the entire body of its wearer, and
went over the head like a ski mask. The eyes and mouth
were sewn-on letter *O*s; the arms were lightweight reed
grasses—no doubt to fly about wildly during energetic
ceremonies; and the chest . . . Jill leaned forward to
examine the intricate weave of the chest—and felt herself
go rigid with terror.

The chest was slowly rising and falling, rising and
falling.

Jill gasped. She lifted her gaze to the eyeholes, and saw
live eyes looking back at her. The figure was watching her
with mocking eyes; full of cunning, full of hateful triumph
eyes.

With a whipping, thrashing sound, the two grass arms
shot out to seize her as she screamed and ducked, lost her
balance, and rolled over sideways. Blinding pain shot
through her as her head hit a pedestal. She saw the monstrous figure coming at her, and pain was forgotten. Struggling to her knees, she seized the white pedestal that stood
between them and with a mighty heave pushed against it.
Her attacker was clumsy in his heavy costume. The falling
pedestal knocked him backward, against the wall, and with
a convulsive jerk Jill scrambled to her feet and broke into a
run. She heard him running behind her, but didn't look
back. Her heart was bursting out of her chest. A little cry,
a soft, squealing scream, began to come from her throat.

She raced around the corner and saw the open back door
about fifty feet ahead. God bless Henry Clark, she thought,
remembering the door wedge. Behind her a rough and
muffled voice shouted, "You bitch, I'll get you!" He was
getting closer. She stopped, reached up and grabbed a
brutish-looking javelin—decoration over a water bubbler—

turned, and hurled it awkwardly at him. She saw the
pointed tip whack wood and the straw-covered figure fall
back, surprised.

She also saw the absurdity of green running shoes on
her pursuer's feet.

She turned and raced out the door, her breath coming in
heaving gasps as she tore over back lawn and then pavement, up the drive to the ambulance bay.

For the first time she was aware of something hot and
sticky trickling down her cheek. Slowing down, she raised
a hand to her forehead and felt the sharp sting of a
laceration.

In a blur she saw a blue uniform rushing toward her.
"You okay, ma'am? Hey, what the . . . "

She felt faint. She was breathing too fast to answer.
Fearfully she turned and looked back, but no one was
following her. The Gothic tower of Madison Museum
loomed in a sky gone suddenly darker, and the only sign
of life was the play of heat lightning that crackled over its
spikes.

26

LIKE A CHILD, she shut her eyes tight while he stitched her
up. "You still there?" he asked.

She opened her eyes. The light from the examining lamp
made her squint. Dimly she could see David's gloved
hands set the curved suture needle on a sterile towel, then
pick up a cotton swab dipped in merthiolate.

"One more dab," he said grimly, "and then we talk."

Jill gripped the edge of the exam table and fought to stop the trembling.

She looked over again at the top of the sterile table. It was littered with an empty Procaine syringe, used mosquito clamps, and a pile of bloody cotton swabs. She took a shuddering breath. She was not used to seeing her own blood.

Levine applied a gauze dressing to the laceration on the side of Jill's forehead. Then he stood back, folded his arms and regarded her for a brooding moment.

"You look terrible," he said.

"You said you wanted to talk," she said. She felt defensive for some reason and avoided his glance. With a knowing gesture she reached out and pulled down the gooseneck lamp, diminishing the glare.

David pulled up a circular stool. He sat on the edge and stared in disbelief at the dressing on her forehead.

"From the beginning," he said. "Again."

"I *told* you. I went to the museum to ask about Mary Jo Sayers. While I was there a giant grass creature jumped out and attacked me. He was wearing green running shoes."

Chin in his hand, David's eyes fixed on hers. She looked back steadily. They held each other's gaze for several seconds, and then he looked away.

Jill realized that she had just passed item number four on the Physician's Psychiatric Evaluation Test.

Leaning forward intently, Jill said, "I found out that Sayers wasn't married, David. She had no next of kin, no boyfriends—nobody."

He looked back at her. She was surprised to see his expression empty of skepticism.

"Nobody's called the morgue yet about the Sayers infant," he said in a low voice. "And since ten this morning the hospital's been investigating Sayers' abrupt transfer to Psychiatry yesterday. A hundred calls have been made. People have been questioned."

"Nothing?"

"Nothing."

Jill stared. For the first time in almost thirty-six tormented hours she felt vindicated. Absolved, she realized. It had to be. She had been the only one to correctly assess the patient's status, and then dare to defy orders.

Orders which turned out to be fake.

She felt a chill. "But *someone* placed that call . . ."

"Yes. The psychiatric nurse couldn't remember the doctor's last name. Said it began with an *M*. How's that for sloppy?"

"Typical."

"Right. Anyway, every *M* in the building has had to account for his activities. Waste of time, of course. George Mackey was delivering twins at the time. And MacIntyre was in surgery . . ."

"Somebody wanted Sayers out of this hospital," Jill said. "Clever job, wasn't it? *Too* clever, David. Too quick! You have to admit—only somebody on the *inside* could have pulled that off."

She had regained a measure of control. Now, she decided, was a good time to tell David some of the more bizarre aspects of the Sayers case.

She told him about the patient's insistence, on Tuesday morning, that she had been "betrayed"; of her battles with the university over her "far out" thesis; and her refusal to divulge her sources.

"It was supposed to have been some weird secret," Jill concluded. "That's what the museum curator said."

The cubicle curtain suddenly parted and a man in a white jacket peered in. It was Warren Duffy, the surgical resident who had been on hand when Jill was brought into Emergency, crying for Levine.

"How's it going?" Duffy asked. He looked worried.

David turned on his seat. "We're lucky," he said. "Could have been a lot worse."

Duffy pursed his lips. "Yeah, well, happy ending this time, huh?" The specter of doctors getting mugged in the neighborhood was a dread that everyone lived with. It was becoming a more frequent occurrence.

"Let me know if you need anything, okay?" Duffy smiled uneasily at Jill.

"Yeah," said Levine. "Thanks."

Duffy went out. There was a commotion in the hall, and then MacIntyre, Greenberg and Donovan came rushing in. All hell broke loose. "Oh my God," Tricia said, "look at you!" MacIntyre kept hollering, "Did you get a description of the guy?" Woody was gibbering something as he gaped at the pile of blood-soaked cotton swabs.

"This girl hasn't even eaten yet!" Tricia exclaimed as she turned from talking to Jill. "I'm going to get a pile of grinders—for all of us!"

Tricia ran out and there was a moment of silence before MacIntyre said, "By the way, David, how come the ER's crawling with cops?"

Jill looked up.

"Yeah," said Woody. "The ambulance bay, too. They're all *over* the place. What's going on?"

"A lot is going on," Levine said quietly. He looked at Jill. "It's been bad here. When you were first brought in, weren't you a little surprised at how fast I got here?"

"I . . . well . . . yes—come to think of it."

Levine shoved his hands into his pockets. "I got here fast because I was *already* here. Since 6:30. The police were asking a lot of questions." He looked at his three colleagues, one by one. "They're still here. Waiting in the ER lounge. They want to talk to us."

"Well, damn!" protested MacIntyre. "Whatever it is, they're going to have to conduct their little tête-à-tête in the cafeteria. I'm starving!"

"Tricia's bringing sandwiches," Woody reminded him. He turned to David. "I don't get it. Why all the questions, anyway?"

"It seems," David said, "that one of our clinic patients didn't make it home this afternoon. Murder, folks. Details to come, but the police are beginning their investigation here. This department."

He looked uneasily at Jill's pallid face and bandaged forehead. "Jill," he said. "On second thought maybe you ought to—"

"Where did you say they are?" she interrupted.

"A homicide detective and one sergeant are waiting in the ER doctors' lounge."

"So let's go then," she said, and unsteadily got down from the table.

They told a nurse to tell Tricia where they'd be, and then headed for the lounge, where they found a black-haired, heavyset man in a dark suit who was spreading photographs across a table. He looked up when the four physicians walked in.

" 'Lo again, doctor," he said, looking at David. "We're in luck. Police lab just delivered these."

David introduced the other three to homicide detective Lieutenant Gregory Pappas, who in turn introduced his serious-faced assistant.

"Well, doctors," said Pappas, indicating the tabletop. "Recognize anybody?"

The photos were grisly. Levine stepped forward, grimacing as he picked up a black-and-white of a dead girl. Her pug nose was encrusted with blood, her skin badly macerated, and her dead eyes were propped open—how *did* they do that for morgue shots? he wondered.

Feeling sick, he put back the picture. "Never saw her," he said. He glanced over his shoulder to the others who hunched around him. "What do you think?"

They stared at the photos in stunned silence.

"Hard to say," muttered Woody Greenberg. "This girl might have been here. So many who come to the clinic are about that age, and . . . well, *look* like that. We call it the 'runaway look.' "

"Funny," said Pappas. "So do we." He looked at Jill. "And you?"

"I definitely don't place her," she whispered. Involuntarily her hand had come up to her throat.

Sam MacIntyre moved forward and picked up the photograph. There was tension in his face. He turned to Pappas, who stood poised with a notebook and pencil.

"I've seen this girl," said MacIntyre. "She wasn't a

regular but I saw her today. Strictly Ozarks. She was about five months pregnant, if I remember correctly.''

"Jackpot," said Pappas. Grunting satisfaction, he lowered his heavy body onto one of the straight-backed wooden chairs that circled the table. Levine and MacIntyre sat at the table, Greenberg and Jill Raney took nearby armchairs.

Pappas stared thoughtfully at the group before speaking, then cleared his throat. "This case is pretty far out of the ordinary," he said.

Pushing the three photographs to the center of the table, Pappas folded his burly hands and began to talk in a flat, police monologue. "Victim's name is Bonnie Lee Gaines. Caucasian, aged sixteen, traced by a fingerprint check to have a record for prostitution. Found at 3:07 today, Wednesday, July 13, jammed into a bulkhead behind a Third Avenue restaurant. Death by strangulation. Her wallet had a recent prison release form. On the line requesting name of physician, she listed this clinic."

Pappas looked over to MacIntyre. "She ever have any checkups here?"

"I doubt it," said MacIntyre. "What she came for was an abortion."

"At five months?"

"Right."

Pappas shook his head.

Jill Raney leaned forward. "You said this case was . . . unusual," she said.

Pappas looked at her. "I haven't gotten to the sick part."

The room became very still. Pappas gathered up the photos and shoved them into a black plastic briefcase.

"The medical examiner has already gone over her, and says there's no doubt about his findings. The fetus she was carrying was about twenty-two weeks along and—" Pappas coughed, took another breath, continued.

"M.E. found a tiny hole, puncture mark like . . . from a needle, between the folds of the victim's navel. Her womb had been completely drained of amniotic fluid."

Jill stared at him, swallowing rapidly.

"What?" yelled MacIntyre. "My God," David said.

At that moment Tricia ran in with the sandwiches.

David stood leaning on the doorjamb, facing out, tall and brooding. The others had gone: the police back to their cars, the OB threesome, white-faced, back to their floor. A pile of uneaten grinders lay on the table. Behind him, he heard Jill's voice. She had called him.

He turned. "What?"

He watched her rise slowly from her chair. She was, he thought, a sight to behold. The bandage had soaked through and the blood had turned brown. Add to that the blood-stains on her pink blouse, the dark circles under the eyes in the pallid face, and you had a typical mugging victim.

A typical mugging victim.

The thought made him feel helpless and terrified; it also made him mad as hell. He had known plenty of women in his time, but he had never fallen for any this hard, this fast. He thought, we've just begun and she nearly gets herself killed. What is happening in this hospital? What in God's name is going on?

She came and stood by his shoulder. He touched her arm and said, "We might as well change that dressing while we're down here. Maybe get you into a new scrub suit, too."

"Okay," she said. Despondently they watched the bed-lam outside. It was 8:30, and the evening tide of accident victims had begun to pour in, some ambulatory but bloody, others on stretchers. Crying relatives added to the rising level of noise, and one woman, screaming hysterically, was being subdued by a nurse and two orderlies.

"David?"

He looked at her. "What?"

"Want to bring me up to date on things upstairs?" she asked. "I mean, after four o'clock did anything . . . else happen?"

He pursed his lips and looked away, resigned. "Hollins miscarried," he said dully. "Around five o'clock."

"Holl—*Hewitt*-Hollins?" Jill's eyes widened. "The lady lawyer? The fever of unknown origin?"

"The same."

"But she was getting better!"

"She got worse."

Jill's cheeks reddened and a long moment passed as she let the news sink in. "That poor woman," she murmured.

"Just as well you weren't there," he said in a low voice. He stared down at speckled squares of linoleum.

"And how many casualties on *Monday?*" she said suddenly. "And the week before? And before I *started* this lousy internship?"

"For God's sake, Jill—" He flushed. "Look. This place has been upside down. Everyone in the freaking hospital has been speculating, investigating, but nothing's *connected*. These patients all have different backgrounds, different treatments, different problems. There's just no common thread!"

She followed his troubled gaze as he watched some bloodied teenagers being wheeled past.

"No common thread? David, do you have a few minutes? There's something I'd like to show you."

He turned to her, looking pained and exhausted, feeling something ready to snap. "*No,* Jill. I *don't* have a few minutes. I'm behind on paperwork upstairs and I *still* haven't gone over today's charts. Besides, you're on call tonight and you've had a slightly traumatic experience. Shouldn't you be trying to get a little sleep? *Now?* We'll go over the charts together. *After.* Deal?"

A thought struck her and she said, "We can go over the charts in my on-call room. It'll be half the work for you and maybe they'll make me sleepy. What do you think of that?"

He looked at her. The foul mood of moments before vanished. "You strike a hard bargain," he said.

"Come *on,*" she said.

27

DAVID FROWNED AT the screen before him, his lips moving slightly, like Peter Gregson's. David was counting. Finally he leaned back in his chair and said, "Yep. Same as the other one. It's unbelievable. It's just fantastic."

Jill said, "Trisomy 14 *and* a 12–17 translocation. Both of them had it. The Sayers infant and"—she tapped the screen with her finger—"Moran here." She paused. "Rather, her baby must have had it. Moran's body was riddled with fetal hemoglobin marker. Well. *Now* do you see a common thread?"

Levine rubbed his chin in thought. "I see they're the same," he said, "but"—he threw up his hands—"two cases don't make a *pattern*. You can't leap from two twisted chromosomes to a deadly hospital intrigue without more evidence than that. It could be just chance. Or I can think of a dozen causes from outside the hospital."

Jill was exasperated. "David—"

"Wait." He held up a hand. "Hear me out. They could have been exposed to the same environmental contaminant. Radiation, or pesticides in the water, for example. Maybe they're distant cousins; or maybe they both had the same boyfriend—a guy with a peculiar genetic makeup." He gave a wry smile.

Jill looked at him. It was his logic versus her instinct, she realized. She felt frustrated, disappointed; but at the same time she knew that he could be right. Crestfallen, she reached out and flicked off the EM beam. The steady hum

of the motor ceased; the nearly empty laboratory seemed
suddenly hollow.

"Sure," she said drily. "They both went on a picnic to
Three Mile Island." She turned and went to stand at the
window, gazing vacantly out into the dark.

David came to stand by her. "Jill," he said. "You've
made an important finding. It is definitely provocative.
But . . . what are you going to *do* with it?"

She did not reply. He noticed that she was staring down
in the direction of the research wing. A long row of
windows on the fourth floor was brightly lit. It was Stryker's
lab.

"They go at all hours, don't they?" Her voice sounded
depressed.

David looked. "So they're dedicated."

"I think they're weird."

He grinned. "By the way, you never told me how you
got the skin specimens from the morgue up here without
incubation."

"Oh." She looked sheepish for a moment, then told
him.

He laughed, and kissed her, and told her she was nuts.

There was a sturdy bed in Jill's ninth-floor on-call room,
and onto it Levine tossed a pile of "trouble charts"—as
the residents were now calling them, he told her.

"Hollins is on top," he said, pulling up a chair. "Aren't
you getting tired?"

"Yes," she said, kneeling over the bed. "As soon as I
whip through these, I'll call it a day."

He watched as her delicate hands flipped expertly through
the charts, then dealt them out separately in a line that
stretched from the pillow to the foot of the bed.

"Will Hollins be leaving in the morning?"

"Yes. Provided her blood count's okay."

Jill looked pensive. "I'll do her hemoglobin, if that's all
right. I'd like to see her again."

"Be my guest." David reached out and changed the
position of two of the charts in Jill's lineup. "These are

Warner and Tarasov," he said. "Two miscarriages from
last week." He placed them next to the Hollins chart. She
surveyed the line of charts and sat back thoughtfully on her
heels.

"There's too much here for now. I'm just going to take
down all the names and chart numbers. Tomorrow I'll
study them more carefully." David rested his head on his
folded arms, and closed his eyes. "Are they all miscarriages?" she asked.

"No." His voice was muffled. "Chang isn't. I thought
you'd be interested in that one. It happened about ten days
before you came."

"Who? What?"

"This one." He opened his eyes and picked up the last
chart, teetering on the foot of the bed.

"Sheri Chang," he said. "Her child was a stillborn."
He seemed to come awake as he held the chart. He regarded it for a long moment, remembering, then placed it
back on the bed.

Jill opened her notebook and began copying the information she needed. She wrote each patient's name, number and diagnosis at the top of a different page. She
flipped the pages of each chart, moving down the length of
the bed as she worked.

"These done?" David indicated a group near the pillow.

"Yes. Till tomorrow. My knees hurt."

"I recommend bed rest." David got up and began
stacking the charts. Minutes later she was finished. David
carried the pile out into the hall, where she heard him stop
a nurse and ask her to return the charts to the eighth floor.
When he returned he found Jill straightening the sheets and
fluffing the pillow.

He closed and locked the door. He held up his watch.
"Eleven-fifteen," he said. "Anyone plan on sleeping around
here?"

"Only if you stay," she said, and smiled.

He embraced her, careful not to hurt the site of her
laceration. He pulled her down onto the bed, and then

reached up to turn off the lamp. She snuggled under his chin.

"David?"

"Hmpf?"

"I've got a question."

Silence. Then: *"What?"*

"Um . . . how do you go about conducting an investigation into something like this? I mean, where do you begin?"

He was silent for another moment. Moonlight streamed in through the window, and outside in the parking lot he heard the wail of an arriving ambulance. He rolled over onto his back, and put his arm under his head.

"Well." He breathed in resignation. "First, you have to define exactly what the 'something like this' is. What is it that you've been seeing?"

In the darkness, Jill frowned. "Pronounced increase in the rate of maternal death, spontaneous abortions, stillbirths, and fetal monstrosities."

"Okay," he said softly. "Fine. Next you look for patterns of causative factors. You look for drugs, or radiation exposure, or chemical pollution in the water. Look for geographical clusters—who knows, maybe it'll turn out that all of these women lived or spent time at Love Canal, or near a Nevada test site, or—"

"David! Mary Hollins spent time in Nevada!"

"On her honeymoon. Six years ago. Phipps already checked that out."

"Oh." Jill was silent. In the darkness he could sense her disappointment.

He turned back toward her. He pulled her to him and kissed her. "Any more questions?" he asked. With his right hand he stroked her cheek.

"No." She put her arms around his neck. "Oh, David, you've been so wonderful!"

He caressed her, tugging upward on the top of her scrub suit.

She pulled back. "What if the damn phone rings? I'm on call."

"If you get called, I'll go with you. You've had one hell of a day."

"But—"

"No buts," he whispered, kissing her. "Listen, in your shape—what if you have to deliver twins?"

The phone did not summon them till nearly four hours later.

28

IT SEEMED TO Jill that the newest pressure was time. All through patient rounds on Thursday morning Jill was tense, and tried to get Greenberg and Donovan to move faster. They loved making small talk with the patients, and seemed puzzled by her fidgeting. They were more puzzled still when she asked to do Hollins alone.

"Suit yourself," Woody said. With Tricia looking on, he flipped through the pages of the Hollins chart. "She has to have her hemoglobin checked. She lost a fair amount of blood."

Jill said, "I know. I plan to do it."

"Don't discharge her till you get the report back," Tricia said. "God, is she in a hurry to get out of here!"

"Can you blame her?" said Woody. "Okay, kid"—he handed Jill the chart—"you're on your own." He smiled at her.

Jill watched them go. From a supply closet she loaded some things onto a sterile table and wheeled it toward room 828. She checked her watch before entering. It was 8:17.

She knocked at the partially opened door. "Mrs. Hollins?"

Mary Hollins, in a chiffon robe, looked up. Jill was surprised to see her setting out her clothes on a bedside armchair—a white linen skirt, a plum-colored silk blouse, underwear.

"My getaway outfit," Hollins said, continuing her packing.

Jill pushed the sterile table alongside. She frowned: What do you say in such circumstances? She hated lame, consoling clichés that never made anyone feel better. She decided to say exactly what she felt.

"You'll be back," she said, looking at Hollins. "In six months you'll already be back for prenatal care. Maybe less. Why, there are women here—"

Hollins shook her head. "No, I couldn't take it." She sat heavily on the edge of the bed, as if the act of laying out clothes had left her exhausted. "I'm just tired of feeling like a walking laboratory," she said.

Jill's hand stopped in midair as it reached for an otoscope. *Walking laboratory?*

She turned slowly. "Mrs. Hollins, do you suppose we can do a predischarge exam? It will be brief, I promise."

The patient became compliant. "Please call me Mary," she said taking off her robe and sinking back dejectedly against the pillows.

"Okay, Mary." Jill smiled.

She helped the patient back under the covers, pulled the sheet up to her hips and raised the hospital gown to breast level. Putting the stethoscope to her ears, she listened to the heart and lungs, checked the abdomen and palpated the uterus. It had contracted nicely. Hollins showed no reaction until she saw Jill reaching for a five cc syringe.

"What's *that?*" she said, looking alarmed.

"Hemoglobin test," Jill said, already snapping the rubber tourniquet onto the woman's arm. "You lost some blood. We can't discharge you until we're sure you're not anemic."

"No!" Hollins' body went rigid. "Not another needle! I'll lose my sanity!"

Jill lowered her chin and peered up at the patient with calm, authoritative eyes. It was a gesture she had learned from the older doctors. Many swore it had a steadying effect.

"No, you won't," she said.

"I can't watch," Mary Hollins said weakly.

The tourniquet was tightly in place. "Open and close your fist," Jill ordered. The veins on the inside of Hollins' elbow bulged. Jill stroked the area with an alcohol sponge, and placed the needle on the skin surface. The patient's body stiffened. "Easy now," Jill breathed. She gave a deft push; the needle flashed and then popped its way in. An instant later the syringe began filling with dark blood.

"One second more," Jill said. Hollins was rigid. Her head was turned away and her eyes were shut.

"Done." Jill first removed the tourniquet, then the syringe, and placed them on the sterile table. Hollins turned back to her with open eyes and inhaled with relief.

"And now, there's just one more thing I have to do—"

"*What's that?* I thought you were—"

"It's nothing. I just want to take a look at your throat. It'll take a sec."

"Whew, is that all?" Hollins looked relieved again.

Jill took a tongue depressor, told the woman to say "Ah," and peered in. "Hmm," she said, then "Hmm," again. As she withdrew the tongue depressor, she gently scraped the edge of the wooden blade against the inside of the cheek. She casually slid the blade into a transport pack—a thin, plastic envelope about eight inches long—and closed it. Hollins failed to notice that Jill did not place the pack on the sterile table, but continued to hold it, tight, between her fingers.

She gave a warm but hurried goodbye. Then she pushed the sterile table to the doorway, where she turned and gave a thumbs up sign to Mary Hollins.

Jill dropped off the blood sample and raced up to Pathol-

ogy. Peter Gregson was nowhere in sight. She took a
culture plate off the rack, and removing the lid, dragged
the tongue depressor, still wet with mucosal cells, across
the amber-colored nutrient. She replaced the lid, labeled it
and inserted the plate inside the incubator, next to the skin
specimens of Sayers and Moran.

With trembling fingers she slammed the door.

Inside, the living cells of Mary Hollins responded to
their new environment by stepping up their metabolism.
Several, when taken from their donor, had already been
primed for cell division. Before Jill had even left the
room, their chromosomes had begun to move.

Sam MacIntyre called to Jill when she reached the eighth
floor. He was scowling as usual.

"How's your forehead?" he said in a rush. "Listen, I
want you to go down to X ray for me. There's a hystero-
salpingogram I want you to check, the right Fallopian
especially, plus another film—see, this lady's expecting
twins but her belly's *too* big, so check the skeletal
structure of the babies. I think one's head-down and the
other's head-up, but check anyway"—he pushed a piece of
paper at her—"and here are the two patients' names."

"No," Jill said.

"What?" MacIntyre looked as if he hadn't heard right.

She raised her hands in a pleading gesture. "Sam,
please understand. There's something else I have to do.
It's important. Couldn't you get someone else to go down?"

"No, dammit!" His face reddened. "Anyway, what's
so important that you can't take ten lousy minutes to run
down to X ray?"

"I have to go over some charts."

"Holloway already did chart rounds!"

"Different charts."

"From a different hospital, right?" MacIntyre's voice
became exasperated. "Jill, what in Hell's Bells are you up
to now? And where by the way were you ten minutes ago?
You left the floor, right? Jesus, we had an admission!"

Jill looked at him fondly. "And you covered for me, right?"

He wagged his finger at her. "Ba-a-d intern."

"Sam, I swear I'll make it up to you. Anyway, if I'm so terrible why did you rate my performance to Stryker as superior?" Stryker had admitted as much two days earlier in her confrontation with the Genetic Committee.

She let the question hang in the air as she gave a little wave and headed for the nurses' station. MacIntyre watched her, still red-faced, then hollered, "I lied!"

Jill thought: Is there *any* place where you can be alone around here?

Three minutes later she was wheeling the charts under a pile of towels into the shower section of the women doctors' lounge. On a long wooden bench she arranged the charts in a stack, with the ones which had troubled David on top. She began with them.

At first glance, the cases of Tarasov and Chang—one a miscarriage, the other stillborn—were random and unconnected. The women were relatively young, with benign medical histories. Neither smoked, used drugs, or had suffered fever in early pregnancy. They came from different social backgrounds. They had had different physicians.

Different *delivering* physicians, that is.

Jill turned a page, and dug deeper.

Tarasov had been a clinic patient; Chang a private patient, treated initially in the Sturdevandt wing. Jill chewed on her ballpoint. Well, the fact that a woman had been a patient of any doctor on the Genetic Counseling Committee didn't necessarily mean anything. Those doctors saw regular patients as well as high-risk cases. Indeed, Jill knew that in Manhattan it was a status symbol to say that your obstetrician was William Stryker or Ben Rosenberg or Clifford Arnett. They had been written about so much in the newspapers. Their private practices were a magnet for wealthy women.

Jill turned back to the Tarasov report. She was turning pages slowly when something caught her eye. A messy scrawl on the bottom of a green page reporting that on April 2 Tina Tarasov had come in ''demanding''—that was the wording—a second pregnancy test.

Jill stared at the page. Now why would anyone ''demand'' a second pregnancy test?

Maybe if she *doubted* the first . . . if the pregnancy had taken her completely by surprise . . .

The door behind her swung open, and horse-faced Carole Shelton appeared, wearing a flowered shower cap and carrying body lotion.

Jill looked up at her. *Oh damn,* she thought.

''Well! Of all places to be doing charts! Really! Are charts *supposed* to be worked on in here?''

''I thought it was going to be quiet,'' Jill said testily.

''Quiet, maybe,'' Shelton said. ''But it's going to get *steamy.*'' She nosed closer. ''What charts *are* they, by the way?''

''They've been stolen from the Pentagon,'' said Jill.

Shelton turned with a snort of disgust and disappeared into the shower. Billows of steam began to pile out. Carole Shelton was the only intern who actually got coverage just to take a shower. Long showers were necessary, she insisted; short ones did not clean the pores.

Place is getting hot, Jill thought. Back to business.

Let's see. So Tarasov came in ''demanding'' a second pregnancy test on April 2 . . .

She did some rapid calculations. Tarasov had miscarried on July 12, at four months' gestation. Jill leafed back through the pages to find the date of Tarasov's initial visit. March 10—sure enough, right around ovulation time—and felt a prickly sensation rise on the back of her neck.

But there was more. On the exam report Jill found that Tarasov had undergone a cervical mucous exam. Jill frowned. *Just like Mary Jo Sayers,* she thought. An unusual test, neatly tucked in with all the other routine tests . . . nobody would notice . . .

And Tarasov and Sayers had been clinic patients.

Jill went through some other charts. Chang's reports were in a surprising jumble, considering she was a private patient. Several pages were out of order, and lab tests ordered had not come back.

Or *had* they come back? And been removed?

The steam was getting thick and pages were beginning to curl. Frustrated, Jill piled up the charts and carried them back to the nurses' station. On the way she reviewed facts she had noticed just before having to stop. She had found a note, in the wrong place, stating that on November 24 Sheri Chang had undergone . . . something, but there was no telling what, since the rest of the line had been inked out.

Could it have been the same test that Sayers and Tarasov had undergone? The cervical mucous exam? But that was a prefertility test! There was no indication on the charts that these women had requested it. Jill bit her lip. She wanted to call someone higher up, ask if there were any other indications for it, and what was it being administered for?

Then she realized that there weren't many hospital higher-ups whom she trusted. David was showing around a group of third-year med students who were beginning their OB clerkship. And Sam MacIntyre was down in X ray at the moment, mad at her.

Who else?

Arnett?

Arnett had said to drop by, if there was ever anything she wanted to talk about, and he *had* pretty much rescued her at Strykers inquisition.

No, not yet. She'd have to find out a lot more before she approached the likes of Clifford Arnett.

Her mind went back to Sheri Chang. The Chang infant had died stillborn on June 20, after a seven month and seemingly normal pregnancy. Jill mentally calculated: November 24, the date of whatever inked-out procedure that Chang had undergone, was exactly seven months before the premature birth that ended in tragedy . . .

She reached the nurses' station, deposited the stack on the counter, and stood back disconsolately to survey it. There had only been time to go through the Tarasov and Chang charts, which left at least a dozen she hadn't gotten to. Then one name—Warner, a miscarriage David had mentioned last night—came suddenly to her. She looked around. No one threatening was near, and the nurses behind the counter were busy with other things.

She pulled out the Warner chart, tore through it—and again found irregularities.

Jill scribbled down three addresses and phone numbers in her notebook. Warner lived on Fifth Avenue; Tarasov lived in Greenpoint, a part of Brooklyn Jill had never heard of; Sheri Chang lived in Chinatown.

Done. Jill slid the chart pile off the counter and handed it to a student nurse. "Will you take these back down to the record room? I'd appreciate it if you'd hurry. They're waiting for them."

"Sure thing," the student nurse said with a smile. And Jill thought: Isn't it wonderful. Nobody around here ever asks who "they" are.

Mrs. Anna Romero didn't show up for her 11:40 clinic appointment, but Mrs. Chichi Miranda *did*—at 11:46 in hard labor. She had to be rushed up to delivery, which left Jill unexpectedly with two empty time slots, and enough time to tend to some important business.

In a phone booth opposite the coffee shop Jill called the Fifth Avenue residence of Mrs. Caroline "Sunny" Warner. She wasn't surprised when a butler-sounding voice answered. "Wohnah residence."

Jill stated who she was and where she was calling from. "May I speak with Mrs. Warner?" she asked.

The nasal voice informed her that madame was resting; would the caller care to speak to the housekeeper, Mrs. Kenworthy?

"I've got it, Thomas," came a sudden, rasping voice. Jill realized that another extension had been picked up. The butler voice muttered something and clicked off.

She hesitated. "Is this Mrs. Warner?"

"Sometimes," said the voice, and then let loose with a wild bray of laughter. Jill was too taken aback to respond.

The laughter subsided, and the voice resumed its tipsy decorum.

"I was *eaves*dropping. You're calling from Madison Hospital and you're Dr. *who?*"

"Raney," said Jill. "I wanted—"

"Well! Aren't you the dear heart! Called to find out how poor little me is doing?"

"Mrs. Warner, I'm sorry, but I have to talk fast and I'm hoping that you'll be able to help me. I've been doing a follow-up study of your miscarriage, trying to understand what might have affected its course, and I find that the information on your chart is incomplete or confusing. For example, there's a—"

"Incomplete? Of course it's incomplete."

For a moment Jill thought she hadn't heard right. "I don't understand," she said.

Mrs. Warner was silent for a moment, then said, "Oh, what the hell. Listen, that's how Dr. Stryker protects his patients. Their *privacy,* I mean. You know, anyone who's had in vitro fertilization or even artificial insemination, like I did, gets hounded by everybody from press to relatives and—"

"You had *artificial insemination?*"

"Yes. Not so *loud.* It'll be in Suzy Knickerbockers column by morning, for God's sakes!"

Jill was thunderstruck. Throughout her training she had been taught to believe what she read in charts—to assume that all objective data had been collected and was *there.* But this . . . It couldn't be called unethical, since there was no deliberate falsification. It was just—what had the woman called it?—omission for the sake of patient privacy.

Jill closed her eyes. How many other prenatal records were worthless?

"The worst is the *sensationalism,*" Mrs. Warner was saying. Her voice was slurred. "So do you know what that dear man does? He even meets with his patients after hours—you know, at night. There's a private entrance and it's *nobody's business* who comes and goes."

"That certainly is dedication," Jill murmured.

"Yes, well, frankly, I'm overdue for a little TLC in my life." She was becoming garrulous. "I divorced two jocks because they were skirt-chasers. Well, hah, good news and bad news. Husband number three leaves the little girls alone, but he's got a low sperm count. He—"

"Another question," Jill interrupted. "In the course of your treatment were you seen by any other members of the Genetic Counseling Committee?"

"Of *course.*" A pause. Time out for what must have been a long pull, a swallow, then: "They all have a go at you. Dr. Rosenberg did the epidemiology and Simpson did the genetic background study . . . I have *terrific* luck, you know that? There's muscular dystrophy up my family tree! Most common in families of northern European background. Isn't that just peachy?"

"And what about Arnett. Did you see him, too?"

"Sure. But he only did the amniocentesis. I'm thirty-six, thash why."

"I have to hang up now," Jill said. "Many thanks for all your help."

"Quite welcome. I might even meet you there one of these days."

"You'll be coming back?"

"As long as Dr. Stryker will have me, of *course* I'll be coming back. The man is a *god*. Well, thanks for calling."

Jill hung up.

It was 12:10. She rushed back to finish her clinic duty.

The next free time slot was gained by skipping lunch, which enabled her to visit the Cytology lab. The place was bustling. Long counter tops were lined with technicians bent over microscopes. Refrigerator and incubator doors clicked open and slammed closed. Bottles—tier upon tier of them—glinted blue and purple and red. The hum of a centrifuge stirred the air.

Jill approached an open-faced young technician. "Would you have a minute?" she asked.

The technician looked up from the sink she was rinsing and glanced at Jill's name tag.

"Sure," she smiled. "You from Pathology?"

"Obstetrics," Jill said.

"Oh," said the technician, wiping her hands. "We get plenty of them, too."

A moment later they were standing before the Cytology computer terminal. "What I need," Jill said, reading from her black book, "are the results of some cervical mucous exams done on a series of women." She read off the names of Moran, Sayers, Hollins, Warner, Tarasov and Chang.

"You've come to the right place," said the technician. "Got their unit numbers?"

"Yes. Here's the list." She held open the notebook.

She watched as the young woman keyed in the six patients' names, then added their unit numbers and the code for the cervical mucous test. There was a silence of several seconds, then brightly lit letters began to march across the screen. First the name Maria Moran appeared and the machine spewed out the information:

CYTOLOGY MEMORY UNIT RECORDS NO SUCH PATIENT OR EXAMINATION.
RESPONSE: NEGATIVE.

"What?" said Jill. "There must be some—"

But already the machine was clacking out the names of Mary Jo Sayers and Mary Hewitt-Hollins:

MEMORY UNITS RECORD NO SUCH PATIENTS OR EXAMINA-TIONS . . .

"There's something the matter with your computer," Jill said tonelessly.

"Nope. Never sick a day. Wait a sec, here comes the rest."

The names of Warner, Tarasov and Chang appeared on the screen. The message following them was the same:

MEMORY UNITS RECORD NO SUCH . . .

"Turn it off," Jill said.

The technician did. "Are you sure you've requested the right test?" she asked. "There's no record of it being made for any of these women, but maybe if you—"

"Could any other lab have done this procedure?"

"No," said the technician, covering the console. "Only this lab. Always. Same with Pap smears, breast biopsies, pleural taps, sputum specimens to look for lung cancer—"

The young woman broke off as she saw the expression on Jill's face.

Tightly Jill said, "Run the same names through again. See if you have any record of their blood types."

"I can't do that," the technician said, taken aback. "For that, you'd have to go to Hematology and use *their* access code. *Our* only access to the main computer bank is limited to Cytology data."

Jill watched her, nodded slowly. "I get it," she said. "And Radiology only knows Radiology's access code . . . and so on. Right?"

"Right."

"Blind men and the elephant," Jill murmured.

"What?"

Jill did not answer. It was just dawning on her that the whole hospital computer system was a hoax: a collection of private lines with unlisted numbers, each department jealously protective of its own internal secrets.

She looked at the covered console, thinking. "So only those cleared for *total* access can extract any information they want."

"You got it," said the technician, clasping her hands. "Only the top brass have the Master Code—they can ask it any questions they want to."

The two began walking toward the door. Jill said, "I wonder how somebody could get hold of that Master Code?"

"Easy," said the technician, smiling brightly. "Steal it!"

At 1:30 Jill went on rounds led by Willard Simpson.

Simpson seemed to be watching her, singling her out from the other interns every time a difficult question came up. If he was surprised when she answered well, he didn't show it. He would nod and then lead the group to the next patient. As if he's keeping an invisible score card, Jill thought.

Or a report card for Stryker?

When rounds were over Simpson called her aside. "Glad to see you're back on the straight and narrow," he said.

Jill looked into his eyes and smiled. "Why Dr. Simpson," she said. "I'm working harder than ever!"

At 2:30, with her beeper in her pocket, Jill sat in the anteroom of Cliff Arnett's office, looking around. Jill glanced at books and framed snapshots, an antique lamp. For a moment she stared absently at a thick red and white book on the bottom of a messy pile, and then she sighed.

"Do you think Dr. Arnett will be much longer?" she asked his secretary.

The secretary looked at her watch. "My goodness," she said. "He should definitely be finished by now, but you know how these things go. Just think: three tubal ligations back to back—quite a lot of surgery in one go."

"Is that how he schedules them? In bunches like that?"

The secretary opened a box of paper clips. "Has to," she said. "It's becoming the most in-demand procedure." Noting Jill's quizzical glance, she gave a matronly smile and went on. "I suppose with all this controversy about conception and when does life *really* begin, women are feeling troubled about which birth control method is . . . the most moral. Tubal ligation wins hands down, of course. Tying the tubes prevents fertilization in the *first* place, so everyone can relax. Except our poor doctor, of course."

"Mmm," said Jill, stifling a yawn. "By the way, that's a marvelous *aspidistra* you have there."

The secretary looked up, beaming. "Oh, you think so? Why, thank you! In three years it has *never* failed me. It's tough, and *look* how the leaves shine. I don't even polish them!"

Jill smiled. "I can tell you love plants," she said. And then she looked sad. "It's too bad about the *syngonium*, though, isn't it?"

The secretary looked concerned. "The *syngonium*? Not the one out in the hall . . ."

"Dry as a bone," Jill said gravely. "When I passed it just now, I swear I heard a tiny voice crying 'wa-ter.' " She made a pained expression.

The secretary jumped to her feet. "Oh, those cleaning women!" She grabbed a plastic watering can. "All they know how to do is empty wastebaskets. I've told them and *told* them to check that all hallway plants are watered."

Jill watched as the woman disappeared into an adjoining washroom. There was the sound of splashing water, then she reappeared, trying not to spill as she hurried toward the door.

"Be back in a jiff," she said. "It's the one by the elevator, right?"

"Yes, better hurry."

Jill waited till the anxious footsteps retreated down the hall. It was a distance of about sixty feet, she calculated.

She crossed to the desk, lifted the pile of books and periodicals and placed them in the center. Her hands were trembling. She pulled out her black memo book, and opened the red and white International Classification of Diseases Adapted book. Toward the front she found the "Directory of Access Codes" of all Madison Hospital departments. Too many to copy, she knew, but no matter. Furiously, she copied only the Master Code. It was all she needed.

Now: backwards! She closed the ICDA book, moved the tower of debris back onto it, and pushed the tottering stack back to the desk corner.

She raced to her chair and sat, heart whamming, just as Arnett's secretary came rushing back in. She had a curious expression on her face.

"Well, I watered it," she said. "But you know? It didn't look so dry to me."

Jill was breathing almost too rapidly to talk. "*Syngonium* needs m-more water than people think . . ."

Forget it.

She stood up. "It's 2:45. I guess I can't wait any longer for Dr. Arnett. Would you please tell him I stopped by?"

"I'm so sorry," the secretary said. "Is there any message I can give him?"

Jill looked back at the tangle of leaves on the secretary's desk.

"Not really," she said. "I came to ask his help in an important matter, but while I've been sitting here I guess I worked things out for myself."

The secretary beamed approvingly. "My, aren't you an enterprising girl!"

"We'll see," Jill muttered. And then she turned and left.

29

WHERE WAS JILL?

David had failed to see her at lunch and with a troubled feeling connected her absence with an earlier glimpse he had had of her, around 10:26, running like a shot down the hall toward the clinic.

Nobody *ever* ran to the clinic.

Unless they were very late, coming from some hospital activity that was not part of the schedule.

It was now almost 3:00. David sprawled in an easy chair in the eighth floor lounge checking his schedule sheet. Jill had been terrific today—she hadn't missed one minute of conference or clinic or ward duty. Simpson himself had gruffly pronounced her "back to normal, and see that you keep her that way," after his 1:30 rounds.

But why did she disappear *between* chores? David looked around at the relaxing interns and residents. Some were drinking coffee; Greenberg and Holloway were reading different sections of the *New York Times*, and Ortega was dozing on the sagging couch.

When it was lull time in OB, you learned to grab it—except that Jill . . .

His words came back to him:

"I suppose what you do with your free time is your business, and if it will get this thing off your mind . . ."

"And get me back on the track," she had cried. *"I'll be a normal intern again!"*

David frowned now, figuring things out. So she was *making* free time—skipping meals, running around God knows where . . . The strange thing was, the hospital's conventional investigation methods had turned up nothing so far in those bizarre cases. Jill's discovery in Pathology was the most dramatic thing yet . . . and still it wasn't enough. Those two cases *could* be freaks . . .

David felt torn. He wanted to defend her, yet he didn't want to see her jeopardize her career—jeopardize his own standing, for that matter—for something which might only be a wild-goose chase and damage both of them.

Should I have her paged? he thought. No, don't bother her. She's probably upstairs looking at her bugs in Pathology. Relax, that's where she must be.

So why do I still feel so nervous?

When the taxi pulled away from the curb, Jill didn't look up. She was busy with her black notebook, checking off a list she had made in her memo book. She had arranged coverage with Tricia for the next two hours; she had left a message for David that she'd be back around five (it was now 3:10), along with a cryptic note to look at the Hollins culture; and she had reached Sheri Chang, who sounded reluctant to speak on the phone but had given her Chinatown address and agreed to meet there.

Chang, in fact, had said the timing would be perfect. Jill had called at her place of work: a St. Agnes School-for-something-or-other, where Sheri Chang was a teacher. Her pupils, enrolled for the summer, would be getting dismissed at the time that Jill would arrive.

The taxi driver was confused by the maze of streets, so Jill asked to get off at Pell Street, where she would ask directions. She walked down the busy thoroughfare and looked at the signs in Chinese, the exotic-smelling markets, and the people. Most of all, the people. When she was sure she had lost her bearings she turned into a small import shop.

The place was a dark, narrow aisle squeezed by counters jammed with silk embroidery, boxes of tea, and carved ivory arcs with little elephants walking over bridges. Chimes tinkled; the smell of incense was heavy. Jill approached a young man who stood behind one of the counters, adding up columns of figures.

He looked up. "Yes?"

"Would you help me, please? There's a school near here called St. Agnes', on Doyer Street. Only trouble is, I can't find Doyer Street."

The young man smiled. "Right across," he pointed. "Don't blink, you'll miss it."

A moment later Jill was crossing into the narrow, winding street, looking for numbers.

She walked until she saw a building with children streaming out—little girls in plaid skirts and white blouses, boys in navy pants and white shirts. Across the lintel read the inscription, St. Agnes School for the Artistically Gifted.

Artistically gifted? Sheri Chang was a teacher of artistically gifted children?

Two older women were supervising the lines, and between them stood a pretty young woman who looked to be in her late twenties. She was wearing a navy blue skirt and filmy white blouse. She kissed several children as they left, and her eyes followed them as they headed down the street.

Jill approached. "Hello," she said. "Are you Sheri Chang? I called before. I'm Dr. Raney."

They shook hands and Jill followed the teacher back into the building. In a classroom Sheri Chang sat behind her desk and Jill took a chair facing her.

"I've been studying your case." Jill chose her words carefully. "What is so puzzling about the . . . outcome is that there was nothing preceding it to indicate trouble. According to your chart, the fetal signs were all running normal. *Everything* seemed normal. I—"

The schoolteacher's voice was soft and hesitant. "I'm thirty-five," she said, as if that in itself were an explanation. She went on haltingly, telling how she and her husband had been married for six years before deciding to have a child. "Separate careers, very modern," she said ruefully. Jill was about to protest when Sheri Chang's voice became suddenly stronger.

"We tried for the next two years but—nothing. Couldn't get pregnant, so a friend suggested Madison Hospital. The . . . infertility clnic."

"You were Dr. Stryker's patient?"

"Yes. He discovered that I had blocked Fallopian tubes, and performed an in vitro fertilization." Chang shook her head. "I cannot describe to you our joy when we found that the implantation had been successful. That I was pregnant . . ."

Jill nodded slowly. "I can imagine," she said.

Sheri Chang folded her hands, as if in prayer. "We have *such* faith in Dr. Stryker. He did everything. He induced my ovulation with hormones. He did that ultrasound thing . . . monitoring the ovarian follicle growth, you call it?"

Jill smiled. "You've been doing your homework."

"Not homework. Obsession. That man is everything to us. Yes, we grieve, but"—she opened her palms—"at least he *proved* that we can be fertile! Do you know what that *means?*"

Jill was pensive. "You said that Dr. Stryker induced your ovulation with hormones. Do you know which ones?"

"No. He said they were new. The very latest drugs."

Jill made a mental note to try to find out what those drugs were.

They talked for another five minutes. Had Sheri Chang's husband worked in any environment containing pollutants or chemicals? No, he was a lawyer. Jill pressed on with the other standard questions: Chang had had frequent fetal monitoring; an amniocentesis performed by Arnett; a family gene study done by Simpson, all the usual things. Nothing seemed out of the ordinary.

Except for the matter of the "new drugs"; and the fact that Chang's in vitro fertilization had never appeared on her records, like Sunny Warner's artificial insemination; and that finally, eyes shining, Chang referred to Stryker as "a god." Again, like Warner.

And then, in the same breath, Sheri Chang mentioned the Infant School.

Jill looked up. "The Infant School? You know about that?"

The teacher looked surprised. "Why, yes. All of Stryker's children go to the Infant School. They get signed up practically on the day of conception. It's a *privilege*"—she looked away—"provided they make it to term."

Jill stared at her. "Stryker's children?" she echoed. A sense of beforeness touched her.

Chang smiled faintly. "I guess that's something the mothers say among themselves. And thank heavens for *them*. It's a wonderful support group. We attend class together—"

"Class?"

"Yes. An informal discussion group, really, but Dr. Stryker wants to prepare us for being mothers of children in the Infant School. You see"—her voice became faraway—"Dr. Stryker's philosophy is that it's not enough to cure infertility and correct birth defects. That's only the *beginning*, the physical aspect of life. But from the day of birth onward he wants to give every intellectual advantage *possible* to a baby. It's a privilege! *Think* how those children will be better able to cope with this increasingly complex world . . ."

Jill's sense of *déjà vu* was giving her goosepimples. "I see you've met Corrine Dewitt," she said, rubbing an arm.

Chang seemed not to have heard her. "Dr. Stryker's going to win a Nobel Prize for his work in perinatal research," Chang said. "Oh, I'm *sure* of it!"

"You're not alone there," Jill said, frowning. "It's just that I wasn't aware the Infant School was . . . part of the genetic counseling program. A graduate school, sort of."

"Oh, yes," said Sheri Chang, sweet-faced and smiling now. "All of Stryker's children," she said. "All of Stryker's children!"

From a pagoda-shaped phone booth at the corner of Mott and Pell, Jill called Tina Tarasov.

"Yes?" came a tense voice.

Jill explained who she was and why she was calling. "I wondered if you could shed some light—"

"My God, you've got a nerve! After what that hospital *did* to me you want to *interview* me? That's a laugh. Listen, if that place ever hears from me again it'll be when I sue—"

"Did to you?" It was very hot in the booth. Jill was sweating. "Mrs. Tarasov, please hear me out. I'm calling independently because I was mystified by your case. It will help others if you help me. *Please.*"

Tina Tarasov was silent for a moment, then said, "Oh, all right. You want to know what that hospital did to me? They got me *knocked up,* that's what! I happen to be sure of it!"

Jill stared unseeingly out at the traffic on Pell Street. "They . . . what?"

"Listen. My husband Alex and I are super—and—I— mean *super* careful. We're both twenty-four. It's too soon to start a family—in fact, the only reason I came to the hospital was for my annual physical and to ask about switching birth control methods." Her voice rose. "Something was *done* to me there, goddammit!"

"Your husband never knew . . . about the miscarriage?"

"The truth is, I was considering an abortion. Weeks passed, and I kept losing my nerve. I never told my husband, but I was a wreck." Tarasov gave a high-pitched laugh. "Then I miscarried at eleven weeks! How's that for irony? Alex was in Houston job-hunting at the time. When he got back I told him a hormonal imbalance had caused heavy bleeding. That happens to women all the time, doesn't it? I read about it in *Cosmopolitan*."

"Yes, it happens," Jill murmured. For a long moment she was silent. It was too incredible—Tarasov was the first patient who had *not* wanted to be pregnant.

Jill asked, "You wouldn't know if you had something called a cervical mucous test, would you?"

"A what?"

"Skip it." Sweat trickled down Jill's back. "Do you remember the names of any doctors who examined you? Not counting the second pregnancy test, there were two visits."

Tarasov gave a snort. "That clinic of yours is like Grand Central Station. One guy starts on you and he gets called away, and then someone else comes in—who can keep track?"

"Old or young?"

Tarasov thought. "The first one old—well, not *really* old—and then two younger ones. The older one wore glasses."

They *all* wear glasses, Jill thought.

"Hey, wait a minute!" Tina Tarasov said excitedly. "I do remember a couple of doctors. The two younger ones. One because he's mean. His name began with a *G*. . . ."

"Gacey?"

"Yes! Gacey. God, is he bad. When he examines, it *hurts*."

"And the other doctor?" Jill asked. She tried to flatten the tension in her voice.

Tarasov thought some more. "Can't recall the name but—tall. Very tall. And absolutely gorgeous."

"Levine?" Jill said, casually.

"Yeah! Levine! You know him?"

Jill thanked Tarasov for her help and hung up.

She thought for a moment, wiping her brow with the back of her hand, then began turning the pages of her address book. She found the number of Maria Moran's home in Queens, and dialed. A woman's voice answered, somber and tense. "Hello?"

Jill's voice was just as tense. "Hello, this is Dr. Raney from Madison Hospital and I'm *terribly* sorry to be calling you at this time—"

"I'm sorry," said the voice. "I can't talk to you. The"—a swallow—"the funeral's in less than an hour. I have to leave."

"Please. It's *about* Maria. If you could just answer *one* question. It's important."

Silence. Then: "I'm her sister, Mrs. Mastroianni."

Jill said, "Maria and her husband. Were they *trying* to have a baby? Or was the pregnancy unexpected?"

A long moment passed. Jill sensed the shock at the other end. "They were trying *not* to. Kevin—that's my brother-in-law—Kevin said they couldn't afford it yet." Another swallow. "And Maria liked her j-job." Jill heard the woman's voice crack.

"Mrs. Mastroianni, wasn't Maria *surprised?* Or upset? What was her reaction to hearing that she was pregnant?"

Other voices were in the room with Mastroianni. Jill heard someone calling to her, agitated. Then footsteps going away. Tensely the woman said, "I have to go now."

"What was their reaction? Please!"

Silence stretched for seconds. "They were surprised. Yes . . . upset. They even thought of . . . doing something about it."

"But they didn't—"

"No!" And now the voice burst into tears. "The priest told them it was the will of God!"

The line went dead. Jill slowly replaced the receiver. The time was 4:30.

30

THREE DOCTORS DESCENDED in the elevator together, the older two surprised that the meeting was to take place in the conference room next to the office of Howard Graham, the hospital director.

"Why there?" whined Sam MacIntyre. "Christ, I hate Graham. I haven't been down to Administration in six months."

"Maybe he's missed you," said David Levine. Woody Greenberg was fidgeting behind them and childishly counting backward as the car dropped past the floors. Nervously he said, "I'll bet it's the cops again. Hey, maybe they want to invite us to the policemen's ball!"

They want to play croquet on the lawn, Levine thought. He tensed and held up his watch.

It was 5:15. Why wasn't Jill back yet?

When they arrived at the assigned room, it was already crowded. William Stryker presided stiffly at the head of the table, flanked by Arnett, Rosenberg and Simpson, other members of the teaching staff and a scowling Howard Graham. Thomas Gacey and Stryker's junior attendings sat at the table, looking uneasy; behind them milled interns, residents, and nurses, looking bewildered.

The three newcomers stood near the door.

Woody nudged Levine with his elbow. "What did I tell you?"

Levine nodded. Like everyone else he was staring at Detective Gregory Pappas, standing to one side of Stryker at the head of the table. The detective's probing gaze watched everyone who entered the room, glancing only occasionally at his briefcase on the table. Behind his chair, with their backs to the wall, stood two uniformed policemen. One of them was resting a hand on his gun.

MacIntyre leaned past Levine and said to Woody, "I don't think they're here about the policemen's ball."

Peripherally Levine saw Tricia Donovan separate herself from a group of interns and elbow her way toward him. "David, is Jill back?"

He shook his head. "I've left word for her to come down as soon as she checks in."

Stryker stood, cleared his throat, and brought the room to order. Frostily he introduced Pappas, and sat down.

David checked the time again. 5:22. He glanced uneasily at the closed door. Damn, he thought. Stryker's going to notice that Jill's not here.

Pappas, hands in pockets and beginning to pace, launched into a rapid-fire police monologue, announcing that two recent homicides might be connected to this hospital, this department, and that he was opening a formal investigation.

David, stunned, looked at Pappas. *Two* homicides?

"Both pretty damned unusual," Pappas went on. "First"—he held up an index finger—"for those of you who don't already know, there's the case of Bonnie Lee Gaines, a five-months-pregnant teenaged prostitute seen once by your clinic, found strangled yesterday, her belly drained of all amniotic fluid."

Those who didn't know conveyed the fact by their expressions.

"The syringe used, by the way, was new," Pappas continued. "The puncture track was straight and clean. You won't find that with a junkie's needle. Also, the site of the puncture was found between the folds of the navel. Very clever, very professional. A lot of medical examiners would have missed a tiny mark like that." He stopped, considering the group. "Not ours."

Levine saw Woody and Sam look at each other. Reflexively he glanced up at the wall clock.

Where was Jill?

" . . . another one, also a prostitute, eighteen years old," Pappas was saying. "In this case the victim had no direct connection to the hospital, but it looks like it was the same guy using the same m.o.—"

"They need that explained," Stryker interrupted, as if he were talking about children.

"Okay. M.o. means method of operation. This morning, 6:00 A.M., harbor cops picked up a floater. About six months pregnant, no amniotic fluid, strangled like Gaines was. M.E.'s working on it now, but this one's harder. Been dead about two weeks."

Ben Rosenberg scowled and leaned forward. "You mean, dead and *floating in the water* for two weeks?"

"Yes," said Pappas. "In July."

He appeared uncertain for a moment, then rummaged through his briefcase. He pulled out a glossy, eight-by-ten photograph.

"This picture's only a preliminary," he said. "They have to, ah, reconstruct certain parts of the face. This hot weather, you know. Things decompose overnight." He turned to MacIntyre, who was standing with his back to the door.

"Doctor," he said, "you remembered Bonnie Gaines. Does the face of this victim look familiar to you?"

With a jerky movement Pappas held up the photograph.

Sam MacIntyre looked at it and turned red. "Chrissakes!" he said. "You expect me to identify *that*?"

"MacIntyre!" said Howard Graham sharply.

"It's a reasonable reaction," murmured Clifford Arnett, sitting next to Stryker.

Willard Simpson looked angry. "Detective Pappas," he said, "I'm afraid your whole premise is on the wrong track. There are a million junkies in this city, and not all of them have bent and rusted needles. Furthermore, there are about twenty thousand M.D.'s practicing in Manhattan alone. Why connect this business to Madison Hospital?"

Pappas looked at him and shook his head. "The murders of both these young women happened within blocks of this place. Victim number two, incidentally, was found floating not a hundred yards from Pier 70, which you can all see from this window.''

Instinctively, faces turned to look at the long window overlooking the East River.

David Levine's hands went cold. He rubbed them against each other, thinking: she's late because it's the rush hour. Hard to get a cab at this hour. Hard to . . . oh, hell. He began pushing his way toward the door, barely hearing the sudden barrage of questions, the angry rebuttals, the shouting voice of Gregory Pappas that carried above it all.

''For starters, I've got a list of people I'm going to have to question further, and the rest of you—keep your eyes open. Consider the neighborhood unsafe until further notice—especially for women. I'm putting more manpower onto the surrounding streets. Also at all of your entrances.''

He turned to Stryker. ''How many guards on your security force?''

Stryker said coldly, ''I assure you, our security is more than adequate—''

''We'll see about that.'' Pappas began picking up his things.

Levine eased behind MacIntyre, who turned and saw his friend's hand on the doorknob.

''What are you *doing?*''

''Leaving,'' said Levine thickly. ''Neighborhood's turning up murdered women and Jill's still out there. He yanked open the door and turning back saw Stryker frown at him. To David's surprise, it was not Stryker who called him back; it was Pappas.

''Oh, doctor,'' the detective said. ''Where are you off to? I had a few questions I wanted to ask you.''

''What?'' David stood in the doorway, annoyed and impatient.

Pappas corrected himself. ''Actually it wasn't just you I wanted to talk to. It was that young woman intern who was with you. Where *is* she, by the way?''

31

THINK, SHE COMMANDED herself. The cab is cool at least.

But her whirling mind refused to cooperate. There were too many pieces. Some fit, some didn't. Moran and Tarasov trying to *prevent* pregnancy. Tarasov convinced that something was "done" to her at the hospital. Misleading prenatal records. Warner and Chang trusting so blindly . . .

The taxi swung left and entered the heavy traffic on First Avenue. Jill, increasingly anxious, was half an hour late. It had been a mistake not to reckon on five o'clock traffic.

The Infant School . . . "new drugs" . . . The rapt expression on Sheri Chang's face: "*All* of Stryker's children . . ."

Which one of the older doctors *didn't* wear glasses?

She reached the hospital and hurried inside. Near the front desk she picked up a red phone beneath a sign that said HOSPITAL STAFF ONLY, and checked in with the page operator. She was told she had three messages: one logged at 4:48 from Dr. Levine, telling her to come straight to an all-department conference at 5:15; the other from Dr. Stryker, logged just nine minutes ago, demanding her immediate presence in the second floor office of Howard Graham.

"And the third message?" she asked, her voice shaking.

Sheri Chang had called at 5:05. She had just remembered something that could be important. Sheri had left her number and Jill was to call back.

Jill hung up and hurried toward the stairwell.

When she reached the second floor she stood in the hall watching as the obstetrical staff trooped out of the conference room next to Graham's office. Woody and Tricia rushed up when they saw her.

"Are you okay?" Tricia turned to Woody. "See? I told you she'd be back any minute!"

Woody glanced down at Jill's street clothes. "Trip took longer, huh?"

"I'll tell you about it later," Jill said. "I understand His Eminence is waiting to see me?"

"Yeah," said Woody. "He's got the brass in with him. And that detective."

"David's in there, too," said Tricia. "Lord, wait till you hear—"

"I'd better go," said Jill.

"We'll wait for you here," Woody called after her.

The atmosphere in the administration office was tense. Pappas sat in an upholstered chair, watching with an abstracted air as Levine and Thomas Gacey argued heatedly in a corner.

Jill wished she had taken a few minutes to change into a scrub suit. David turned and went to her, his face conveying both exasperation and relief. "Where have you been?" he said in low tones. "God, do you know what's been going *on* around here?" He was about to say more when he heard Stryker's voice behind him.

"Sit down," Stryker ordered Jill in a tight voice.

Jill sat. Levine stood at the back of her chair.

Stryker strode forward angrily. "Breaking rules again, eh, Jill?"

She looked at him.

"I . . ." She collected her thoughts, and decided suddenly that this whole scene was ridiculous. "I obtained proper coverage for a two hour absence, and was half an hour late. Is that why you've called an all-department meeting?"

Stryker glared at her, and turned to Gregory Pappas. "Perhaps you'd better tell Dr. Raney what you told us," he said.

Pappas did—beginning with the two murdered teenagers.

Jill stared at him. "No amniotic fluid?" she asked. "The *second* one, too?"

Pappas said, "There's more." He was silent for a moment, then abruptly changed his line of questioning.

"Dr. Raney," he said. "Last night when I was here . . . You're the one who was wearing the bandage, weren't you?"

She blinked. "Yes, I—"

"The bandage is gone. You heal fast or something?"

Jill wondered what he was getting at. "It was only a small laceration," she said. She pushed aside a strand of hair to show him. "It's already closed and the sutures—"

Pappas stood and began to pace. "Funny thing," he said. "Last night after we left, one of my men mentioned that he had helped into Emergency some lady doctor who had been attacked." He stopped pacing and looked directly at Jill. "Attacked in the Madison Museum. That was you, wasn't it?"

There was a stunned silence. Jill controlled herself with an effort and said, "Yes. I was attacked in the museum."

Out of the corner of her eye she saw Gacey and Stryker exchange glances.

"And why didn't you mention it to me then?" demanded Pappas.

Flustered, she began, "Well, just a common mugging. I didn't think—"

"Nonsense!" interrupted William Stryker.

All eyes turned to him.

"You see, Mr. Pappas," he said, "we've had a bad run of obstetrical mishaps recently. Some were tragedies. Dr. Raney here, like many an overzealous intern before her, has insisted on considering these tragedies as mysteries to be solved. One of the patients worked at the museum."

Gacey, wearing a sardonic smile, leaned on Graham's desk and said, "Mysteries to be solved. That's really too much, isn't it?"

Levine flared. "You're really concerned about the patients, aren't you, Gacey?"

The two looked ready to kill each other.

Stryker glared at Jill. "You were no doubt there asking the curator questions—in secret, of course. Isn't that correct?"

Jill looked at Stryker and felt a deep burning color spread across her cheeks. *Damn* that Pappas, she thought.

The anger she had been struggling to suppress erupted. "Mary Jo Sayers was not married!" she blurted. "This hospital *allowed* her to be kidnapped!"

She felt David's hand on her shoulder, saw Pappas pull a small notepad from his breast pocket and begin writing. She saw in Stryker's expression the astonishment and fury at being caught off guard.

Pappas finished writing and snapped his notepad shut. "*That* will take some looking into," he said. He seemed to remember something and turned to another tack.

"Oh, by the way," he said. "There's something minor I didn't mention at that meeting. The museum was troubled further during the night by a very strange theft." He looked around, sizing up reactions. "Apes," he said bluntly. "Well, not exactly apes. Those . . . you know, ancestor-of-man dummies?"

Jill leaned forward. "Hominids?"

"Yes, that's it. I'm told two hominids are missing. Now don't that beat all?" He looked directly at William Stryker, picked up his briefcase and headed for the door. With his hand on the knob he said, "We haven't linked the theft to the murders and Dr. Raney's attack, because, well, the hominids . . . that sort of thing is usually the work of vandals."

Levine looked incredulous. "You're saying that someone carried off two life-sized dummies from a burglar-proof museum?"

Pappas gave him a sunny smile. "Unless they walked off by themselves." He held up his watch. "Got to go. Alert your staff and tell everybody that by eight tonight this place"—he patted the door frame—"is going to be crawling with cops."

A moment later he was gone.

And several moments later William Stryker was coolly telling his colleagues why he thought department records should be immediately impounded.

"Impounded?" said Clifford Arnett. His eyebrows knotted together.

Jill stared at Stryker openmouthed. Impounded? Locked away? Her heart sank as she realized that she had given him the perfect excuse, had played right into his hands.

Stryker's voice rose. "The only way to approach this problem is to expand the investigation we've already begun. I want every chart from the past six months taken from the record room, scrutinized by the most highly trained staff members and *protected"*—he shot a furious look in Jill's direction—"from any further meddling and misinterpretation."

Jill sprang to her feet. "Cover-up!" she cried. Ignoring David's look of dismay, she took a step forward. "Sure, get there first and sift out anything that would imperil the reputation of the hospital . . . of *yourself,* for God's sake—"

She stopped, surprised at her own vehemence.

Clifford Arnett said mildly, "Jill wasn't meddling, Bill. And this idea of impounding charts won't work. There are thousands of them. It would take months."

Rosenberg said abruptly, "I think it's a good idea."

Simpson, glowering at Jill, said nothing; and Gacey sent her a nasty, self-congratulatory look.

Stryker looked at all of them and turned to Jill. To her astonishment his voice changed, and sounded very sad.

"And you, young lady. I am truly filled with regret. It was for your own good that I implored you to stop what you were doing. You ignored my requests. Your histrionics and your wild and unsubstantiated charges have placed our department in an intolerable situation." He hesitated. "Tomorrow I'm going to call a faculty-wide hearing to see that your internship here is terminated."

"No!" David said involuntarily.

"Yes," said Stryker.

Jill gripped the back of her chair with white-knuckled

hands. "You," she said to Stryker. "You're just *using* this police business to get me out of the way!"

Levine grabbed her by the arm and began pulling her toward the door. "Come on, Jill," he said.

She yanked her arm free and glowered at Stryker. "Do you actually think I'll disappear just like that? Well, I'm not going to! You may think you're God around here but there's no *way* you can—"

"Come *on!*"

Levine hustled her out, and with a loud bang the door slammed shut behind them.

32

IT WAS TEN o'clock, and sudden rain was pelting the window. Numbly, Jill watched droplets trickle down the darkened panes, then looked despondently into his face.

"Do you believe me?"

"Yes."

"Everything?"

"Yes. Shh, I can't hear. Open a few more buttons."

She unbuttoned her blouse all the way and tried to appear calm, a useless ruse, with David's stethoscope moving across her breast and pressing gently for the truth.

"Heart rate's still 110," he said. He pulled off his stethoscope, and reached from his chair across the bed where she was sitting for the blood pressure cuff.

Her eyes followed his. "You even believe about Tarasov?"

"I believe that what she told you is what *she* believes."

David stopped and looked at her. "Those were her exact words? The pregnancy was *done* to her—here?"

"Verbatim. Chang called me back, you know that? She said there was something important she had forgotten to tell me."

David pushed her sleeve above her elbow and wrapped the blood pressure cuff around her arm. Adjusting the stethoscope again, he pumped up the mercury with his left hand, listened over the brachial artery inside her left elbow, then let the pressure hiss down. He was frowning.

"Don't say it," she said.

"160 over 95," he said.

She shrugged. "I could have told you that."

"Wise guy." David undid the cuff. He tossed it into a nearby armchair and got up to pace the room. He stood by the window looking out at the rain. "I went up to check on Mary Hollins' cultures," he said.

She looked up sharply. "And?"

"Nothing," he said, leaning on the sill. "No resemblance at all to the abnormalities of Sayers and Moran." Absently he gazed down at a very small light, bobbing and tossing its way up the blackened river. Brave little boat, he thought. That's the way it is, isn't it? Upriver in the dark in the rain—alone. And then he thought: no, not alone, thank God. He turned around.

Jill's hands covered her face. She was crying.

"No, don't." He crossed to the bed and put his arm around her. "Listen," he said. "Sayers and Moran make two, and that's *still* pretty damn bizarre." He stroked her hair. "It's . . . enough. Tomorrow I'm planning to make it exhibit A when Stryker's little sideshow gets under way. We can point a few fingers *too*, you know. They're going to look like a bunch of jackasses when they find out what you've discovered."

Her glistening face looked up at him. "I'm not going to *be* here tomorrow! Didn't you hear what he said? And I've messed you up royally, too. David, I'm so sorry."

He held her tighter. "Jill," he said firmly. "You have

not screwed me up and you *are* going to be here tomorrow. And—''

"But he's so *powerful!*''

"Who *cares!* Listen, what's the worst possible thing that could happen to us? We'll get thrown out of this pressure palace, and we'll find ourselves a nice little hospital in the boonies, and we'll deliver babies for poor people. And you know something? That would be very nice! It would be *damned* nice to feel appreciated for a change!''

"Oh David," she said, very softly, and for a moment he thought that things seemed right again. Her arms went around his neck, her self-control seemed to be returning . . .

And then he sensed the change. It was as if he could feel the fear pumping back into her. Her slow breathing halted; through the closeness of their chest walls he felt the new thudding of her heart.

He pulled back to study her face. "Jill—''

"Don't you realize," she said, her face strained and anxious, "that somebody is getting away with *murder* around here?''

He felt his shoulders sag. He loosened his grip around her waist and looked at her. "You're really obsessed, aren't you?''

She dropped her gaze. "I can't help it," she said.

"Okay," he said quietly. "Okay. Tomorrow we wage bloody hell warfare, but tonight, I'm going to be on call and you, babe, have to get some sleep.''

She shook her head. "*I* should sleep? Last night you slept three hours because you got up to help *me*.''

"I'll survive." He reached out to turn off the lamp. In the dark he said, "Anyway, the phone hasn't rung yet, has it?'' Gently he pulled her face to him and kissed her. He felt her relax a little, then open her lips and kiss him back, hesitantly at first, then not hesitantly at all.

The rain outside drummed softly.

Into her ear he whispered, "Now. Do you think I can get you into this bed?''

*   *   *

The phone rang at 2:00 A.M and she came awake with a start.

He had it off the hook before the second ring.

"Umm?"

Silence. David listening. Then, groggy-voiced: "How much is she dilated? Yep, okay, be right down."

He stood and dragged on his clothes, muttering to her that the case sounded bad; he'd probably be up the rest of the night.

Jill felt a stab of fear. The last dream she had had before awakening was of huge and leering shapes chasing her through endless blackness. She realized she was trembling, bathed in cold sweat.

"David—"

"Sleep," he said. In the darkness he bent and kissed her, then straightened, adjusted his belt and headed for the door. Fighting panic, Jill followed him. It was terrifying to see him leave; she wanted to hold him, beg him to get someone else to cover for him—just for this awful night. But by the door she made herself stop. This was no way to behave, she thought. He would be away for hours; she had no choice but to stay and wrestle with her demons alone.

"Who else is on call?" she asked weakly.

"Woody. Mackey. I forget who else."

He glanced down at her nakedness. Sleepiness vanished from his face.

"Lock the door, Jill. *Double*-lock it."

She looked puzzled. "Of course. I was planning to. What's the matter?"

"Those murders," he said. "I guess they've got me more spooked than I realized."

Jill hesitated. "But that was *outside,*" she said. "The hospital security . . ."

"Hospital security stinks."

"And those extra police?"

David shook his head. "They're worse. You think they can tell staff apart from anyone else?" He drew her to him. "Jill, any creep with a good haircut can come walking into Emergency and then disappear into the hallways, the stairwells . . . Just go back to bed and *stay* there, Okay?''

Reaching down, he adjusted the bolt on the door so it would snap when he closed it. He kissed her on the mouth, then again on the cheek; and then he went out.

The click of the lock engaging echoed in the darkness. Jill stepped away from the closed door, shaking her head. David had to be wrong, she thought: the hospital security was okay, the guards knew every face, and the extra police were there in case the *guards* spotted trouble. That made sense, didn't it?

The thought of dark figures lurking in the corridors loomed up suddenly at her, and she shivered.

Stop it she thought. She went back to bed, lay frowning at the shadowy ceiling, and finally reassured herself. David had every reason to feel jittery, but the murders were police business, and downstairs probably looked like an armed camp.

All I have to worry about, she thought, is William Stryker.

Outside, a high wail heralded the arrival of another ambulance. She realized that it had stopped raining.

33

A TENSE-LOOKING nurse disappeared into the delivery room, and Levine, approaching, quickened his pace. He was preoccupied; he could not shake his uneasy feeling after he left Jill. Ducking into the scrub room, he found an angry Sam MacIntyre already up to his elbows in suds.

"Chrissakes," complained MacIntyre. "They already got Mackey and Greenberg in there. What the hell do they need us for?"

David took the sink next to him. "Problems," he said. He pressed the foot pedal that turned on the water. "Woman's been fully dilated for forty minutes. Labors not progressing."

"She's not getting good contractions?"

"She's not getting *any* contractions."

MacIntyre pounded out some more Phisohex. "Jesus, I hope we don't have to open her up. I want to go back to bed!" He looked at Levine. "Where's Jill, by the way?"

"Sleeping, I hope," said David. "Recovering from her thoroughly rotten day." He sighed and pitched a used nailbrush into the hamper.

MacIntyre stared thoughtfully into the sink. "She'll get used to Stryker's terror tactics," he said. He shook his hands free of water and turned toward the delivery doors. "In the meantime, I hope you chained her to the bed."

"Yeah," David said ruefully, following him. "I should have."

MacIntyre looked at him in mock horror. "You mean you *didn't?*"

34

SHORTLY BEFORE 3:00 Jill gave up trying to sleep. Fatigue was gone and she was excited: she had just had an idea. A crazy idea, but booming with possibility.

Except that she would have to hurry.

She rolled out of bed and pulled on her scrub suit. She

thought: They've got it backward. They're all looking at the problem backward!

The idea had come while she had been brooding about the previous afternoon, and the Master Computer access code she had pirated from Arnett's secretary. She had felt cocky then, but later she was depressed, confused.

What was she going to do with it?

Now she knew.

Running a brush through her hair, Jill pondered human nature and the tricks it played on people. How ironic, she thought. No matter how great one's individual brilliance, it was always emotions that took over first: fixing on major events and tragedies, missing or dismissing smaller clues, smaller events.

Events which just might be part of a bigger, more recognizable pattern.

How big? Jill laid down her brush. That depended on whether one averaged in *everything,* including the many early miscarriages they'd been seeing—some so early the women hadn't even known they were pregnant—the idiopathic bleeding, the strange, low-grade fevers . . .

The computer could tell her a lot, now that she knew what to ask it, and provided no one caught her using it.

She shoved her black memo book into her pocket and glanced at her watch. 3:09.

Why did the computer have to be in the basement, she thought. That awful basement. The idea of going down there at night was unthinkable.

So don't think, she told herself.

She grabbed her large notebook and hurried out the door.

Moments later the elevator jerked to a stop, depositing Jill on the rock-hard tunnel floor. She stepped out and turned, watching nervously as the doors closed behind her. With a thumping sound the car went up again in its shaft.

Her hands tightened around the edge of her notebook, and she looked around.

Even by day this place reminded her of Jules Verne's *A*

Journey to the Center of the Earth. Yellow-painted stone passages ran off in both directions, arrow-straight, then twisted off into darkness. Across from the elevator red arrows pointing left indicated the pathology department and the morgue; those pointing right led to the boiler room, the laundry and the record room.

Jill turned right. She walked for about fifty yards, straining her hearing for the slightest noise. Would anyone be down here? Could a vagabond or some homicidal maniac be lurking around some darkened corner? Jill froze at the thought, and then told herself of course not. One had to be *inside* the hospital in order to descend to the tunnels. And the hospital entrances were well guarded.

The tunnel seemed to narrow. Overhead, fluorescent bulbs buzzed on and off, casting weird, moving shadows on the ceiling. Jill stopped to peer through the glass-windowed door that said Boiler Room. Inside, darkened shapes seemed to be looking back at her. The boiler suddenly thundered on, emitting a blast of steam that made her jump.

She ran. The sound of her footsteps pounding on the concrete seemed abnormally loud. A few more seconds of this horror show and I go right back upstairs, she thought. And then, abruptly, she found herself facing a wooden door with the reassuring sign, Record Room.

She opened the door and stepped into darkness. She listened and waited for a moment. There was no sound. Closing the door softly, she reached out and groped along the wall until she found a panel of light switches. She flicked one on. With a snapping noise, a far bank of fluorescents lit up to reveal a long, rectangular room, musty-smelling, with stacks of patients' charts arranged along aisles and in tiers that reached up to the ceiling.

It's so deathly *quiet* in here, she thought. Like a mausoleum.

She hurried through the room and up a short ramp. At the top was a glass cubicle, the size of a large booth. The sign by the door said Master Computer—Faculty Only. She entered, turned on the light, and felt her stomach tighten. Glass rooms are so frightening, she thought, because you feel watched. Her gaze traveled from the carpeted floor to shelves loaded with complex equipment, then back to the immense piece of machinery in the center.

So that's Ida, Jill thought. People called the machine Ida because it was hard to say International Classification of Diseases Adapted. Ida, with her name making her sound almost human, was the central computer used to store data. Thousands of millions of bits of data. Ida had been programmed to remember every patient's name, admission number, and disease or injury diagnosis, going all the way back to the fifties, some said.

They had different problems back then, Jill thought.

She sat at the console, depositing her notebook on a low counter to her left. Squinting, she studied the empty print-out screen, the myriad buttons and lights and switches, and for a moment she felt apprehensive. Then she reminded herself that she was no stranger to computers. Throughout the first two years of medical school she had been required to study programming—no "computer illiterates" would be allowed to graduate, they'd been told—and now she was glad.

Biting her lip, she raised her hands above the typewriter keys, scanned the red and black buttons until, in the corner of the keyboard, she found the switch marked On.

She flicked it. The machine kicked on with a surprisingly loud humming noise, and she was on her way.

A little frantically, she pressed the button for override, to avoid connecting with the computers more banal circuits used to house hospital financial data, drug inventories, employee records. The machine made several clicks, then resumed its steady hum. Jill peered out through the glass to make sure nobody was there. It was hard to see. The shadows were deep between the tall stacks of charts.

Hurry, she told herself.

The circuits were clear; now it was time to use her stolen code.

She flipped open her notebook and found the place. Using her right index finger, she punched in the six-digit

access code for general patient record information. A green
light flashed; then came a series of clicks, a shifting of
gears and the whirring sound of winding tapes. Jill held
her breath. Suddenly a line of white digital letters began to
march across the screen.

"Instructions, please," said Ida.

I did it! she thought.

Referring back to her notebook, she punched in the
eleven-digit request for the subcategory she wanted. This
was Obstetrics: the section detailing all complications of
pregnancy and childbirth.

Again she waited, as the green light changed to yellow
and the internal metallic units hummed; and then the light
flashed back to green, and the printout blinked the word,
Ready.

She had made it.

Before her lay open the computers forbidden core with
its memory of thousands of obstetrical secrets.

She breathed again. Now the machine was ready to
answer her questions.

Jill had decided to go back only three years in the
memory circuits, then compare her findings with those of
the recent past. Quickly, she asked the computer to give
her the chart numbers of *all* obstetrical disorders—from
tragic to minor—that had occurred in 1982. She waited
five seconds until the machine came back with the answer.
A short column of letters and numbers lit up the screen.

In her notebook she jotted "1982: incidence of complications within normal range." Then she turned back to the
console.

She requested the same information for 1983. This time,
two and one-half long columns appeared, lighting up the
left vertical half of the printout screen.

Jill stared. *Two and a half columns?*

She frowned and typed back: "Please copy." Obedi-
ently, the console's typewriter chattered its message on a
sheaf of paper that came out from a slot into Jill's hand.
She read it again, her frown deepening. She placed it

under the clamp inside her notebook, then turned back to the console.

With trembling fingers she punched out her third request: a list of all obstetrical complications for 1984. This is it, she thought. God, why am I so frightened? If Pandora had known what was in the box, would she still have gone ahead and—

The machine jerked into operation. A few letters first, several numbers, and then an explosion of wildly clacking chatter as the long columns poured up and down the printout. Stunned, Jill half rose out of her seat and peered frantically around. The thing was so noisy! Someone was sure to hear. A tinny bell rang. She turned back. The screen was as full as a telephone page. A red light flashed impatiently. She reached out. "Yes, please copy," she wrote.

Out slipped the crowded sheet. She scanned it quickly and felt cold. The red light changed to green. Another clattering printout began to appear.

More? Jill stared mesmerized at the screen.

The entire booth seemed to be shaking. Jill whirled around again and craned her neck to see if anyone was coming. There was no one. Turning back, she found the page already thundering its way down a third long column. Her hand went to her throat in disbelief.

And then, abruptly, the printout stopped. The room reverted to catacomb silence. Her heart racing, Jill requested the second copy and then stood, gaping at both sheets of paper. One and three-quarter pages crammed with chart numbers! She had had her suspicions, but all this?

The question burned through her: how in God's name was it possible to have so much going wrong without anybody noticing?

She sat down, thinking. Of course it was possible, she realized, because the system was so huge and decentralized. Many doctors delivering many babies, tending different pregnancies, working different shifts. Private patients, clinic patients. Minor disorders lumped together in the records with outright tragedies; all viewed as unrelated statistics . . .

No common thread, as David would say.

Rubbing her brow, Jill thought some more. Even something as minor as a vestigial sixth finger on an infant's hand, which was common, and which the doctor would snip off moments after birth, would still be entered into the records—and the computer—as a birth defect. Jill glanced down at the reams of numbers on the printouts. The question was, how many of these chart numbers represented minor disorders, and how many belonged to women like Maria Moran and Mary Jo Sayers?

There was only one way to find out.

She stared through the glass into the record room beyond. She checked her watch: 3:40. Not much time, she thought. She gathered up her printouts and rushed down the ramp. In the center of the floor she stopped, looking around. So many chart numbers to match. Where should she begin?

Her eye fell on the sign designating the 100s aisle. *Start at the beginning, ninny*. She took a long breath, and then hurried into the shadows of the high, looming stacks.

35

IN ANOTHER PART of the hospital, a telephone rang. It rang again, its tone muted, so as not to be heard beyond this room; and then it rang again, before a hand in a white sleeve reached out to pick it up.

Stiffly, a man listened. The man's face tensed, and then his eyes opened wider as he listened to the tinny voice on the other end.

"It is Ida who speaks to you. The memory systems of the Hospital Classification of Diseases Adapted wishes to inform you that the obstetrics and gynecology section is now being questioned for essential information. Repeat. The obstetrics and gynecology section memory circuits are now being questioned for essential . . ."

The man replaced the receiver. He held up his watch. It was 3:34. Two hours until dawn. Time enough to summon help and deal with this matter.

He picked up the phone again and dialed.

The computer Ida, among her other formidable talents, had been programmed to tattletale.

36

JILL WORKED FEVERISHLY. She started on the most recent records, and had already made her way up and down several aisles. She had skimmed, taken frantic notes, and jammed each chart back into its shelf unless it needed further study.

In which case, she kept the chart out and carried it. Her pile was getting heavy.

In the 700s aisle, she lowered the charts to the floor and watched them topple. She dropped to her hands and knees, oblivious to the dust, and began making two separate stacks: one for fetal disorders, one for maternal morbidity.

Minutes later, she sat back on her heels and contemplated the two growing piles.

The fetal disorder one was higher.

This is insane, she thought. What's really needed down

here is a whole team of impartial investigators, not one weak-armed, scared and exhausted intern who can barely see in this awful light . . .

She glanced up, toward the single bank of fluorescents. She debated turning on more lights, then decided against it. Her eyes were smarting. She rubbed them with soot-smudged hands. Then she resumed her sorting.

Let's see—lacerated bladder and ruptured uterus go *here,* and harelip and pyloric stenosis go *there,* and this one with a trisomy 14 abnormality goes . . .

Jill stared down at the chart she held in her hand. A thin shaft of light angled its way down the side of the aisle, and she shifted her weight so she could see better. There it was, neatly typed and right there on the cover sheet: a diagnosis of trisomy 14 with a 12–17 translocation.

The mysterious chromosomal abnormality of Maria Moran and Mary Jo Sayers. Of their babies, that is.

Jill flipped through the pages. The patient's name was— had been—Sawyer. Her full-term infant had been an over-weight stillborn, and the mother had died of . . . Jill leafed back to the postop report . . . of *apparent* reaction to general anesthesia while undergoing a Caesarean.

Jill looked up, staring unseeingly at a shelf lined with old, yellowed charts. She remembered Peter Gregson's astonishment at seeing this abnormality. A fourth-year Pathology resident and he had never seen it before!

Drop into Obstetrics sometime, Jill thought.

She read on. The tragedy had occurred on May 6 of this year, two months before the beginning of Jill's internship. The attending physicians had been . . . everybody, almost, which was not surprising. When a case turned bad, every-one came running. George Mackey had done the Caesar-ean; the anesthesiologist was somebody named Gibbons; the initial attending physician had been Jim Holloway; and later Stryker was called in . . .

Stryker. Jill paused. A coincidence? Probably not. Jill knew the medical-academic mind. Higher-up doctors came rushing to cases like this not out of passion to save the patient, but because the case was "interesting . . . excellent teaching material."

But who had done the post? And whose idea was it to do a chromosome study? Had Stryker suggested it as a research project? And what made him *suspect,* unless . . .

Jill resumed reading. Beneath the operative report was a terse note penciled in barely decipherable handwriting. She could not make out the first line; but there, on the second line, were the words "important aberrations" . . . and "possibly connected to our" . . . and "preliminary but suggest we use utmost" . . .

A shadow fell across the page she was reading.

She looked up—and froze.

The figure standing at the head of the aisle was grinning at her.

Jill stared at him, at first refusing to believe what she was seeing. Then a swooning, cold terror took hold of her, gripping her body and locking the legs that wanted to jump up and run.

"Who are you?" she asked in a trembling whisper.

The gaunt-faced figure edged toward her. There was something familiar about his shape, the way he moved. She had seen him before, she was sure of it.

He stopped, feet apart, close enough to lunge at her. His face twisted into a sneer. "Been usin' the boss man's computer, eh?"

Jill glanced over his T-shirted shoulder toward the still-lighted cubicle. *Computer? Boss man?* Her mind cleared just enough to realize that a giant piece had just fit into the puzzle.

The printout. With shaking hands Jill folded the two pages and fumbled them into her pocket.

And then she noticed his green running shoes.

Oh, my *God.*

She felt a choking sensation, rose unsteadily and took a step backward—*to where, fool, the aisle's a dead end!* For an absurd moment she tried to place that accent. Midwest? Texas? Her heart was pounding so hard that it was painful to breathe.

She stumbled over a library stool. Before she could regain her balance, he had seized her by the arm and squeezed so hard that she screamed.

"You want to know what happens to pretty women who get to snoopin'?" he hissed. "Want me to show you?" Jill was clutching the Sawyer chart so hard that it hurt her fingers. She could see his eyes glittering in sadistic amusement; could see a hand moving into a pocket, removing a long—

No, a *cord?*

—and the cord looked like a snake in his hand as it thrust forward and grazed her neck between fingers that suddenly squeezed like pincers; as her own hand, shaking uncontrollably, reached back and raised up the Sawyer chart and arched from behind a sickening crack to the side of her attacker's head. The man went down beneath her. She saw the thin line of blood erupt on his right temple; saw his face grow dazed, then clear, then contort to an expression of murderous rage.

"Fuckin' bitch!" He was half up, lunging for her.

She dodged past him, spun, crashed into another shelf sending charts flying, and then she ran. Out past the front line of stacks and through the low door frame. Out into the cement tunnel, past the thumping boiler room, toward the closed elevator door.

She pounded on the Up button—a joke: the thing moved with the speed of a vertical glacier—and then, hearing running footsteps approaching, she raced in mindless terror toward the other end of the twisting corridor.

Which was a mistake. The basement tunnel system was like a maze. She didn't know her way around.

37

"MAYBE WE'D BETTER take her up," MacIntyre said.

Tense, Levine looked up over his surgical mask at the face of the exhausted patient. Take her upstairs for surgery? The transfer alone would take ten minutes; then they'd have to prep and drape her all over again . . .

"No," he said. "She's in trouble now. She'd never make it."

A glistening loop of umbilical cord began to ooze out of the birth canal.

"That's it!" Levine said. "We've got a cord prolapse. Ruthie, get the pack."

George Mackey stepped back. The nurse named Ruthie Stone was quick. She was back at Levine's side in seconds with the Emergency C-Section Pack, which she opened and spread on a stainless steel table.

With his gloved fingers Levine grasped the umbilical cord and felt for pulsation. For two seconds it was bounding. Then, as if the cord were a hose and someone had just turned off the water, the pulse grew weak.

The umbilical cord was being compressed between the baby's skull and the mother's bony pelvis.

Woody Greenberg's eyes were on the fetal monitor. "Trouble!" he hollered. "Fetal heart rate's dropping!"

Levine's voice remained calm. "Carole," he said to another nurse. "Run in 50 milligrams of Pentothal. And Woody"—the first year resident looked up—"start the Halothane."

Seconds later the nurse was injecting Pentothal into the IV tubing; and Woody, having secured a black rubber mask to the patient's face, was spinning open the valve on a green tank. The hiss of gas could be heard.

Levine moved around to the side of the table. Now MacIntyre's gloved hand was on the bloody, collapsed cord: he felt the last feeble beat; and then there was nothing.

MacIntyre's voice behind his mask sounded husky. "You've got one minute to get that kid out, or we're going to have a dead baby."

David nodded. "I know. Start the count."

"Yeah. It's already four seconds."

"Which leaves fifty-six to go," Levine said.

With that he reached for the scalpel.

38

JILL HUDDLED AGAINST the wall of the tunnel, still clutching the Sawyer chart, her heart thudding crazily as she stared at the room across the way. A sign on the door said Morgue, and underneath, in black letters, Unauthorized Entry Forbidden.

As if anyone would *want* to go in that place, she thought. The windows in the upper half of the swinging doors were dark. And she wouldn't dare turn on a light. Not with that maniac coming after her.

But she had to go in. The morgue had the only telephone at this end of the tunnel. It was a wall phone, hanging near the refrigerated drawers at the far end of the room. She had noticed it the day she had taken the Sayers and Moran skin cultures. If she could only reach David . . .

She heard a footstep. She ducked behind a group of tall oxygen tanks and crouched down. More rapid footsteps, and then they stopped just around the corner. The custodial supply room she had just passed?

She heard the door open, the footsteps enter. Then came the sound of equipment being shoved roughly about.

He's right around the corner, she thought. If I don't make a run for it now I've had it.

She squeezed out from the oxygen cylinders and hurried across to the morgue doors. She raised her right hand to open one, then stopped, paralyzed. A hissing noise from behind made her wheel around.

Overhead a thin plume of steam escaped from a joint in the tangle of pipes.

She pushed open the morgue doors and plunged into blackness.

Feeling her way in the dark, Jill ran her free hand along rims of stainless steel tables and then bumped into a floor light. "Ow!" she cried out involuntarily, then clapped her hand over her face. She expected her pursuer to come crashing in at any second. She waited, trembling. Nothing happened. Everything seemed unnaturally silent.

Find the phone . . .

She still clutched the Sawyer chart, and felt in her pocket for the printouts. They were there. Folded. She patted the wad of papers and withdrew her ice cold palm. The printout and the Sawyer chart, she thought. I'll bet Stryker would love to get his hands on them. If she could only reach David by telephone, she wouldn't have to worry about having evidence yanked away from her. And calling Security would be tantamount to reporting more of her own snooping.

But you don't want to get murdered, do you?

Find the damned phone . . .

She left the line of steel tables and moved, groping blindly, across a wide aisle. Ahead, she recalled, rose the wall of refrigerated drawers. She shivered, then looked again. There was a curious, feeble luminescence emanating from the metal surface of the drawers. That gave her some relief: now she could see outlines of things.

She turned right, nearly colliding with a tall card file. Good, she thought. The card file stood diagonally across from the wall phone, about ten feet away. She crossed to the drawers and ran her fingers along the chilly, metallic surface as she walked. One drawer was slightly open. Reflexively she pushed it closed. Something went thud inside.

Still groping, she passed more drawers and then found the phone. In a flood of relief she grasped the plastic receiver. Safe, she thought. She listened for footsteps, but all was quiet. Maybe too quiet, she realized in a panic. Someone could be outside the door this very moment, listening for a sound . . .

She lifted the receiver and dialed zero. She held her breath and kept her eye on the door.

Fifteen floors above, the young woman at the switchboard picked up on the first ring.

"House page." The voice sounded sleepy.

"Cassie?" Jill's voice was a hoarse whisper.

"House page," repeated the voice, still sleepy-sounding.

Jill spoke louder. "Cassie, this is Dr. Raney. Please page Dr. Levine, double stat. I think he's somewhere in the OB suite—"

"You *bet* he's still in the OB suite. They're having trouble, Dr. Raney. They just ordered two units of blood and—hey, could you speak a little louder?"

Jill's mind was racing. Frantically, she watched the door—it hadn't burst open, yet—as she said, "Could you ask him to break scrub? Tell him it's Dr. Raney calling and that it's an emergency . . ." She caught herself regretting her unprofessional impulse. Two units of blood and she wanted him to break scrub?

"Forget it, Cassie. I didn't mean that."

The voice was awake now, friendly and soothing. "I know. How 'bout if I page Dr. Mackey for you? He's on call too. Or Dr. Holloway. He just went back to bed but I can—"

"No, no!" The others knew nothing of what she was doing; they would think she was crazy. She was struck by an idea.

"Cassie, can you reach Dr. Arnett for me? He's the only other person I can—"

"You mean, Dr. Arnett at *home?* Wake him up?"

Jill was silent.

"Hey, where are you calling from anyway? I don't see your light on the panel. Uh-oh! Two ambulances just lit up. I have to take their calls and I'll get right back to you. Can you hold for just a sec—"

The operator never got to finish her sentence.

At the other end the line went dead.

An arriving knife wound and an arriving stomach full of Seconal were quickly relayed to Emergency; then Cassandra Devine leaned back in her chair to ponder Dr. Raney's strange call.

Only at the end of the call had Cassie noticed the tiny white light at the bottom of the panel. Cassie wondered about the light—now a dark button. Dr. Raney was always polite and friendly. Except tonight. There had been something very wrong in her voice tonight.

Cassie pulled off her headset and smoothed down her Afro. Her head ached and she was tired, but she could not push that call from her mind. She frowned, thinking; and then what was wrong about the call finally hit her.

Doctors handled emergencies all the time and their voices didn't *shake*. Besides, where *was* it that Dr. Raney had called from?

Cassie's chair squeaked loudly as she took down the hospital directory and looked up the number under the call button.

She looked up, puzzled. *The morgue?*

What was Dr. Raney doing down in the morgue at this hour?

Those doctors work round the clock, Cassie thought, shaking her head. And if I were calling from the morgue at four in the morning I'd be sounding a lot worse than that. Yessir.

She readjusted her headset and pressed it against her
ears to hear better. Tonight was definitely too busy for one
person, she thought. She was going to complain in the
morning.

At that moment the panel lit up again. Went crazy, in
fact. Five red flashing buttons, then ten. Cassie started
answering and her hands could not move fast enough to
connect all the calls.

There had been a gas explosion. Half a neighborhood
blown away, casualties coming in by the score. All other
thoughts went out of Cassie's mind as she sat up in her
seat and snapped into action.

39

JILL HAD HEARD footsteps. She hung up quickly and crouched
low, holding her breath. The footsteps paused outside the
door. On her hands and knees she crept forward, groping
her way across the wide aisle until her hand found the base
of a heavy desk. She remembered: it was the morgue
attendant's desk that stood back to back with the card
file.

She scrambled under and listened. There was no sound:
she knew he was standing motionless outside the door. She
could hear the beat of her own heart. It's so dark in here,
she thought. So horribly dark. What if the door suddenly
crashes open and he turns on the lights? She recalled the
array of long knives on the autopsy counter. Those knives

. . . a sick feeling spread through her as she remembered the rage on her pursuer's face.

The footsteps started up again. Jill froze, then blinked in the darkness. They were moving away! Their tread was disappearing down the hall, back toward the elevators, it seemed. Jill sat on the floor under the desk and counted slowly to five hundred. He was gone. She was sure of it.

Slowly she let out her breath.

She crept out and stood up stiffly, listened, heard nothing.

With the Sawyer chart under her arm she felt her way around the desk, the card file; went straight ahead, gingerly, down the line of stainless steel tables to the morgue doors, which she opened just a crack.

The light from the outside fluorescents was harsh and made her blink. Which way should she go? Turning left, she feared, toward the elevators, could involve running into that goon. His "boss man" would probably want him to rush back and clean up the telltale mess of charts. She would not go that way. The risk was too great.

Should she turn right?

She didn't know the way.

Then she remembered there was a stairwell somewhere at that end: the north stairwell was supposed to be a quick way to get upstairs from this part of the basement. She would try to find it. Jill peered out, going over the layout of the hospital in her mind. The tunnel continued under the old medical school and then under other sections of the med center. There would be branching tunnels all over, Jill knew; she hoped they were well marked.

Casting a fearful glance over her shoulder, she ran out.

It was a queer feeling, walking *away* from the elevators. And as soon as Jill's eyes adjusted to the lights, she realized that they were *dim,* not bright. She looked up and jerked to a stop, surprised. The overhead lights were not fluorescents but gritty light bulbs encased in wire cages, spaced farther and farther apart as they stretched ahead.

Clearly, this end of the tunnel was used less.

Jill walked faster.

For nearly a hundred feet the way was straight, though the tunnel seemed to smell mustier. My imagination, Jill thought. Abruptly the corridor branched in front of her. There were no signs, but the left corridor was unlit. Jill headed right.

She turned down one tunnel, then another, which brought her to a short, vaulted passageway. A single bulb cast down a sickly glow. From somewhere came the sound of water dripping.

Jill looked up at the clammy, hand-hewn stones over-head. Now she knew where she was—under the old medi-cal school.

Oh, no, she thought. I went too far. I took the wrong tunnel.

But the other tunnel wasn't even lit!

She stood in the dim light for a moment, hugging herself in sudden chill. She looked around. Ahead, a heavy wooden door with a metal bar blocked the way. That was odd: there shouldn't *be* any door here, she thought. Fire laws decreed that no thoroughfare be blocked throughout the entire medical complex . . .

Jill looked uneasily at the closed door.

She *was* under the old medical school, wasn't she?

Cold fear went through her. She wanted to get out of this clammy dungeon—now! She heaved on the door, then fell backward. The door would not budge. Her eyes grew wider, then darted around in sudden fright. Her shove against the door had apparently dislodged the ancient fila-ment in the overhead bulb, because suddenly the passage went dark and there erupted around her feet the sound of sickening little claws scurrying, and she cried out, "Cripes! Rats!" Throwing her entire weight against the door, she found herself crashing through.

The door clanged shut behind her. She stumbled, righted herself, looked around. Moonlight washed feebly through a high basement window, and Jill was able to make out vague, darkened shapes. She was in a hallway of sorts.

Across from her, four feet away, was what appeared to be a tall, glass-fronted bookcase. And to the left, close by in shadow . . . Jill stifled a cry.

A large black shape was moving toward her. "No . . ." she whimpered, too frozen to move until she saw the leering countenance as it was nearly full upon her—

And then she screamed.

40

HIS HAND MOVED so fast that it looked as if he had drawn a red line.

David made a single midline incision from below the navel to the pubis. It was a shallow cut, through the skin and subcutaneous tissue only. Beads of blood enlarged and spilled down both sides of the abdomen. The nurse named Carole placed long gauze sponges on either side of the incision and began to exert pressure.

"Twenty seconds," said Sam MacIntyre.

David nodded and tossed his scalpel to the floor with a clatter. The scalpel had gone through unsterilized skin and was therefore contaminated. He took a new sterile scalpel and cut through the fascia layer and then into the peritoneal cavity.

"Thirty seconds," said MacIntyre.

"Almost there," muttered Levine. His voice rose. "Hey Woody, more Halothane! Carole, change the sponges. Use doubles. Start suction."

Bright blood was welling up. It was hard to see. David was vaguely aware of hearing Sam's voice; of the nurse's busy hands near his and then the gurgling sound of blood being suctioned out. He waited a precious four seconds, until he could see what he was doing, and then with his scalpel tip made a small nick in the uterine wall.

"Fifty seconds," said MacIntyre.

David pushed two fingers down through the hole, exerted slight pressure away from the fetus, then cut an eight-inch vertical incision between his fingers. He looked: the opening was good. He didn't breathe: the child had less than ten seconds left. He reached deep into the cavity with both hands and found two tiny feet. He grabbed the child by the ankles, pulled it out, and held it—her, they noticed—up like a triumph. His eyes were beaming.

"Fifty-eight seconds," said Sam MacIntyre.

"You can stop now," said David, and everyone laughed with relief. Woody rolled up the bassinette. David cut the cord, tied it and handed the infant girl to Sam, who laid her down and began checking her vital signs. "She's pinking up nicely," said Sam.

"Thank God," muttered David. He turned his attention back to the mother, attended by Mackey and the nurses.

Mackey looked up. "She's bleeding faster, David."

"So I see." Levine glanced over his shoulder.

"Call blood!" he said. "Two units on the double!" He calculated rapidly: at this hour the blood bank would not be so busy; they'd get the units here in minutes. He looked back to the patient, one of the lucky ones, he reflected. If she had come in during the peak surgery morning hours, or peak violence evening hours, the situation might have been different.

He sighed. While they waited for the blood he had work to do. He bent over the unconscious woman and, reaching in, peeled the placenta off its attachment to the uterine wall. Moments later he was suturing the uterine wall back together. He looked up only when he heard a lusty wail as the bassinette was rolled out of the room. He returned to his work. The clock on the wall said 4:09.

41

COVERING HER FACE, Jill jerked instinctively backward as she saw the figure coming toward her. She screamed and went down, pounding her assailant wildly as she felt his weight upon her. She cried out again, and in a frenzy rolled over and away.

She cringed back against the wall. He lost his grip! she thought. He lost his grip!

She groped around the floor for a weapon—anything with which to fight back—

And then she realized that she was the one who was making all the noise.

Gasping for breath she waited, trembling. Nothing happened—except for a queer itching sensation in her right hand. In the gray light she saw tufts of hair protruding from her fist.

Hair?

She looked over at the long figure lying motionless on the floor.

Even supine, its shoulders were hunched. The light from the high window cast a weird illumination upon it, making even more ominous the heavy, overhanging brow, the glassy look in the eyes . . .

Glassy . . . ?

Slowly, her heart still whamming, Jill realized where she was. She inhaled deeply, then laughed bitterly in the gloom.

She was in the museum. Overwrought Jill Raney, physically and emotionally exhausted, was in a basement hallway of the Madison Museum of Anthropology at four in the morning, with its headhunters and apemen and . . . the figure before her was a dummy.

A dozen feet away she could make out the base of the mahogany staircase that led up to the main floor. Across from her, in the large glass case, were the shadowy forms of spears and masks and . . . smaller shapes. Bizarre and obscene shapes, squatting roundly, some with long thatches of hair . . .

She struggled to her feet. She had to step over the hominid, and as she did she noticed a long, gaping tear in its belly. Fragments of plaster of paris and some smelly, spongy material spilled out. Jill bent, reached forward to touch, and made a small sound of revulsion as she yanked her hand back.

She stood there, breathing heavily, looking around.

I'll be all right, she thought. I'll be all right if I can just get out of here.

She felt her way back to the door, trailing her hand along the wall until she came to the metal bar. She stood still, remembering the weight of the door; recalling too late the thin, metallic click after the door had shut. Had the lock engaged?

Using both hands, she pressed hard against the door. It would not give. She took a step back and slammed her shoulder against the door, then cried out. Her own voice sounded loud in the darkness, and she held her breath, listening. No one was coming. She wished miserably that she had stayed in the morgue.

Rubbing her aching arm, she considered the mahogany staircase. Should she go up? It was a possibility. But opening any outside door to the museum would surely trigger an alarm.

Yet there seemed to be no other way. The tunnel door was impossible; and the museum doors—Jill supposed that she could bolt through one fast and make a run for it. The thought of bells going off appalled her. I'd make a terrible thief she thought. Still . . .

She tucked the Sawyer chart under her arm and headed for the staircase.

A door opening somewhere above stopped her cold.

She whirled. *Where?*

Footsteps were coming down the mahogany staircase.

Jill froze.

The footsteps sounded two floors up, but were descending briskly, getting closer.

Where could she go? She found it difficult to move. She turned and looked down the hallway past the glass case. That was no escape route—once past the dim shaft of moonlight the hall was completely dark. She would crash into something. Whoever was coming would find her easily.

She ran on rubbery legs back to the tunnel door. As if *staring* at the thing would help, she thought frantically. From upstairs the footsteps hit the first floor landing, starting down.

Now she knew she was trapped.

$$42$$

DAVID LEVINE WAS tired.

He was, in fact, half asleep when the ninth floor elevator doors slid open and he emerged into the hallway. The patient on the floor below was out of danger. They had stabilized her, closed her up, and breathed a collective sigh of relief as she began to come out of the anesthesia. She had smiled at David. He had smiled back and squeezed her hand. And now, walking down the dimly lighted hall, he found himself thinking of the baby. That new little noisemaker was so marvelously ordinary and healthy—already squalling up a storm in the nursery—that it made him want to cry and laugh at the same time.

Fumbling for his keys, he thought of MacIntyre and Greenberg, still down there working: checking that the patient made the full trip back from anesthesia; writing postop orders and dictating the operative summary.

Maybe someday we can all go fishing, David thought wistfully.

But right now what awaited him was a warm bed and a sweet sleeping girl, around whom he wanted nothing more than to wrap his arms and—well—just conk out.

Turning the key, he pushed the door open and stepped in. He headed for the bed. He glanced toward the closet and then the bathroom, debating whether he should shower and change now, or wait until later. He decided to wait. He didn't want to wake Jill, and in any case, in ninety minutes it would be time to get up.

Try to sleep, he thought, and turned back toward the bed.

It was then that he sensed that something was wrong.

The room was too quiet. Jill, sleeping, was a heavy breather: the night before he had teased her that she snored, and she had bashed him, laughing, protesting that it wasn't true.

"Jill?" An alarm sounded in the back of his mind.

He went to the bed, bent, felt for the reassuring mound of feminine hips . . . and found instead a cold pillow and sheets strewn as if she had left in a hurry.

With a corner of the sheet still in his hand, he swore under his breath. "Jill?" he called again, louder, desperately, knowing it was useless.

He dashed out to the corridor. Jill wasn't on call, so where could she be? He remembered their midnight discussion, which seemed like ages ago. Jill was convinced she'd be thrown out by morning. She was angry about the charts being impounded, had been asking questions about the computer.

At the hall phone he dialed the number of the house page.

"Page," answered a weary voice.

"Levine here," he said. "Hey, Cassie, there's a problem. I want you to page Dr. Jill Raney, fast. Page her all over the place. Every station and *especially* the basement. Try the record room."

Cassie Devine's voice sounded worried. "Oh, doctor, Dr. Raney called in already. She wanted to talk to you and sounded upset and—"

"What time?"

"Three fifty-one," answered Cassie, looking down at her night log. "And Doctor Levine, the strangest thing . . ."

David stiffened.

"She wouldn't tell me where she was calling from, but I could tell from the console that she was in the morgue and—"

"The *where?*"

"The morgue. And if I may say, doctor, she sounded pretty shaky. I was going to call someone about that, but then I figured she was working down there, and the explosion happened and all the ambulances started calling in . . ."

For a long moment the line was silent. Then, in a somber tone, Levine said, "Cassie, get me downstairs. Delivery room number four. Get MacIntyre and Greenberg."

"On the intercom, you mean?"

"On the intercom."

As the nurse tidied up, two exhausted doctors were finishing the postop routine. Woody Greenberg was checking the patient's pulse, blood pressure and respiration, speaking gently and smiling to her as he poked about. Sam MacIntyre's hands pressed gently on the woman's abdomen, noting that the uterus was contracting down, but not quite on schedule. He was considering administering a dose of Ergotrate when the intercom clicked on overhead and the voice of David Levine came on.

"Hello again," Levine said. "Sorry to disturb, but this is an emergency."

"*Another* one?" said Woody.

"Call Mackey," said MacIntyre, looking up. "He just went back to bed."

"No." There was a curious tension in David's voice and then a long pause. Sensing that something was wrong, the doctors exchanged glances and then looked up at the ceiling speaker.

Levine was aware that the patient was now nearly awake; he did not want to alarm her, so he tried to speak cryptically.

"Does anyone down there know the whereabouts of Dr. Raney?"

Greenberg and MacIntyre's eyes dropped to each other, and they exchanged headshakes.

"No, David," said Woody. "Dr. Raney must be in another part of the hospital."

"The question is *where!*" said Levine. And that time they heard it—the voice that was usually wry and easygoing was now taut with apprehension.

MacIntyre frowned. "Try paging her," he said. "Have them turn on every—"

His words were interrupted by a flat, female voice in the hall. "Dr. Raney. Dr. Jill Raney. Call operator, stat." The loudspeaker was just outside the delivery room, but another speaker, down the hall, could be heard echoing the same message.

The female monotone repeated its message and then switched off.

"Christ," said MacIntyre.

Greenberg glanced at the nurse, who nodded, and then he looked up at the speaker. "Five minutes," he called. "We'll meet you in the lounge."

"I'm on my way," Levine said.

And then he was gone.

Suddenly, nobody was tired anymore. Woody handed his blood pressure cuff to the nurse and walked out the door. MacIntyre quickly administered a dose of Ergotrate and hurried after him. The patient was falling asleep again. The clock on the wall said 4:35.

43

ON THE OTHER side of a three-foot stone wall, Jill knew it was useless to scream. No one would hear her. There wasn't a soul in that awful tunnel. She heard hurrying feet above her. They were about halfway down. In seconds they would round the bottom of the staircase. All she could do was stare desperately down at her shaking hands on the door bar and wish she had never been so eager to get in here . . .

In here?

She was confused for an instant. Then, in a flash of recall, she remembered how she had gained entry in the first place, and she wanted to howl at her own stupidity. Behind her she heard a footstep hit the floor. She drew breath, placed both hands on the iron bar and pulled at it with all her strength. The door burst open with a rasping sound—as if mocking her for having forgotten that the damned thing opened *inward*.

She squeezed through and ran faster than she had ever run in her life.

The bumpy stone tunnel led the way back. Cobwebs brushed her face, grotesque shapes seemed to reach out for her. She thought she was running through a nightmare. At the corner she stopped, her chest heaving.

She heard a sound.

She turned right, running again. But nothing looked familiar, and in her flight she had lost her orientation. She fled down one passage, then another, and at the next turn she jerked to an abrupt halt. She looked around in astonishment.

Without knowing how, she had found her way back to the main tunnel, with its mustard walls and green painted floor.

For a moment Jill stood, still shaking, her eyes darting right and left as she tried to decide: Which way?

She stepped out into the center of the tunnel.

A single light above her head glowed feebly. She looked left down the hall; a bulb twenty feet away looked brighter, newer. Some clue, she thought. She stared a moment longer, then turned and headed left, casting anxious glances over her shoulder, until she had covered about sixty feet.

She stopped when she saw a small sign: CHAPIN BUILDING, STRAIGHT AHEAD. Jill's stomach turned over. Had she actually raced past that sign? Lost her head and her bearings so disastrously? She felt humiliated, foolish; and then her hand brushed against the wad of paper jammed into her pocket and she thought, maybe not so foolish.

She walked another thirty feet, to a point where the light bulbs changed back to sputtering fluorescents; and there, a step past the cement seam that joined the old building to the new, was a gray steel door with white letters that said CHAPIN NORTH.

Jill groaned. The color makes it look like all the other doors, she thought.

She crossed the hall and pushed open the door. Ahead rose the cinderblock stairwell she had been seeking, with electric lights illuminating the landing. Stepping in, she waited, listening. There was no sound. The door she had come through thumped softly behind her; with a sigh, she began her ascent.

She rounded the first landing at the steel door marked GROUND FLOOR.

There was one more flight to go. On the second floor she planned to walk the block-long corridor to the central bank of elevators, which would bring her back to the ninth floor on-call room and David.

David.

Jill paused in the stairwell, halfway to the second floor. She recalled Cassie's report of the delivery beset by complications, and realized that David had probably just gone to bed. She was floored by a rushing sense of guilt. *He hasn't slept in two nights,* she thought, clutching the rail. *He's been up all night saving lives, and here I am planning to burst in waving this pile of papers at him. What's the matter with me?*

She trudged up two more steps. My holy war, she thought miserably. David had laid his profession on the line for her, had risked everything coming to her defense . . .

And she had let him.

"Selfish," she muttered to herself—her fatigue blowing away logic like the fragile thing that it was.

The tall window on the second floor landing revealed stars turning pale in the sky. The demons of night, Jill thought, give way to the demons of the day. She felt ready to cry. Soon it would be time for the big confrontation, with fingers pointing and titans of medicine shouting and ready to pull any rotten trick to cover up . . . Jill's hand moved anxiously to the bulging papers in her pocket. *My God, they'll impound these right on the spot!* she thought. David will fight them and then the *two* of us will be thrown out . . .

"No," she whispered, and went up the steps faster. She would do this thing alone. She would lie down for a while, and in the morning she would get through Stryker's "hearing" as calmly as she could.

And then she saw the light, and drew in her breath.

By chance she had looked out again, through the tall window on the landing and across the parking lot to the research wing. It was a dim light, barely visible in the last window on the top floor of the building.

Jill gave a start.

Arnett! The light was coming from Arnett's lab! Jill began to take the steps more quickly, her heart quickening with hope. Arnett had been here in the hospital all the time. Doing his research.

She rounded the landing, and jubilantly ran up the next flight of stairs.

Arnett would help, for sure. Cliff Arnett, who had helped her before in tense times; who had risen to a position of authority because he was brilliant and independent-minded, not because he played hospital politics. He would insist on a full investigation into Jill's evidence. And she would get to him two hours before phones would start ringing with antagonists stacking the deck against her.

On the third floor landing she stopped and turned. Grasping the rail, she stared down at a second floor sign which she had just raced past, and which now, oddly, seemed almost to be calling her back. CHAPIN ELEVATORS, said the sign. FOLLOW BLUE ARROWS.

She leaned out over the railing and looked up to the fourth floor landing. On the right loomed the gray steel door which would lead her to the research wing. She held up her watch: 4:50 already? She glanced down again at the Chapin sign, then raced up the last flight of stairs.

44

LEVINE RAN ALONG the corridor to the doctors' lounge and saw Tricia Donovan approaching him. Tottering sleepily, she was still pulling up the elastic pants of her scrub suit.

"They call you?" Levine said by the door.

Tricia looked at him. "Yes, Woody called. David, what's going *on?*"

He put his hand on her shoulder and they went in.

In the lounge Greenberg and MacIntyre were busy dumping spoonfuls of instant coffee into styrofoam cups. MacIntyre looked up. "House brew, Trish. Want some?"

"No thanks. I've slept." She turned to David: "Have you called Security?"

"Yes." He waved off Sam's coffee. "Security says no member of the house staff, including Jill, has been seen leaving the hospital by any entrance. And Cassie's been paging all over, the basement, every broom closet, the whole damn med center." He paced, looking down, then looked up at them with troubled eyes. "She's not on the outside and she's not on the inside," he said. "She's missing."

Greenberg, sitting, pushed away his coffee. "Dear God," he said.

Everyone started talking at once. Woody jumped up saying something about the stairwells; Tricia agreed with Woody, and MacIntyre, half shouting, suggested other places to look.

Levine held up his hands.

"Ida," he said.

The others looked at him.

"The record room," he continued. "Jill *may* have tried to use the computer, and I know from Cassie that she was in the basement because she made one call from the morgue." He ran a hand across his brow, frowning. "Could she have gone *back* to the record room? . . ."

He turned toward the door.

"The *morgue*," Tricia wailed after him. "Jill wouldn't go down *there* in the middle of the night!"

"Wanna bet?" said David softly.

There was a sudden flurry of movement and they all turned to see Woody tearing down the row of steel lockers and begin rummaging in his own. An instant later he held up something that gleamed metallically.

"Uh . . . David?" Woody's voice was oddly quiet as the others watched him, startled.

"Last year," he said, "I lost my beeper. Well, by the time I got a new one, I had found the old one." He held up the rectangular page device and flicked it on. "See?" he said. "I can call myself."

The room filled with the chirping of the two gadgets, one of which was attached to Woody's belt.

He handed the other one to David. "If you need us . . ." he said.

"I can use the house phones," protested Levine.

"Take it anyway."

"Yeah," said MacIntyre, stepping close to Woody. "Can't hurt."

Tricia tugged on Woody's sleeve. "And *we* have a few places to look into, don't we, Dr. Greenberg?"

MacIntyre was reaching for the wall phone. "Get me Emergency," he said. He turned to the others as he waited.

"Maybe this is nothing," MacIntyre said. "Maybe she's sleeping in one of the alcoves off the emergency area. I'm going to have them look for her."

"Doubtful," said Levine, hooking the extra beeper onto his belt and turning to go. Woody and Tricia followed him out.

At the elevator the three exchanged hurried words and then parted company. Levine watched as Woody raced for the south stairwell. Tricia, lingering a moment, peered up into the anxious, lean face before her.

"It's going to be all right," she insisted quietly.

David stared grimly ahead at the closed elevator doors.

"I hope so," he said. "I damn well hope so."

45

IN THE EMPTY, half lit hall of the research wing Jill's footsteps echoed ahead of her. She felt cold and hugged herself. It was strange not to hear typewriters clacking, telephones ringing. She hurried past locked doors and darkened portraits and—she averted her eyes—the office of William Stryker. Arnett's lab door was the last on the right. Jill raised her hand and knocked. While she waited, she turned and absently contemplated the blank wall which marked the end of the corridor. Something about that wall niggled at the back of her consciousness, and she was trying to figure out what it was when the door opened and Clifford Arnett was there, looking tired and rumpled in his white coat.

"Well, Jill! And I thought I was the only wee-hours lunatic around here. What brings you at this hour?"

Jill awkwardly held the Sawyer chart in one hand and with the other fumbled in her pocket for the wad of papers.

"Before they throw me out of here," she said, tight voiced, "I think you should take a look at these."

Arnett smiled and shook his head. "Nobody's going to throw you out, Jill. But come on in. You can tell me what's on your mind while I'm straightening up."

He held the door as she entered the room. Turning, she saw him watching her, studying her clothes. She looked down sheepishly. The scrub suit that had been fresh two hours ago was now torn and filthy. She raised a hand to her disheveled hair. Was he thinking that she had gone crazy? He's doing the humane thing, she told herself. Calming down a colleague who looks like she's on the brink. I'll try to sound calm and rational.

"Dr. Arnett—" she began.

"Wait," he said. He turned and shut the door. Jill heard the faint click of the lock.

He looked back to her and smiled. "Speak," he said.

She hesitated, then walked over to a lab counter. She put the Sawyer chart on top, carefully spread three pages of computer printouts, and began pressing out the creases. She heard him approach. Without looking up she said, "Dr. Arnett, I'm entrusting this information to you. Tonight, in the record room, I discovered the true magnitude of recent morbidity in the Obstetrical Department. Just *look* at the year 1984!" She pointed with her index finger. "The first six months of this year alone are already four times the total of all of last year. And the years before that there was practically nothing—"

"Oh my," she heard him say. He was leaning forward, peering at the printouts like an owl suddenly startled by a flashlight. "On my," he said again, and then: "May I?" He picked up the printout sheets and held them in his hands, studying them one by one.

Jill felt her heart pound. Her excitement told her that she had come to the right place.

As he read she plunged on. "Something horrendous is going on, Dr. Arnett. Something as yet unnamed but with a definite and deliberate pattern." She gulped air and dropped onto a stool. "Before I only suspected," she said. "Now I have proof. Obstetrical problems here are hideously above the national norm. I've found three—*three*—identical cases of rare chromosomal disorders, two in the last week alone, and the third, this Sawyer chart here, from last May." She patted the chart with her fingers.

Arnett looked up from the sheets. "Sawyer?" he said, frowning. "Sawyer?"

"Yes." Jill leaned forward, breathing rapidly. "And the printout speaks for itself wouldn't you say? Dr. Arnett, I have . . . interviewed a few former patients. I found one who is *convinced* she was unknowingly impregnated here, at the hospital, during a routine gyn exam. Now, normally one would dismiss such an assertion as irrational and hysterical, except that this girl sounds sharp as a tack, and in view of the *pattern* of the printout you're holding—the *huge* upsurge of *all* kinds of OB problems—well, I really think . . ."

She stopped, suddenly apprehensive about finishing the sentence.

She saw Arnett's eyes lift above his spectacles and look at her. "Yes?" he said.

She drew a long breath. "I have reason," she said, "to believe that Dr. Stryker and his DNA research associates—Gacey, certainly—have been experimenting on unknowing human subjects. The evidence gathered thus far merits an open investigation. Perhaps the matter should even be brought to the District Attorney . . ."

For a long moment Arnett looked at her. There was no expression on his face. "Well now," he said, "you certainly are a clever girl." He sighed and turned away. "I must be getting old."

Jill sat up on her stool. "I did nothing special," she called after him *"Everyone* in Obstetrics was getting alarmed at what was happening. It was just a matter of time—"

"Not the same," said Arnett. He sounded far away. He walked past another lab counter and stood at the window, gazing out. Jill noticed a thin gray line beginning to appear on the horizon.

"Not the same," he said again, and turned. He waved the printouts. "Oh, they may have noticed," he went on in a louder voice, "but . . . herd minds, you know. Too timid or ungifted to put the pieces together." He was walking back toward her, casually, stopping on the way to peer into a line of test tubes. "But that's what you did, Jill. You put the dissimilar, conflicting bits of information together and saw a pattern. Asked the right questions. God, what a great researcher you'd make!"

Jill frowned, feeling vaguely uncomfortable. She had a

sense that something was happening, something beyond her grasp.

"That's kind of you, sir, but after this I'm afraid—"

"Nonsense!" he said. "You've got the whole department over a barrel." He snorted laughter. "Pretty good for someone who's still an intern." He held up a test tube and examined its contents. "Have you told anyone else about your . . . findings?"

"Well, no, how *could* I? It was barely an hour ago that I . . ." Jill found herself staring at a pattern on the floor. It occurred to her that she was still waiting for Arnett to display more emotion, appropriate outrage, at her discovery. Why was he so calm, so . . . distant? Looking up, she watched him replace the test tube. Then, with another casual gesture, he folded the printouts and put them into his breast pocket.

Jill felt the first vague prickling of alarm.

He caught her gaze and touched his pocket. "They'll be safe here," he smiled. He resumed walking toward her, his lips pressed together in what appeared to be deep thought. Three feet away he stopped, hands in his pockets, feet apart. His muscular bulk strained at his white coat. For the first time Jill noticed that the front of his coat was faintly streaked with grime.

With a start she looked down at her own smudged scrub pants. Same color? Hard to tell. Her scrub pants were green; his coat was white. She was tired, she thought. Her mind was so strung out with exhaustion that it was playing tricks on her . . .

"Jill," he said. He turned and began to pace solemnly. "What if I were to tell you that you've got it all backwards? That nothing is what it seems? Your motivation, of course, is to help humankind. That is why you have entered medicine. But"—he turned to face her—"what if I were to tell you that calling attention to the hospital's . . . problems at this point would be *harming mankind?* Or that each of these . . . statistics was a tragic and highly, *highly* regrettable event on the road to the greatest and most

final medical breakthrough in all of human history? What
would you say to that? Hmm?''

She stared at him, speechless.

But he had asked her a question. He was waiting for an
answer, his head cocked expectantly.

"Greatest and most final . . . breakthrough? Greater than
. . . the discoveries of anesthesia and antibiotics?" She
began to ease carefully off the stool.

Arnett smiled and shook his head patiently. "Anesthesia
and antibiotics won't even be *necessary* any more!" He
waved an arm grandly. "Such is the *magnitude* of this
astounding breakthrough!"

Jill stood without moving, looking at him.

"Ah, don't mind my excitement," he said, striding
away from her, shoving some notebooks into a cabinet.
"In a minute you'll see why. Let's go look at my rats!"

"Your what?"

"My rats! No one else *knows* about them! You'll be the
first!"

Jill stood with her back against a blue steel cabinet, and
glanced quickly toward the door. "You mean your rat
embryos?" she said. "I heard about that experiment. Embryos fertilized in Petri dishes, and *kept* there—to see how
long they'd last? But yours all died, didn't they? That's
what I heard."

"No, *no*," he said. "It's just that I didn't want my
breakthrough techniques to be *copied!* You can understand
that, can't you?" He came to her and took her by the arm
and his manner became urgent.

"I am convinced," he said, "that after you see the
extraordinary things I am about to show you, you will put
everything—including this investigation of yours—into a
new and more *responsible* perspective."

She stared open-mouthed at him. He released her arm
and was suddenly off like a child, rushing ahead to new
toys, under the Christmas tree. Confused, Jill glanced
again over her shoulder toward the door. He *was* acting
rather manic, she thought, but maybe Arnett got like this
every night, like in the werewolf movies, and returned to

normal in the morning when the hallways filled with people and he was forced to don his controlled social facade. At the south end of the lab he was flinging open doors under the formica countertop, calling out "Come! Come!" to her over his shoulder.

What *were* these "extraordinary things" he wanted to show her?

Curiosity took hold. Uncertainly, she moved down the gleaming room and then watched as he yanked the top off a squat-shaped supply box in which she saw something moving.

Things moving, actually. The light was dimmer at this end of the lab, but Jill could just make out the interior, with its writhing mass of something mammalian. The fur was unlike any she had ever seen. Arnett reached in, detached one of the scuttling shadows from the rest and, grasping an evil-looking tail, held it up.

"Redesigned rats!" he said. His face was beaming.

"Redesigned . . ." Jill's eyes were riveted on the coat of the wriggling beast. Black and white, black and white; a near-perfect checkerboard. The animal seemed larger than any rats she had ever seen, with a larger brain area. But by far the most striking feature was the bizarre fake-fur design on the rodent's coat.

Jill found her voice again. "You . . . dyed it?"

Arnett smiled a magician's smile and lowered the animal back into its box. He slid the top back, but not all the way, Jill noticed. One of the corners still gaped open and she was about to mention this when Arnett's voice cut into her thoughts.

"My dear," he said, "I've rewritten their *entire* genetic code. You might even say I have created a whole new race of creatures to put on the face of this earth!"

"Genetic engineering . . . but how . . . ?"

"Long story. Has to do with fusing white rat embryos and black rat embryos. But come over here"—he took her arm—"I've got something even better to show you."

Jill was pulled toward a steel tank tucked unobtrusively under a lab table. Arnett kneeled and hauled out the tank, produced a key, and with trembling hands began to wrestle with the lock.

"Frogs!" he announced. "And every one of them a test tube tadpole!" He looked up into her disbelieving face, chortled, then threw back the cover, revealing what Jill at first thought were floating lumps of dough. Then, reacting to the light, one of the lumps began to move, then another, until in a moment the entire tank was awash with the crazy-car movements of perhaps a dozen albino frogs.

Jill's hands went to her throat. "But they're white," she said.

Arnett nodded happily. He picked one up, dripping, and held it firmly by the hind legs. The tiny pair of red eyes bulged. "These are really just ordinary bullfrogs. Or were, I should say. The first lot were all fertilized in vitro, kept alive in a liquid broth—*my* secret recipe!—and switched to water when the eggs were ready to hatch. At first I was pleased with the success of merely keeping frog embryos alive. But then it got dull. So I began to insert the most *wonderful* DNA into their cells." His features became thoughtful. "I thought white would be nice—so, with the next lot, I used ultraviolet light radiation to destroy all native genetic material in the eggs. Then I inserted a brand new nucleus from a cell removed from a true albino frog"—he looked at her—"they're tiny and rare. Have you ever seen that species?"

"Only in textbooks . . ."

"Very rare, very rare." He sniffed. "Well, one albino went a long way with me, because I used the intestine for a constant supply of my . . . designer genes. Ha!" He smiled coyly. "That's what the med students are calling it, aren't they? Designer genes?"

Jill did not answer. She couldn't take her eyes off the white bullfrog.

Arnett stroked the frog as if it were a prize spaniel. "I've also introduced enzymes into their genetic core that will guarantee them longer lives and immunity to disease." He eyed his frog, rapt. "Just think. Hereafter, you'll be able to rewrite an organism's whole genetic code to develop *any traits you want!"*

Arnett leaned forward to put back his little creation. He was muttering something that sounded like ". . . would've taken God fifty million years to pull off that one . . ."

Then he stopped, swearing softly. He switched the frog to his left hand, and began to tinker with a hose that looked like an oxygen supply unit for a fish tank.

In a flash the frog, still wet, squeezed free of the doctor's hand, landed on the floor, took one look around with his bulbous eyes and vaulted in three leaps across the floor to safety.

"Hey . . ." Jill started, checked herself, then stared at the place where the last trace of white had disappeared under a liquid nitrogen tank. Then she watched as Arnett shoved the tank back under the table. When he stood, he waved at the air dismissively.

"Don't worry about that little dickens," he said. "I'll catch him later."

"Why did you pretend failure?" Jill asked abruptly.

He looked at her and said reasonably, *"Had* to. Had a series of experiments I wanted to complete before I got *any* kind of attention. Don't you know that everyone *ignores* failures? It's the only way I could get any peace around here! And speaking of peace . . ."

He grabbed Jill's arm and began to push her toward the far wall lined with bookcases. "My dear, you haven't seen the most important thing of all. In no time this place will be crawling with ordinary mortals, and my work is not yet ready for just *anybody* . . ."

She pulled her arm away. "Dr. Arnett, I . . ." She was breathing rapidly, tried to control herself. "Your discoveries are astonishing, but somehow . . . we got off the track, didn't we? I mean, I came here to talk about human suffering and you . . . well"—she pointed toward the steel tanks—"those animals seem to be faring a lot better than the women on my computer printout. Now I really have to—"

"All your answers and more are right here," he said

patiently. *"Promise."* He rushed on ahead—a tactic that had worked before—and, mystified, Jill followed after him.

He had reached the wall crammed with bookcases and was busy pulling things off the shelves. A group of leather-bound books was heaved onto a stainless steel table. A jade figurine on top of the books toppled over with a clatter. It was an elephant. Jill's mind was in a whirl. She had seen that figurine before. Where? Where?

Arnett cleared away more things. "You will do nothing about that printout," he said. "After you see what I am about to show you, you will not *want* to."

With that he reached out and flicked a lever behind where the figurine had stood. There was a click and then a creaking noise. The wall moved; a six-foot rectangle detached itself from between a pair of mahogany columns, and groaned outward an inch or so. A gust of musty air wafted out.

"I ran out of room," Arnett said in a reasonable tone, "so I'm using space in the adjoining building."

Jill peeked in, squinting, wrinkling her nose at the faintly familiar odor. "Lab?" she asked. "Does anyone—"

"Better than a lab," he said. "And the *best* secret of all within. We'll have to hurry, before janitors and secretaries start arriving."

He smiled his most reassuring smile. She hesitated. What could be more amazing than what he had already shown her? He touched her arm, smiling again, and nudged her forward—over the threshold and into the darkness. Behind them the door closed. And then all was quiet.

46

THE DOOR TO the record room was open, and that was the first bad sign.

David stood inside the entrance, looking around, feeling his rapid heartbeat. She had been here; that much was clear. The lights were still on in the glass computer booth, and, he noticed, one set of fluorescents glowed dimly at the far end of the room.

The lights were the second bad sign. It wasn't like Jill just to go off and not close up properly. PLEASE TURN OFF LIGHTS WHEN FINISHED, read signs by the door, the cubicle entrance, and points in between. David rubbed his face with a shaky hand. What is it, he thought. What's going on?

"Jill? You in here?"

The only answer was silence. How could she still be here anyway? The page system reached the record room. She would have answered.

David hurried up the ramp to the computer booth. Entering, he could only guess at what had caused the turmoil. The chair seemed to have been flung away from its usual position, and the blue plastic cover of the console lay in a jumbled heap on the floor. David stared, looked around. No. This wasn't Jill. Fighting panic, he pushed the chair back into position, feeling foolish at the gesture, then bent to retrieve the cover.

It was then that he saw the black memo book.

It lay near the base of the machine, the pages dog-eared,

the corners of the cover curled from constant thumbing. *Compulsive* thumbing, David thought. Jill never went anywhere or made a move without consulting that notebook. He leafed through the pages. On the day marked July 15—today—he stopped. Here the handwriting was abruptly larger, and visibly agitated. He tried to make it out, turning so that the light fell directly onto the crowded page. Now the ballpoint scrawl fairly jumped out at him: quick notations of a few code numbers and chart numbers; the words "1984 8X mort rate!" and, in tall capital letters, "TELL D AND A!"

She tried, he thought. She tried.

Cursing under his breath, he shoved the memo book into the pocket of his jacket. Cassie said that Jill had tried to reach him around 3:50. That was when he was in surgery. Could she also have tried to call Arnett? No, that was unlikely. She was not about to jolt him awake at four in the morning.

Levine turned around in a slow, restless circle, looking for clues, wondering what to do next. Where had she gone after her call to Cassie? And why did she make the call from the *morgue?* Why not from here? He glanced at the phone on the counter next to the console. He peered through the glass, and saw the house phone that hung by the door.

Two phones right in the room and she had to run to the morgue?

He went out and started back down the ramp. His mind was working furiously. What bothered him most was Jill's handwriting. It was erratic, out of character. Amateurs would insist that this implied impaired judgment, but David knew better. He had seen Jill at her worst moments, and always, despite the strain, she had remained in his eyes a person of order and good sense. Which was why, halfway across the room, he jerked to a stop and stood staring in disbelief.

The floor between stacks six and seven looked as if someone had launched a wild and destructive charge up and down the aisle. Charts were strewn crazily, their contents spilling out.

David stood immobile. "I'm not seeing this," he said out loud. He thought for a moment that his mind was playing tricks on him; that this was what loss of sleep did. It made your head go bad and killed the power of logic and caused all kinds of hallucinations . . .

He came closer and hunched down like an explosives expert about to dismantle a bomb. He stared unblinking at the mess. His face was stiff with shock.

And then it hit him that Jill had not been alone down here.

He turned and looked up at the cubicle. She was up *there* alone; he knew it intuitively. The disorder was simply that: disorder caused by a person in a frantic rush, in a panic.

He looked back down at the destruction that stretched before him. Someone else had come. David knew it just as surely as he knew that character in crisis was still character, period, and that even under terrible duress Jill was not capable of . . . of this. Grimly he poked at the pink-sheeted lab reports that looked as if they had been trampled. He looked again. No, he realized, not trampled. They looked as if they had been *struggled upon:* black, dusty footprints of two different sizes tore across a battleground of littered, pastel papers. A library stool lay overturned in the aisle. A mashed, green-sheeted operative report lay under it.

"Oh, my God," David whispered, feeling terror shoot through him. He searched urgently through the sheets, finding reams of bad cases he hadn't even known about. So many! And Jill was attacked while discovering . . . this?

You can't leap from two twisted chromosomes to a hospital conspiracy, Jill.

Do tell.

1984 8X mort rate!

A picture rose in David's mind, an insanely tame picture of him taking Jill's blood pressure as she sat on the bed. He saw her talking. Telling him something. What? What? He tried to think, but his brain was careening. He pictured

her face. She was upset, insisting about *things* she had
discovered while interviewing patients . . .

He pulled out Jill's memo book.

He began to riffle slowly through the pages—and then,
because what had been lying just beyond memory suddenly came back, he found his hands moving faster as he
searched for what he needed.

Five seconds later he was across the room, yanking the
phone off the hook and dialing the number of Sheri Chang.

That was it. Jill said that Chang had called back with
something important, something she had forgotten to mention. David pictured an angry *Mr.* Chang answering the
phone, and was preparing a hasty apology when a woman's voice came on, groggy and confused. "Hello?"

David identified himself and spilled out an apology
anyway. "You called Dr. Raney back? What about? It's
important?"

"What? Oh. Yes, I called to tell her about a low-grade
fever I had. A few months before . . . the baby . . ."

"Fever? Fever? Why didn't you call your doctor?"

"I did. Dr. Arnett said it wasn't important."

"What?"

"He said it didn't mean anything at all. It started the day
after he did the amniocentesis, but he said low grade fevers
were common just after. He said to take aspirin, but I didn't.
I don't believe in drugs. He even offered to call in some
penicillin—"

"Penicillin?" Levine stared at the wall phone. No ethical doctor phone-ordered penicillin without examining the
patient. You had to find out first if the infection was
bacterial or viral. Any doctor knew that.

"Dr. Arnett didn't suggest that you come in to be
looked at?"

"Oh, no! He said it was *imperative* that I stay in bed
until the fever passed. And it did, finally. Doctor, that
fever *wasn't* important, was it? So low! Only 99.8."

David closed his eyes and said, "Yes, that is low. Well,
thank you. Sorry to have awakened you."

"That's okay," Sheri Chang said. "You'll give Dr. Raney the message?"

He hung up; the phone rang in his hand; he picked up again.

"David? It's Tricia."

"And Woody!" a deeper voice hollered from the background.

And then they both started to shout at once. First Tricia, sounding out of breath, telling David they had been all over the place, up and down the stairwells, but no sign of Jill. Then Woody, interrupting, to say that maybe they should try the cafeteria; and Tricia, shrilly insisting over Woody's voice that that was ridiculous: why would Jill be *there?*

David's mind was darting elsewhere, not paying attention, when he heard Tricia's voice again; and the words "strangest thing" were what pulled his attention back to the phone.

"What did you say, Tricia?"

"I said," she repeated patiently, "that while we were in the north stairwell, Woody noticed the strangest thing."

Woody was yelling in the background, and Tricia's voice pulled away from the phone to hush him. David could barely hear. "Get *on* with it, Tricia."

"Well. Woody noticed a light on in Cliff Arnett's lab! Now what do you make of that? Maybe somebody forgot to—"

"Gotta go," David said. He was on the point of hanging up, listening not patiently anymore to Tricia's pleas to phone in more often, then hearing Woody's voice again, stronger now, on the phone.

"My beeper!" shouted Woody. "Just don't forget you have it and for God's sake, if you need us, *use* it!"

Levine said he would, told them he was heading up to Arnett's lab, and hung up. A moment later he was tearing down the basement tunnel as if the rest of his life depended on it.

47

AHEAD THE DARKNESS was impenetrable. Jill turned to where Arnett had been standing.

"Can't see . . ." she said shakily.

She heard his footsteps move past her across dry wood. A low-voiced "wait" came to her from somewhere off to the right, and Jill swung around to try to guess where—

And then the lights came on. Not fluorescents, as in the research building, but low-hanging lights so dim, so yellow, that the tall figures on the opposite side of the room appeared as no more than a line of dark and formless blurs.

"Have a look," invited Arnett behind her.

Jill stood looking across the room, not breathing, then slowly moved forward, only half believing what she saw. When she reached the silent group, she blinked at them, then blinked again. Now she understood.

"Well?" Arnett called to her.

She did not answer. Slowly she made a complete circle around the first of the figures, staring at the apelike skull, the almost human, erect posture. In the half light she stopped to scrutinize the glassy-eyed face, and felt fear sweep through her. This was not the apeman that had toppled over her in the basement. This was the original, the first she had seen in the hominid workshop.

The one which had been stolen?

Glancing to the right, her eyes passed down the line of other figures: *Homo erectus*, a professional looking job (the *other* stolen hominid?); *Homo habilis,* looking a little mangy and badly put together; *Homo neanderthalensis,* taller, less amateurishly crafted; and finally, a Cro-Magnon couple, a man and a woman, the tallest and largest-brained of all. The man, his expression intelligent, held a spear in one hand and some sort of tool in the other. The woman, her face nearly obscured by a mass of black hair, held a knife and cooking tools in her clasped hands.

"Welcome to *my* museum!" Arnett was suddenly beside her, and she jumped. "You know," he said, "it's not hard at *all* to make these things. All you need is a knowledge of anatomy and a few . . . borrowed materials." The comment seemed to strike him as funny, and he laughed.

"Borrowed . . . materials," Jill repeated, staring at Cro-Magnon woman's black wig. He's insane, she thought quietly. It came to her just like that; the doubts and misgivings that had been tugging at her for the past thirty minutes now came rushing to the surface. The man steals museum property. Falsifies his research findings. Conducts secret experiments . . .

Jill turned to face him. He was watching her attentively.

"This . . . is your . . . big breakthrough?" she asked, gesturing unsteadily toward the lineup of mannequins.

In the gloom she could see Arnett's mouth slowly widen into a grin.

"You're not *serious,* of course."

Her fear deepening, Jill backed away.

"You have seen nothing," said Arnett. "Nothing! This is merely the evolutionary ladder that had to wait three million years for what *I* have accomplished in eighteen months!" He motioned with his hand. "Do you know where you are?"

The heavy rafters looming overhead, reeking of age; the antique fan window; the unmistakable smell of the place . . .

She nodded wordlessly. They were in the attic, of course. The attic of the Madison Museum of Anthropology. Arnett was using it as his lab "extension." *My museum,* he had called it. Jill's gaze traveled up the shadowy wall and she

saw an incongruous array of objects: medieval looking
amulets, a Civil War saw—the kind used for amputations—
and a collection of nineteenth-century obstetrical instruments that made her feel ill.

She turned back to Arnett, who opened his hands and
turned around grandly. "Someday this room will be more
famous than Edison's Menlo Park or Einstein's *mess* of a
library at Princeton.'This is where Arnett worked,' people
will say. Oh, yes!" He went to the wall and reached to
flick a switch. There was a snapping noise, and suddenly—
illumination. Real illumination. Fluorescents recessed overhead crackled on with blinding brightness.

Arnett smiled at Jill from his place by the wall. He
seemed almost to be toying with her. "Turn around," he
said. "Turn around very slowly."

Heart pounding, she rotated in a stiff jerky movement.
And then she looked.

In the center of the room, closer to the fan window,
sprawled a cluster of machines, most square or oblong in
shape, one soaring upward like a silo. The cylinder seemed
to be transparent, but the contents were dark. Around it were
monitors with banks of gauges and dials; tubes and colored
wires fed into it and then crisscrossed with each other.

He was at her shoulder. "Come closer," Arnett said.
Jill stiffened, ready to pull away. "Oh, come, come," he
said impatiently, and, taking her arm, led her firmly down
the room to the darkened container. "Look," he said, and
pointed to the cylinder.

She could see a vague shape inside. It seemed to be
floating. Arnett reached beyond her, turned a switch, and
illuminated the interior.

"Ohh!" Jill gasped. Her eyes flew open; her mouth
gaped, and for a moment she felt close to fainting. The
glow emanating from within was a soft, mellow pink. A
tranquilizing color.

And a perfect color, no doubt, for the temporary environment of a five-month-old fetus. Its eyes were closed; it
appeared to be sleeping. Its head was the size of a small
grapefruit. The rest of its tiny body was perfectly formed.

Jill brought both hands to the sides of her cheeks. In a voice full of incredulity she said, "A baby . . . ?"

"Five months!" Arnett said. "Five months of incubated life outside the body, and only four to go. Then its mother here"—he patted the silicone cylinder—"can get immediately to work on the next embryo. I'll have one ready *long* before then."

Jill looked at him, slowly lowering her hands from her face. "Mother . . . ?"

Arnett ignored the question. He was looking at the floating fetus and his eyes had taken on a look of exaltation. His voice when he spoke was trancelike.

"This fetus," he said, "has perfected gene systems. He is immune to all disease, including cancer. He will have an IQ in the range of two hundred, and will live at least to age one hundred and fifty, perhaps longer. I have given him an anti-aging gene into his cells. I've also given him a self-regulating enzyme that can convert carbohydrate to protein or fat, *and* vice versa, depending on his nutritional needs." Arnett's eyes gleamed. He turned to Jill for a reaction. "Not bad for a little chap who started life in a Petri dish. Well, now! What do you think of that?"

Jill stood in stunned silence.

Her face was ashen. She took an unsteady step backward. "No," she whispered. "Monstrous . . ."

She took another step back, and then another—

"See here!" he said, hurrying after her. "Monstrous, you say? *Monstrous?* Good Christ, girl, are you a physician or a fool? You are witnessing the . . . the *Creation* and you call it monstrous?" He released her arm and considered her for a moment. "Of course, it's a shock at first. No one is immune to emotions. However—"

"You left that *out?*" Jill interrupted. "Immunity to emotions?" Her face was clearing now, becoming angry.

" . . . however, you must recognize the absolute necessity of this new breed of human. *Homo sapiens* as we know him will be either extinct or living in misery in one hundred years. Less, probably. The world's resources will have been used up or poisoned. The last humans will die of famine, or in warfare over the last crumb, or the last drop of oil to light their lamps.'' He raised his fists; he was breathing hard through his nostrils. ''For tens of thousands of years man has survived by one thing only—his ability to adapt. But now, in the last quarter of this century, man has fallen *behind*. And is falling behind at a faster rate! Evolution, as we know it, taking thousands of years, has become ineffective!''

He unlocked his gaze from Jill's and let his hands drop by his sides. Watching him, Jill saw her chance. Appear to placate him, she thought suddenly. Pretend to shift away from resistance, or you'll wind up as dead as . . .

She was hit with a devastating thought.

She wiped her sweating palms on her scrub suit. She raised her eyes to the floating infant, struggled for a neutral voice. ''What kind of fluid is he floating in?''

''Synthetic nutrients,'' Arnett snapped. ''My own formula.''

She swallowed hard. ''Human amniotic fluid doesn't work? You've tried it?''

He made a dismissive gesture. ''It doesn't work as *well*. It's useful in other experiments, though.''

Jill thought of the two murdered girls. She felt the beginning of nausea, forced it down, forced herself to go on.

''And you say this infant is . . . immune to all diseases,'' she fumbled, ''and will live to *at least* one hundred and fifty?'' She looked at him. *''Really?''*

There. Done. She exhaled. The implied note of awe had been there, must have been there, because Arnett suddenly switched moods again and with a volatile gesture flung up his hands.

''She understands!'' he said, his heavy face coloring as he saw her gaze fixed—wondrously, she hoped—on the floating fetus. He pointed in its direction. ''And you understand the rest, don't you? Certainly a person of your immense gifts can see that we are living at the end of an era! That the old way of seeing the world is outdated. Destructive, even!''

He stepped closer to the cylinder and peered in musingly at the tiny sleeping face. "I feel like the Fates, you know, weaving in my little strands of DNA. I kept him in his dish until he had grown to thirty-two cells. By the way . . ." He turned back to Jill. *"That's* my first innovation! Not four cells. Not even eight. That doesn't give you enough time to *do* things to the embryo! That's for fools like Stryker who are too stupid—"

Jill gave a start. "You mean William Stryker had no hand in these experiments? He doesn't know anything about this?"

Arnett looked offended. "Do you really think *that* mediocrity is capable of *this?* Stryker is a drone! Good only for posturing, for calling conferences and school-marming residents. Indeed!"

Jill watched, feeling lightheaded, as he began to pace angrily around the container.

"People like Stryker," he said. "They and their so-called medical ethics *force* real genius into hiding. Force . . . real genius to do things which were once unthinkable. But for the greater good!" He paused. "Oh, they think they're benefiting mankind because they help a few individuals. Hah! Finger-in-the-dike medicine is what I call *that*. Could they even *dream* of human salvation on the scale I have achieved?"

He raved on, and Jill glanced furtively toward the door, calculating her chances of escape. Was the door locked from the inside? Was the distance, the length of the attic, too far to make a run for it? She glanced back to Arnett. He was standing in front of her with his back turned.

". . . Stryker's children are all *failures!*" he said. "Bright, yes. Geniuses, maybe. But all are as miserably mortal as man has ever been! Prey to illness and disease and absurdly short life spans—"

Jill started to move backward, step by step, not daring to take her eyes off him.

He still had not turned. She held her breath. Suddenly he slammed a fist into his open palm with such violence that she jumped.

"To think that fools should try to bar me from such advances! Don't you see? I have discovered the means to *accelerate human evolution!* It's a race against time. We *must* do this or the human race is doomed—"

Her feet were moving faster. Her body was half-turned, her wide eyes staring so fearfully at the ranting, white-coated back—". . . anti-aging genes were my *worst* problem!"—that she did not hear the soft, metallic sound of a doorknob turning, the rubber-soled shoes stealthily crossing the room, until they stepped on a floorboard behind her, and she wheeled and saw the face and screamed and tried to make a run for it. But it was no good; her attacker from the record room would not let go, had seized her by the wrist and was leering down at her as she flailed at him. And then she screamed again.

Arnett turned and stood unmoving, watching.

"Damn you!" he exploded, his eyes on the newcomer. "I buzzed you five minutes ago! What in hell took so long?"

48

TAKING THE STAIRS in twos, David whammed open the fourth-floor fire door and raced down the hall of the Sturdevandt wing. At Arnett's door he knocked loudly. No answer. "Jill?" he called out. "Clifford Arnett?"

Silence. He knocked again, loudly, and the sound of the pounding echoed the length of the floor.

Silence again.

He tried the door. It was locked. He frowned in alarm.

Woody and Tricia's call had come only four minutes ago. The light they mentioned must still be on. *Somebody* had to be in there.

He turned and dashed to a wall phone a few steps away.

He picked up the receiver, dialed, heard the familiar voice.

"Cassie, listen." He was breathing almost too fast to speak. "Send a security man up to Research North, fourth floor. Stat! You got that?"

"I'll send you an angel," Cassie said.

"Send me all your angels!" hollered Levine.

"Sorry, honey," said Cassie. "I'm down to my last one. And even *he* don't move too fast."

David hung up. Three minutes later the elevator doors opened and a small, olive-skinned man in uniform stepped off, carrying a giant ring of keys. When he saw David, he grinned.

"Hey, Angel," shouted David down the hallway. He gave the name its Spanish pronunciation. "How come the elevators only give the doctors a hard time?"

Approaching, Angel Torres grinned again. He put the key in the lock and turned it, looking at David. "Maybe you in the wrong business," he offered cheerily.

David grimaced. "No doubt about that," he muttered.

They went in. The place was dazzling with light. Every bank of fluorescents buzzed and flickered.

Angel whistled. "Dr. Arnett got a swell way a conservin' 'tricity." Then he turned to David. "Now what seems to be the problem?"

David smiled involuntarily. It was a joke. Angel had used the line he heard a hundred times a day from the doctors.

David thrust his hands in his pockets, grateful for the moment of levity. Then misery closed in again.

"I'm looking for Dr. Raney," he said. "She's missing."

Angel's eyes opened wide. *"Dios!"* he said. "I know all about that. Dr. MacIntyre, he's downstairs tearin' the place apart! He got extra guys watching the entrances, and he keeps calling the room she sleeps in. Can you eemachin *dat?* Calling an empty bed?''

"I know, I know . . ." said David. His eyes moved dejectedly about the room.

Across from him he saw something move. He stiffened. Angel started to speak but David held up his hand. He pointed to an unplugged dialysis machine. The two men stared.

It was just a whisper of movement at first, then nothing. After another moment, a pair of whiskers poked around the corner, then a rodent head.

"*Un ratón!*" said Angel, stooping to see. David made a sign to be quiet but the startled animal suddenly darted from behind its hiding place, scurried across the floor and disappeared under a liquid nitrogen tank.

Their faces froze. Angel straightened, shaking his head. "Now I *know* I got to switch to the daytime shift. Whew! I coulda swore that rat looked like a checkerboard."

"Shh," Levine whispered. Angel followed Levine's gaze and his jaw dropped. The top of a long, metal box under one of the lab counters was askew, and through a small triangular opening at one end another rat was squirming his way out.

A rat with black and white squares on his fur.

The physician and the security guard exchanged identical looks. Angel drew his gun. David gave another mirthless smile.

He crossed to the metal box, bent and lifted the lid slightly. Underneath, a sickening commotion of more squirming checkerboards.

He replaced the cover, carefully adjusting the clamps on all four sides. He was thoughtful for a moment. Angel came to stare over his shoulder.

"Oöcyte fusion," David muttered. He looked down incredulously at the metal box. "Arnett said he was having no success with this . . ."

Angel still had his gun drawn.

And it was a wonder the thing didn't go off right then and there, because suddenly Angel shrieked.

"Dr. Levine! Dr. Levine! Aye, chihuahua!" A torrent of Spanish followed that David, jumping up, could only partly make out because he was too busy subduing the hand that was wildly waving the gun.

Still gasping, Angel told him what had happened. Something had crawled over his foot. No, he corrected himself. Something had *waddled* over his foot, and it was *heavy*, and it was somewhere still here on the floor. He pointed here, there, looking apoplectic.

David glanced around. "There's nothing, Angel. I don't see a damn . . . ah . . . omigod."

In long strides he crossed to a wooden stool, bent, and seized the ready-to-lunge frog.

Angel stared. He would definitely go to church this Sunday, he decided. "A white fr-frog? With eyes like a leetle devil?"

David, studying the creature, had grown very still. Obviously its genetic makeup had been dramatically altered, an oddity, he realized, that surpassed even the bizarre phone call to Sheri Chang. The rats and the frog represented major research triumphs—and neither had been reported. Add to that the lights, the way the room looked as if its occupant had left just a minute ago, the scene of destruction in the record room . . .

He tossed the frog into a sink, watched it hop over to the wet drain. Then he turned to Angel.

"I'll be needing your gun, Angel."

"Wha . . . ? You gone crazy? You're not supposed—"

David took a step toward him. "If you don't give it to me," he said gently, "I'll have to take it."

Angel Torres looked up at Levine, who he realized, probably outweighed him by at least forty pounds. Besides, Angel *liked* Levine. The guard's small, dark features worked in confusion.

Levine's voice was soothing. "As soon as you give it to me," he said, "I suggest you go immediately back down to Security and tell them I took it from you."

Angel hesitated, gave a bewildered sigh. "You're the boss," he said.

He removed the .38 from his holster and handed it to David.

"Thanks," said David.

"Yeah," said Angel. Looking a bit subdued, he turned to go.

An incongruous thought popped into David's head. "Oh, by the way," he said to the departing guard. "What happened to the two other Angels on the force?"

Angel Torres stood in the doorway. "Them? Well, Angel Solano's working in a computer place. And Angel Vega? He's a night watchman now in a church that's been getting vandalized. You know, nuns getting raped, the works."

"Vega's a good man," said David.

"Yeah." Angel Torres' gaze dropped to David's right hand.

"That gun," he said. "Use it *good* okay?"

49

JILL GAPED AT the gaunt face, the pointy chin.

Seeing him in this setting jogged another memory, buried and barely perceived the first time, of having seen him before, this sallow-faced young tough whose fingers were still clamped painfully around her wrist.

"Close the door, Sonny," Arnett ordered.

Sonny. Sonny . . . Sears? The young assistant sweeping scraps in the hominid room?

Peking's light bulb is broken, Sears.

Jill jerked her arm away, shaking, backing away from

Sonny Sears. Her gaze dropped to the green running shoes that he wore, and in all-out horror she looked over to Arnett.

"I *said*, close the door!"

Sears looked at Arnett and then jerked his thumb at a door located across from the one Jill had passed through.

"You know what took so damn long?" he whined. A definite Southern drawl, Jill noticed. "First she nearly cracked my head open. Then I couldn't find her. And you should see the freakin' mess she made downstairs! Busted things and knocked over a dummy, and his guts is lyin' spilled all over the place!" He leered at Jill. "That should be *you* with your guts lyin' spilled all over—"

"That will be enough, Sonny," Arnett said. He thought a moment, then said, "All right, I guess you'll have to go back down. Clean up whatever is there before the guards come to open the museum."

"*What?* Not when I got *her*, I'm not gonna go! She ain't *easy* to catch, and you said you—"

"There's been a possible change," Arnett said mildly. He looked at Jill, silent and frozen-faced. "The important thing is that she has *seen* you, isn't that right, Dr. Raney? You know that I am very . . . serious. And Sonny, if there's any further trouble and I call, I want you here on the double. Do you understand? Now off you go, please."

Sonny lifted his chin high and tucked his thumbs into his belt. "I don't take orders from nobody."

Arnett smiled pleasantly. "Then you shall get heroin from nobody."

Sears gave Jill a murderous look. "Shee-it!"

"*Now*, Sonny."

Sears made no reply. Scowling at Arnett he turned, crossed the floor, and disappeared through the door that led down the museum stairs.

Jill closed her eyes. Don't react, she thought. Keep your face blank. If he gets hostile you're dead. She opened her eyes and saw that he was watching her. She tried to control her voice.

"You . . . give him h-heroin?"

"I also give him money—more than he's worth, you can be sure—but . . . he's done some important errands for me."

Such a wonderful young man, Jill remembered. Thank you, Vera Crowley. "Yeah, right," she said.

Arnett eyed her appraisingly. "Of course, not the kind of errands I *need* for my present stage of experiments . . ."

He had walked around and placed himself, arms folded, feet apart, between Jill and any escape route to the door. Might as well roll over and play dead, she thought. She sank onto a chair and gripped the edges of it tightly, avoiding his eyes.

"You . . . said there's been a possible change," she said. Events, she realized, were beyond her control; and perhaps because of that she was surprised to feel her fear receding. I flattered him once, she thought. Now if only I can keep up the pretense, maybe I'll survive the night, find out more about this experiment, what he knows about the women on that grotesque printout . . .

"Excuse me?" she said.

He had said something she hadn't caught. That was bad; Arnett must think she was impressed by his work, hanging on every word. Careful, careful, she thought, and then: No, I can't, I'm so tired.

"I said that I'll be blunt." Arnett pointed to the cylinder with the floating fetus. "I had second thoughts after sending Sonny for you, and was *so* delighted when you showed up at the door. It has occurred to me that I could use you."

She stared at him blankly.

"You see," he continued, "starting tomorrow and thanks to your damnably ingenious snooping, I, like the rest of the faculty, will be under close scrutiny. I won't be able to come in here every two hours to monitor this fetal life-support system. I would like you to do that for me." He smiled at her congenially. "Wouldn't you prefer that to having to worry about Sonny tracking you down? Think of the irony! You're the last person in the hospital anyone would suspect of something like this!"

Jill held her breath. I'm not hearing this, she thought. She kept her body still and her expression solemn as the cunning voice went on.

"Your printout, of course, must not be divulged, at least not until the child is born. Only four more months of silence, and then it needn't even *be* a secret any more! The astonishment in the medical community will offset any . . . sacrifices that were made along the way, I'm sure of it." He bent to check his instruments. Across an oscilloscope screen beeped a continuous green tracing of the fetal heartbeat: a healthy one hundred sixty per minute. He adjusted a knob, then straightened.

"Now about the electrolyte solution," he resumed. "You must be sure that—"

"What sacrifices?" Jill blurted.

He turned to face her. "Now, see here! I thought we would discuss this like—"

"But I have to know everything if I'm going to help you," Jill said, just a little too sweetly.

He hesitated. Jill could see he was torn between the habit of secrecy and the desire to brag.

She said calmly, "Those two teenage girls. You were referring to them, weren't you?"

Arnett stared at her. The blood seemed to rush into his jowly face. "Of *course* not!" he said. "You call trash like that a sacrifice? They supplied me with amniotic fluid for some tests, that's all! It was simplicity itself teaching Sonny to use a twenty cc syringe. He's been putting stuff in for so long, it was easy to teach him how to take it out. I told him, you sink it in just three inches, no more or you'll—"

Jill felt a wave of nausea. She calculated—two girls, two unborn infants. Four lives. For some *tests*. She felt close to tears. Then she heard Arnett moving again.

He had made a half circle around the cylinder and now stood, looking up, his hands held tensely behind his back. Jill could see his face through the silicone. Like all rounded lenses, it distorted the image on the other side. Arnett's features looked broken and grotesque.

"My surgical patients were a regular spawning ground," he said. "I scheduled *lots* of tubal ligations for ovulation time. Even an occasional hysterectomy would yield an egg or two. Well, I did what *had* to be done to those eggs, and then my reimplantation program began about eighteen months ago. Clinic patients, private patients, every female *Homo sapiens* I could get my hands on.

"Well, you know the story! You saw it right there on your damned printout, which fortunately no one is ever going to duplicate. *They'll* never put the pieces together the way you did!"

Jill avoided looking at him. "I . . ." Her voice shook. "I had no idea those statistics were connected to . . . anything so awesome as this." That much at least was true. She lifted her eyes to the fetus with an expression that was genuinely astonished.

"Ah." Arnett looked pleased. He walked the rest of the way around the cylinder and stopped a few feet from her. Over his shoulder Jill could see the fan window at the end of the attic. Outside the light was becoming murky; it was the last few minutes before dawn.

"At any rate," he said, "*those* are the sacrifices I regret. The hospital patients. I anticipated fewer problems, of course." He exhaled heavily. "Jill, I understand how you feel. Experimenting on human beings without their consent goes against the code of medical ethics. But consider it this way—a few sacrifices made toward the betterment of all humankind! Also, the failures are in the *past*. With the help of this prototype"—he pointed at the fetus—"I have perfected every technique. Hereafter I can impregnate women at a faster rate with a *much* lower risk factor—and think how society will benefit! Think also," he said, coming closer, "that you'll be my assistant. You will *share* in the glory!"

Jill looked at him. She saw that he meant it, the part about her being his assistant, at least, and it made sense: he needed her; he was insane; he was convinced the world would swoon over his triumph when he revealed it.

In four months.

After he impregnated and endangered the lives of how many more women?

I could save my skin if I wanted to, Jill thought.

She rose stiffly to her feet. In a daze she walked past Arnett, past a metal box that was making soft, pumping sounds, and stopped at a temperature gauge attached to the side of the cylinder. The mercury read 98.6. She saw the fetus, sleeping, give a little twitch.

"But how did you *do* it?" she asked softly. "How did you get all those women pregnant so easily?"

Arnett followed after her so hurriedly that he knocked over a chair. "I didn't *get* all of them pregnant," he said with sarcasm. "Oh, I would have *liked* to: indeed, my in vitro fertilization and embryo transplant methods were already more sophisticated than Stryker's. The problem was"—he gestured angrily—"many patients came to me already pregnant. That's when I recommended amniocentesis as often as I could. You know, of course, that I lowered the maternal age requiring amniocentesis to thirty—"

She spun to face him. "*That* was the reason? But I thought—"

". . . and then it was simplicity itself to load the syringe with my altered DNA solution." He scowled. "But that's not as good as getting your *own* egg in from the outset. The clinic patients were the best for *that*. And the private artificial insemination cases were also good. They're considered so routine now; you don't have people *standing* over you, watching—the way Stryker does over every single in vitro job!"

Jill heard the sound of paper crumpling. Arnett had taken her printouts from his breast pocket, and was twisting them, twisting . . .

She asked carefully, "You mean you never . . . altered any of the in vitro fertilization cases?"

"Who could get *near* them? That Stryker thinks he's the moral watchdog of the Western world! He has been *such* an obstacle to me that I'd like to . . ." The hands were twisting harder now; trembling. Abruptly Arnett threw the mangled printouts into a wastebasket and shoved it under a table.

Jill thought, he's getting hostile again, I mustn't lose him. She steadied herself with a hand on a monitor and forced a sympathetic look. "Well, that certainly made it hard for you, didn't it? Limited to amniocentesis and artificial insemination cases?" She thought of Warner and Chang and her heart turned over.

"No! I told you! Every clinic and private patient I could get my hands on, remember? They had artificial insemination too, they just didn't know it! It's easy. You just use that syringe with the soft plastic tip, and inject your embryo. The patient barely feels it entering the cervix."

"But the nurses—" Jill was breathing too fast again; she knew she was pushing her luck. "A *nurse* has to be present during every exam—how did you explain that special syringe unless . . ." Her face went slack; she remembered. "Oh," she said, looking down. "The cervical mucous tests . . ."

"Very *good!* Oh my! You certainly have been doing your homework." Abruptly Arnett whirled away, distracted, rubbing his hands. Jill went after him, stumbling over creaky floorboards. They were approaching the line of hominids. She listened as he waved his arms in complaint.

"Such a pity! Such a pity! To have *wasted* the most perfect protoplasm in human history on requisite test runs. I had inserted the most *marvelous* DNA into every cell! Stocked those little Petri ponds with the most advanced enzymes!" He stopped to brood. "Well, I suppose it was necessary . . ."

"Human incubators," Jill murmured, and her voice cracked a little. "Only most of the pregnancies didn't take, right? Miscarriages, fetal abnormalities, a maternal death here and there . . . right? The human factor backfired."

He shook his head angrily. "I *told* you I have perfected every technique. Those things are in the *past,* I am confident. Starting tomorrow, in the clinic . . ."

Jill turned away from Arnett; saw painful images of Maria Moran, Mary Jo Sayers, and tiny Christopher Sayers.

She looked back. A stillness overtook her, as if all the cards had been dealt, the most frightening plays made. She could quit here, she knew, and probably still get out safely. Yet some lunatic part of her mind pushed her to ask one more question—the one that would not rest.

"So, Dr. Arnett," she said, drawing a breath. "You must have known all along what became of Mary Jo Sayers."

Arnett's back was to her. He was staring moodily out a pair of derelict French doors, located near the door Sonny Sears had used, and giving out onto the highly pitched Gothic roofline. The sky beyond was turning a lighter shade of gray. Slate shingles glistened, wet with dew.

Nervously, Jill began to speak faster. "It's just that she was the only case who disappeared under such mysterious circumstances, and her chromosomal abnormality matched Moran's and Sawyer's, and I thought maybe you . . ."

She thought she saw his back stiffen. When he turned, he fixed her with a look that sent a chill through her.

"Mary Jo was my colleague," he said in a low voice.

Jill looked at him.

Arnett nodded, then gazed over Jill's shoulder with a fond expression on his face. "We became acquainted when she came to interview me on certain aspects of my research. For her doctorate. I was delighted to meet her, of course. Her feelings about accelerating human evolution were as urgent as my own."

Jill stared blankly at him, trying to absorb this new bit of information.

Arnett turned back to face out the window. "It was a catastrophe, that birth. She turned against me. I pleaded with her, promised that an egg from the current crop would turn out brilliantly—but she refused to try implantation again. She was vehement . . ." Jill saw his hands clench.

"You mean, Mary Jo Sayers *knew?* You impregnated her with one of your DNA embryos and she *knew?*"

He spun around. "She *requested* it, for God's sake! She *wanted* to be the mother of the first . . . the first . . ."

"Superhuman?"

"Goddamn it! Stop sounding like a comic book!"

Jill felt dizzy, as if the floor had shifted under her feet. "But where is Mary Jo *now?*" she persisted. "A person doesn't just disappear into thin—"

"Enough!" Arnett said. "I cannot tell you more. Suffice it to say that she is . . . involved in another phase of the project."

"That's the truth?"

"That is the truth."

Jill turned away. "Dr. Arnett . . . you must realize that this is a lot to take in in one go. I haven't slept all night. I'll be back soon"—*and not alone, you madman*—"and you'll show me what you want me to do . . ."

She took a step toward the door.

"Yes," said Arnett, watching her go.

She continued babbling, forcing herself to walk. She could not believe her feet were moving toward the door . . . and he wasn't stopping her. Had she actually made it? She had pretended to be impressed, and he had bought it, and he was letting her go so she could run to David and the others as fast as—

"You never mentioned my hominids," he called after her.

She looked back across the short space she had covered. "Hominids?" Her voice was reedy with fatigue.

"Yes, I'm rather proud of my evolutionary lineup. I had to learn a whole new skill! Sonny appropriated the materials, of course, but still—well, what do you think of my craftsmanship?"

He was looking at her with his head to one side, as if awaiting praise.

"Oh," she said. The door was a good twenty feet away. It could be locked, she realized. There was no choice. She would have to humor him, play one more little game, steel herself for just another minute . . .

She retraced her steps and stood before the first three figures in the lineup. Under different circumstances she would have laughed. The *Australopithecus* was so amateurishly done it looked almost like a huge, stuffed rat; the *Homo erectus* was a little better, but a far cry from any Peking or Java man she had ever seen pictured; and the Neanderthal—

Arnett said, "They get better as you move up the line, don't you think?" He was leaning casually on the jamb of the French doors.

Jill nodded uncomfortably and moved on. "Your . . . Neanderthal man is good," she said, and felt a prick of alarm as soon as she said it. *Why is he doing this?* I've seen the source of his vanity; he doesn't care about this bunch of stuffed dummies. Confused, she remained standing, scanning the other mannequins, trying to pinpoint what it was about Arnett that had suddenly changed. Was it the way he stood, affecting casualness, yet somehow rigid? Or those eyes, watching her, waiting for . . . for what?

"Intelligence!" exclaimed Arnett. "It's the hardest thing to depict, don't you think? That's why the Cro-Magnon pair gave me the most trouble. They're the most advanced, of course, coming just before *Homo sapiens.*" He stood erect, his gaze growing more intense. "Tell me, do you think I did a good job on the Cro-Magnons? I'd be *most* interested in your opinion."

A ruse. He was using the mannequins as . . . as what? A delaying tactic? Had he seen something that she hadn't seen? She spun around, looking for trouble, or Sonny Sears, or some new kind of threat . . .

There was nothing. In the ticking stillness she turned back, moved to the Cro-Magnons. The details *were* well-done: the man with his tool and his spear; the woman with her knife and cooking utensils in her clasped hands. And the black, long-haired wig; that was what Jill had remembered most vividly. She looked again from the man to the woman, and then stopped, her eyes locked on the woman's face. She went cold. Arnett had been testing her; she knew it now with sickening certainty, just as she knew that under the wig and beneath the thin, doll-like layer of plaster, the distorted features of Mary Jo Sayers stared grotesquely, tragically out at her.

The game was over.

She went rigid with shock and then she screamed, but not before powerful arms had yanked her savagely off her feet.

50

LEVINE WAS CHECKING the .38 revolver. The cylinder was full, which he expected. He half-cocked the hammer and spun it several times, checked the safety, then slammed the cylinder back into position.

And then he wondered what to do next.

As he shoved the gun into his belt, the thought came to him that the weapon had already served a purpose of sorts. It had kept his hands busy, his mind momentarily occupied. The respite had lasted all of ninety seconds. And then the grinding worry came back with a vengeance. He hadn't found Jill after all. The trail had led here, and the trail had gone cold; yet some intuitive pull kept him from leaving. He began to pace, glancing at his watch. It was a little after five. Outside Arnett's long line of windows the black of night had lifted. It was almost dawn.

David stopped by a lab table, looking absently around at the equipment, the lines of stools, the far end of the room. Arnett's bookshelves looked messy, even from here. David sighed heavily. A feeling of futility had begun to envelop him. Dear God, no, he thought. I have to find her!

A muffled thud came to him, and his head jerked up. It had been a distant sound, as if from the other side of the wall. He looked around, confused. Dammit, there *wasn't* any other side of the wall. Two exposures—east and north— were exterior walls. That left the wall running along the corridor and . . . Stryker's office?

David scrambled for the door and hurried outside to the hallway. It was empty. He sprinted one door down and peered through the glass in Stryker's door. The glass was dark, and inside was thick with silence.

He stepped back, frowning.

A moment later he was back in Arnett's lab, standing motionless, straining his hearing; but the place was silent and he began to suspect that his exhausted mind was imagining things. His eyes smarted from lack of sleep and he felt too dizzy to think. That sound . . . had he actually heard it?

He turned to close the door to hear better, and then— unmistakably—he heard a scream. He whirled around, his pulse rocketing sickeningly. It was in *here*, somehow, but . . . *where?*

"Jill!"

He scanned the room, frantically trying to decide which way to run. Another moment passed; he stood, frozen and listening, waiting for the next sound, and then it came—a muffled struggle, another dull thud from—his head jerked around—*from the other side of the north wall?*

It wasn't possible. That meant from *outside* the building. David ran the length of the lab, then stopped, uncomprehending, at the wall crowded with antiques and bookshelves. Stacks of books were leaning precariously, ready to topple. He turned, saw another pile of books and a carved jade elephant on its side sitting incongruously on a supplies table. Slowly his gaze traveled back, traveled up the mahogany columns in an expression of dawning comprehension that barely had time to register before he heard— but just barely—a man's shout of anger and a girl's sobbing pleas.

"Jill!" he shouted at the top of his voice.

David heaved books and crashed paraphernalia to the floor, clearing a wide space, palpating with trembling fingertips for a hollow place, a way through. The sounds of struggle on the other side were receding, as if someone were being dragged . . .

He pounded the wood with both hands. It would not move. In a frenzy he rapped in a line going straight across, right to left; nothing but masonry behind the layer of wood, and then—hollow!

He spent seconds rapping up and down. Big and hollow. *A door?* He stepped back and flung himself against it with a force that splintered wood and exposed large areas of old brick. He looked: part of a heavy door had been exposed. He stepped back, shaking from effort, realizing the door was probably bolted from the other side. His shoulder was throbbing.

Please God, he thought.

Desperately he looked around him. He reached down instinctively and flicked on Woody's beeper. Then he dashed fifteen feet to the fire alarm and pulled the red lever.

The next seconds passed like a bomb going off in slow motion. Woody's beeper began its insistent bleat; and then the ear-piercing alarm came on in the rising and falling wail of an air raid siren. Elsewhere in the building other sirens could be heard going off.

David ran back to the wall. He raised his foot and crashed through the door with a force that left a gaping hole. He tore wildly at shards of splintered wood and then scrambled through.

He was unaware of the sirens, the musty smell and rotten floorboards that he was racing madly across. One image only burned into his brain with a horror that drove him harder, his feet pounding furiously toward a pair of open French doors with their panes badly shattered.

Beyond the doors stretched the rising slope of a gabled roof. And struggling near the edge of the roof were two figures. The hulking figure of Clifford Arnett was only inches away from hurling the smaller figure to its death. And the smaller figure was Jill.

51

THE OTHERS HAD regrouped on the second floor, outside the Administration office.

Sam MacIntyre, back from a search of the emergency and outpatient areas, stood in the hallway talking to an ashen-faced Tricia Donovan. Inside, through the open door, Woody Greenberg could be seen replacing a receiver on one of the front desks. A gray-haired security guard stood at his side.

Woody came out. "Stryker's on his way," he said. His voice was husky. "I've never heard him sound so upset."

MacIntyre looked at him. "What was the second call?"

"Stryker said to call the police."

Tricia peered down at a soggy Kleenex in her hand. "*Cannot* believe this," she whispered. "Oh, my God . . ."

There seemed nothing else they could say or do. The two men, grim-faced, stared down at their shoes, and Tricia Donovan burst into tears.

And that was when Woody's beeper went off.

The rhythmic chirping filled the hall and reverberated off the walls and raised three sets of eyes to each other in sudden, heart-stopping comprehension.

And then the fire alarm. Far off at first, somewhere in the building but above them, followed seconds later by the hospital-wide alarms. One went off right over their heads and Tricia screamed.

"Sounds like the north wing!" shouted MacIntyre.

The security guard was already hollering into a house phone. "Arnett's lab!" he said, slamming the phone down.

MacIntyre, taller and faster, took the lead with Woody only yards behind. And Tricia, doing her best and screaming "Wait for me! Wait for me!" followed after them as they charged madly for the stairwell.

52

LEVINE BURST THROUGH the smashed double doors. Without breaking stride he jumped onto the steep-angled roof, landed off balance with one foot higher than the other, corrected his skid on the slates and then stumbled ahead.

They were struggling twenty feet away from him, now fifteen, now—

He saw Arnett shove Jill over the edge.

His heart stopped. "No!" Then he saw Jill's hands, scraped and bleeding, clinging for life to a wrought-iron gutter. Arnett, crouching, was trying to peel Jill's fingers away.

"Bastard!" David screamed. The diversion worked. Arnett released his grip and, looking up, looking like a mad animal suddenly cornered, reversed his weight and began to clamber back up the slates.

Levine let him go. He flung himself forward, pitching headlong onto his belly and sliding down another six feet toward the edge. His left foot hit the gutter, and he felt it start to give way. He thought he and Jill were both going to plunge down the sixty-foot drop—but the gutter held and appeared only bent.

She was out of his reach.

"Jill!" he yelled.

Still on his belly he inched his way forward. She was now scarcely three feet away. He heard her scream, saw one bloodied hand quit and let go. With a convulsive jerk he pulled himself closer, then heard a cracking noise as the gutter began to pull free. He heard his voice shout her name again; leaned out over the edge, and tried not to look down as his left arm hooked down and under her shoulder. He grabbed tight and pulled, using his other arm for leverage as he struggled upright again—heaving her over the top to safety.

With a crashing noise, the gutter collapsed and fell away from the building.

A yard from the edge, Jill lay facedown and sobbing. David lifted her to him and cradled her in his arms. He heard a noise. Turning he saw Arnett inching his way back down toward them. Levine thrust his hands under her shoulders, getting ready to carry her in a fireman's lift. Peripherally he saw a quick movement from above, then felt a sharp and painful crack on the side of his head.

Dazed, he looked up. Arnett, his expression gone to demented fury, had thrown a loose slate shingle at him; and, tugging at stony points along the roof's surface, was about to pull out another.

Ignoring the spreading, warm stickiness on his temple, Levine turned back to Jill. She was reaching for him, struggling to speak. He bent his head closer. "I can walk," she said.

"Come on," he said, pulling her up. He pulled one of her arms around his waist and they took a step. He saw the burly arm above them curving up again and he shouted, "Down!" just as another razor-edged piece of slate struck the side of his head, and he reeled, feeling momentary blackness.

The second hit was worse. He tried to get up, and stumbled. He struggled to think, but it was as if a curtain of fog had closed over his mind, and all that he knew was blind rage.

For the first time, he thought of the gun. Angel's gun, heavy inside his belt. Use it! his senses screamed. He saw Arnett fifteen feet above him tugging at another piece of slate. He reached under his white jacket for the gun and his fingers tightened around the grip. And then the reality of that grip brought him to his senses—partway, at least.

No, he thought. Doctors don't shoot doctors.

I'm going to kill him with my bare hands.

He did not know where his strength came from. He pulled Jill like a rag doll up another eight feet and then left her there, on her hands and knees. "Go!" he yelled. He saw her begin to crawl. He twisted around, possessed by a rage he had never known, and went after Arnett.

Arnett saw him coming. He turned, clambered up the roof to the ridge and stood clutching at a chimney.

Stumbling and slipping on the slick surface, David scrambled toward him. A yard away he stopped in a half-crouch. Their eyes met. Arnett's lips stretched into a mocking grin. David was below him—an easy target. Still hanging on to the chimney, Arnett drew back his free arm and made a fist. David made a quick ducking motion, allowed his adversary to swing wildly, then stepped up and inside the swinging arm and punched him hard in the face. The force of the blow drove Arnett backward against the chimney, a whole side of which crumpled, sending bricks in a dusty avalanche skidding down the roof.

"Help me! Help me!"

Struggling to regain his balance, David did not see Arnett lose his footing. By the time his head cleared, Arnett had hurtled downward fifteen feet, grasping at a tile that had momentarily stopped his fall.

"Help me, damn you!" Arnett screamed; and even now, in this desperate moment, David saw madness blazing out of his eyes.

David looked over to Jill. She was halfway to the French doors, looking down at Arnett in horror.

Warily, David began to pick his way downward. Even a monster like this, he thought with disgust, has a right to a trial. The fog was lifting from David's mind. In the distance he could hear the wailing police sirens. You'll get your due process, you bastard, he thought; and just as he came close enough to hunch down and extend a hand, he heard Jill scream. Glancing up, he saw the expression of *new* horror on her face. She was looking behind him, at a point halfway up the sloping roof. He turned to see, and as he did, he heard a sudden snap of tile and a hideous scream as Clifford Arnett slid plunging to his death.

There was no time to look back. Up to the right David saw Sam MacIntyre burst through the French doors, yelling, "Levine, behind you!"

Levine already had his gun out. He had seen the fast-approaching figure of Sonny Sears with his upraised arms carrying a cinder block which he was about to bring crashing down on David's head.

He never had a chance. David spun away and raised his gun. He fired only once. It was the best shot—the only shot, actually—he had made in years. Sonny Sears fell, rolled over once on the roof grade and then lay, watching the sky with two sightless eyes—and a gusher of a bullet hole lodged right between them.

53

SHE WAS AWARE of hands, most of all.

David's first, gripping her protectively as they stumbled their way back. Then other familiar hands, reaching out, grabbing her arms and helping her through the window to safety. She saw her friends' faces as though from a hazy distance: Tricia, whimpering encouragement, trying and failing to get her to sit down; Woody, his rapid voice

blurred as his thumb and forefinger pressed the inside of
her wrist; MacIntyre, a hand on the back of her shoulder,
telling someone to run for something which she could not
make out.

And still she clung to David.

"It's all right," he was whispering. "It's all right." He
had his arms around her and was holding her tightly. She
realized she was shaking violently.

Someone came running with gauze and alcohol swabs.

Jill heard Tricia's voice, very gentle. "You've got to let
go, hon."

Jill released her grip, pulled back, and looked at David.
Her fingers went to the side of his head. Bright blood ran
from his temple down the side of his face. "Oh David,"
she said. Her eyes filled with tears. Levine grinned weakly
at her. "We'll have matching scars," he said. He patted
her cheek; then, still standing, he slumped back against the
wall.

Tricia climbed up on a chair and began sponging his
wound.

"Ow, dammit, that hurts!"

"You make a terrible patient," Tricia said.

The alarms had been turned off and Jill's shaking had
begun to subside. She gripped the back of a chair and
watched as the others dressed David's wound; MacIntyre
had actually got him to sit down.

When she spoke her voice sounded hoarse. "That creep
on the roof worked for Arnett, you know."

They stopped what they were doing and looked at her.
Tricia said, "Do we dare guess the rest?"

"I'll be right back," Jill said.

She half-limped down the room, hard work because she
hurt all over. She bent, groaning, reached into the brown
wastebasket, retrieved her printouts, walked painfully back.

People were rushing into the room. Some of the white
coats stopped to stare, bewildered, at the door they had not
known was there. Two surgical residents—she vaguely
knew one of them—had joined the group around David
and were talking excitedly.

"The *roof?*" one was saying. "Arnett? Oh, my God!"

Jill, approaching, said, "There's more."

She felt their eyes on her as she sank into a chair, pried open the three twisted sheets with the printout figures and smoothed them on her lap. She looked up for a second. MacIntyre was busy taping a gauze square to David's forehead; David and the others were watching her intently.

Stammering slightly, stopping often to catch her breath, Jill told them about Arnett's experiments, using women's bodies as human incubators for his DNA-treated superembryos.

They stared at her, white-faced.

"Mostly clinic patients for *that* approach," Jill went on. "Private or already pregnant patients got their DNA in a syringe during amniocentesis. He did private artificial inseminations too." She held up the papers. "These printouts tell the story. Look at the jump for this year. His implantations all turned out badly in *different ways;* that's why no one could figure it out."

Tricia pulled in her breath.

"Labs!" Jill said. "He used women's bodies as *walking labs!*"

They gaped at her in disbelief. Woody Greenberg leaned on the mangled doorway looking as if he was going to be sick. David reached across to Jill for the papers.

"Let's see," he said.

As he read she told more. About the two murdered girls, their amniotic fluid used for experiments. *Yes, just experiments.* She told them of the fetus floating in the cylinder, and saw their eyes go, squinting, toward the other end of the attic. It was hard to see much from here. The attic was a good sixty feet long; from this distance the array surrounding the cylinder looked like any jumble of medical equipment.

David finished scanning the printouts and looked up. He wore the expression of a man just let off a plunging elevator.

Jill leaned forward. "David! *Nobody* figured it out. Not Stryker, not Simpson or Rosenberg, nobody! Arnett was too—"

"She's right, David."

Jill turned in her seat. Above her stood William Stryker, his face ashen.

"Oh, Dr. Stryker—"

"Jill," he said. He seemed awkward, at a loss for words. Then: "Thank God you're alive. Please . . . accept my apology."

She stood up to face him, her mouth slightly open. "I . . ." Words failed her, too. She saw that he had thrown on a pair of old pants and a shirt that looked as if it had been yanked out of the laundry. He looked older, thinner inside his clothes.

Jill felt a sudden surge of sympathy for him. All along this tight-lipped, cold authoritarian had been . . . was it afraid? Not afraid for himself, she thought; but for his still-controversial program which could be torpedoed by one breath of scandal; which hundreds of infertile couples were still depending on desperately for help.

And the worst of it was, she hadn't told the whole story.

She looked at Stryker, at each of her friends. "There's one more shock to go," she said quietly.

No one spoke; their silence seemed to fill the room.

She inhaled. "I found Mary Jo Sayers," she said.

She led them to the mannequins and they stood before the Cro-Magnon woman. One minute was enough; they turned, one by one, each face taut and disbelieving.

"That monster," Stryker said between his teeth. His face reddened; his blue eyes burned. "That *monster!*"

The commotion level was rising in the room. Excited voices milled around, their owners looking around bug-eyed like children at a creep show. A group of med students asked Woody what had happened; he answered, sketchily, and the word traveled fast. Soon others were coming over to check—"She's okay?"—then going back to look stupefied at the mannequins.

David said, "Let's get a look at that fetus before it becomes a sideshow."

They started toward the cylinder, then saw that blue-uniformed policemen were arriving. Homicide Detective

Pappas strode directly over to David. "Broke laws getting here!" he said.

The two conferred for several moments, David with his arm around Jill, Pappas abruptly pausing to send two men out to retrieve Sonny Sears. "We've already removed the body from the parking lot," he said. "That was the doctor who . . ."

David nodded. Pappas looked at Jill, giving her a tired, fatherly smile. "How's the patient?"

"Okay." She smiled faintly. "We're *both* okay."

And then, because she realized it was true, she smiled openly, lifting her chin and taking what seemed like the first long, deep breath in an age.

Pappas looked around. "So where's the weird experiment?"

"Over there," said Sam MacIntyre. He and Woody had been staring again at the Cro-Magnon woman. Tricia had slumped into a chair and was staring at her hands.

Pappas turned and looked.

The cylinder had been discovered. A small crowd was gathered around it, and more people were pushing close. Policemen craned their necks and hospital personnel stood, hands to their faces. "Unbelievable!" someone said, and someone else cried, "Arnett? Never!" A break in the crowd occurred, and as Pappas and the others began to move forward, the lower, pinkly illuminated half of the cylinder became visible.

Pappas' jaw dropped. "A *baby?*"

"No," Jill said. "A fetus. A five-month-old fetus as yet unborn."

Pappas stopped and stared. The tiny floating human seemed to weigh about four pounds. The doll-like knees were drawn up, and the hands, curled into miniscule fists, were tucked in over the face.

Jill stepped closer and the others followed her. Pappas was still aghast. "Fertilized in a Petri dish," she told him quietly. "Nourished since four days—"

"Louder!" came a voice from the rear. "Can't hear back here!"

Jill turned to see who it was. She saw med students and interns and residents. Lots of nurses. Pop-eyed policemen. All wanting to hear what she was saying. She glanced at Levine, who stood by her side. He nodded encouragement, and she continued.

"This child, this fetus," she said in a louder voice, "was fertilized in a Petri dish. Just sperm and egg brought together, that's all. Since four days after conception he's been nourished in this . . . tank which you see here."

She paused self-consciously.

"And?" bellowed a voice.

Jill coughed. She saw David peering intently into the cylinder. "Well," she said, turning back. "The author of this experiment claims to have succeeded in, ah, altering the child's human heredity. Various strains of DNA have been implanted. The child, it is claimed, will be longer-lived, resistant to all disease including cancer, and will probably possess an extraordinarily high intelligence."

There was an incredulous silence in the room.

A medical student standing near Jill was looking dubiously into the cylinder. *"If* he makes it to viability," he said.

Tricia Donovan turned, annoyed, to the student. "He's *already* viable," she said.

A red-haired policeman in back yelled, "Aw, he looks like a regular kid to me."

Another policeman yelled, "Hey! Isn't it illegal to experiment with yoomans?"

There was an agonizing pause. Stryker, his face dull with fury, turned and answered the question. "Experimentation with unknowing human subjects is not only against the law, it's an abomination against all of humankind, a betrayal of every code of medical ethics . . ."

He stopped, and took off his glasses to wipe his eyes. Jill felt miserable. It was the rotten apple theory. One ruthless scientist, driven by his ambition, had destroyed so much . . .

"Excuse me," said Stryker.

Jill watched as Stryker shouldered his way out of the

crowd and went to stand by the large fan-shaped window. Through the window she could see the first faint pink of dawn.

"Okay, okay, let's get a move on!" There was a grating noise and, turning, Jill saw the police loading Sonny Sears' body onto a stretcher. Jill caught David's eye and, understanding, he motioned to Pappas.

"That one, too," David said, pointing to the Cro-Magnon woman.

Pappas looked over and stared. "*Which* one?"

David explained, and watched the detective's face drain of color.

"You'll give me details in the statement?" said Pappas thickly.

"Every sordid one," said David.

Hospital personnel, still shaking their heads, began slowly filing out.

And before another five minutes had passed, most of the police and the two stretchers bearing their gruesome dead had gone, leaving behind only Pappas and a young-faced sergeant. Pappas wrote rapidly on his pad. David and the others supplied what they could, but Jill did most of the talking.

Closing his book, Pappas signaled to his assistant and headed for the door. "By the way," he said. "That Sears goon. They don't come more vicious. Would you care to guess how long his record is?"

Jill had walked with him a few steps to the door. "No," she said wearily, "I don't think I would." She returned his wave, then heard a new surge of excitement sweeping the room.

"Hey! You gotta see this!" Woody cried to her. David and the others were staring into the cylinder as if mesmerized.

Jill hurried back. Out of the corner of her eye she saw Stryker, still at the window, glance balefully over at them, then turn to look out again.

"Do you *believe* this?" said Tricia, as Jill approached.

Jill looked. And then she looked again.

The fetus was moving. At first he made a wide kicking

motion with his feet; and then, raising his tiny fists and elbows, he began to rub his eyes. "Well, I'll be," murmured David, leaning closer. "He looks like any baby just waking up."

Five pairs of eyes watched in astonishment as the fetus stretched, rubbed its eyes again—and then opened them.

"Ohhh," said Jill.

Blinking, the tiny babe looked out, unseeingly at first and a little sleepily. Then, opening his eyes wider, he seemed to realize he had company—

Because he *smiled*.

The five young doctors erupted into exclamations of surprise and delight. And, seeing their reactions, the fetus in the cylinder grinned more widely—*beamed*, in fact; his toothless, tiny mouth opened in an expression of exquisite and impish delight.

And then the most astounding thing of all: a tiny hand went up, fluttered ineffectively, bumped against glass and tried again. It was an instinctive reaction, a gesture intrinsic to every human from time immemorial. The fetus was trying to wave. *Was* waving now, both hands going at once in an infantile, floppety wave, but the communication was there. The communication was there!

"It's not possible."

They all turned, saw that Stryker had left the window and was approaching them. His expression was dumbfound.

"It simply isn't possible!" His voice rose as he laid both hands on the glass and peered in. "A five-month fetus isn't . . . developed enough to communicate, to have command of his body movements like this . . . his nervous system doesn't reach . . . until after . . ."

Stryker was sputtering. Thirty-five years of training and experience told him what he was seeing was impossible.

"This one's supposed to be different," said Jill softly. "Remember?"

The fetus had spotted him. Was knocking on the glass. Was grinning at him!

Stryker, relaxing for the first time in what was probably years, smiled back.

When at last he spoke, his voice was husky. "Jill," he said. "What else did Arnett tell you about this . . . this child?"

"Let's see," she said. "Resistant to all diseases, will live to maybe two hundred years, will have an IQ around two hundred, and, oh yes, possesses a system that will require less of the environment."

"Gee," said Tricia.

"That's all?" said Woody Greenberg.

"What else would you like? Arnett said *any* new traits could be implanted . . ."

David spoke up. "I like what that policeman said."

"What policeman?" asked MacIntyre.

David knocked gently on the glass, then bent, his face miming the kitchy-coo antics of a new parent. "You know," he said. "That red-haired cop who said this little one looked like any kid. And he does! Just *look* at that face."

David straightened. Jill came closer and laid her head on his shoulder. She looked thoughtful.

"Do you ever think," she murmured, "that in some awful, roundabout way, good can sometimes come from evil?"

Now it was David who appeared thoughtful. "Can I have some time to think about that?" he said.

She smiled up at him. "All you want and more."

His eyes crinkled and he looked at her, pulling her closer. They both looked back at the fetus, who was now very busy making swimming motions.

"I think he's going to do just fine," said David.

Stryker said, "It certainly looks that way, doesn't it?"

The others nodded and smiled in agreement. Behind them, the light in the fan-shaped window was growing bright. The sun had come up, and a new day had begun.

By *New York Times*
Bestselling Author

ROBIN COOK

"The master of the
medical thriller."
— *The New York Times*

*The chilling new
novel of...*

MORTAL FEAR